MEL
the Chosen

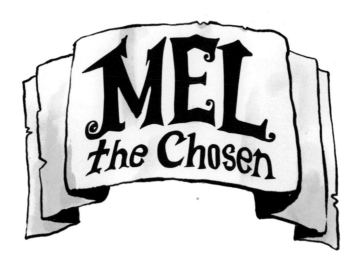

Mel the Chosen was illustrated with pencils
and inks and colored with watercolors.

Text, cover art, and interior illustrations copyright © 2021 by Rachele Aragno
Translation copyright © 2021 by Bao Dieci

All rights reserved. Published in the United States by RH Graphic, an imprint of
Random House Children's Books, a division of Penguin Random House LLC, New York.
Originally published as a hardcover in the Italian language in Italy by Bao Dieci, in 2020.

RH Graphic with the book design is a trademark of Penguin Random House LLC.

Visit us on the web and sign up for our newsletter! RHKidsGraphic.com • @RHKidsGraphic

Educators and librarians, for a variety of teaching tools, visit us at RHTeachersLibrarians.com

Library of Congress Cataloging-in-Publication Data is available upon request.
ISBN 978-0-593-30123-4 (pbk) — ISBN 978-0-593-30124-1 (hc)
ISBN 978-0-593-30125-8 (lib. bdg.) — ISBN 978-0-593-30126-5 (ebk)

Interior design and lettering by Patrick Crotty
Translation by Carla Roncalli Di Montorio

MANUFACTURED IN CHINA
10 9 8 7 6 5 4 3 2 1
First American Edition

A comic on every bookshelf.

Rachele Aragno

MEL
the Chosen

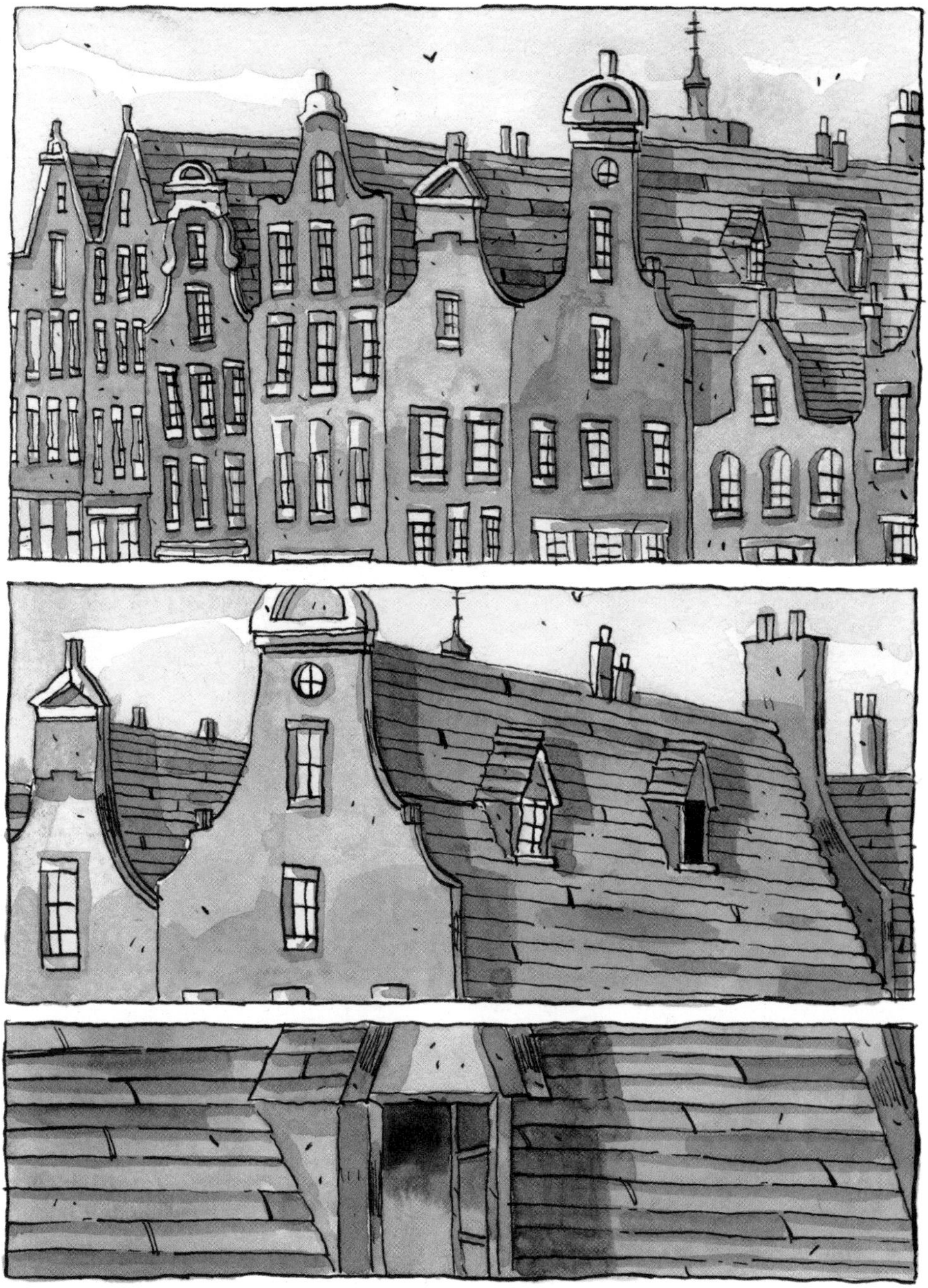

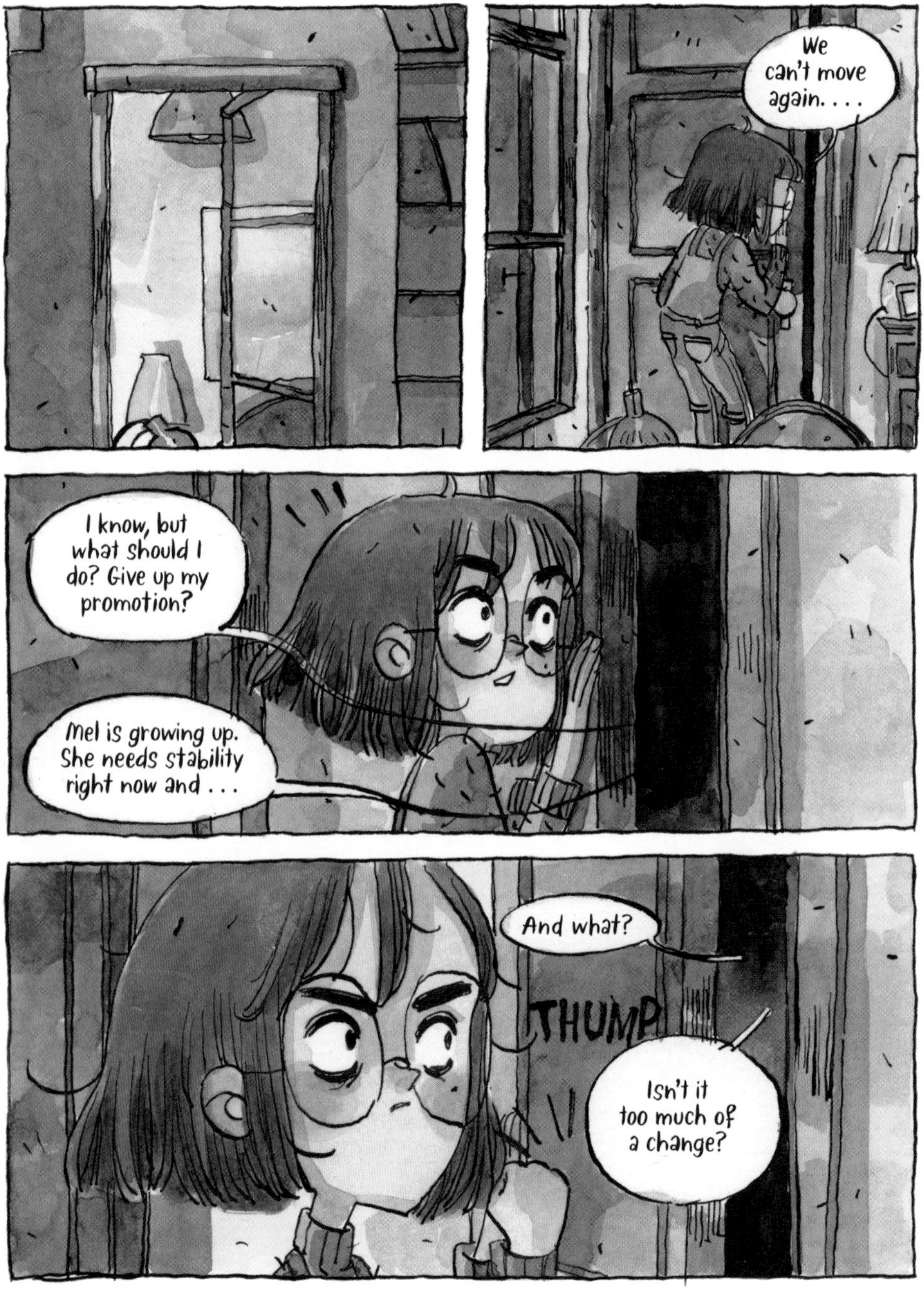
We can't move again. . . .
I know, but what should I do? Give up my promotion?
Mel is growing up. She needs stability right now and . . .
And what?
THUMP
Isn't it too much of a change?

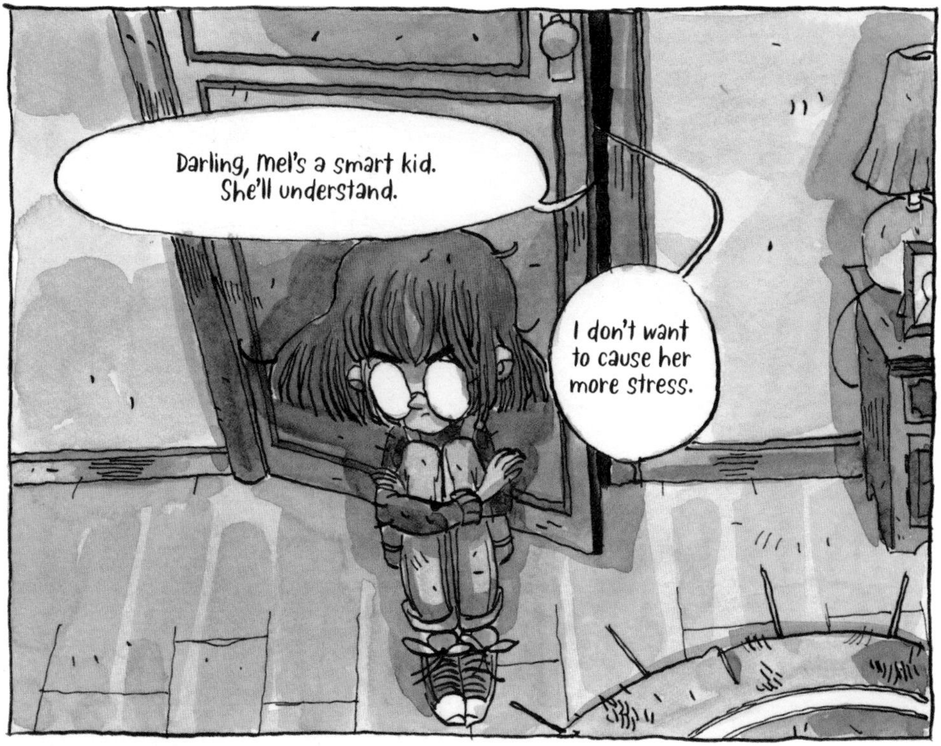
Darling, mel's a smart kid. She'll understand.
I don't want to cause her more stress.

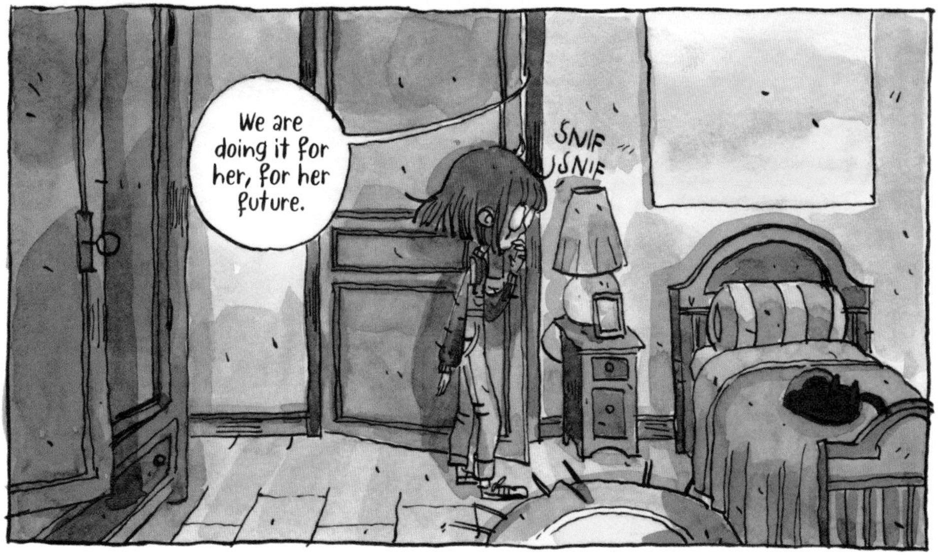
We are doing it for her, for her future.
SNIF
SNIF

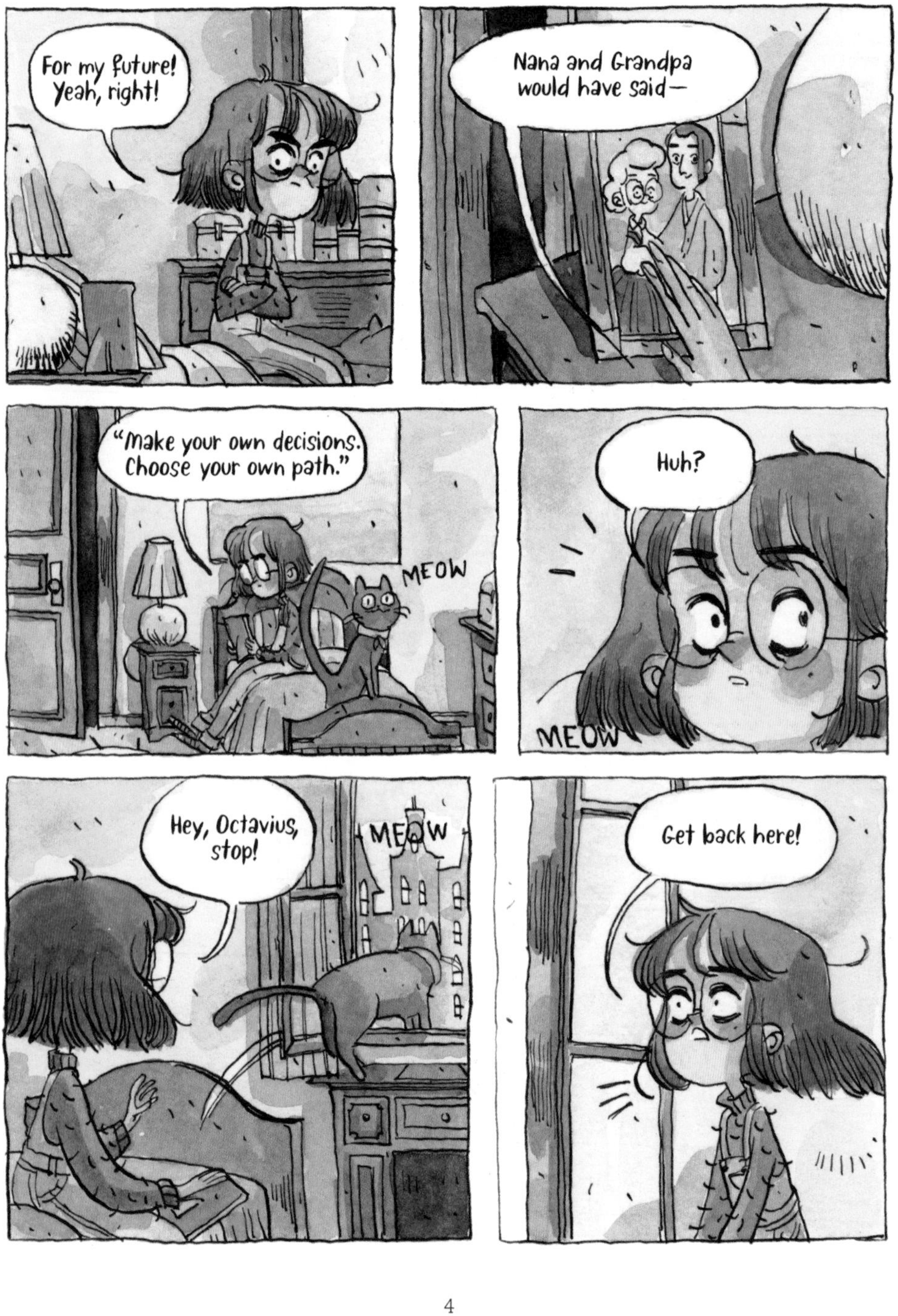

For my future! Yeah, right!
Nana and Grandpa would have said—
"Make your own decisions. Choose your own path."
MEOW
Huh?
MEOW
Hey, Octavius, stop!
MEOW
Get back here!

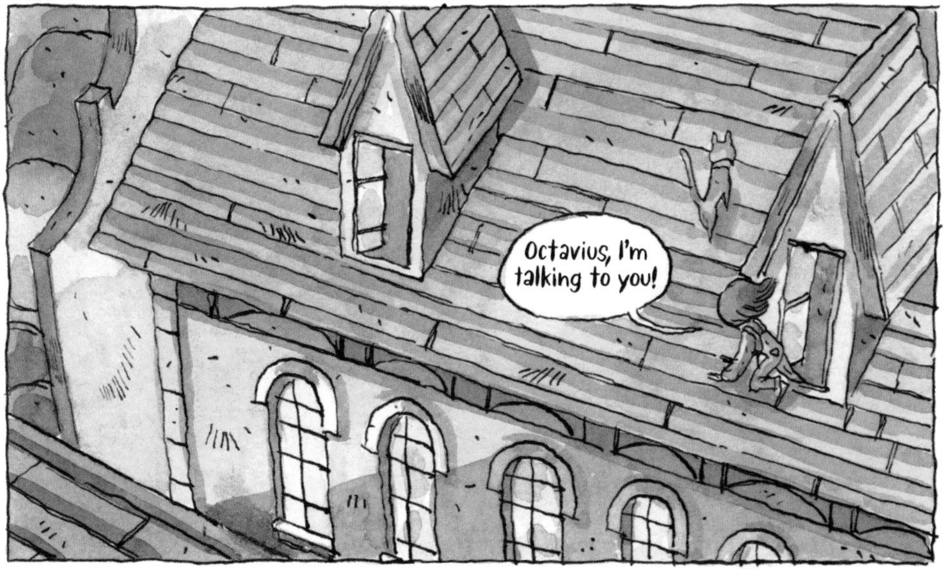
Octavius, I'm talking to you!

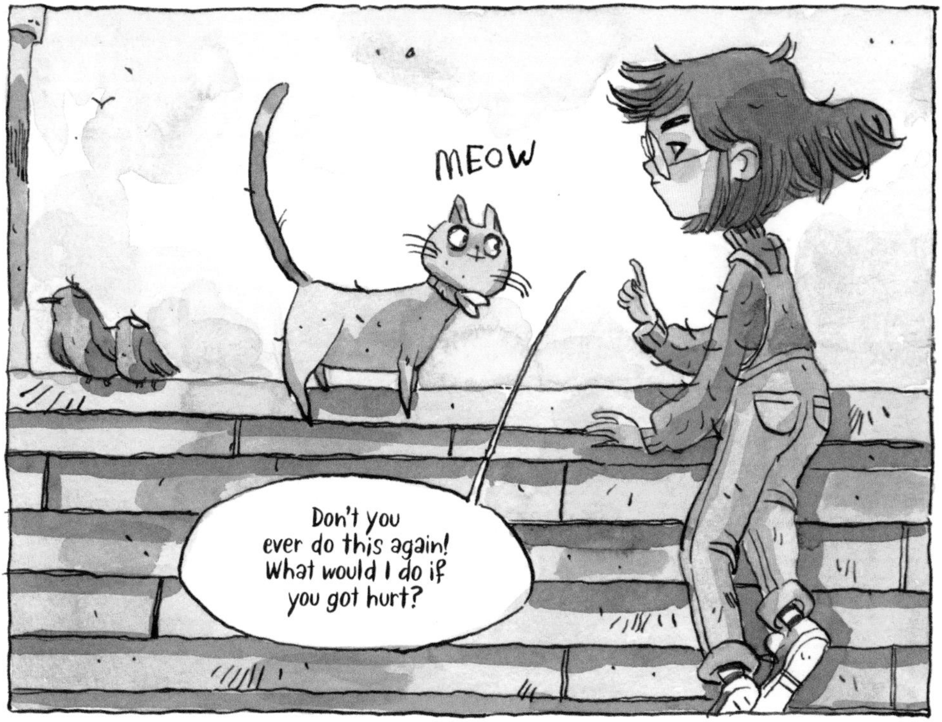
MEOW
Don't you ever do this again! What would I do if you got hurt?

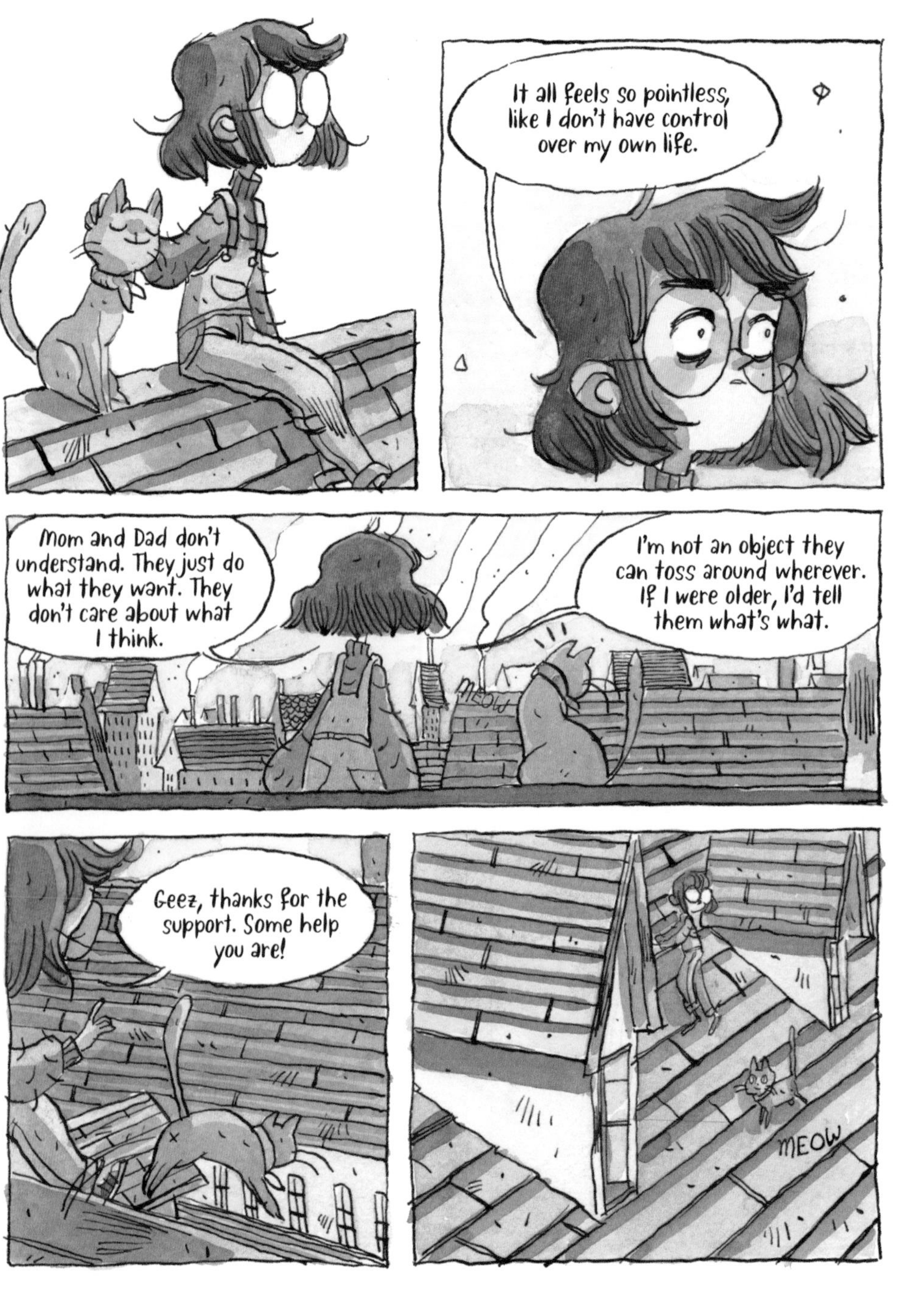
It all feels so pointless, like I don't have control over my own life.
Mom and Dad don't understand. They just do what they want. They don't care about what I think.
I'm not an object they can toss around wherever. If I were older, I'd tell them what's what.
MEOW
Geez, thanks for the support. Some help you are!
MEOW

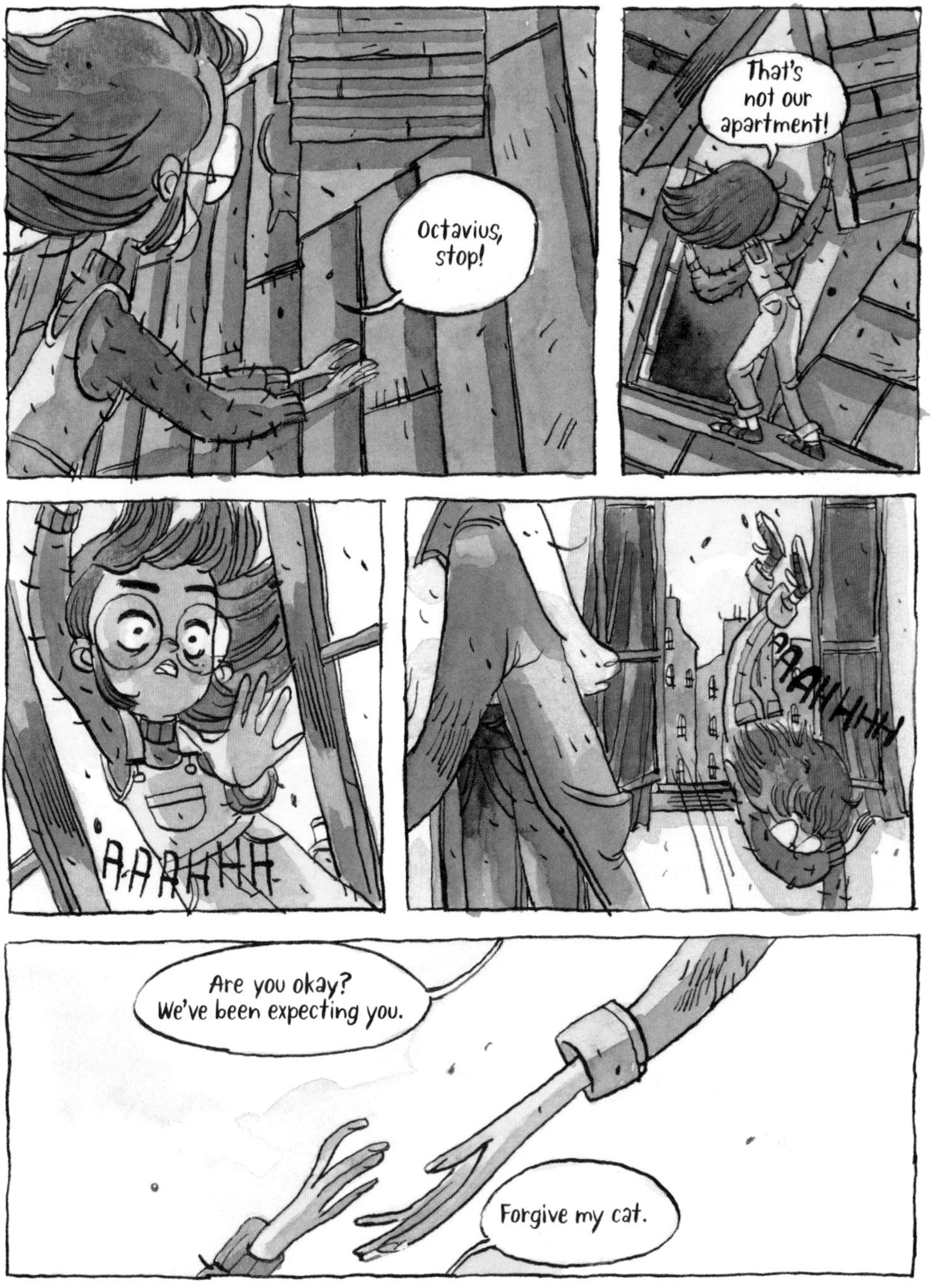
Octavius, stop!
That's not our apartment!
AAAHHH
AAAHHHH
Are you okay? We've been expecting you.
Forgive my cat.

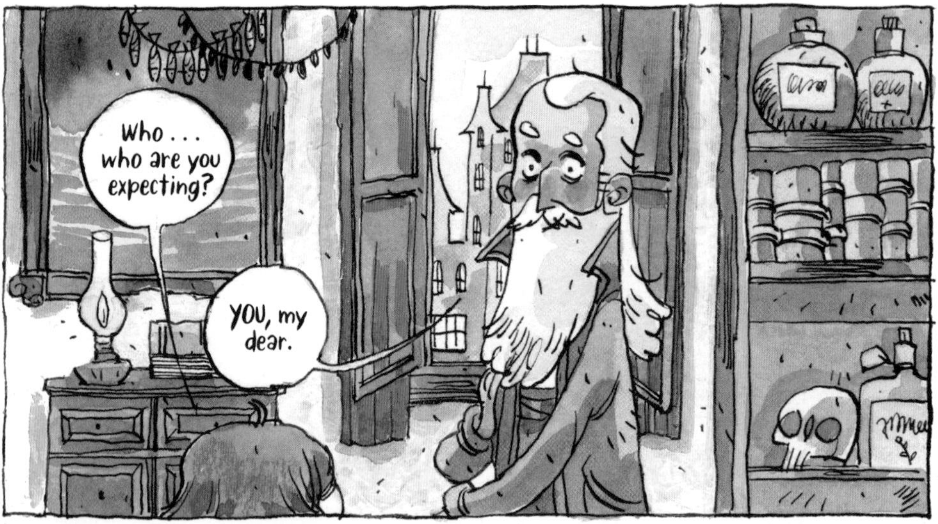
Who . . . who are you expecting?
YOU, my dear.

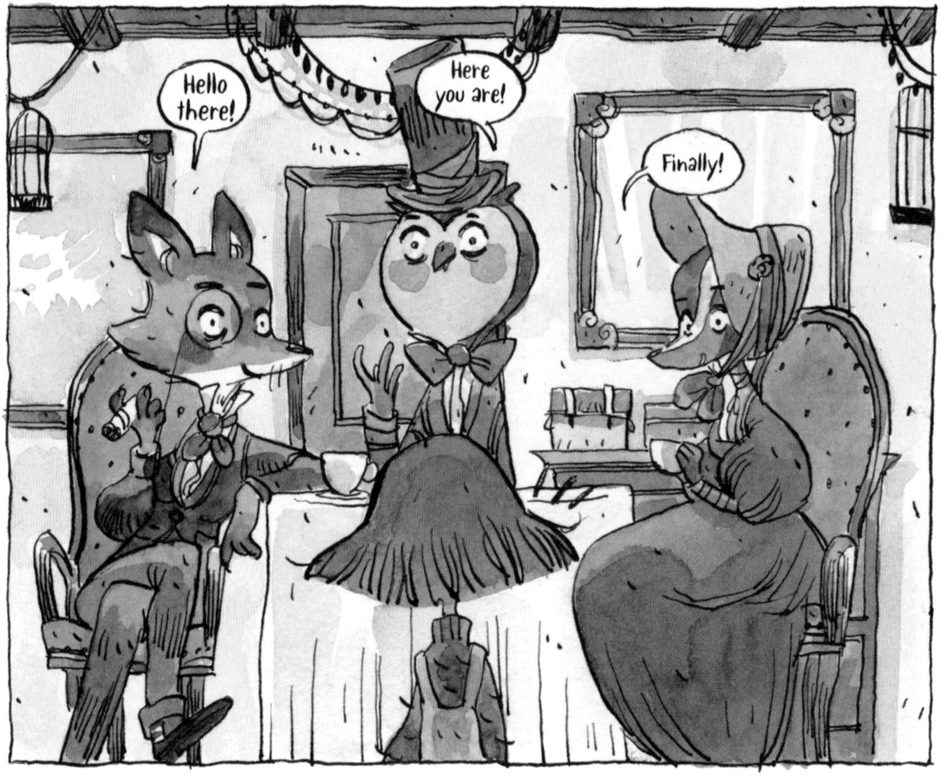
Hello there!
Here you are!
Finally!

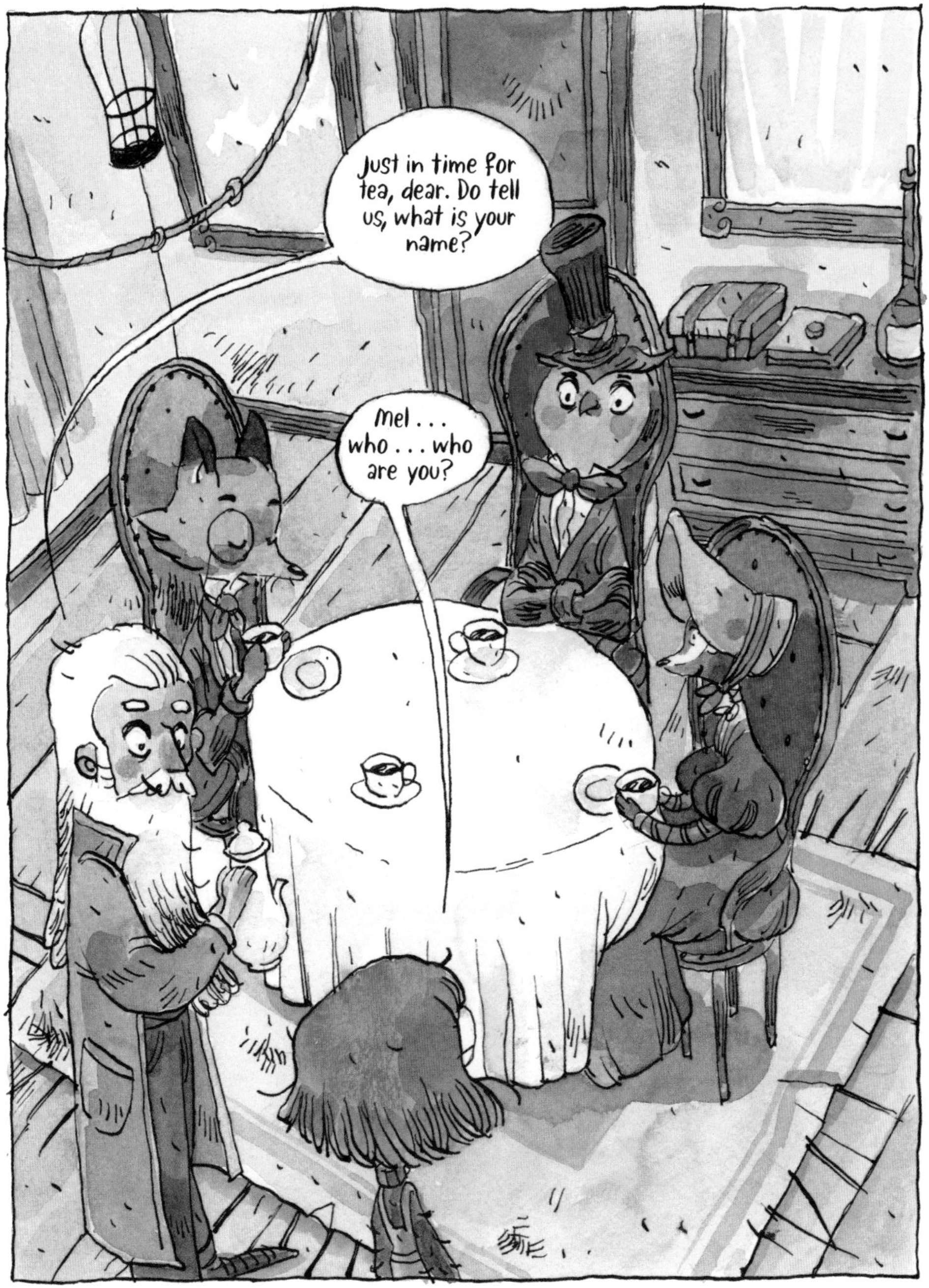
Just in time for tea, dear. Do tell us, what is your name?
Mel . . . who . . . who are you?

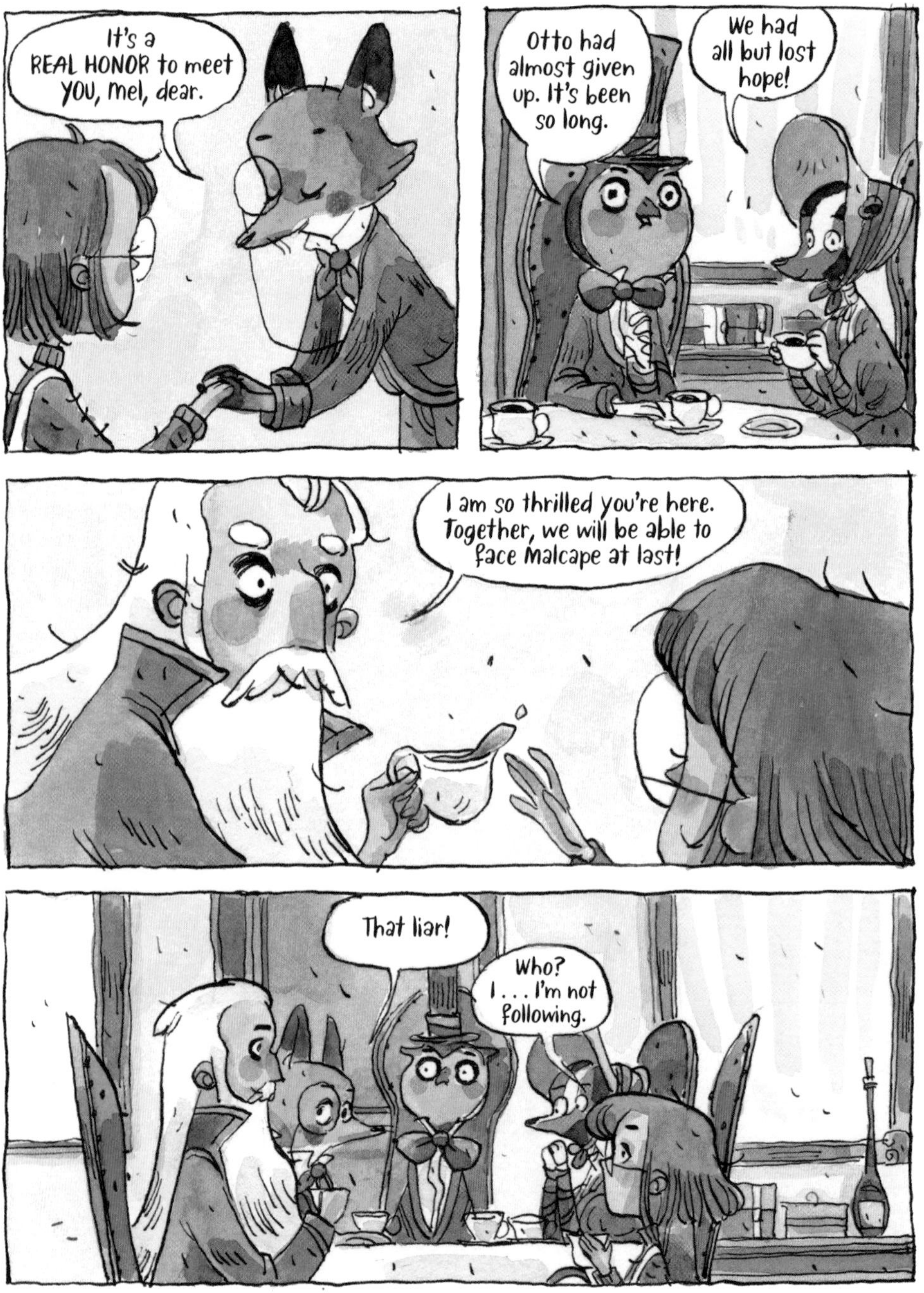
It's a REAL HONOR to meet YOU, Mel, dear.
Otto had almost given up. It's been so long.
We had all but lost hope!
I am so thrilled you're here. Together, we will be able to face Malcape at last!
That liar!
Who? I . . . I'm not following.

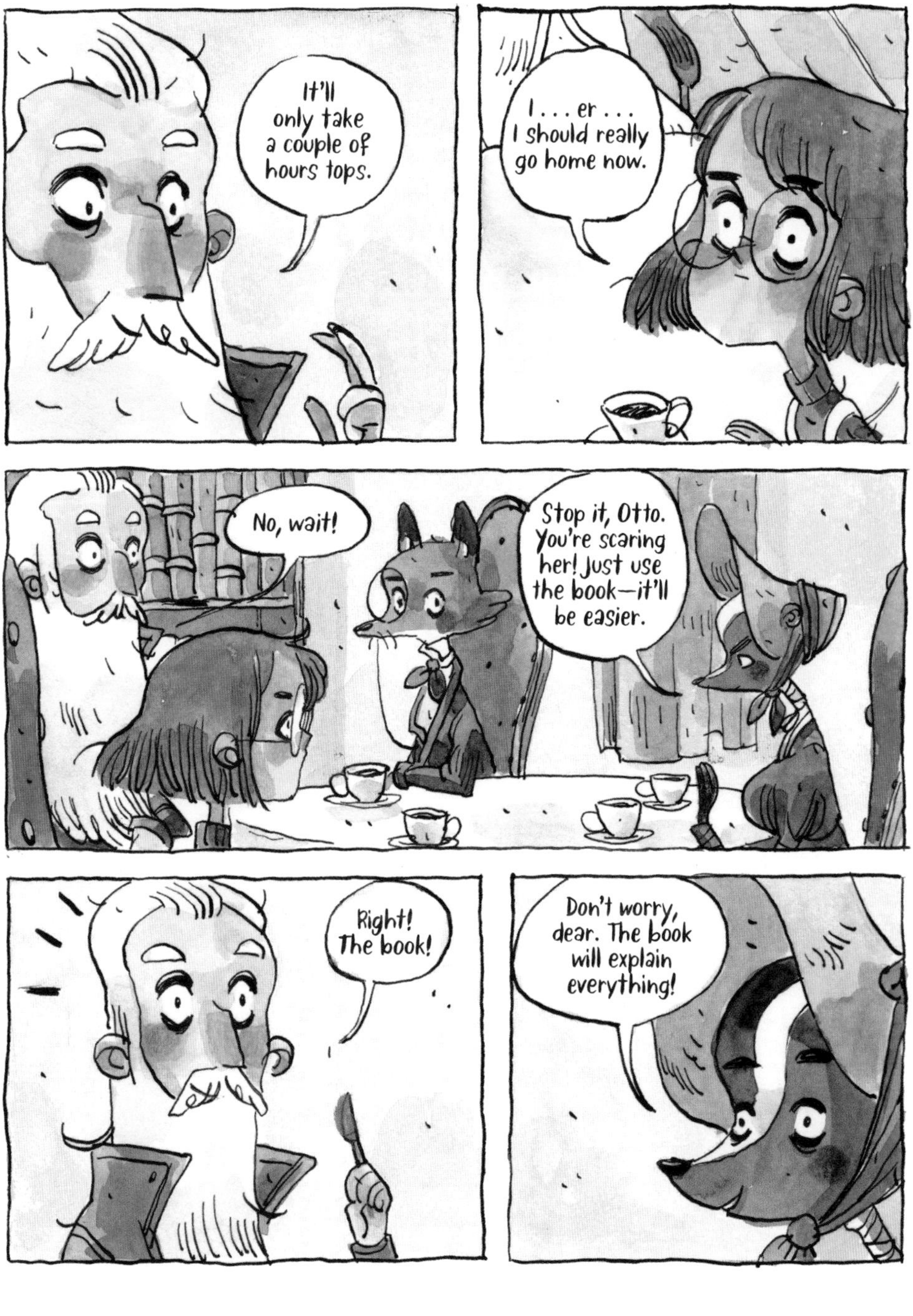
It'll only take a couple of hours tops.
I . . . er . . . I should really go home now.
No, wait!
Stop it, Otto. You're scaring her! Just use the book—it'll be easier.
Right! The book!
Don't worry, dear. The book will explain everything!

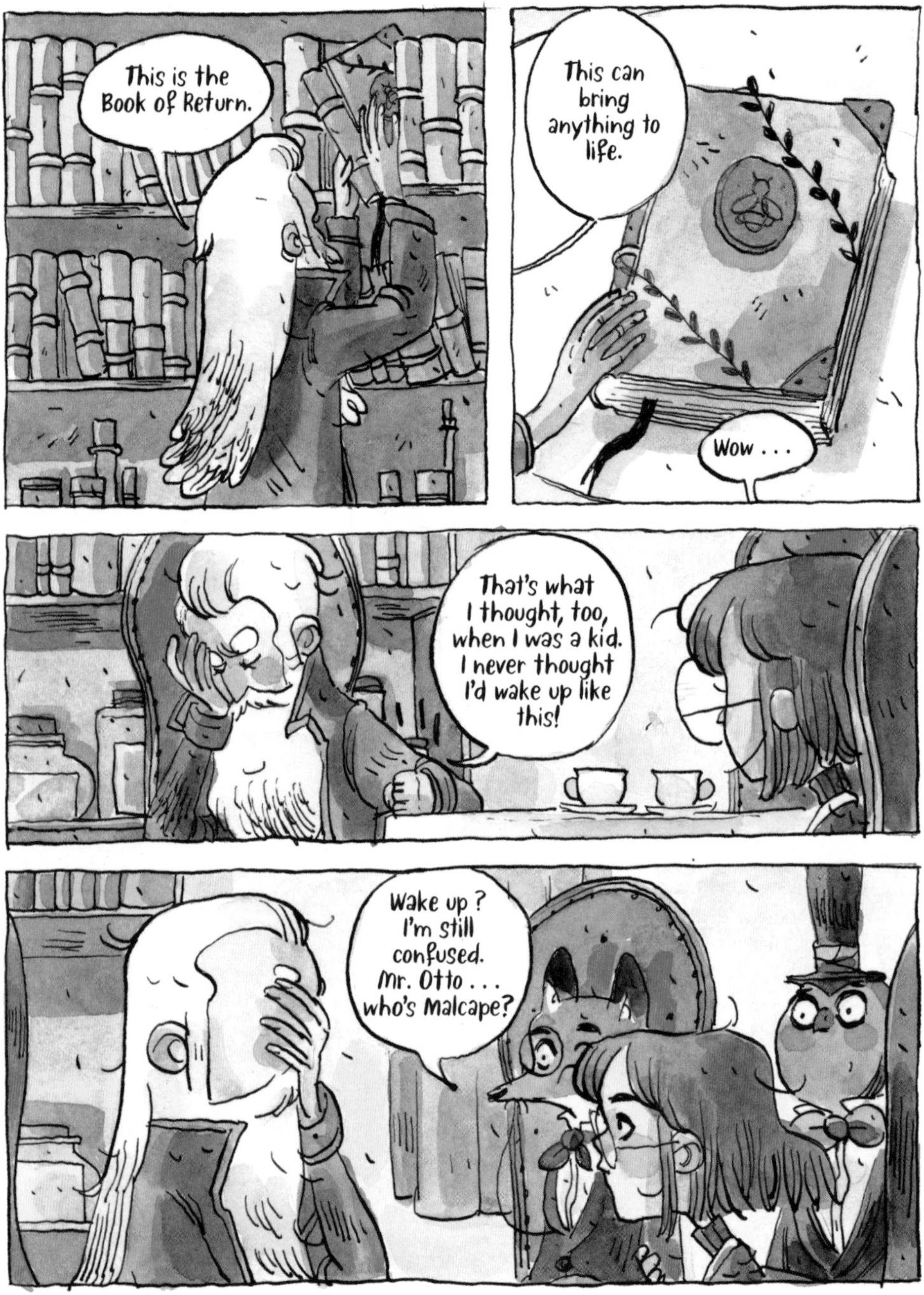
This is the Book of Return.
This can bring anything to life.
Wow . . .
That's what I thought, too, when I was a kid. I never thought I'd wake up like this!
Wake up ? I'm still confused. Mr. Otto . . . who's Malcape?

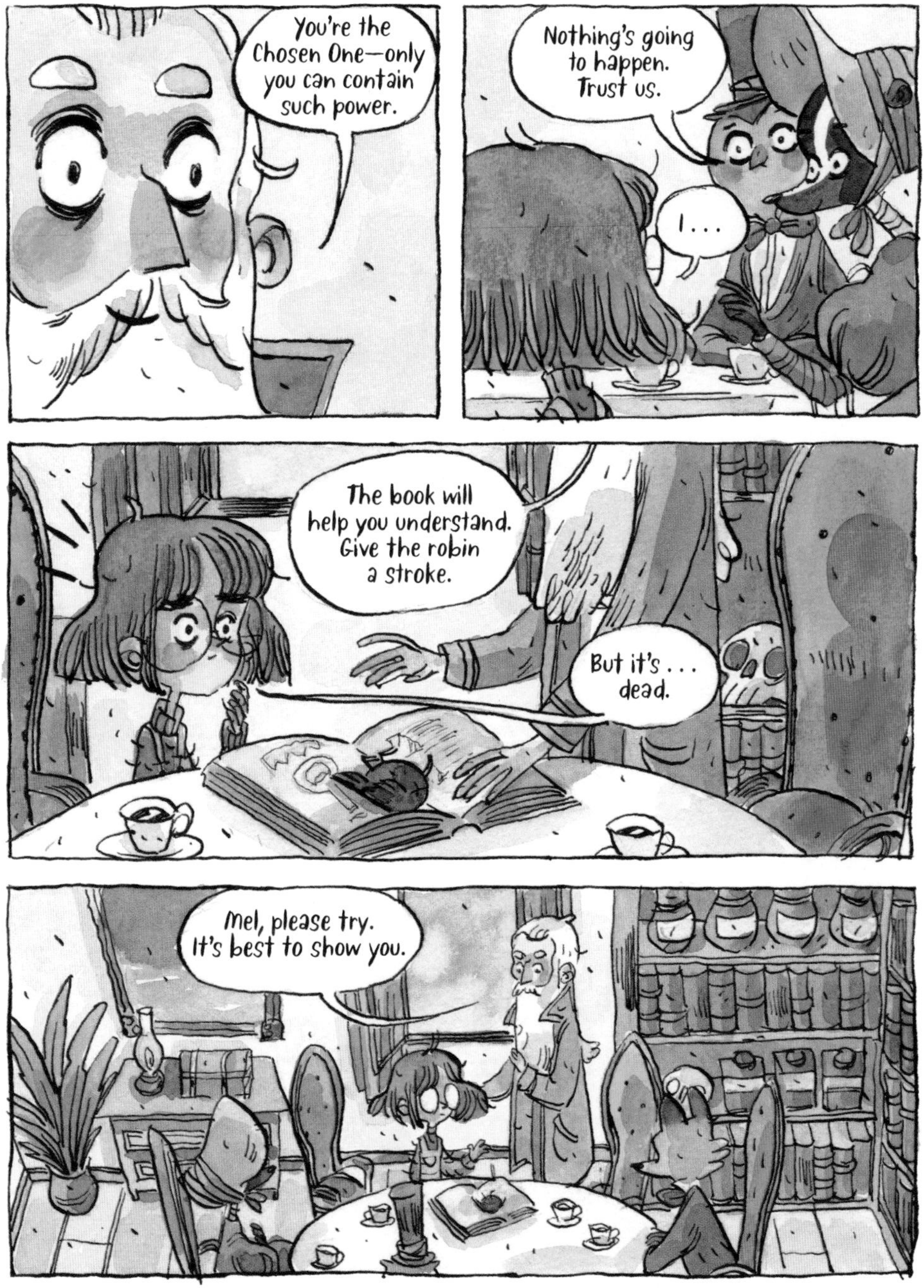
You're the Chosen One—only you can contain such power.
Nothing's going to happen. Trust us.
I . . .
The book will help you understand. Give the robin a stroke.
But it's . . . dead.
Mel, please try. It's best to show you.

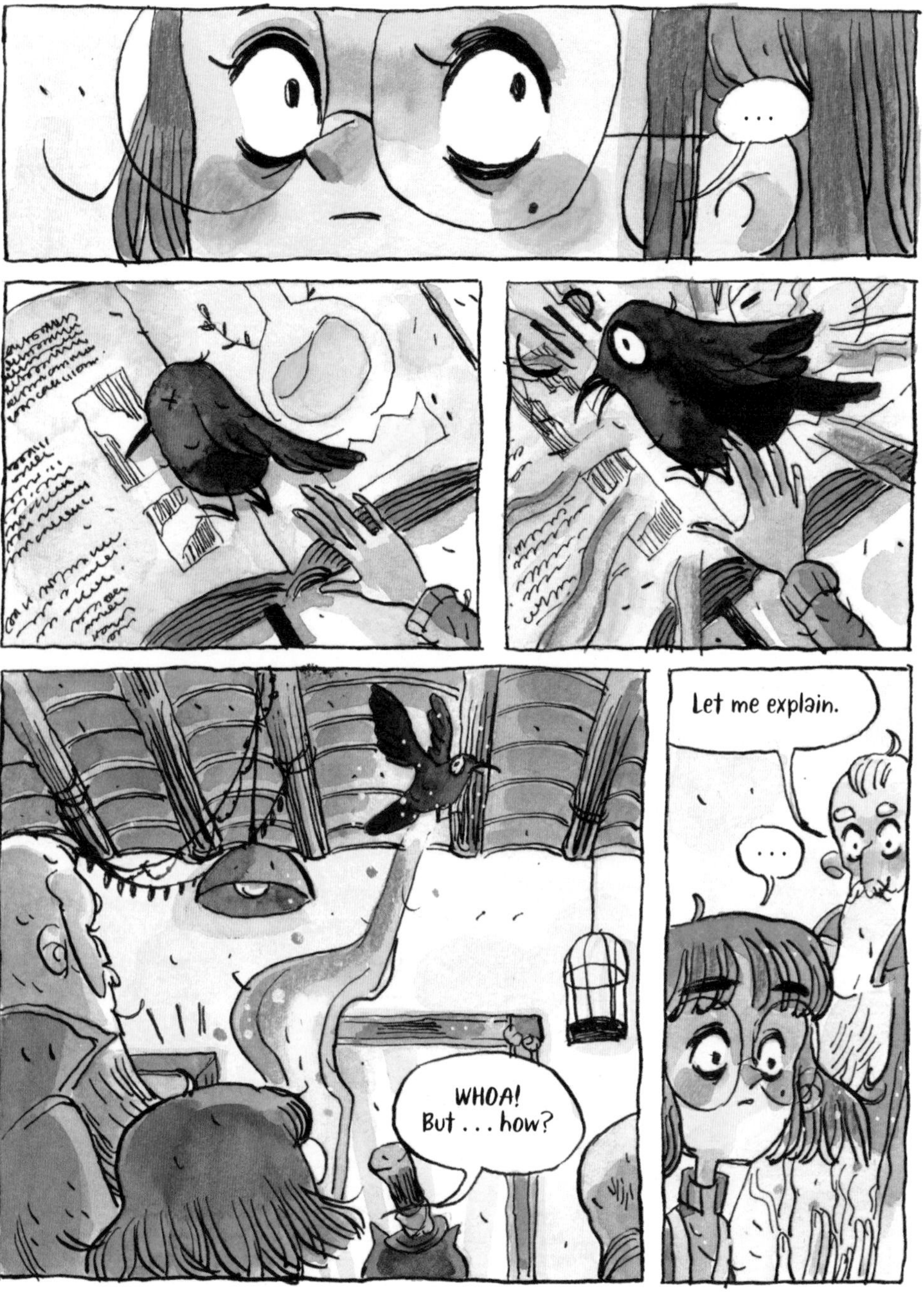
. . .
WHOA!
But . . . how?
Let me explain.
. . .

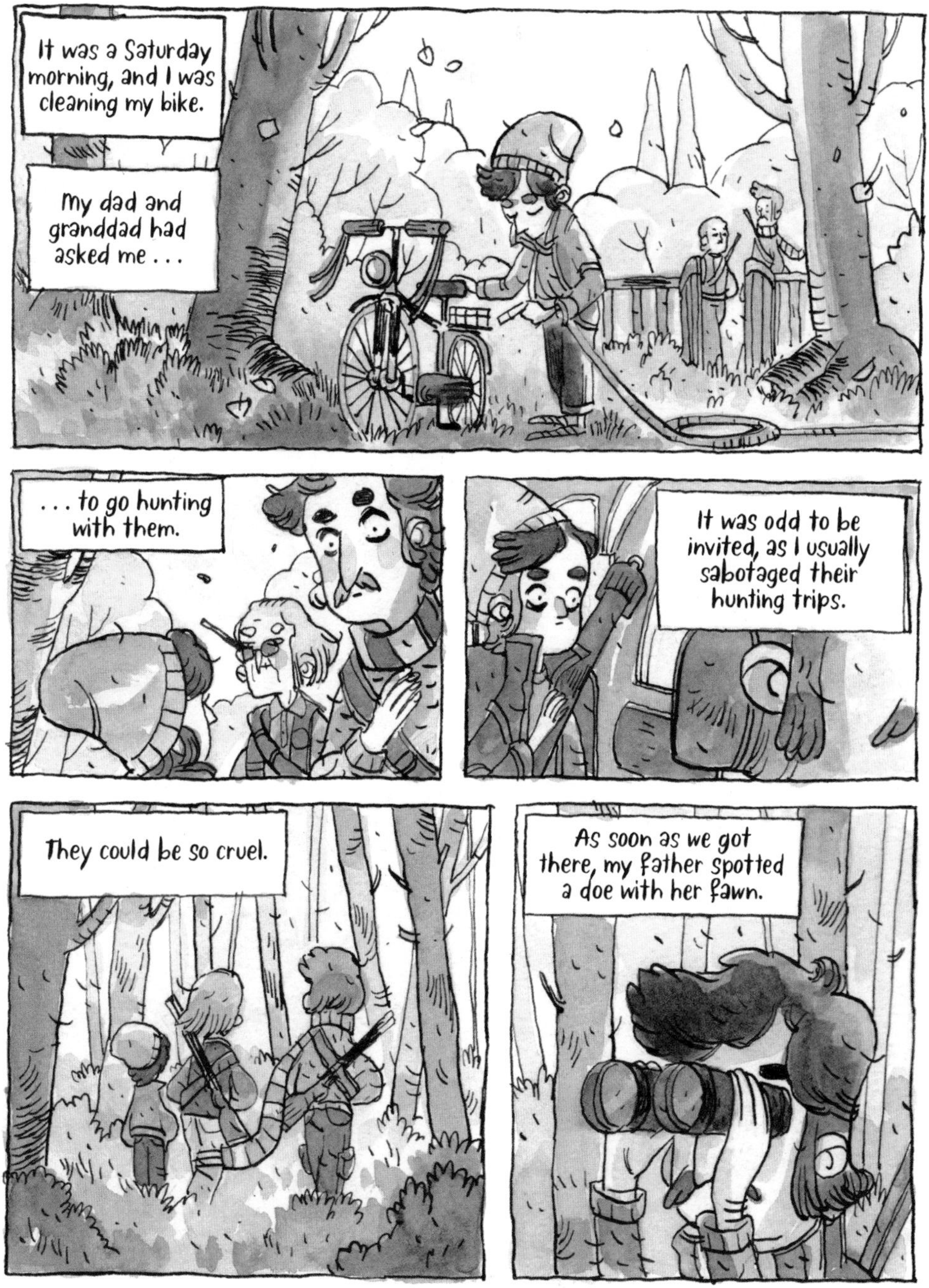
It was a Saturday morning, and I was cleaning my bike.
My dad and granddad had asked me . . .
. . . to go hunting with them.
It was odd to be invited, as I usually sabotaged their hunting trips.
They could be so cruel.
As soon as we got there, my father spotted a doe with her fawn.

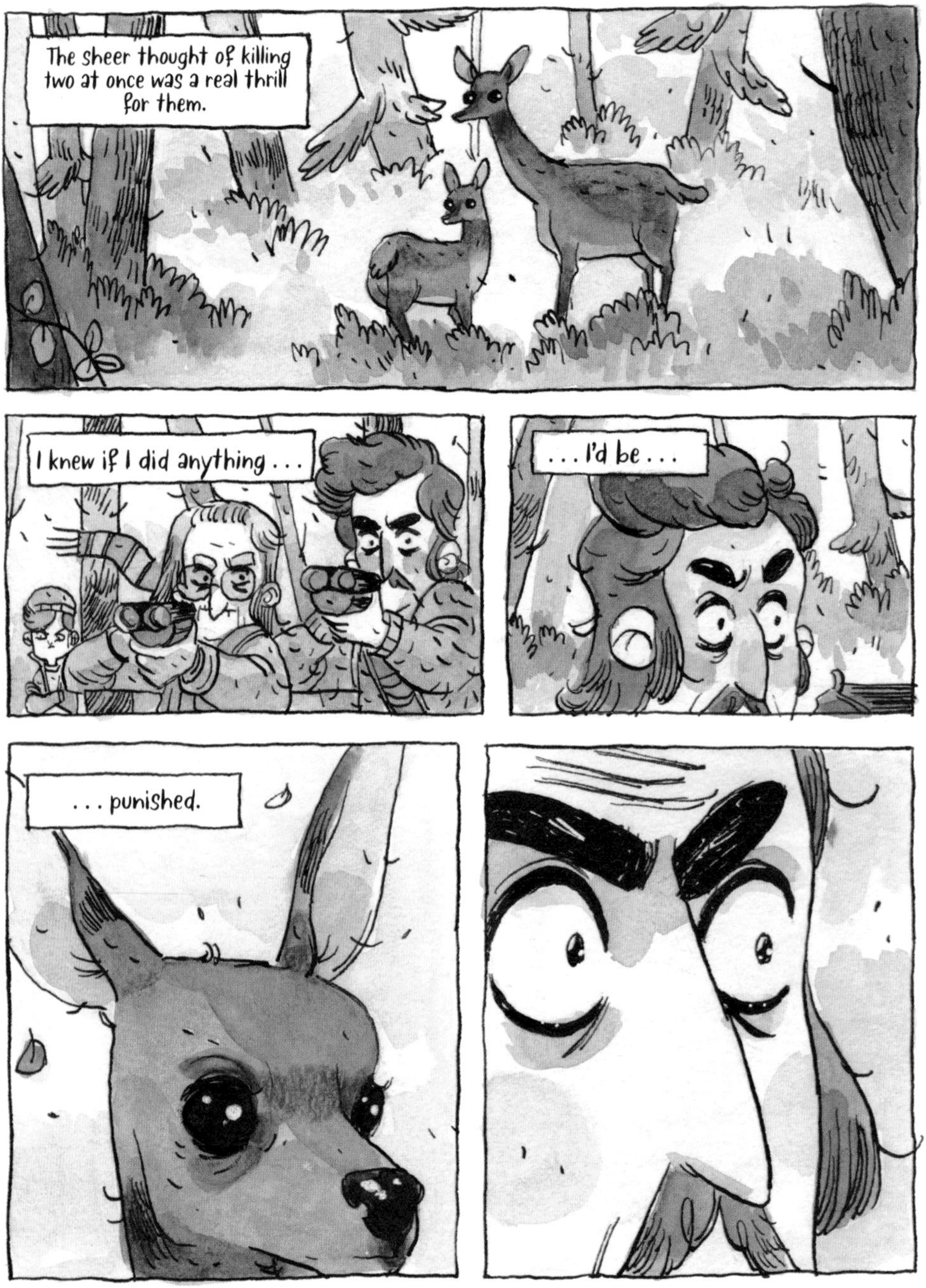
The sheer thought of killing two at once was a real thrill for them.
I knew if I did anything . . .
. . . I'd be . . .
. . . punished.

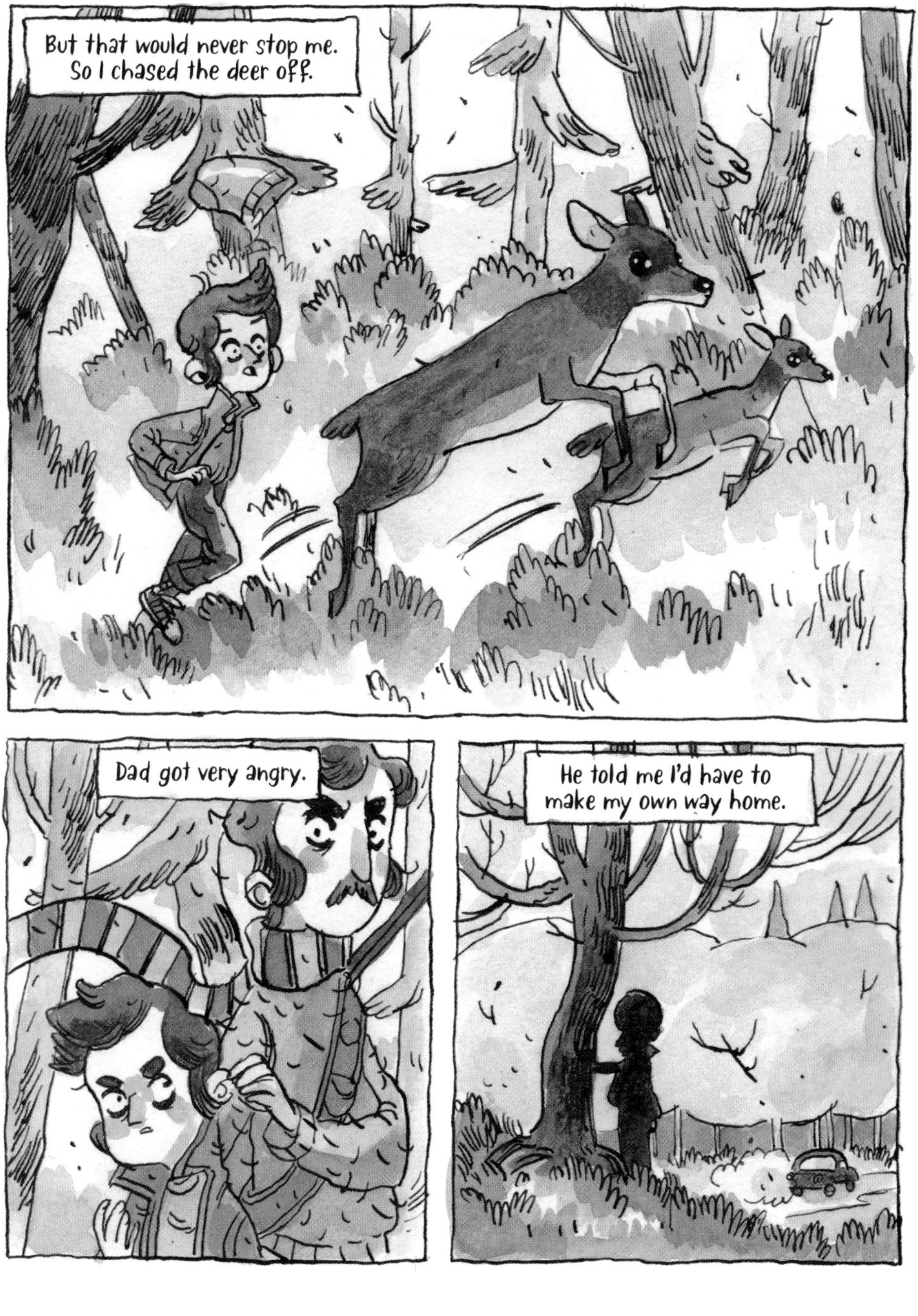
But that would never stop me. So I chased the deer off.
Dad got very angry.
He told me I'd have to make my own way home.

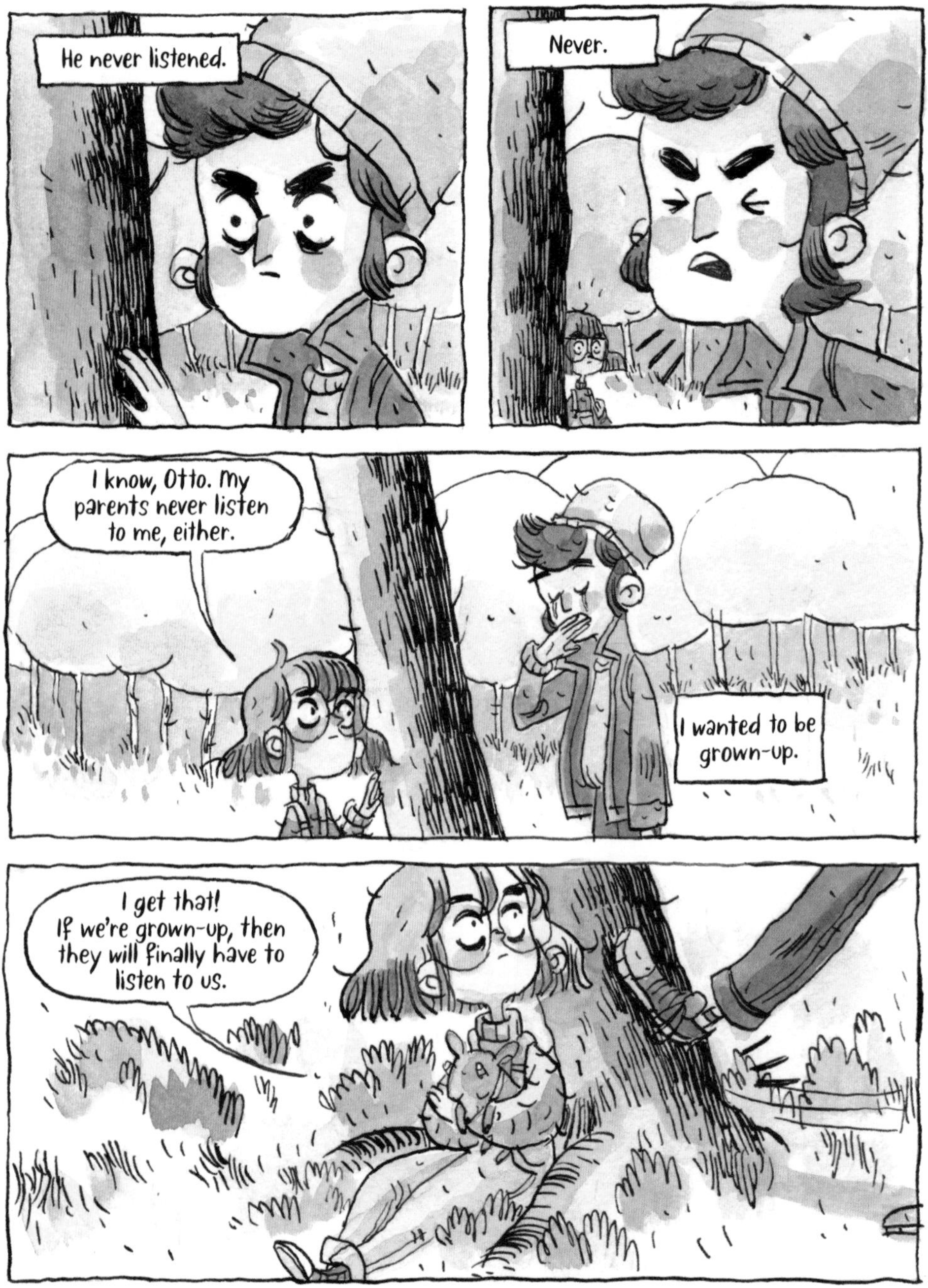
He never listened.
Never.
I know, Otto. My parents never listen to me, either.
I wanted to be grown-up.
I get that! If we're grown-up, then they will finally have to listen to us.

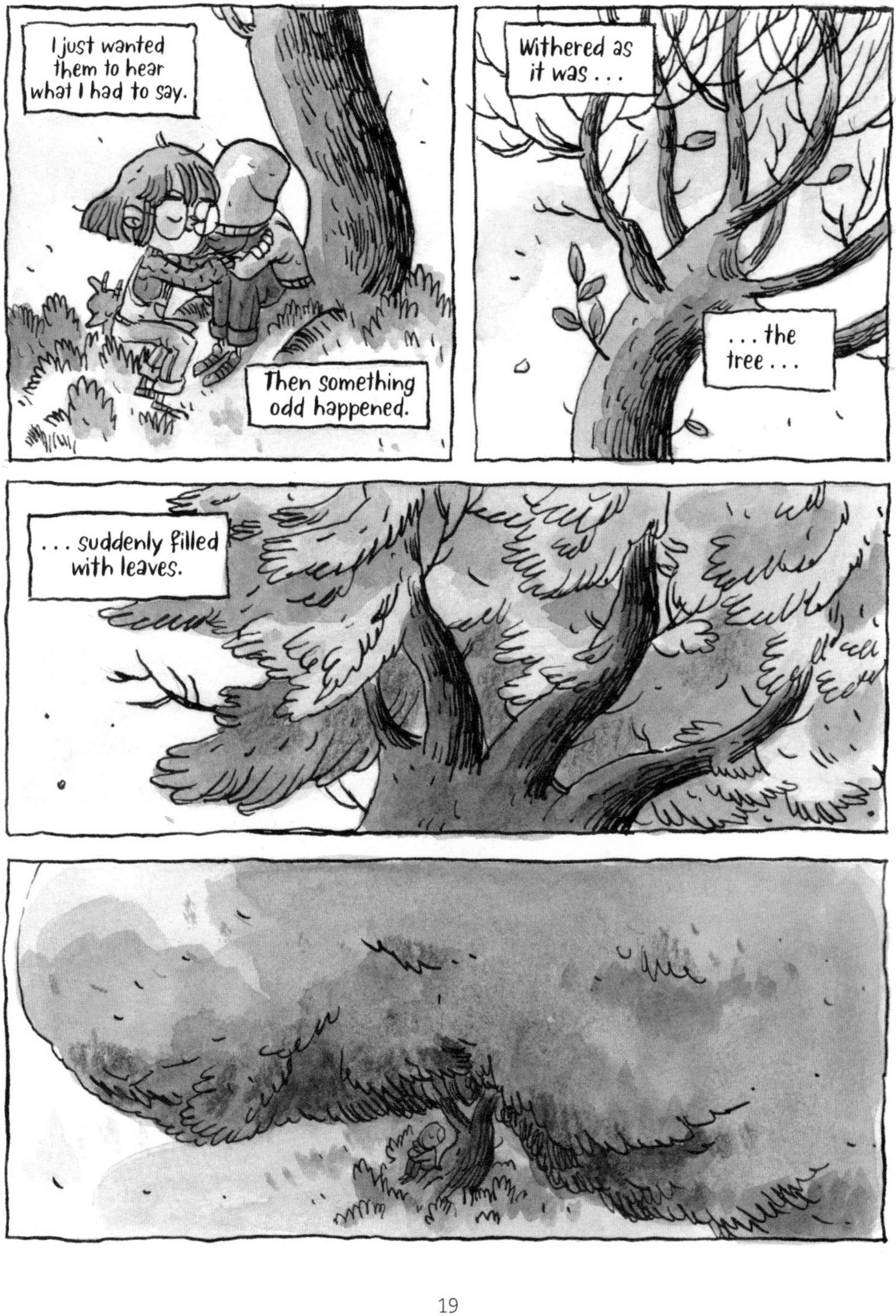
I just wanted them to hear what I had to say.
Then something odd happened.
Withered as it was . . .
. . . the tree . . .
. . . suddenly filled with leaves.

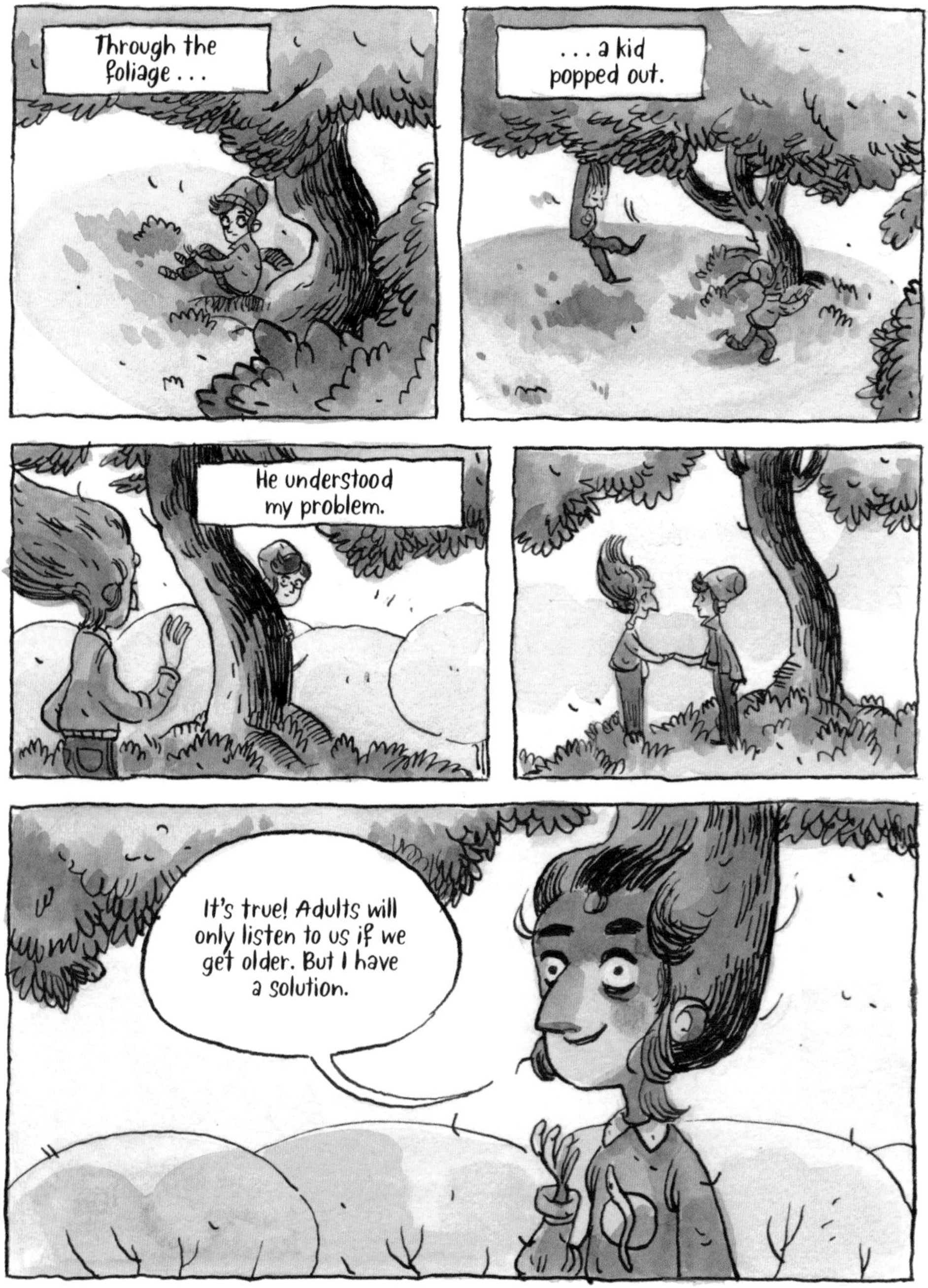
Through the foliage . . .
. . . a kid popped out.
He understood my problem.
It's true! Adults will only listen to us if we get older. But I have a solution.

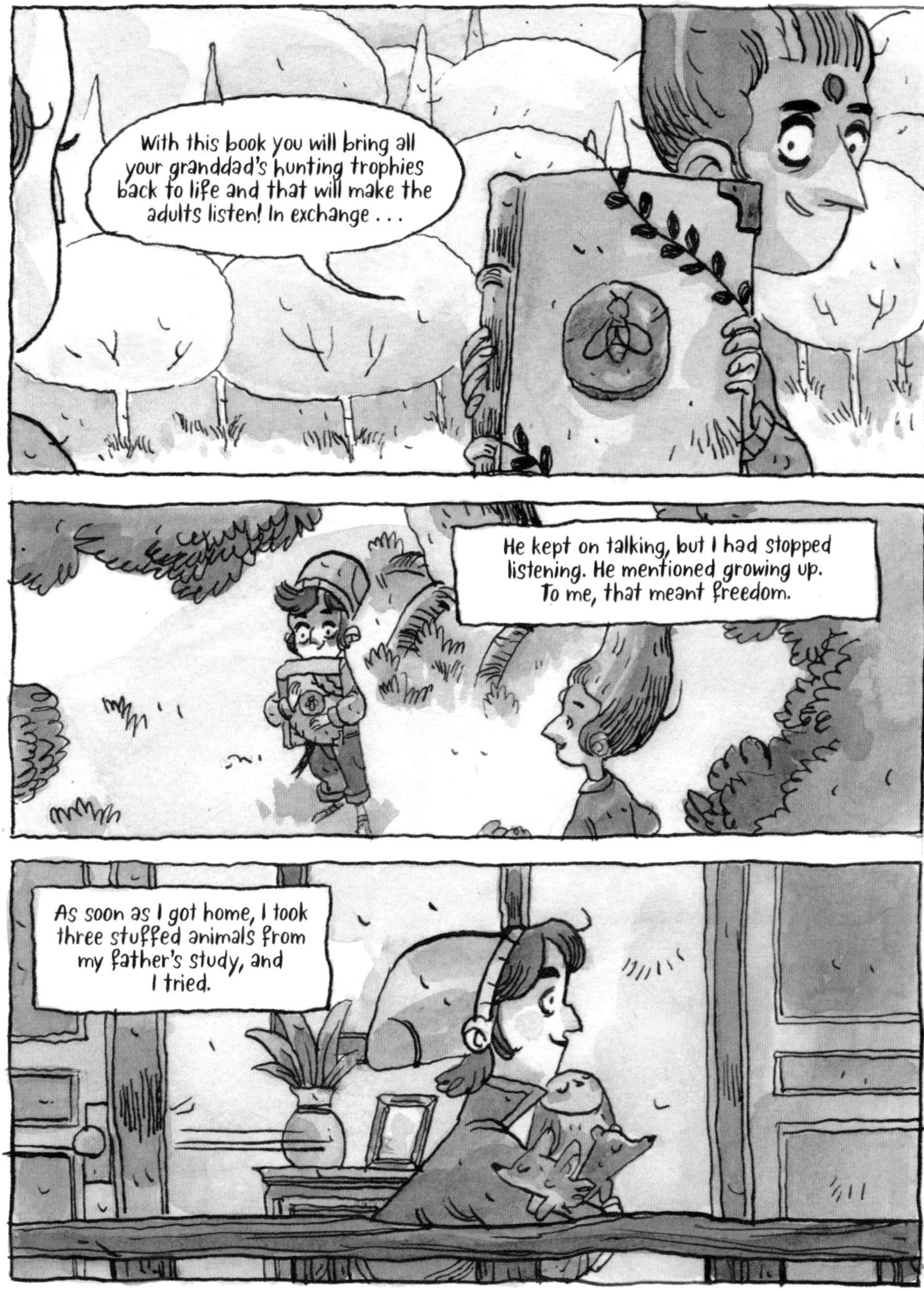
With this book you will bring all your granddad's hunting trophies back to life and that will make the adults listen! In exchange . . .
He kept on talking, but I had stopped listening. He mentioned growing up. To me, that meant freedom.
As soon as I got home, I took three stuffed animals from my father's study, and I tried.

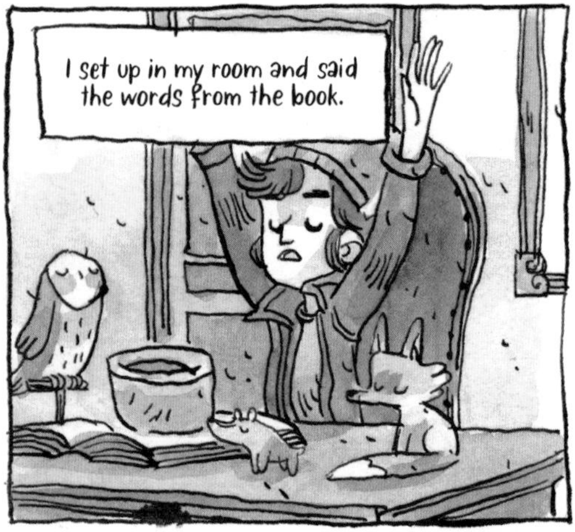
I set up in my room and said the words from the book.

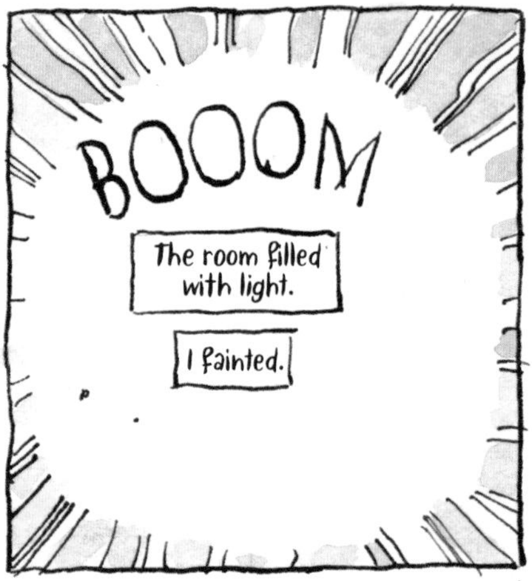
BOOOM
The room filled with light.
I fainted.

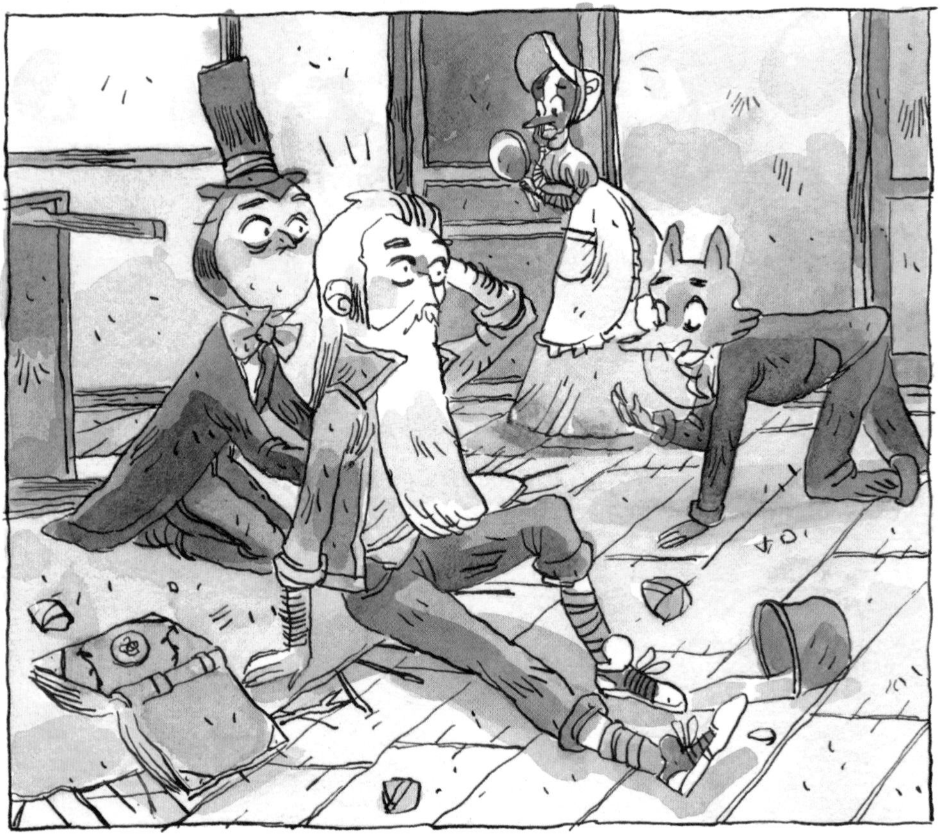

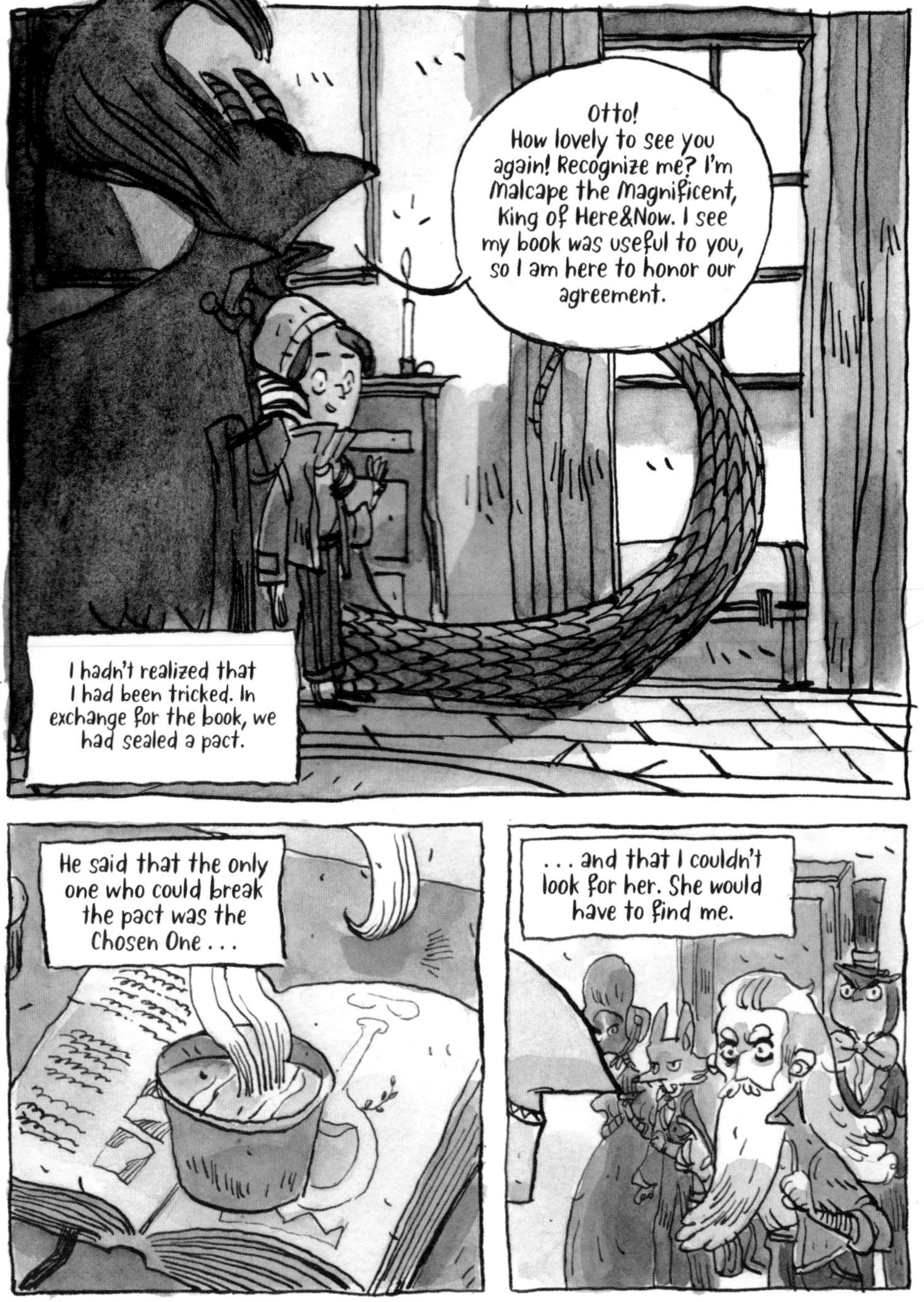
Otto! How lovely to see you again! Recognize me? I'm Malcape the Magnificent, King of Here&Now. I see my book was useful to you, so I am here to honor our agreement.
I hadn't realized that I had been tricked. In exchange for the book, we had sealed a pact.
He said that the only one who could break the pact was the Chosen One . . .
. . . and that I couldn't look for her. She would have to find me.

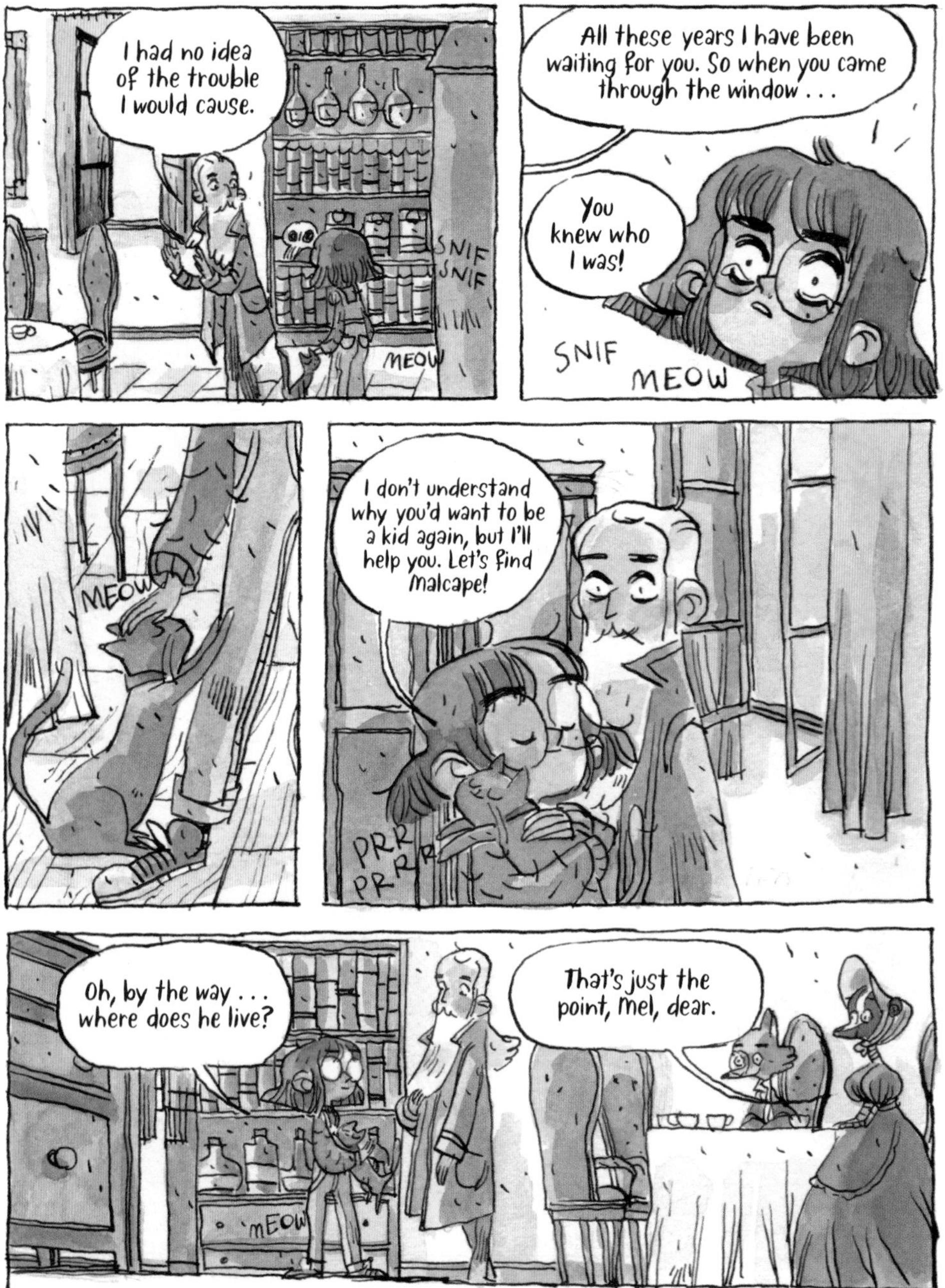
I had no idea of the trouble I would cause.
SNIF SNIF
MEOW
All these years I have been waiting for you. So when you came through the window . . .
You knew who I was!
SNIF
MEOW
MEOW
I don't understand why you'd want to be a kid again, but I'll help you. Let's find Malcape!
PRR PRRR
Oh, by the way . . . where does he live?
MEOW
That's just the point, Mel, dear.

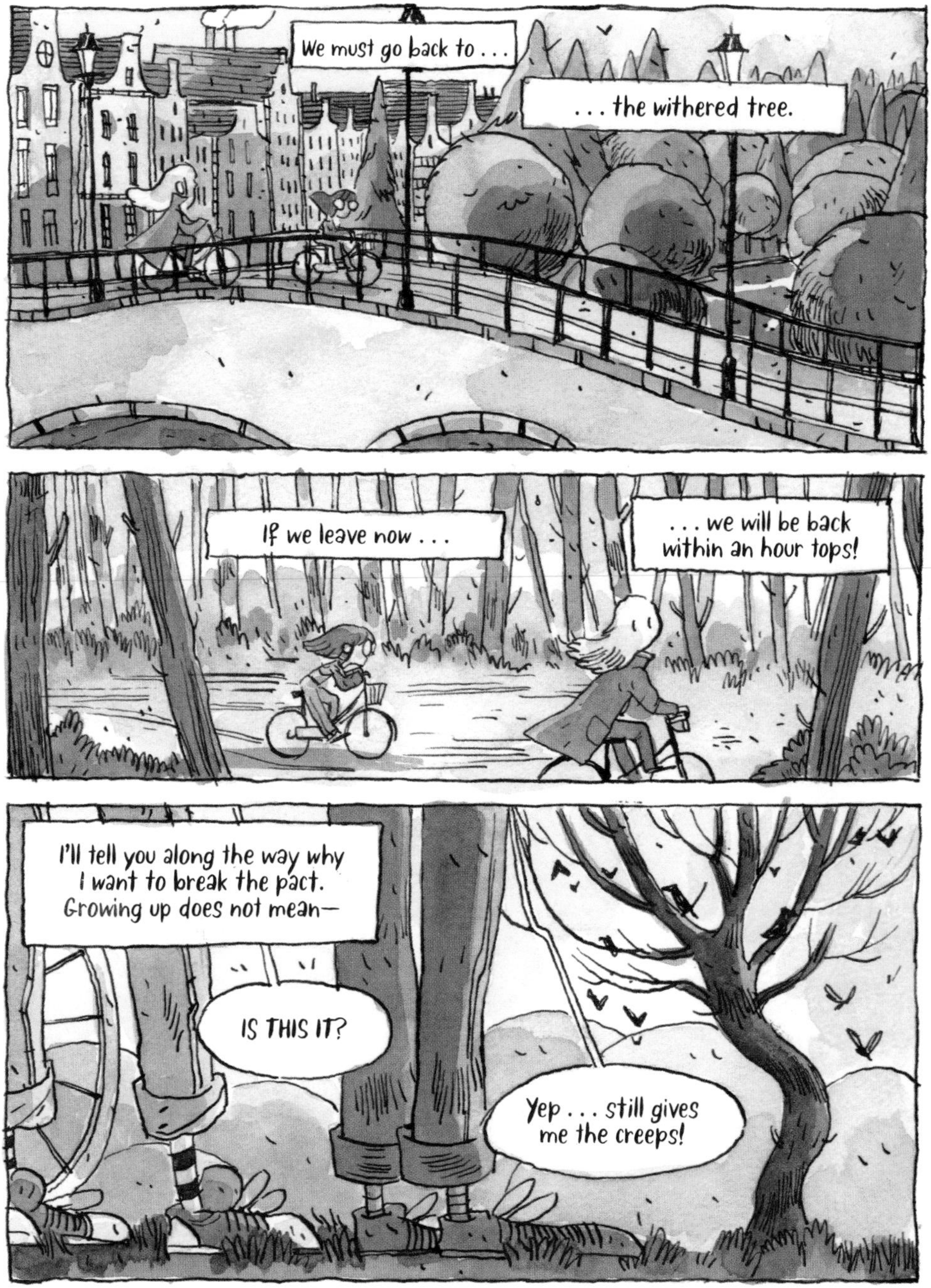
We must go back to . . .
. . . the withered tree.
If we leave now . . .
. . . we will be back within an hour tops!
I'll tell you along the way why I want to break the pact. Growing up does not mean—
IS THIS IT?
Yep . . . still gives me the creeps!

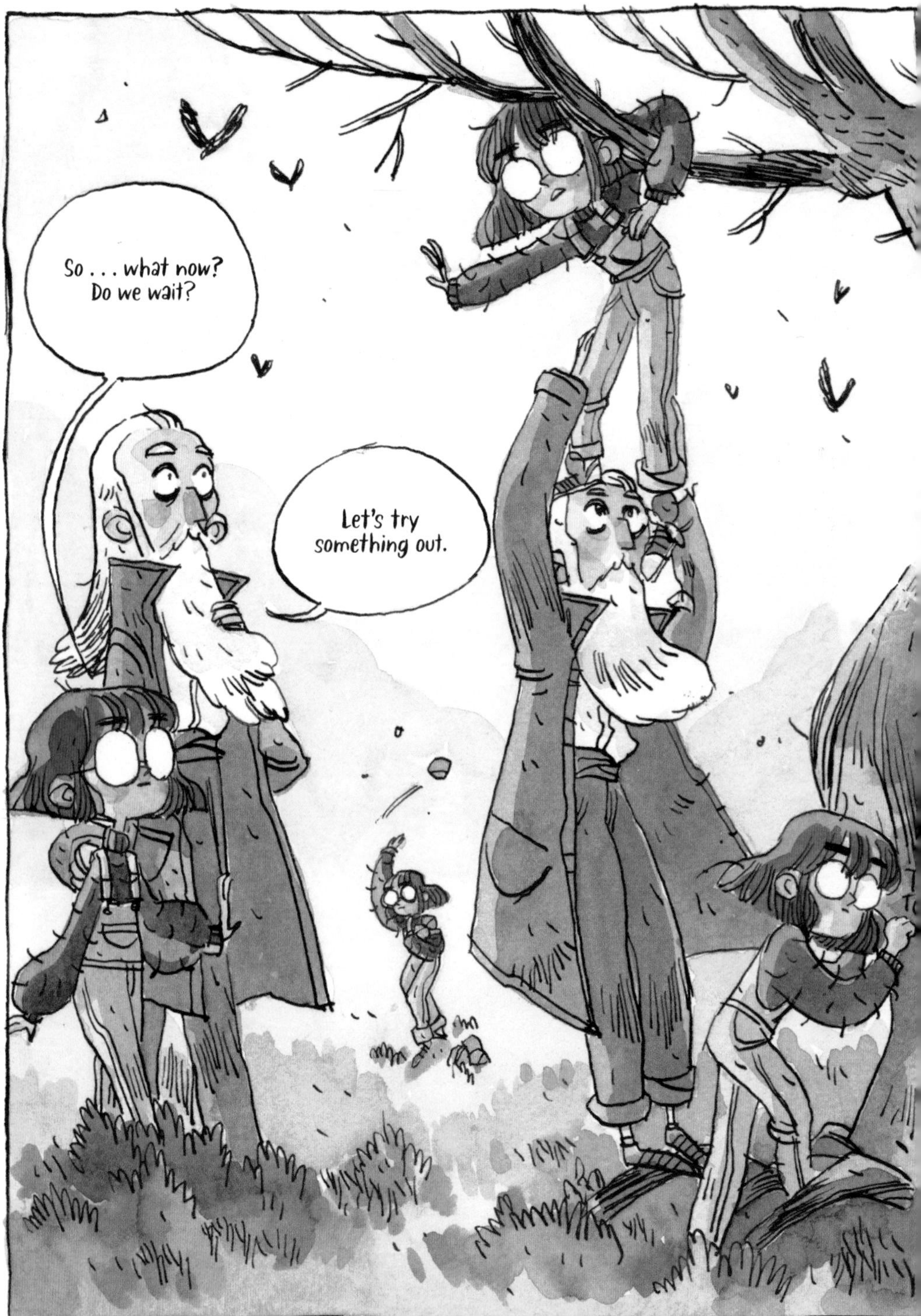
So . . . what now? Do we wait?
Let's try something out.

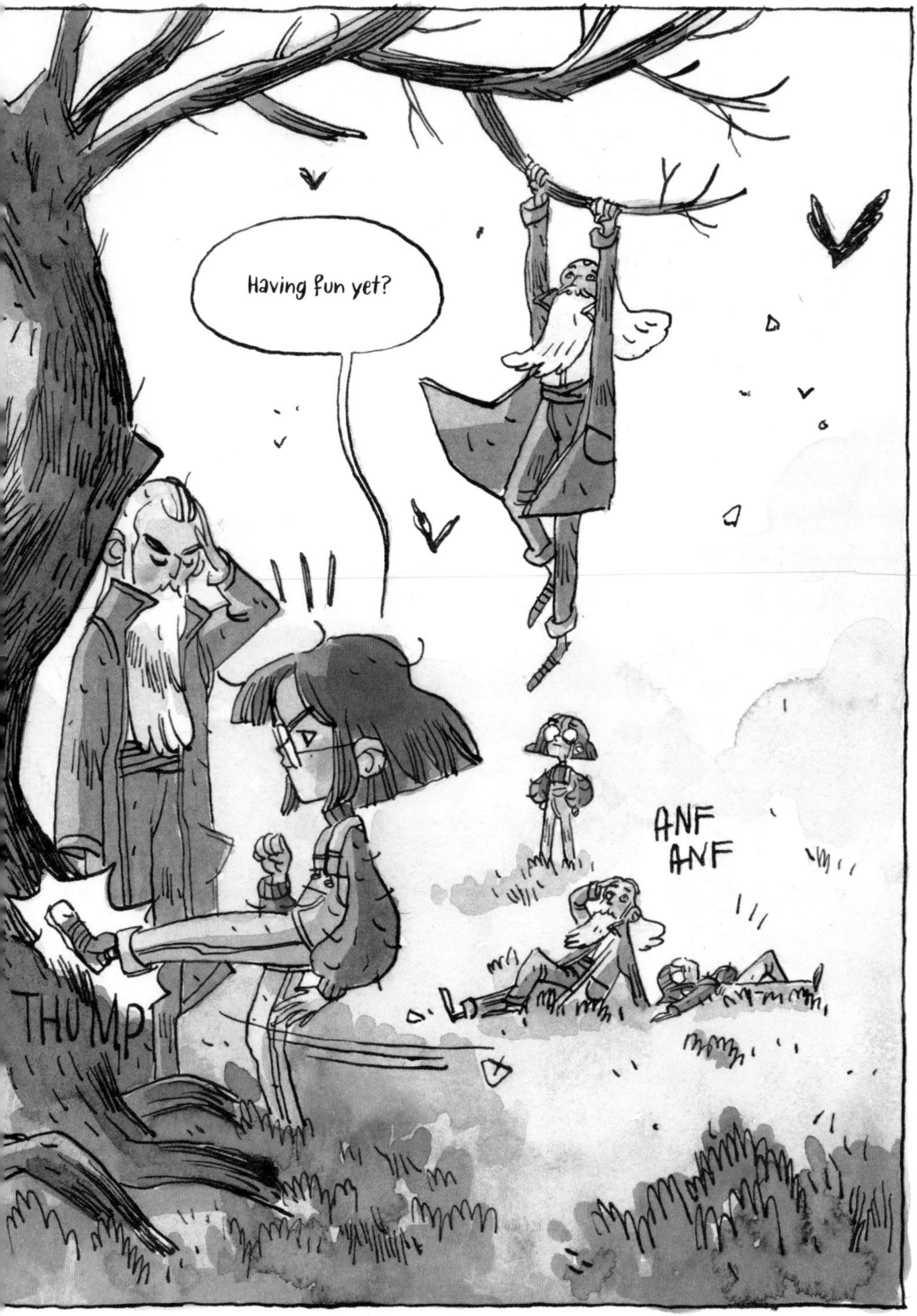
Having fun yet?
THUMP
ANF ANF

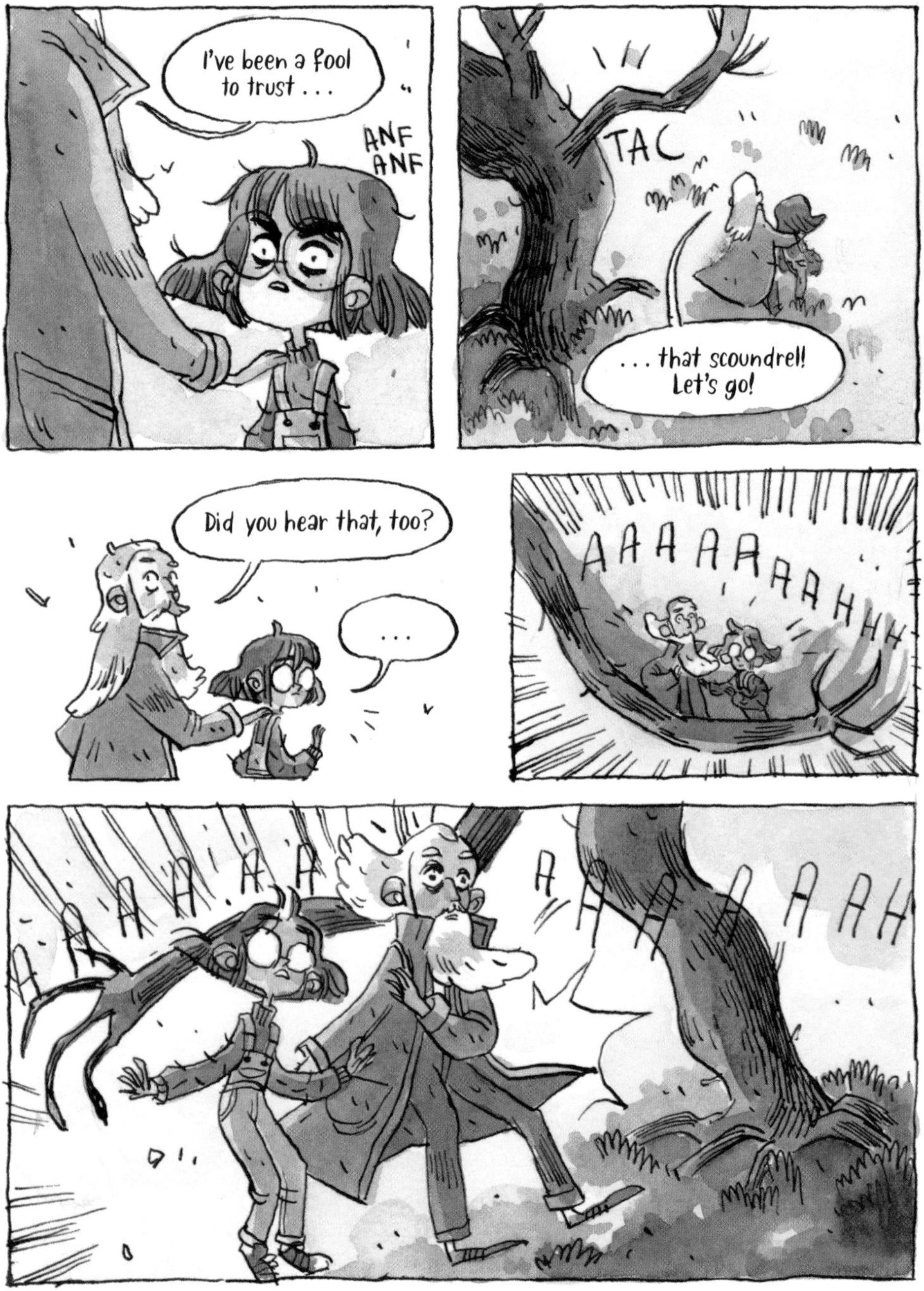
I've been a fool to trust . . .
ANF ANF
TAC
. . . that scoundrel! Let's go!
Did you hear that, too?
. . .
AAAAAAAAHHH
AAAAAAAAAAAAAAH

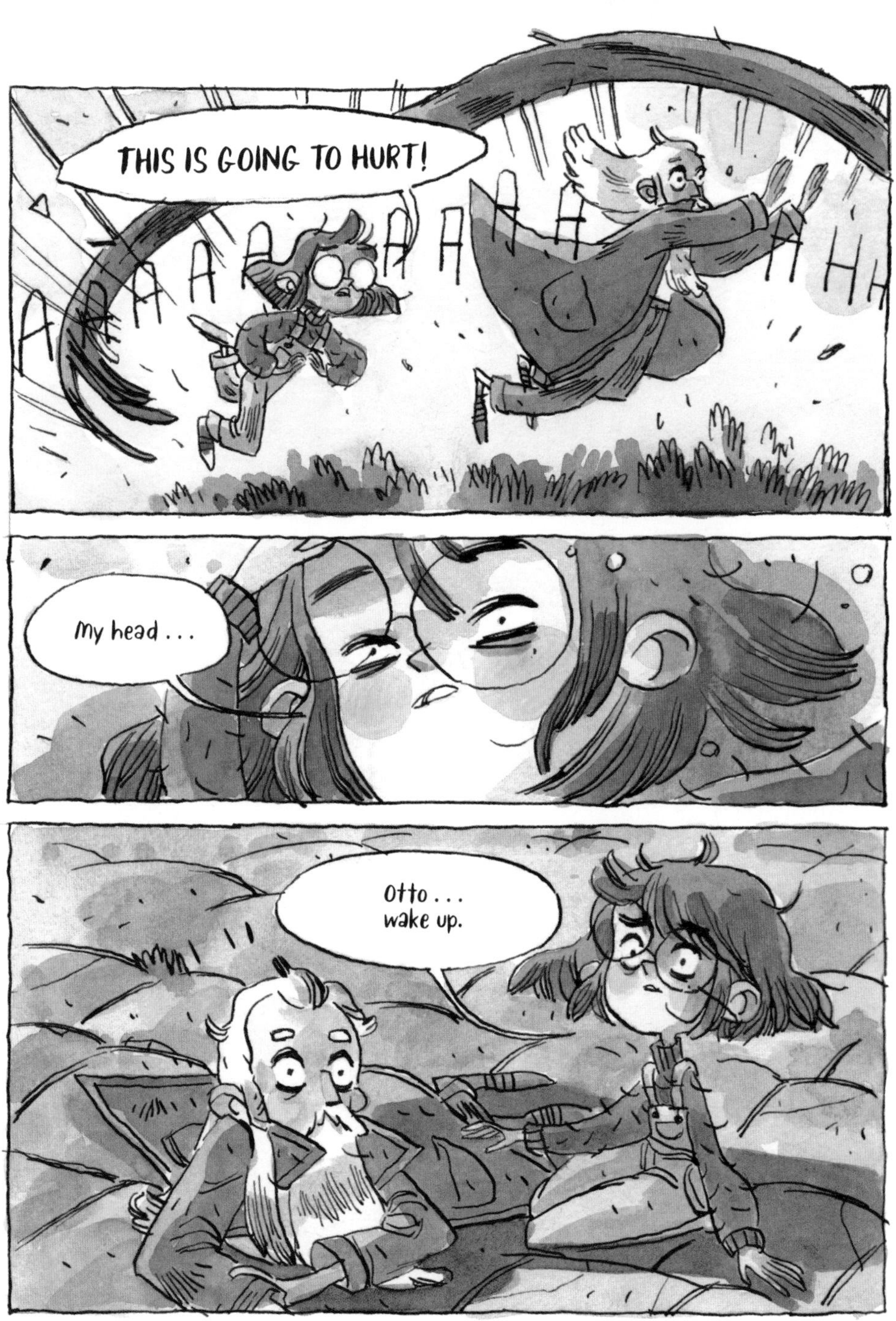
THIS IS GOING TO HURT!
My head . . .
Otto . . .
wake up.

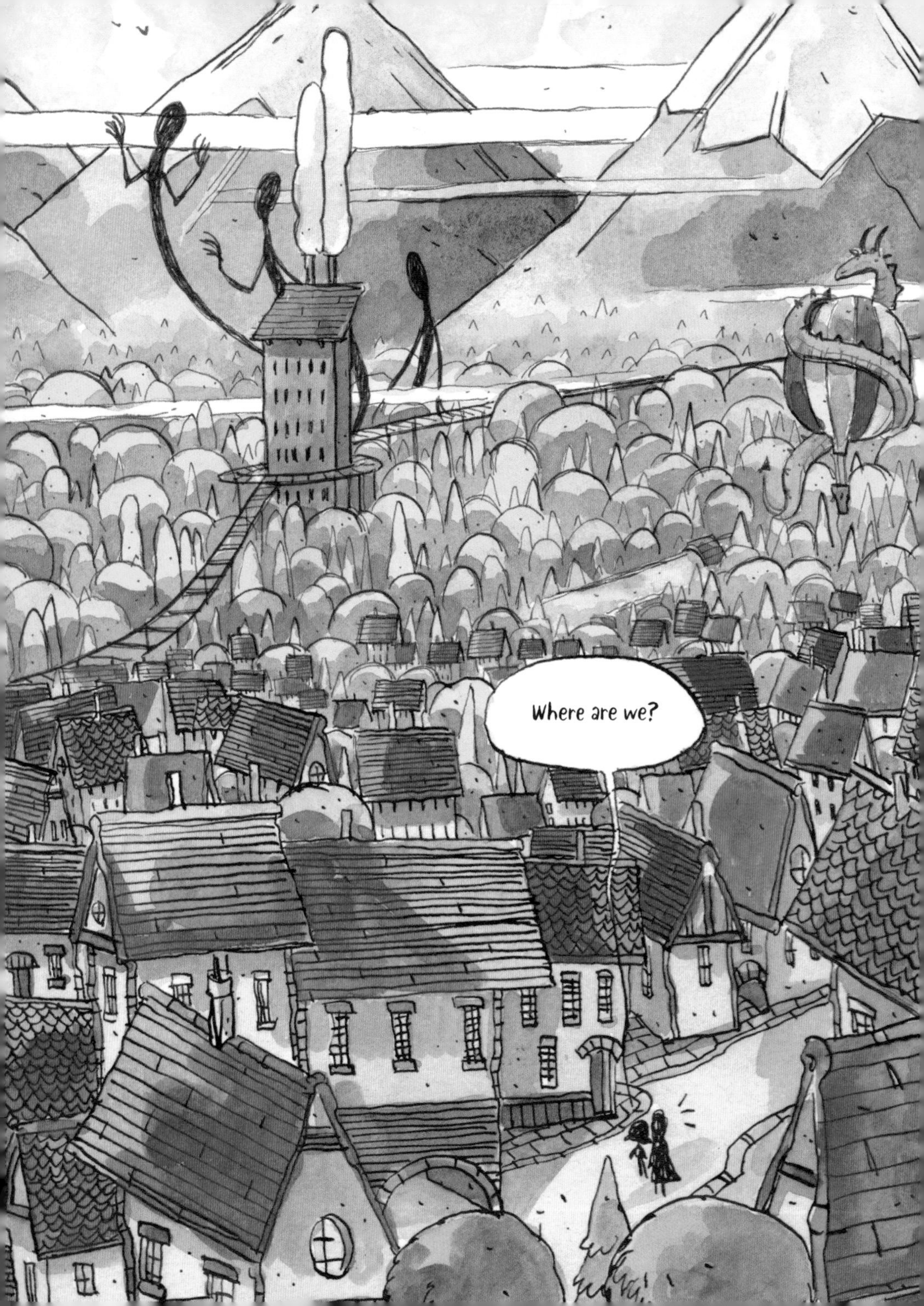
Where are we?

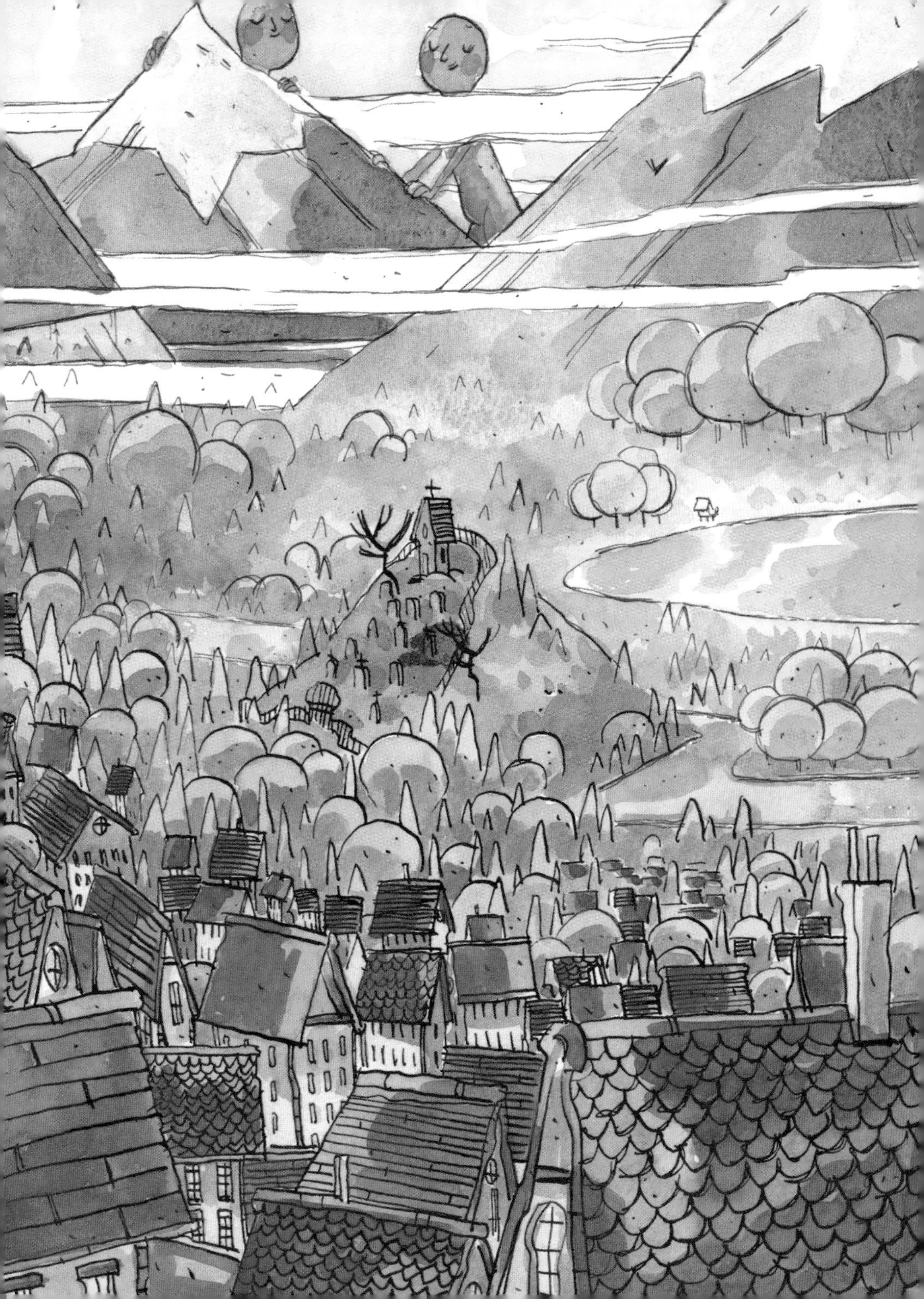

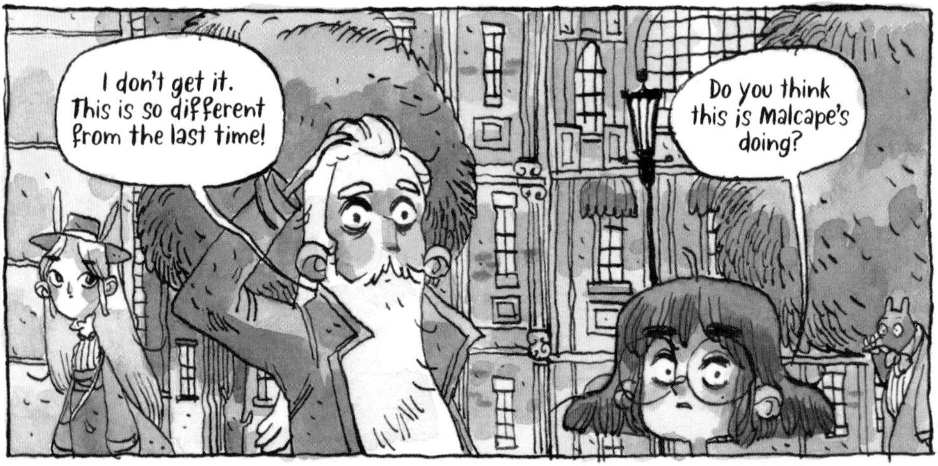
I don't get it. This is so different from the last time!
Do you think this is Malcape's doing?

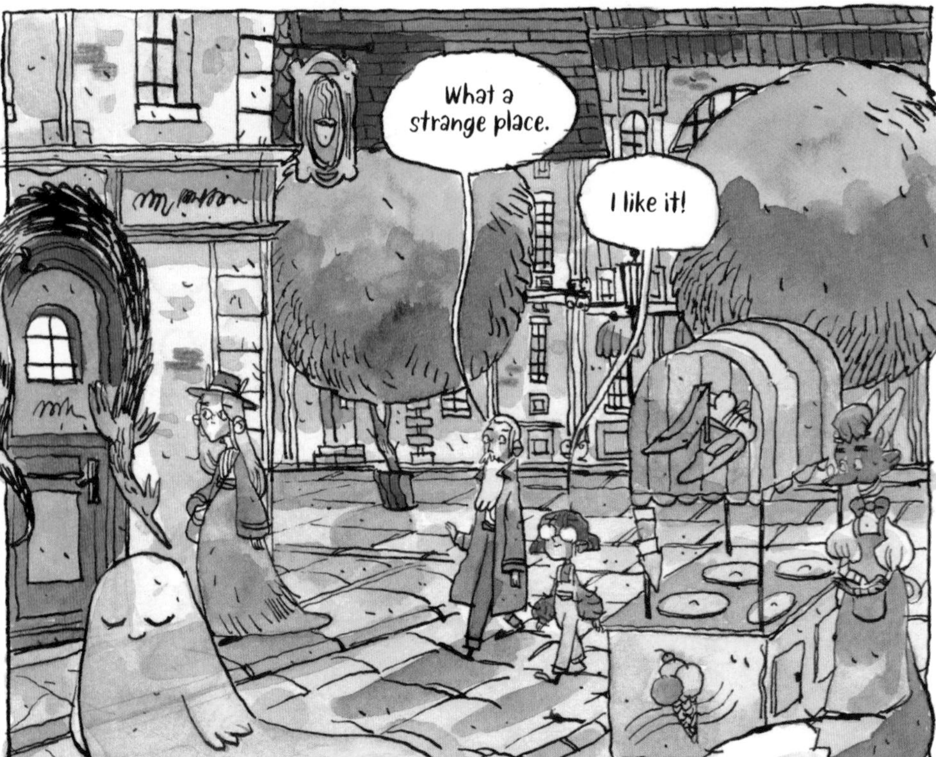
What a strange place.
I like it!

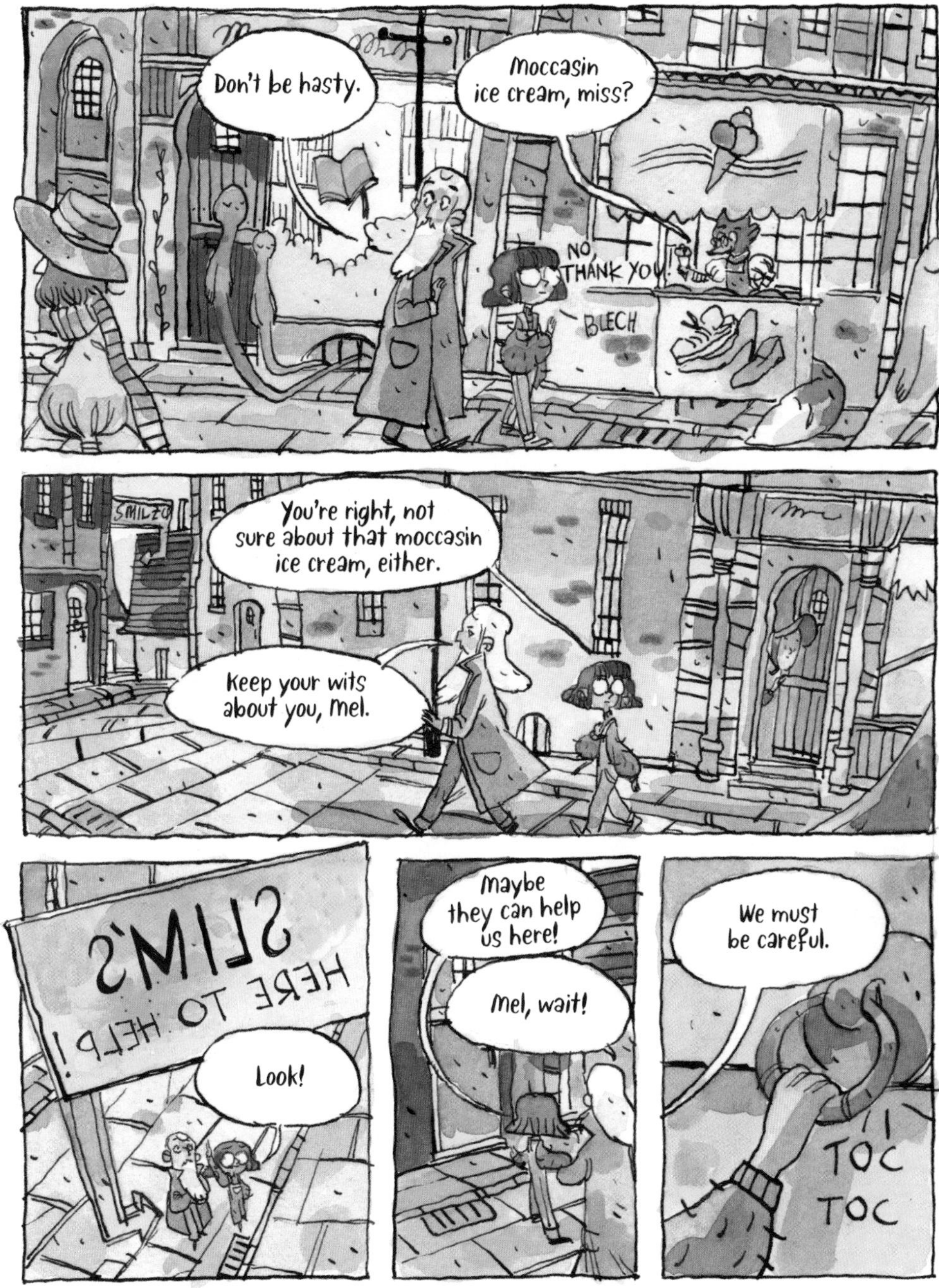
Don't be hasty.
Moccasin ice cream, miss?
NO, THANK YOU!
BLECH
SMILZO
You're right, not sure about that moccasin ice cream, either.
Keep your wits about you, Mel.
SLIM'S HERE TO HELP!
Look!
Maybe they can help us here!
Mel, wait!
We must be careful.
TOC TOC

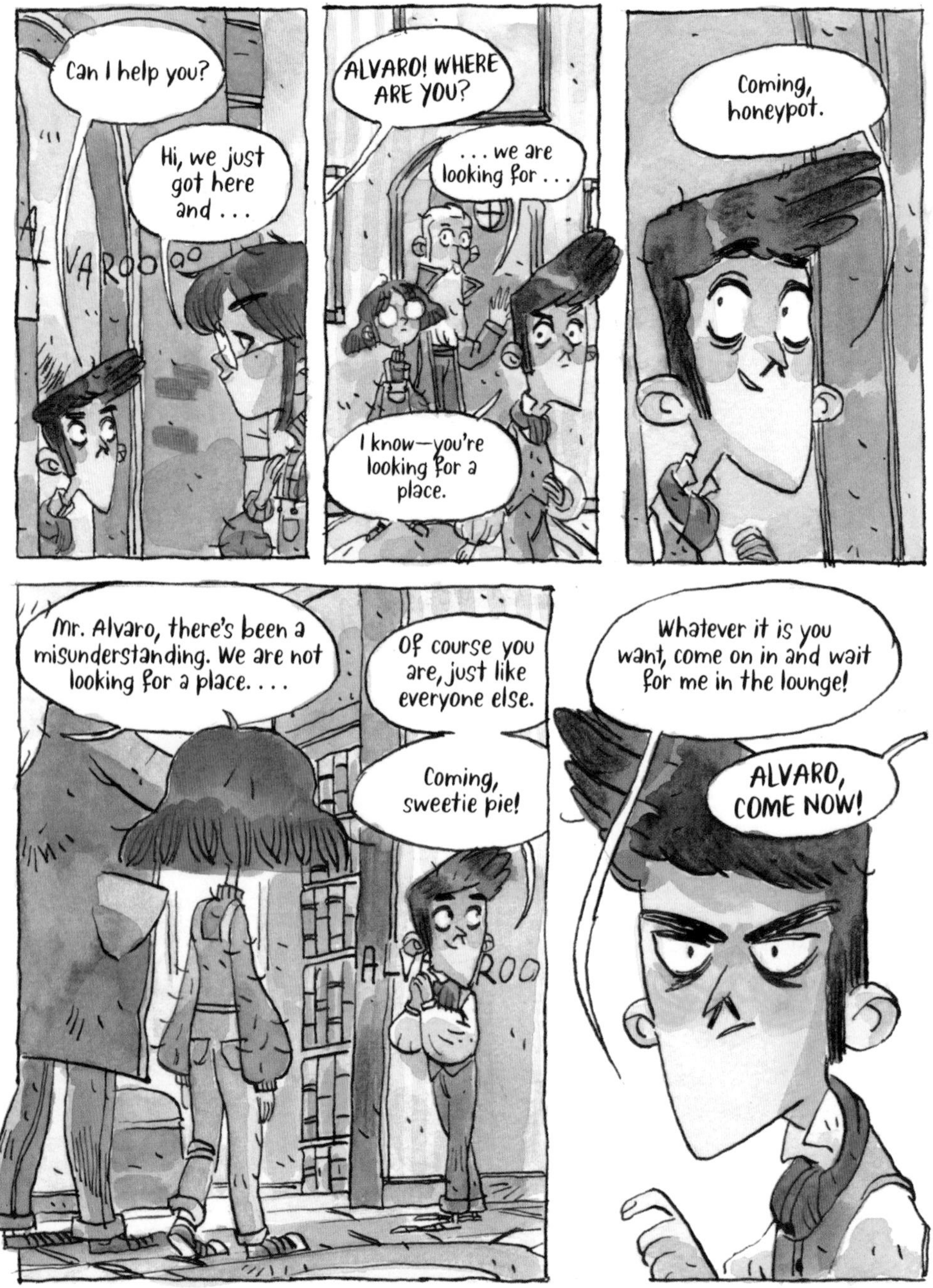

Can I help you?
Hi, we just got here and . . .
VAROO
ALVARO! WHERE ARE YOU?
. . . we are looking for . . .
I know—you're looking for a place.
Coming, honeypot.
Mr. Alvaro, there's been a misunderstanding. We are not looking for a place. . . .
Of course you are, just like everyone else.
Coming, sweetie pie!
Whatever it is you want, come on in and wait for me in the lounge!
ALVARO, COME NOW!

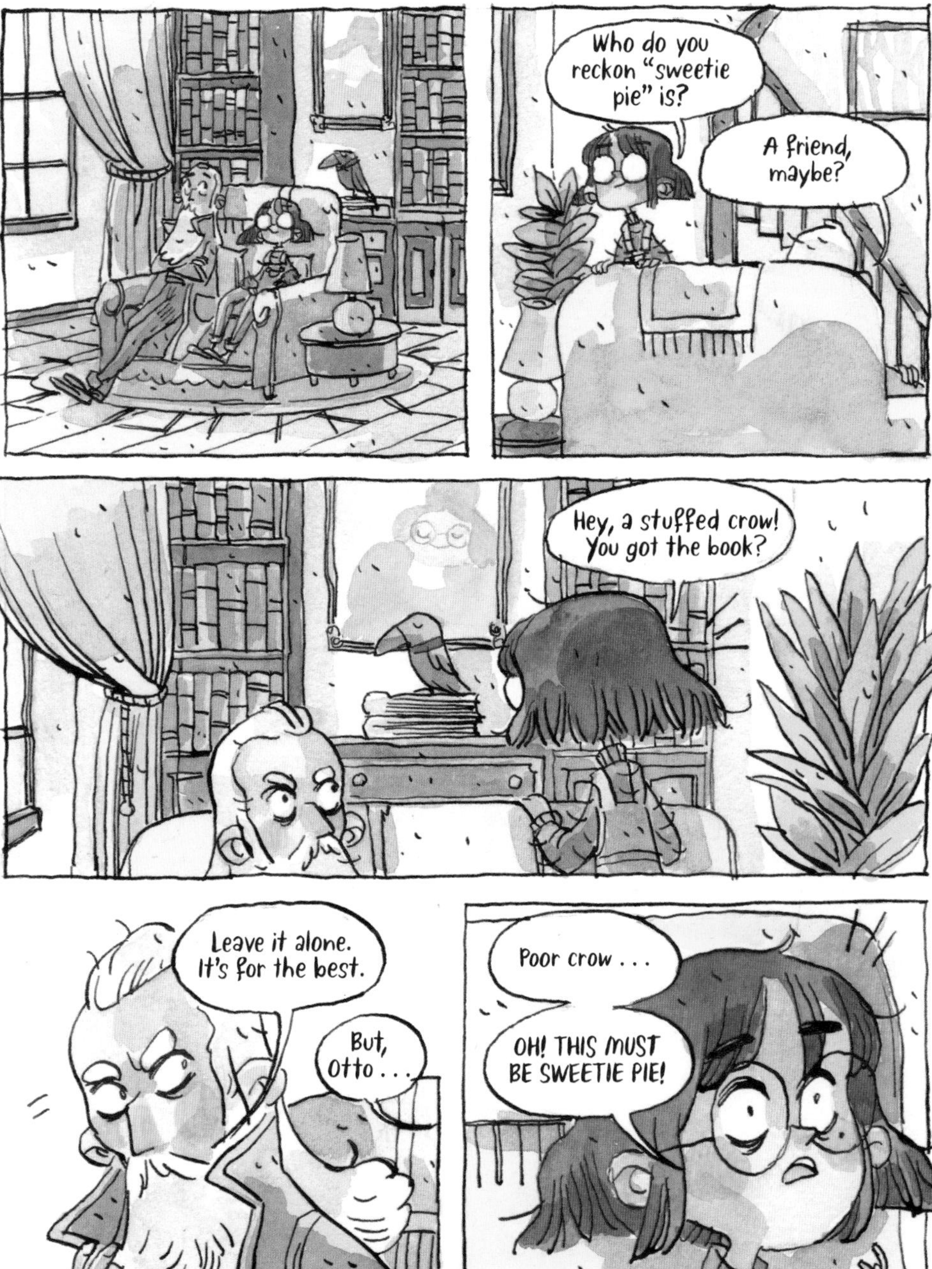

Who do you reckon "sweetie pie" is?
A friend, maybe?
Hey, a stuffed crow! You got the book?
Leave it alone. It's for the best.
But, Otto . . .
Poor crow . . .
OH! THIS MUST BE SWEETIE PIE!

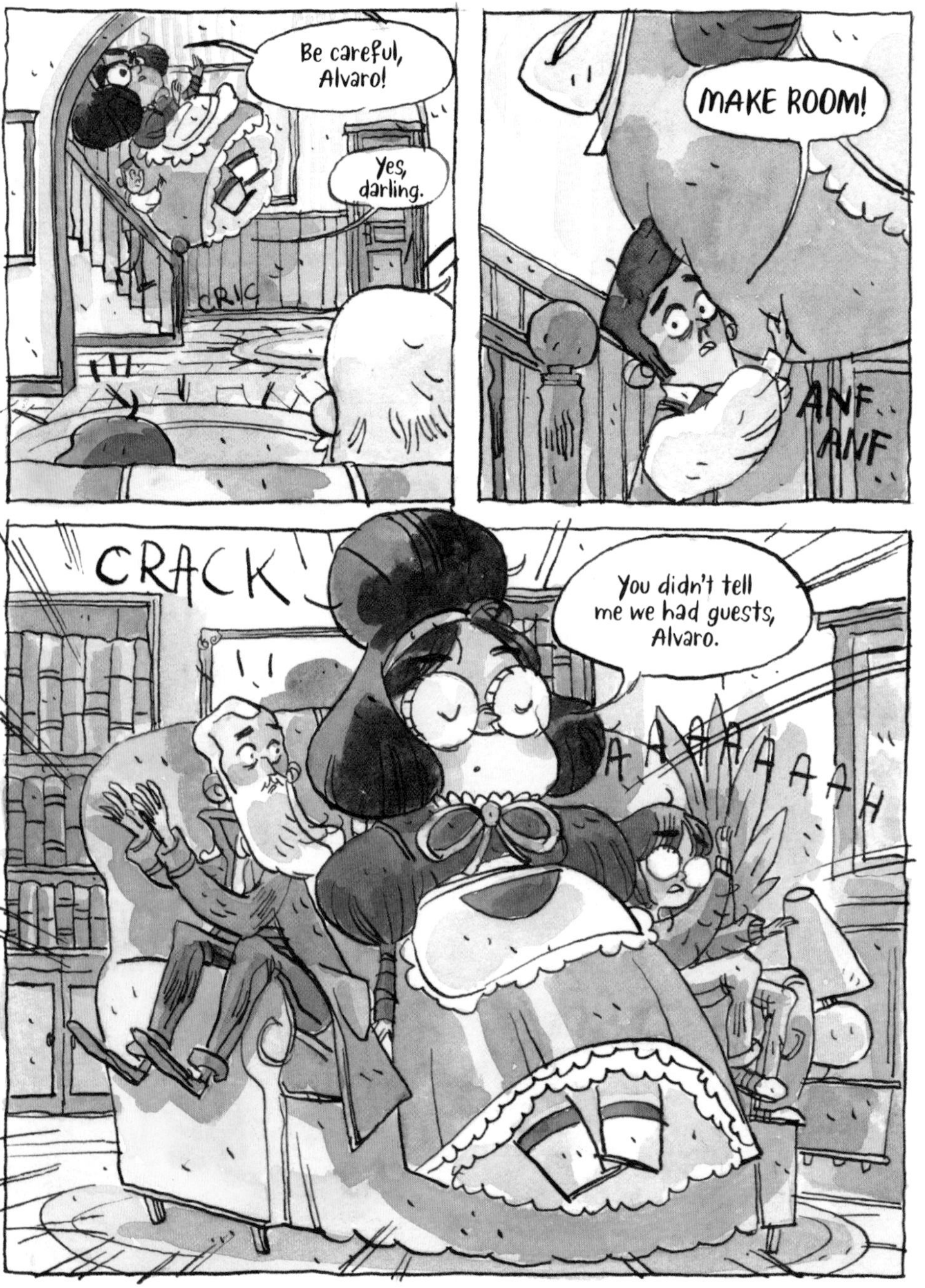
Be careful, Alvaro!
Yes, darling.
CRIC
MAKE ROOM!
ANF ANF
CRACK
You didn't tell me we had guests, Alvaro.
AAAAAAAAAH

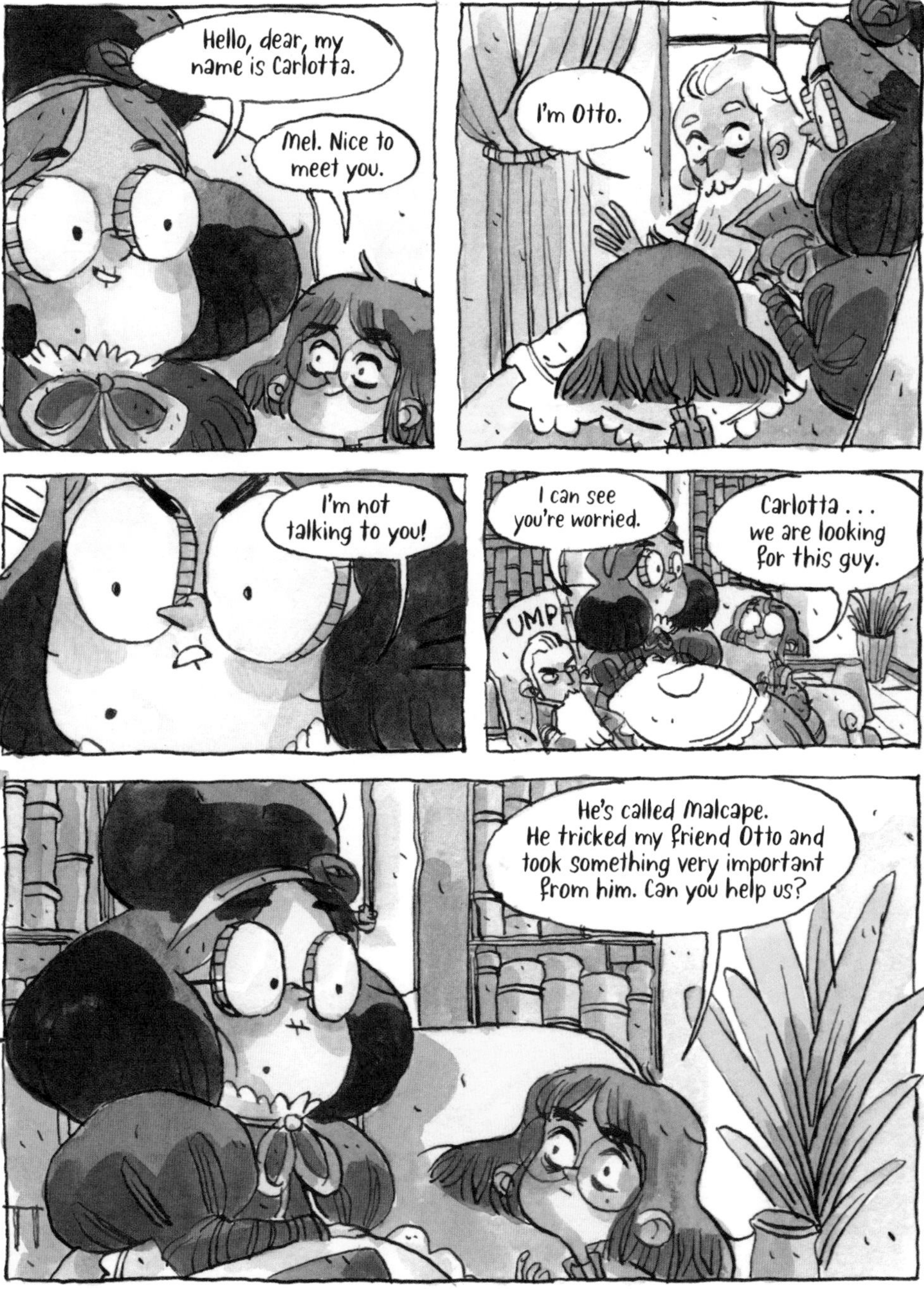
Hello, dear, my name is Carlotta.
Mel. Nice to meet you.
I'm Otto.
I'm not talking to you!
I can see you're worried.
UMPF
Carlotta . . . we are looking for this guy.
He's called Malcape. He tricked my friend Otto and took something very important from him. Can you help us?

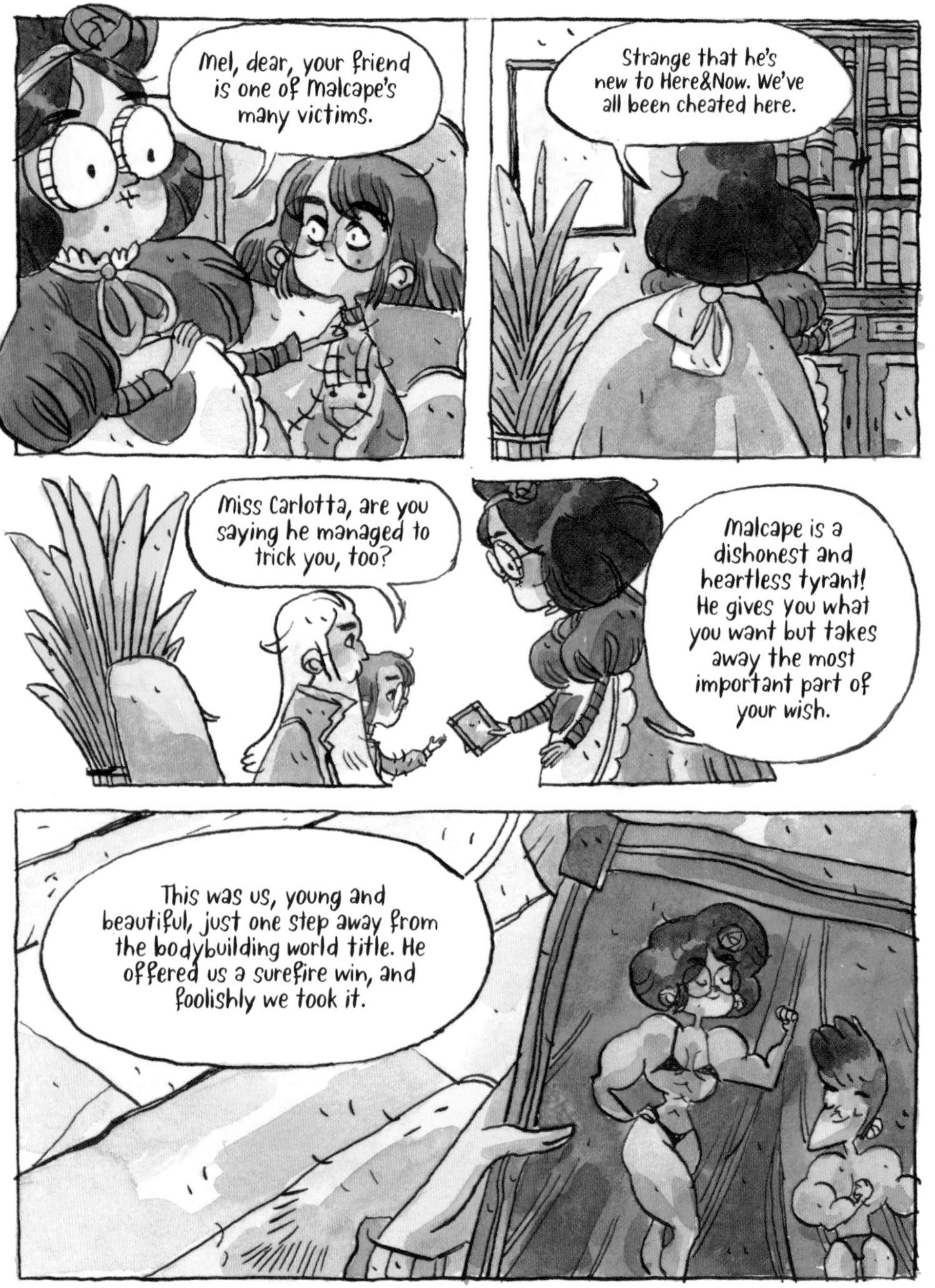
Mel, dear, your friend is one of Malcape's many victims.
Strange that he's new to Here&Now. We've all been cheated here.
Miss Carlotta, are you saying he managed to trick you, too?
Malcape is a dishonest and heartless tyrant! He gives you what you want but takes away the most important part of your wish.
This was us, young and beautiful, just one step away from the bodybuilding world title. He offered us a surefire win, and foolishly we took it.

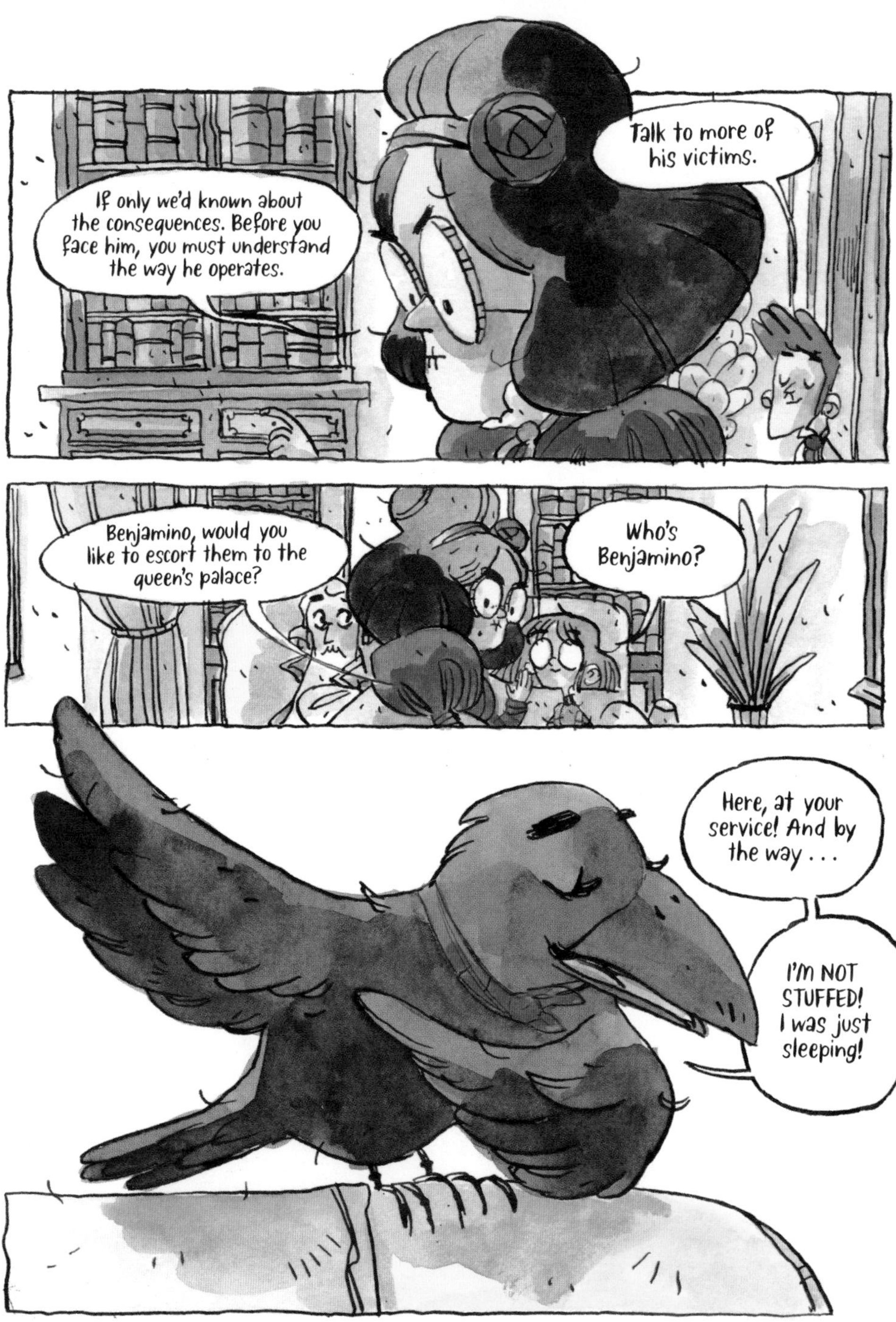
If only we'd known about the consequences. Before you face him, you must understand the way he operates.
Talk to more of his victims.
Benjamino, would you like to escort them to the queen's palace?
Who's Benjamino?
Here, at your service! And by the way . . .
I'M NOT STUFFED! I was just sleeping!

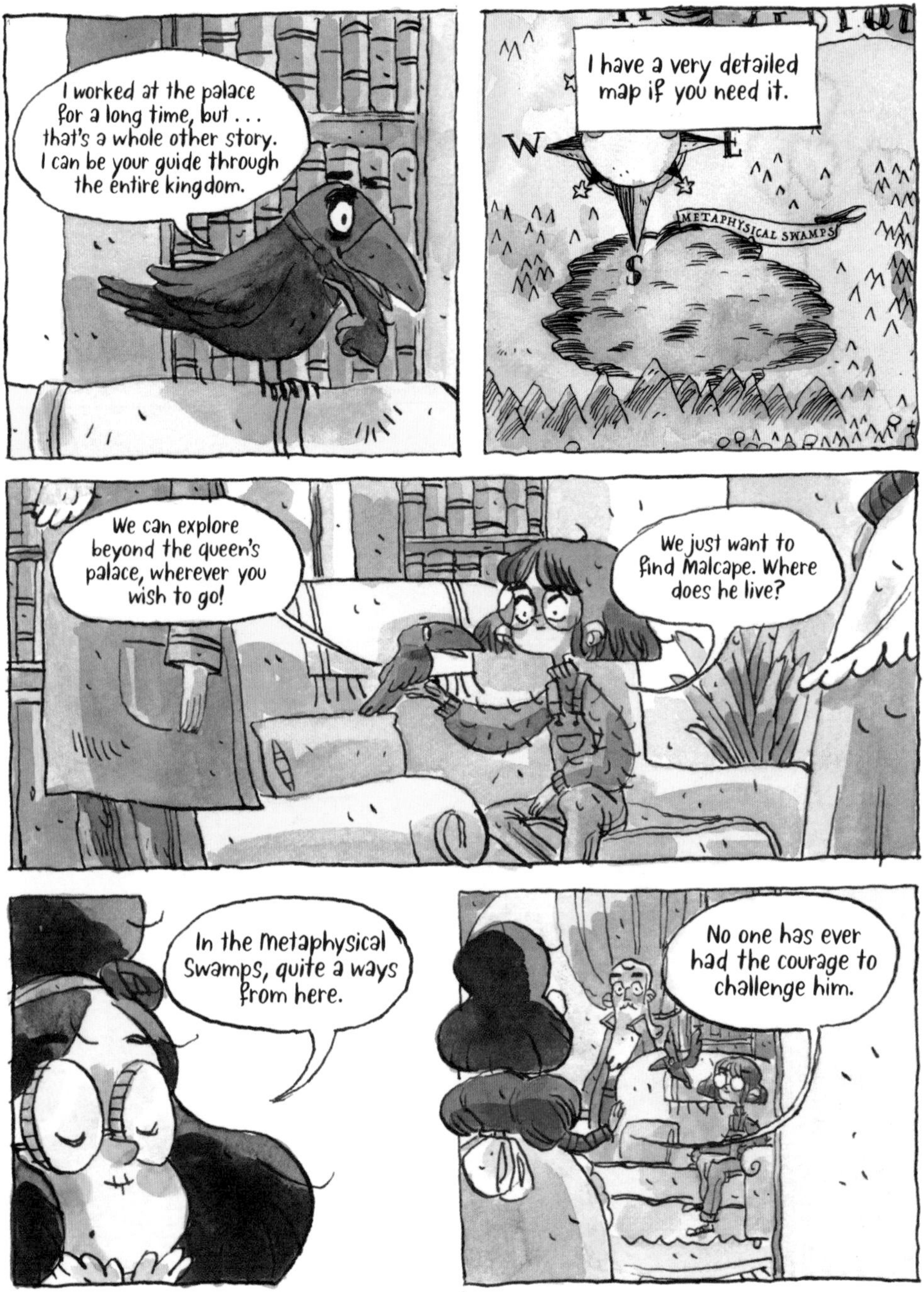

I worked at the palace for a long time, but . . . that's a whole other story. I can be your guide through the entire kingdom.
I have a very detailed map if you need it.
W
E
S
METAPHYSICAL SWAMPS
We can explore beyond the queen's palace, wherever you wish to go!
We just want to find Malcape. Where does he live?
In the Metaphysical Swamps, quite a ways from here.
No one has ever had the courage to challenge him.

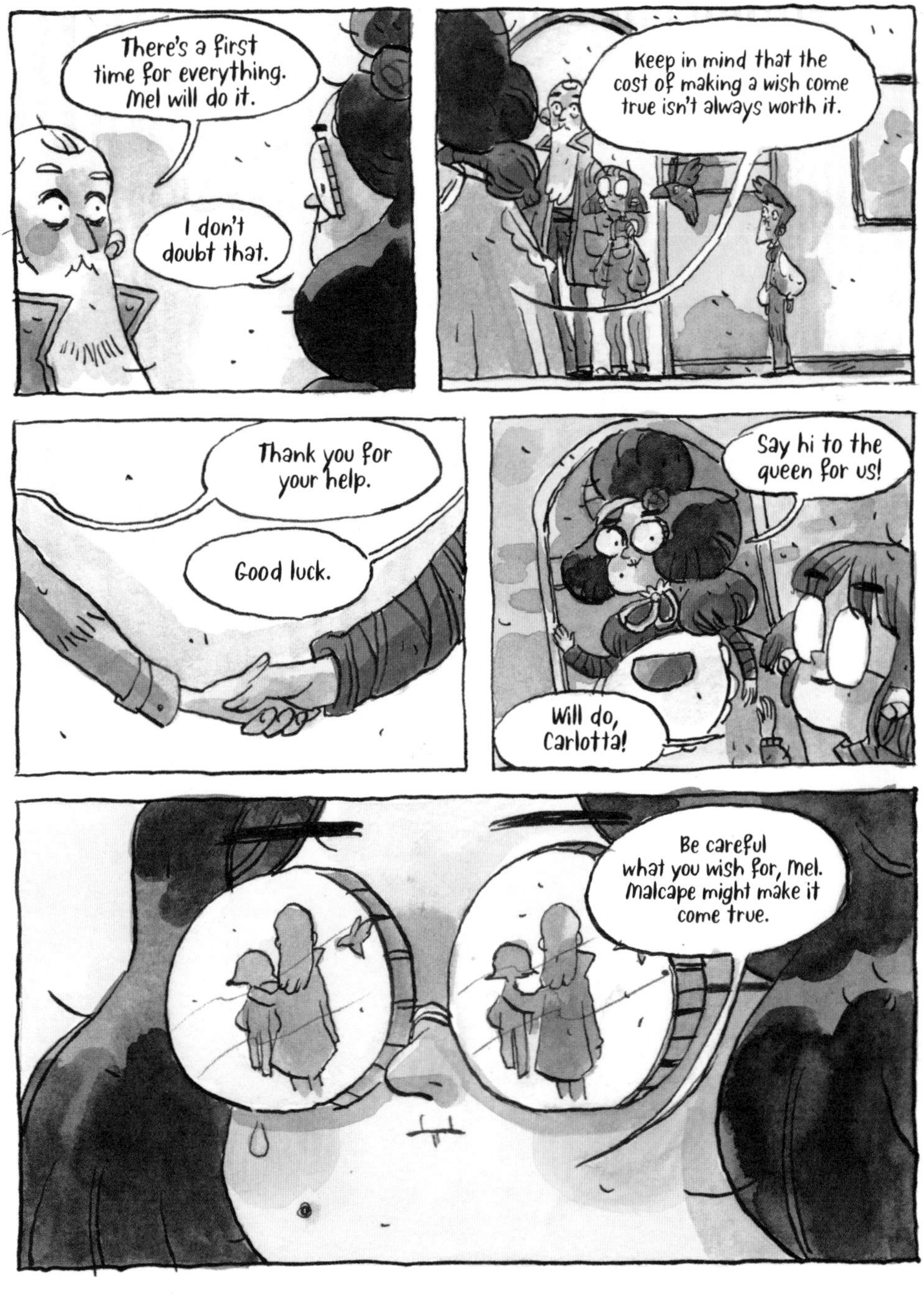

There's a first time for everything. Mel will do it.
I don't doubt that.
Keep in mind that the cost of making a wish come true isn't always worth it.
Thank you for your help.
Good luck.
Say hi to the queen for us!
Will do, Carlotta!
Be careful what you wish for, Mel. Malcape might make it come true.

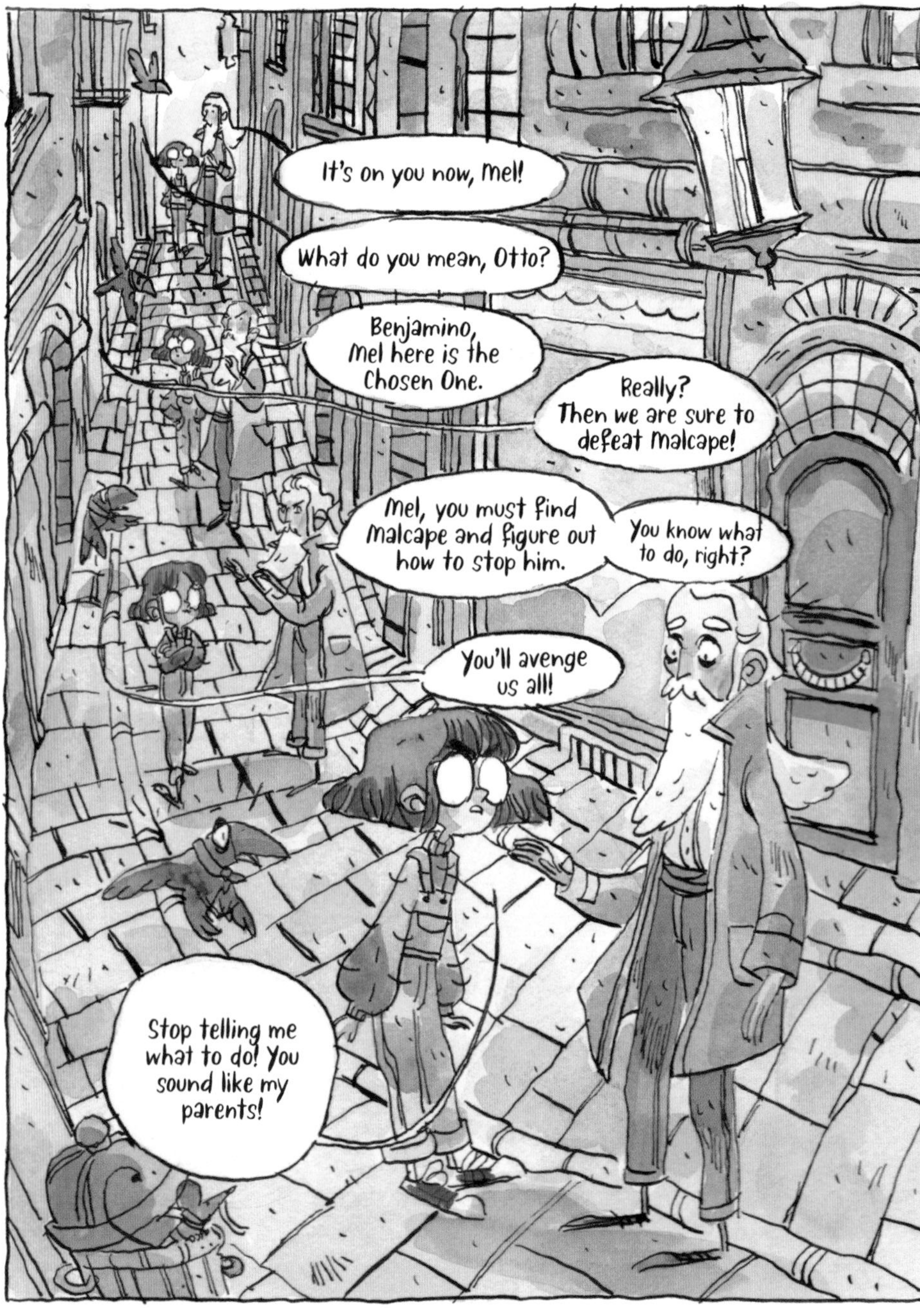
It's on you now, Mel!
What do you mean, Otto?
Benjamino, Mel here is the Chosen One.
Really? Then we are sure to defeat Malcape!
Mel, you must find Malcape and figure out how to stop him.
You know what to do, right?
You'll avenge us all!
Stop telling me what to do! You sound like my parents!

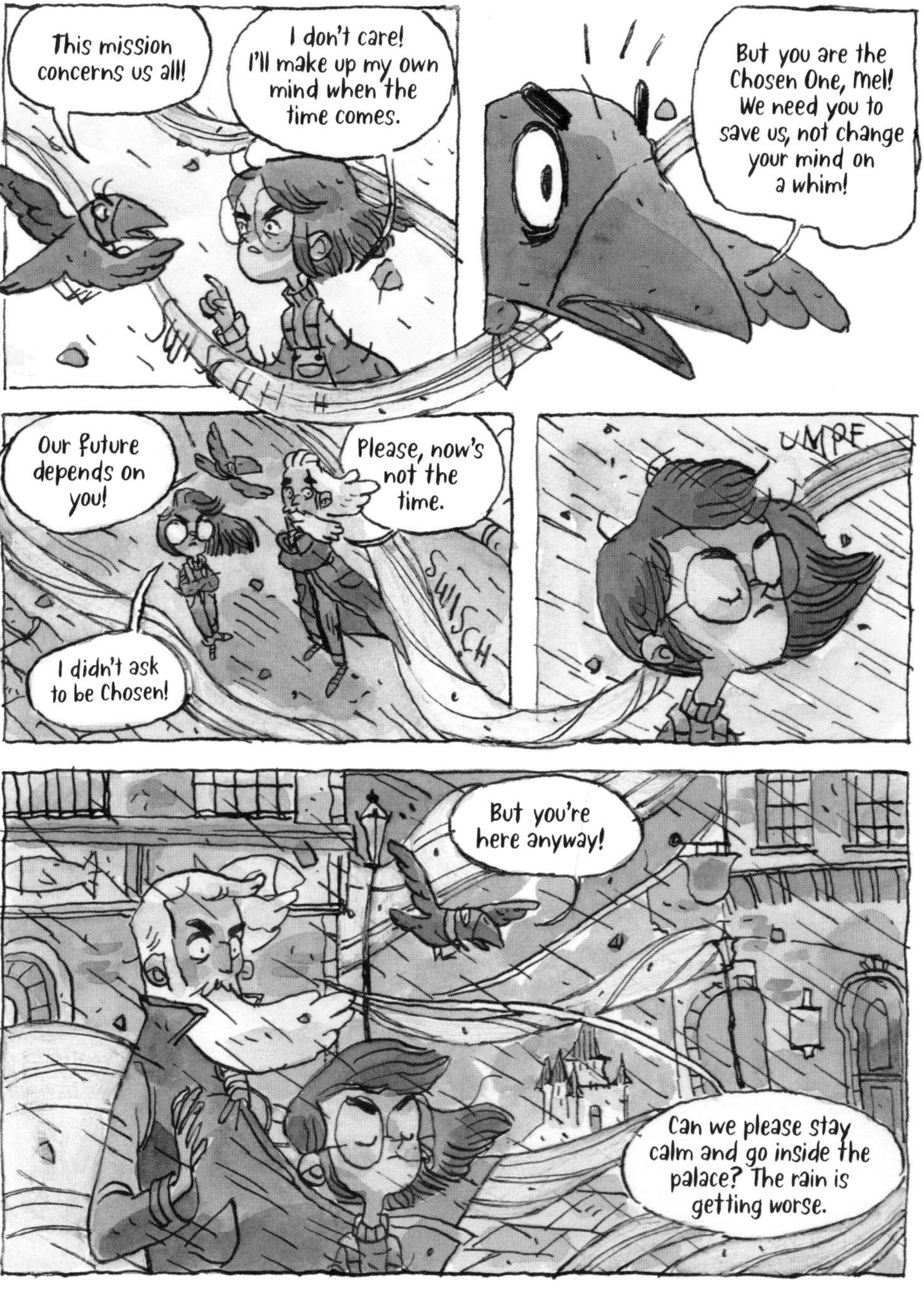
This mission concerns us all!
I don't care! I'll make up my own mind when the time comes.
SWISCHHH
But you are the Chosen One, Mel! We need you to save us, not change your mind on a whim!
Our future depends on you!
Please, now's not the time.
SWISCH
I didn't ask to be Chosen!
UMPF
But you're here anyway!
Can we please stay calm and go inside the palace? The rain is getting worse.

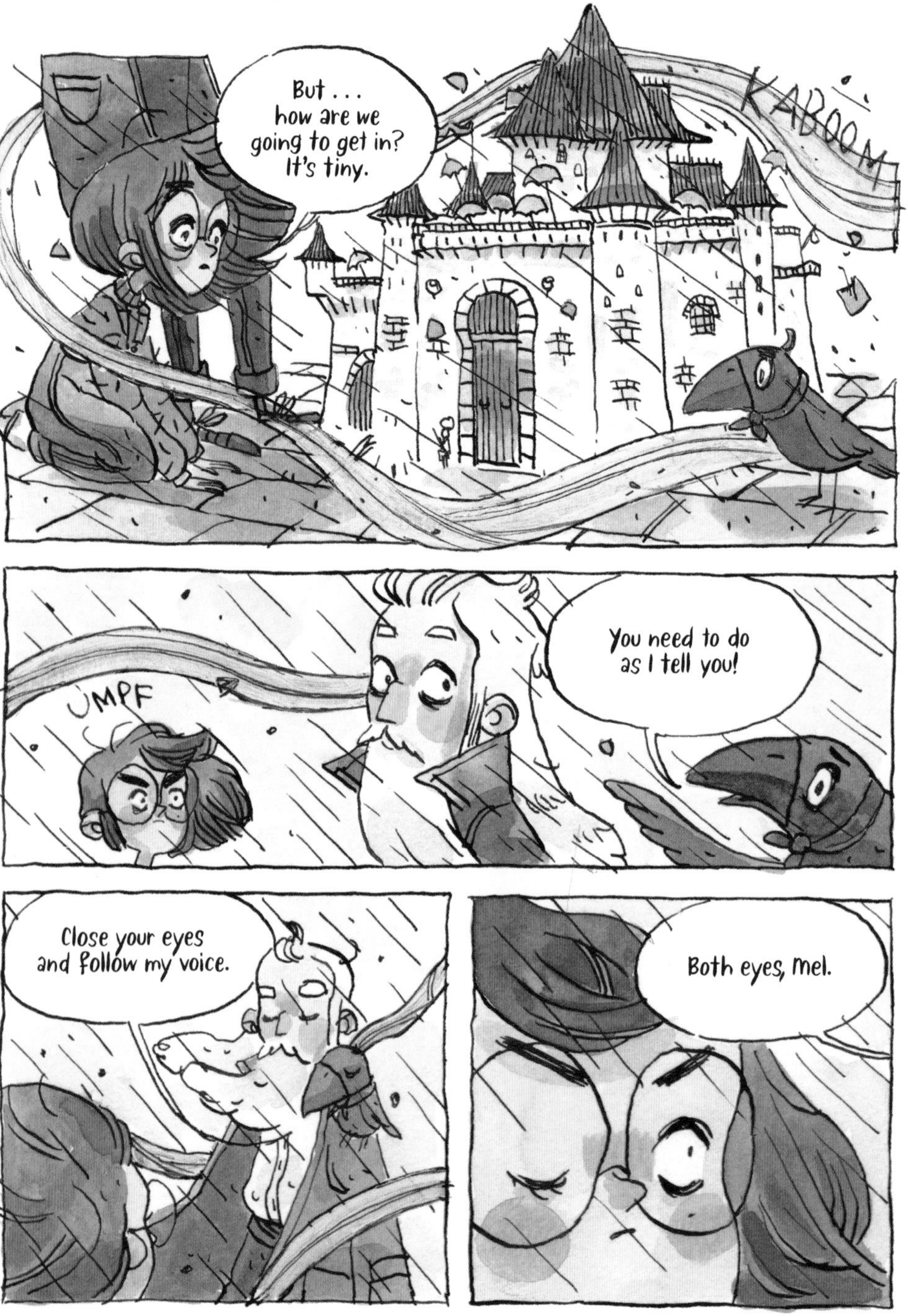
But . . . how are we going to get in? It's tiny.
KABOOM
UMPF
You need to do as I tell you!
Close your eyes and follow my voice.
Both eyes, Mel.

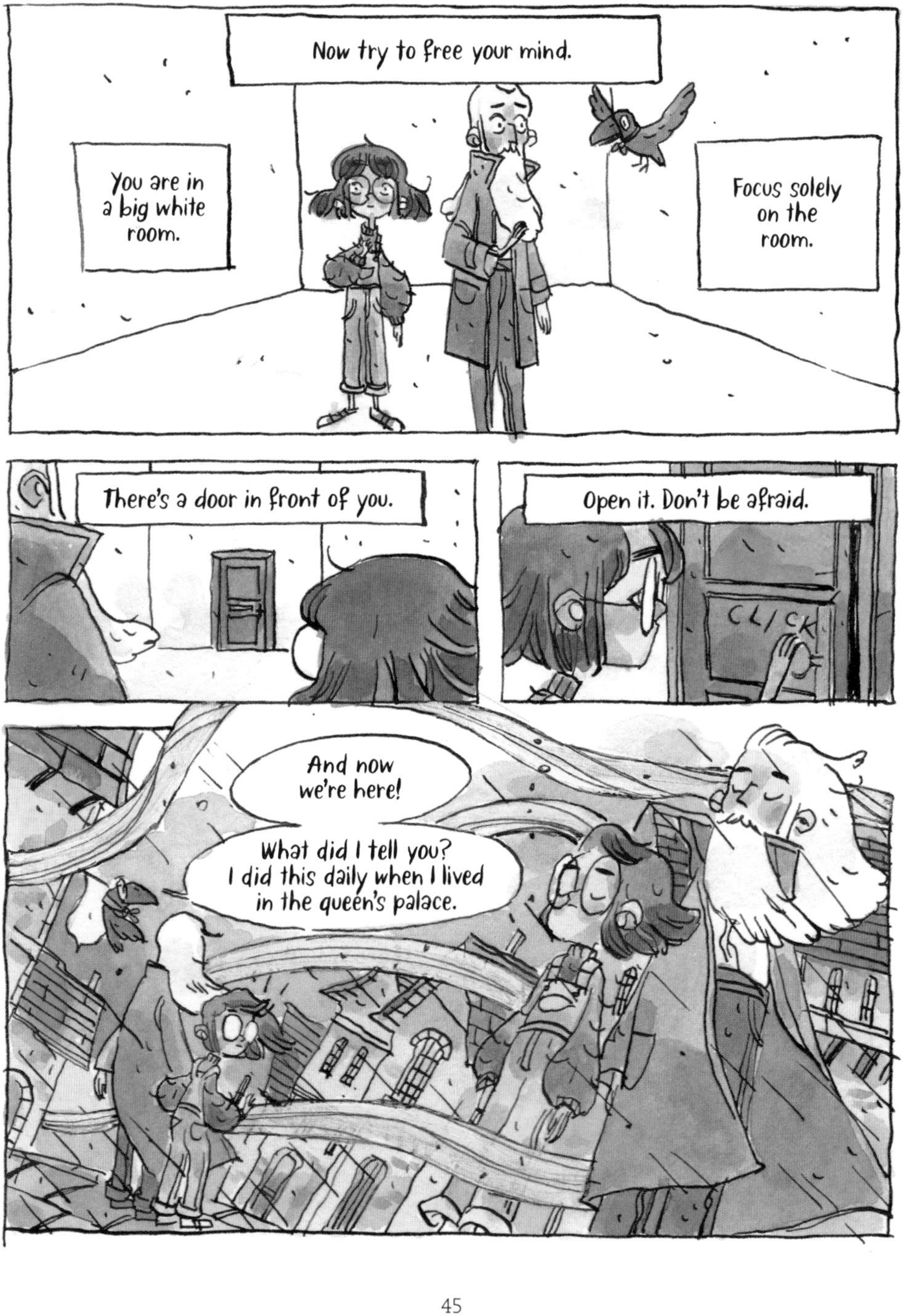
Now try to free your mind.
You are in a big white room.
Focus solely on the room.
There's a door in front of you.
Open it. Don't be afraid.
CLICK
And now we're here!
What did I tell you? I did this daily when I lived in the queen's palace.

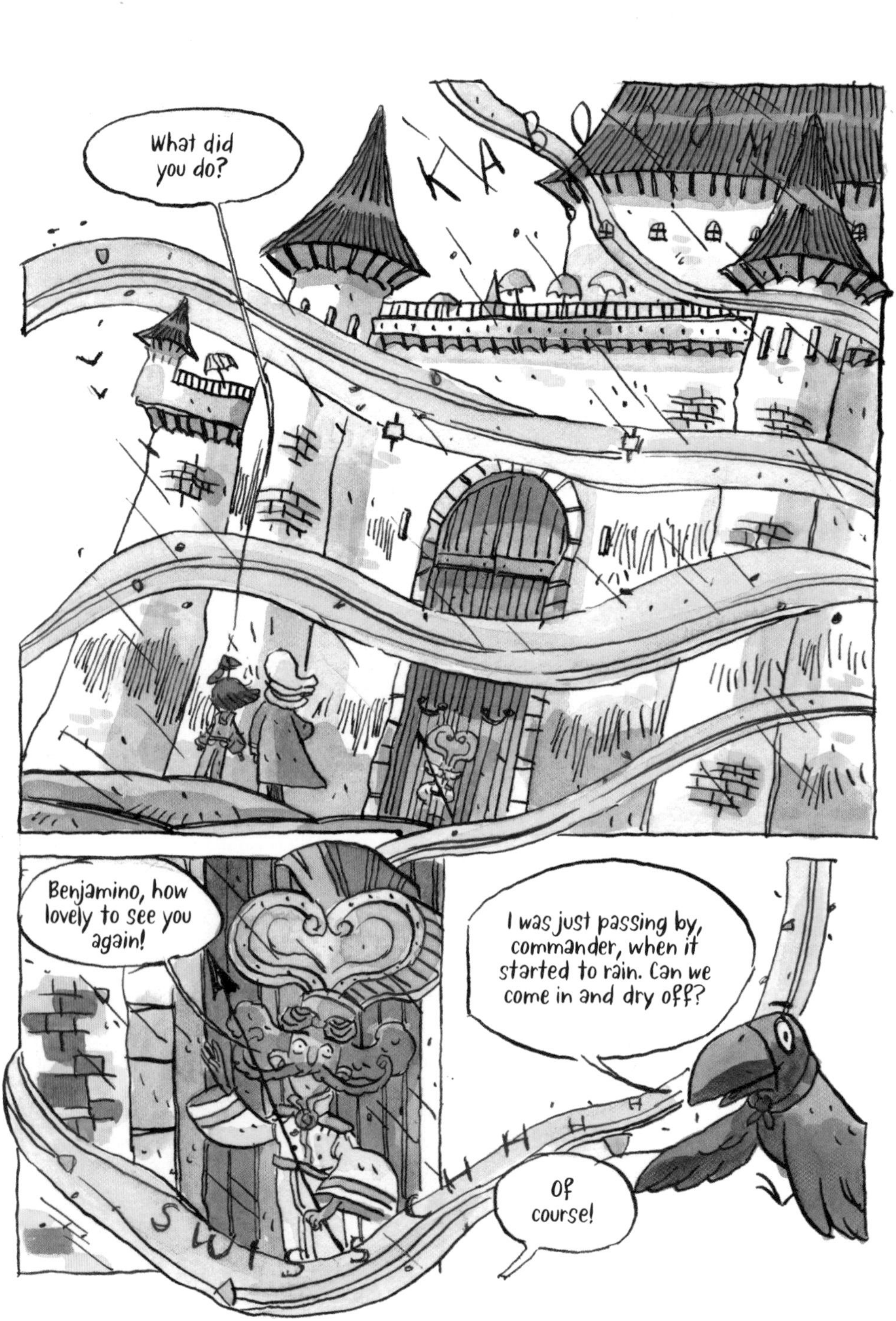
What did you do?
KA-BOOM
Benjamino, how lovely to see you again!
I was just passing by, commander, when it started to rain. Can we come in and dry off?
Of course!
SWISH

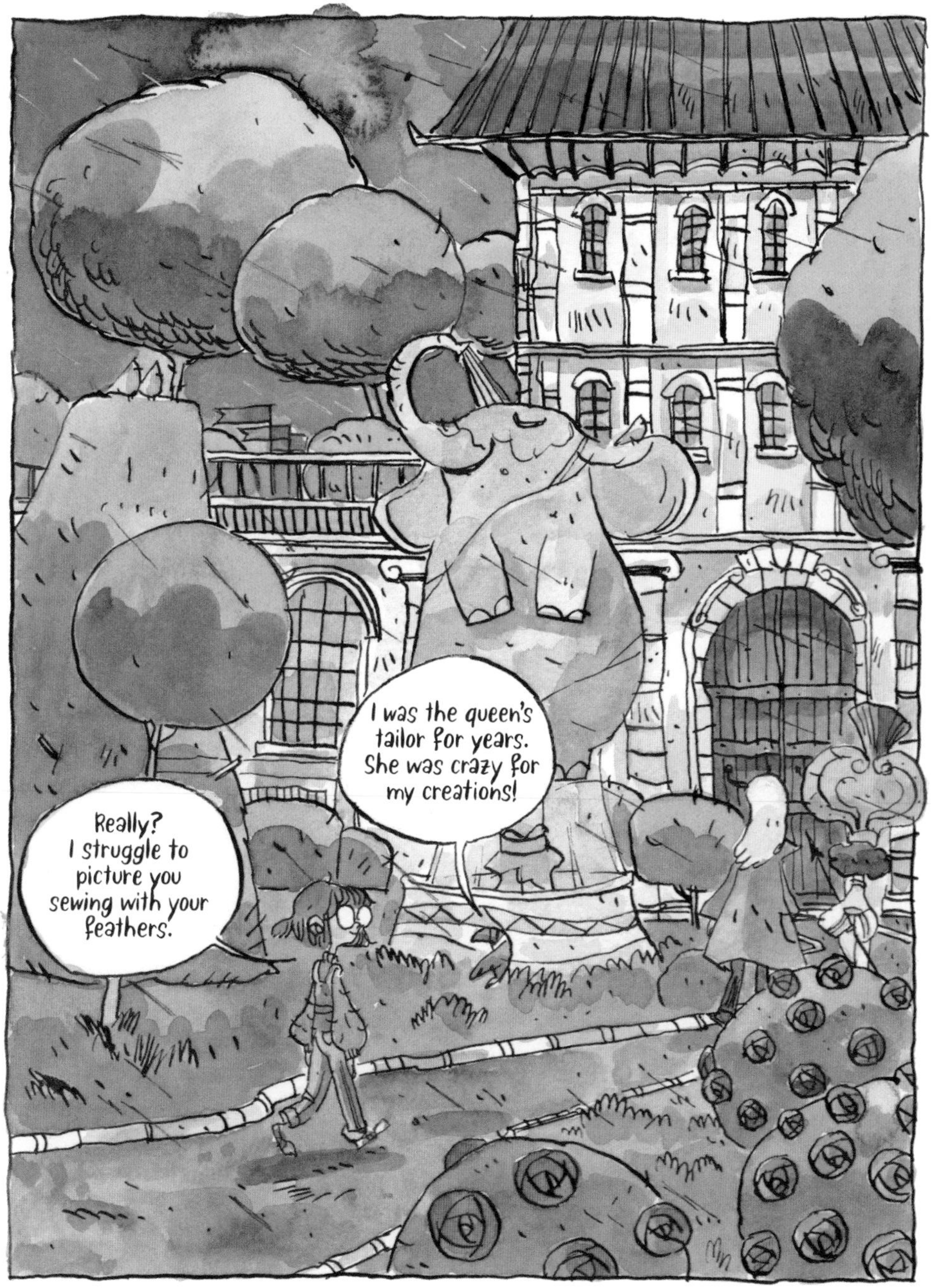
I was the queen's tailor for years. She was crazy for my creations!
Really? I struggle to picture you sewing with your feathers.

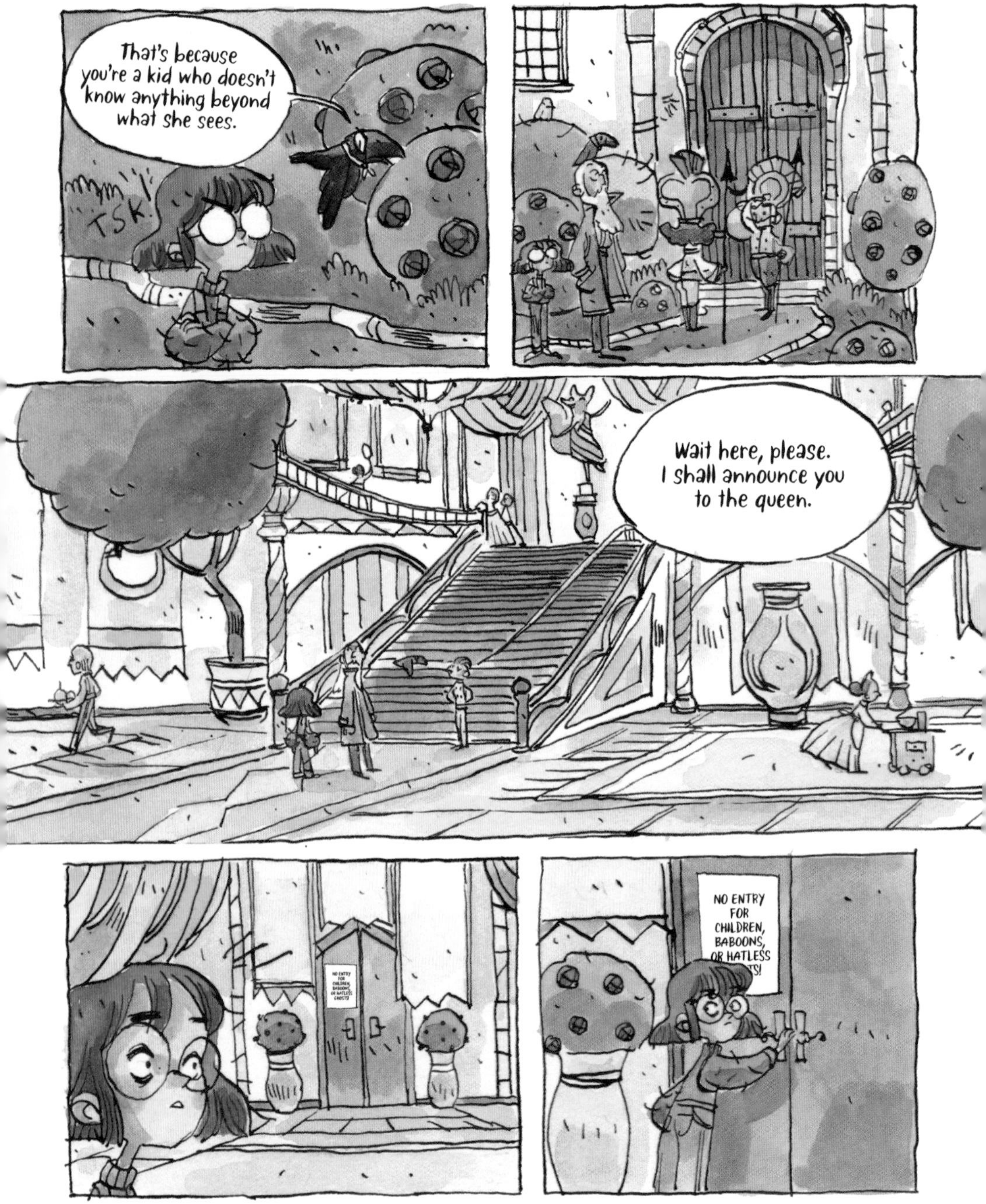
That's because you're a kid who doesn't know anything beyond what she sees.
TSK
Wait here, please. I shall announce you to the queen.
NO ENTRY FOR CHILDREN, BABOONS, OR HATLESS GHOSTS!
NO ENTRY FOR CHILDREN, BABOONS, OR HATLESS

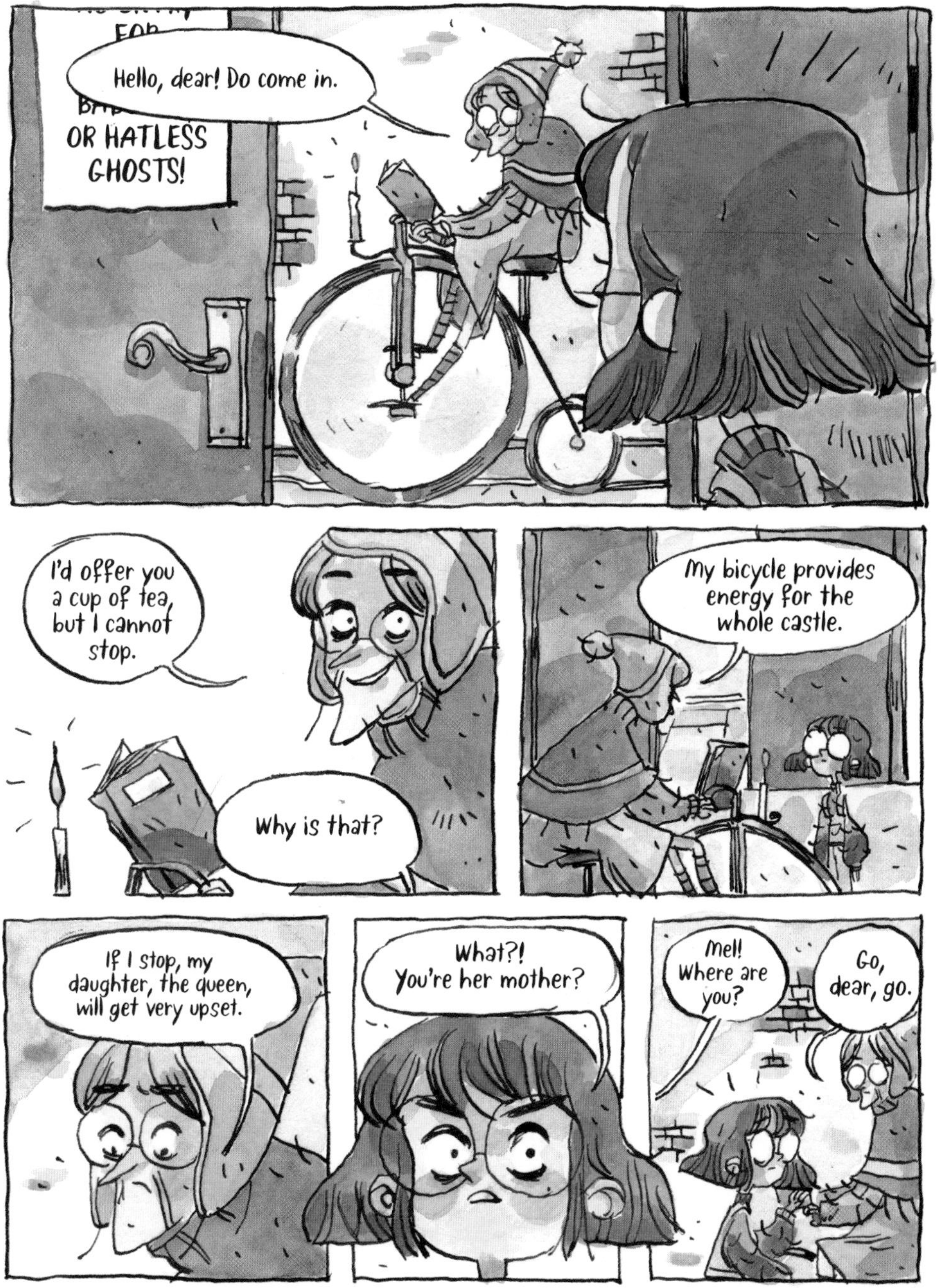

OR HATLESS GHOSTS!
Hello, dear! Do come in.
I'd offer you a cup of tea, but I cannot stop.
Why is that?
My bicycle provides energy for the whole castle.
If I stop, my daughter, the queen, will get very upset.
What?! You're her mother?
Mel! Where are you?
Go, dear, go.

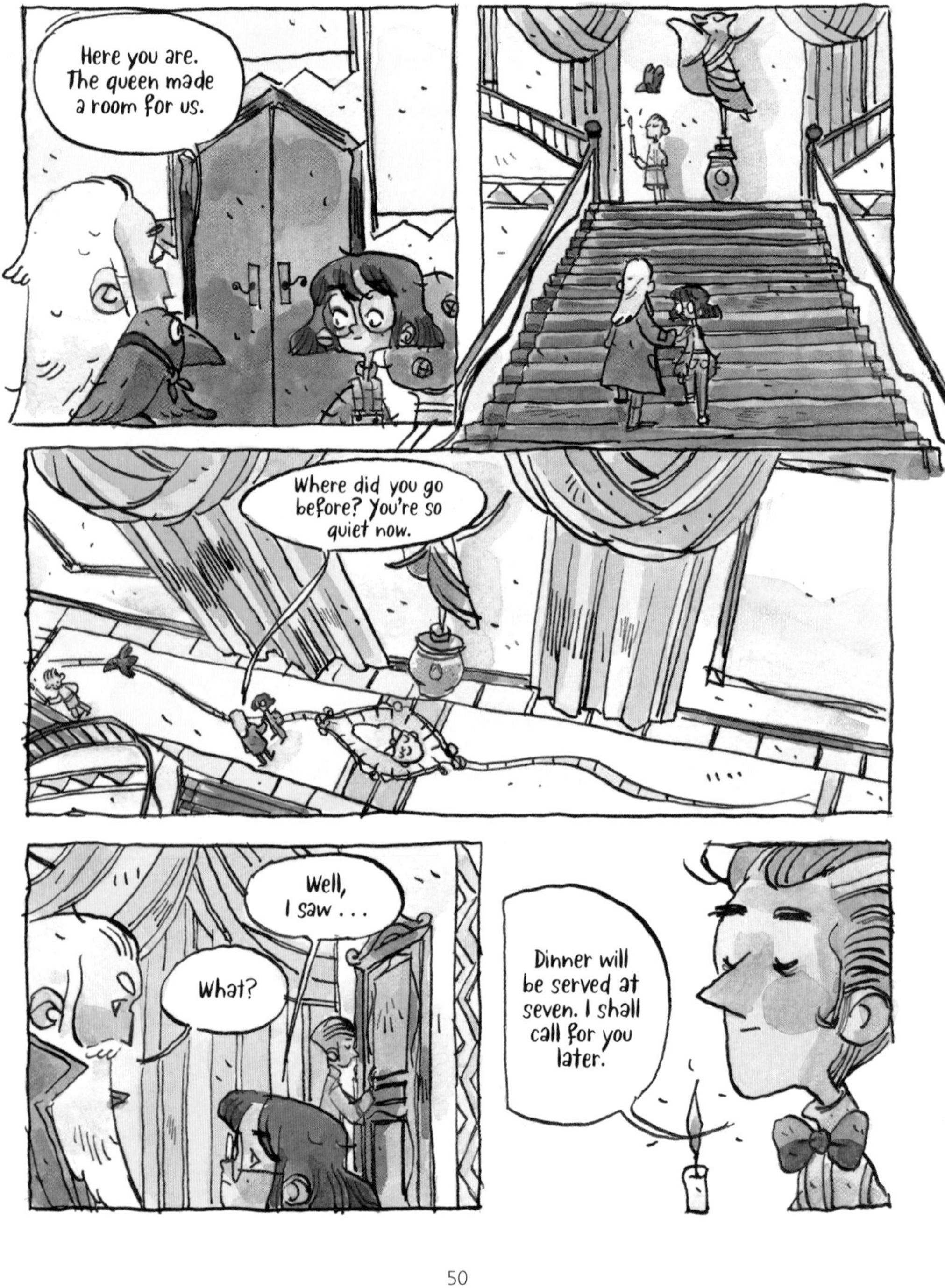

Here you are. The queen made a room for us.
Where did you go before? You're so quiet now.
Well, I saw . . .
What?
Dinner will be served at seven. I shall call for you later.

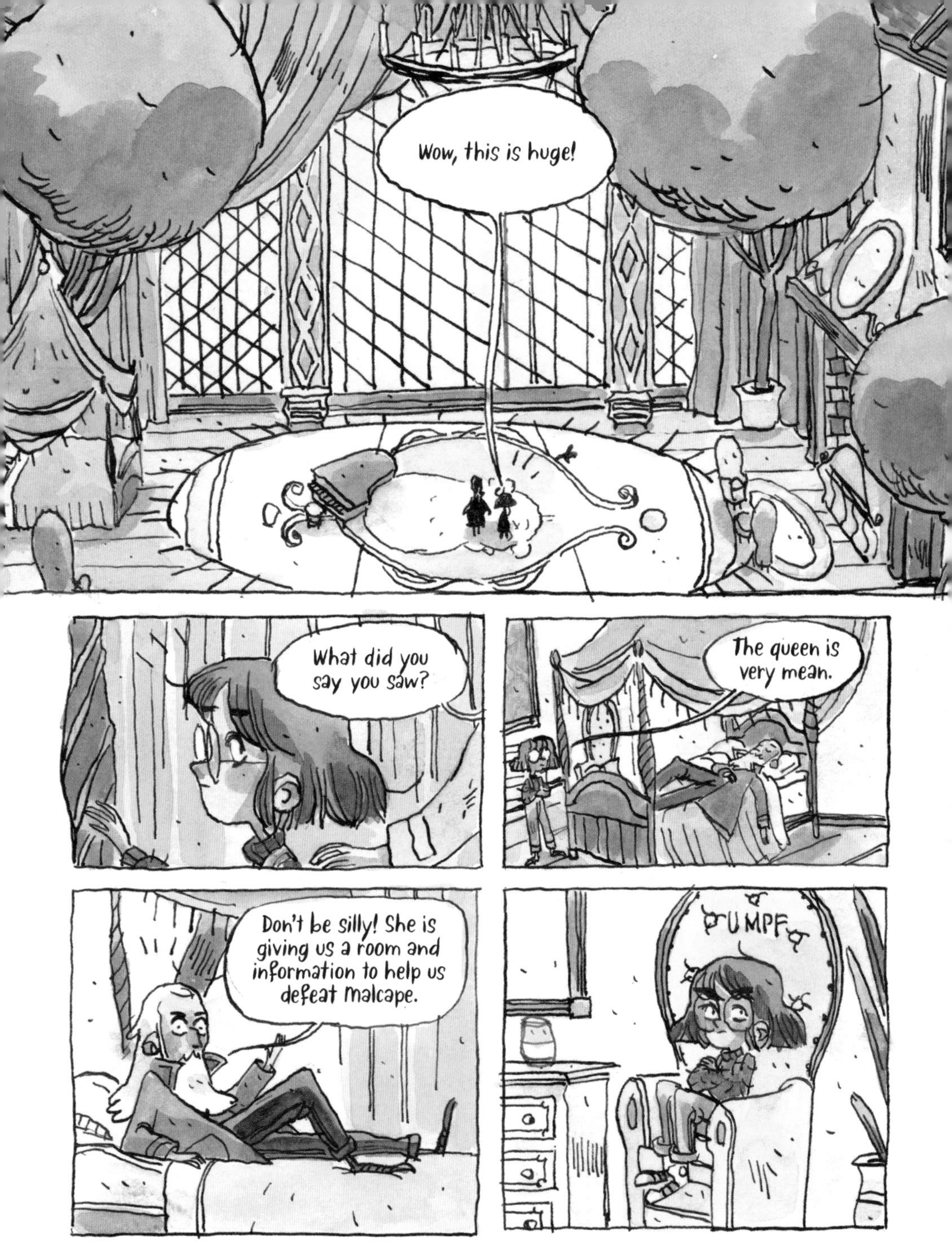
Wow, this is huge!
What did you say you saw?
The queen is very mean.
Don't be silly! She is giving us a room and information to help us defeat Malcape.
UMPF

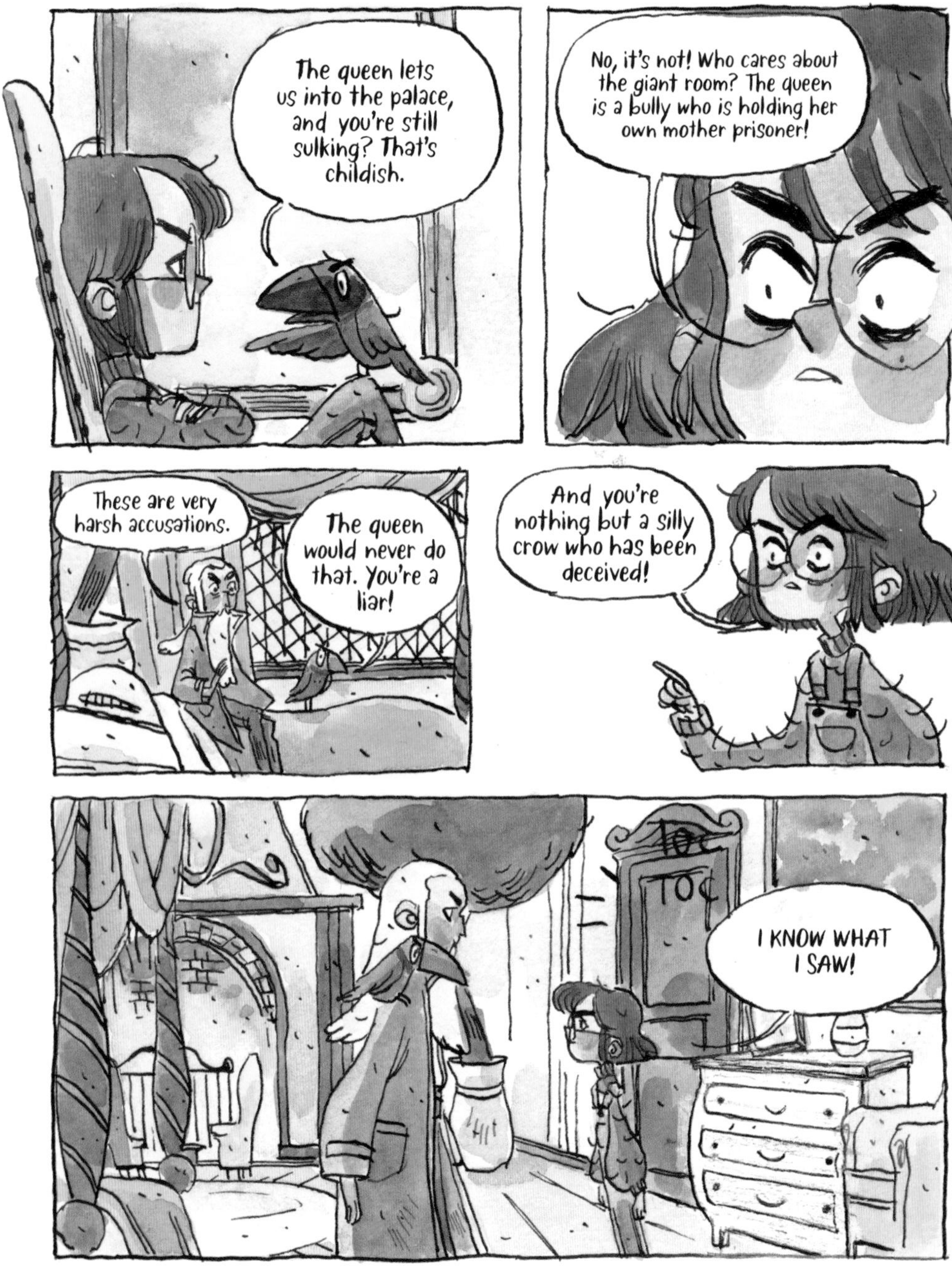

The queen lets us into the palace, and you're still sulking? That's childish.
No, it's not! Who cares about the giant room? The queen is a bully who is holding her own mother prisoner!
These are very harsh accusations.
The queen would never do that. You're a liar!
And you're nothing but a silly crow who has been deceived!
TOC
TOC
I KNOW WHAT I SAW!

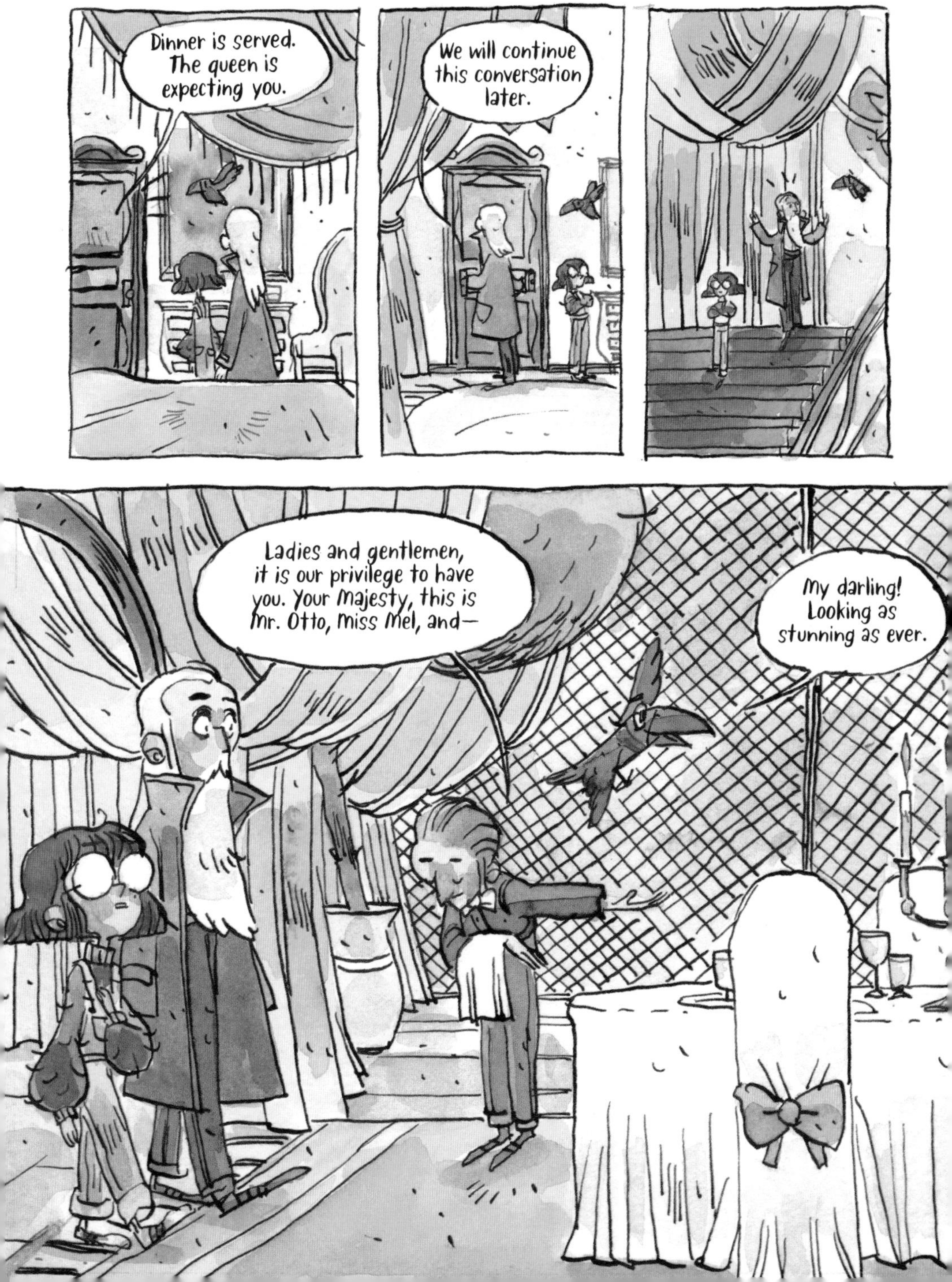
Dinner is served. The queen is expecting you.
We will continue this conversation later.
Ladies and gentlemen, it is our privilege to have you. Your Majesty, this is Mr. Otto, Miss Mel, and—
My darling! Looking as stunning as ever.

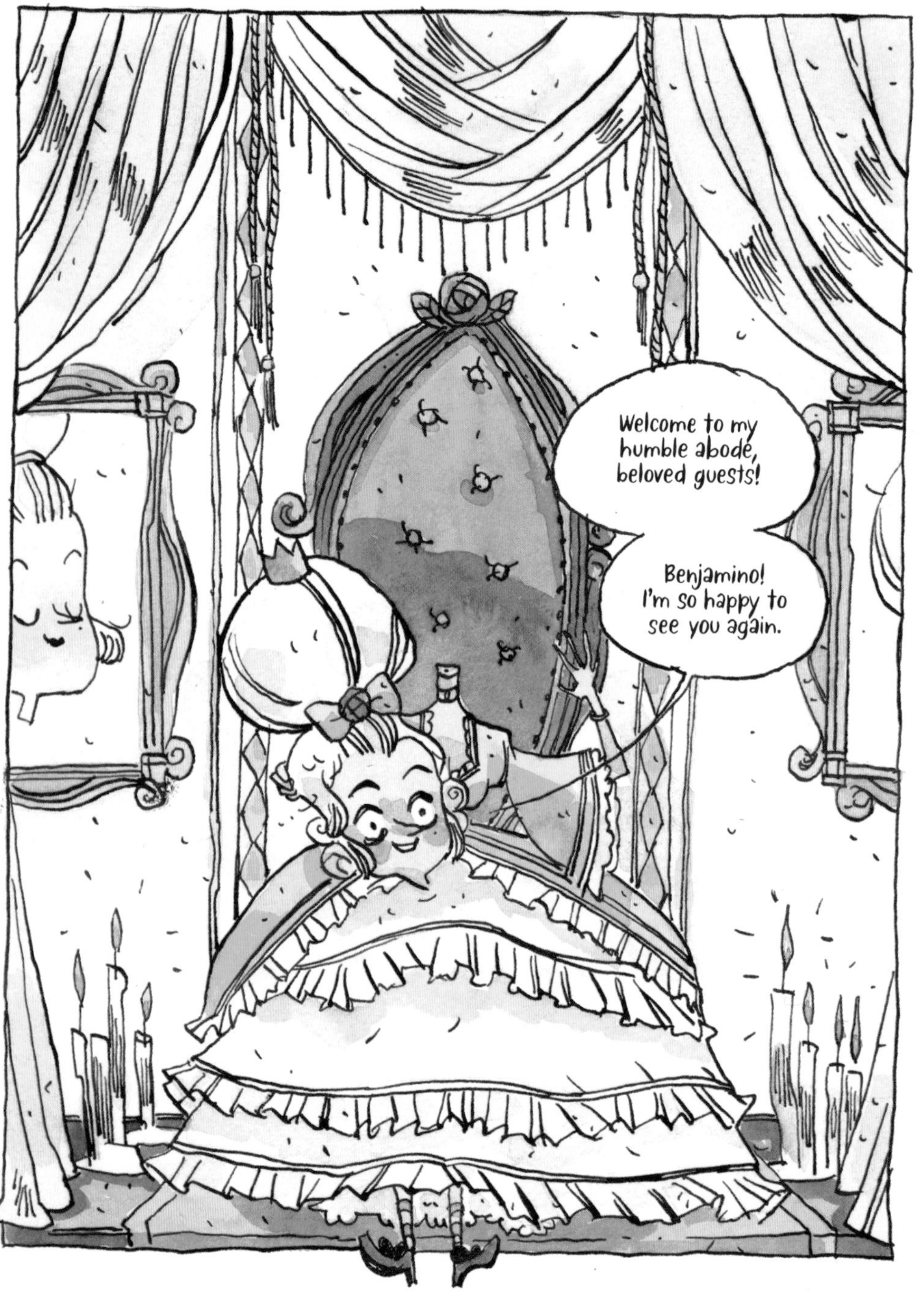
Welcome to my humble abode, beloved guests!
Benjamino! I'm so happy to see you again.

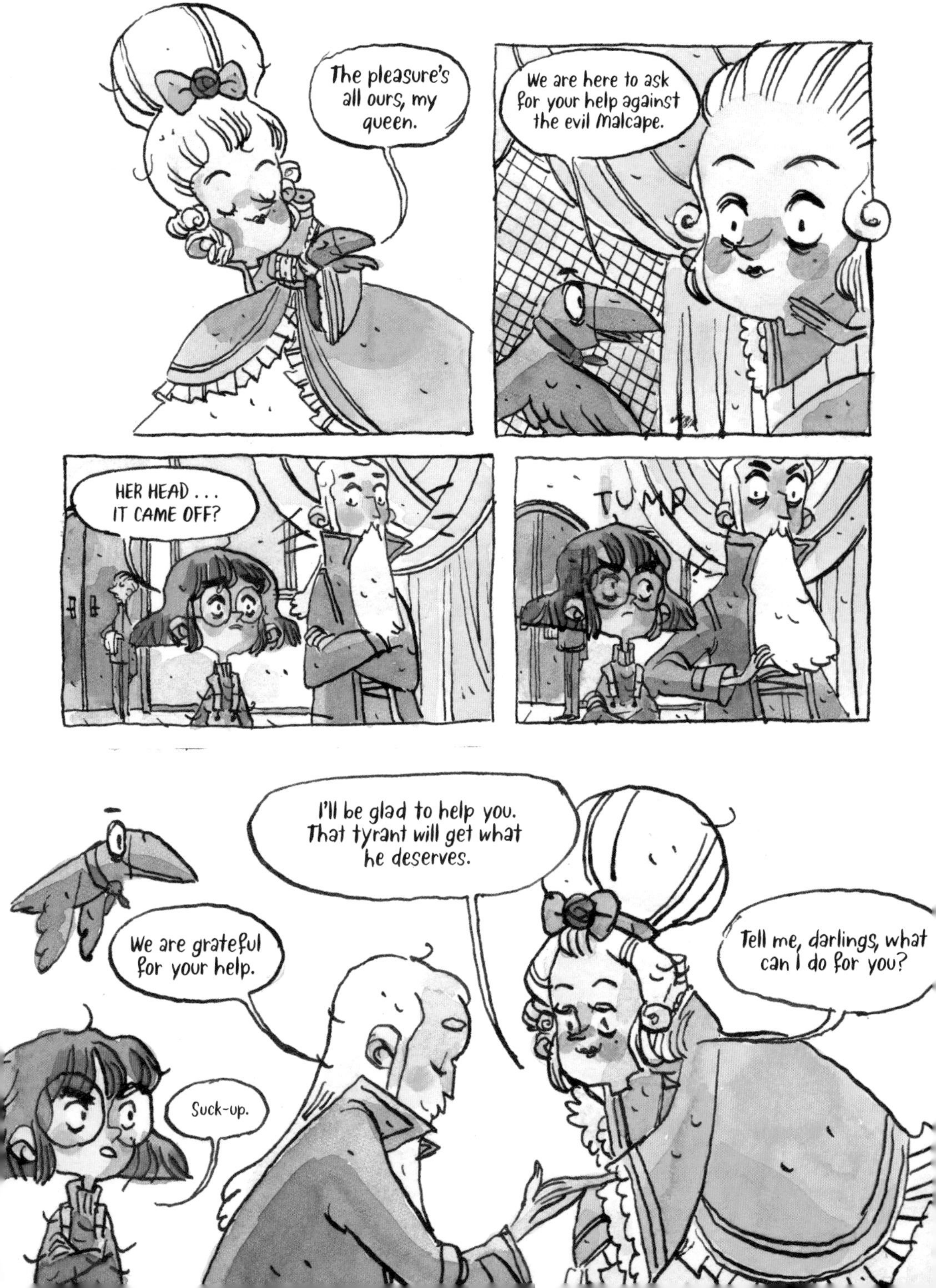
The pleasure's all ours, my queen.
We are here to ask for your help against the evil Malcape.
HER HEAD . . . IT CAME OFF?
TUMP
I'll be glad to help you. That tyrant will get what he deserves.
Tell me, darlings, what can I do for you?
We are grateful for your help.
Suck-up.

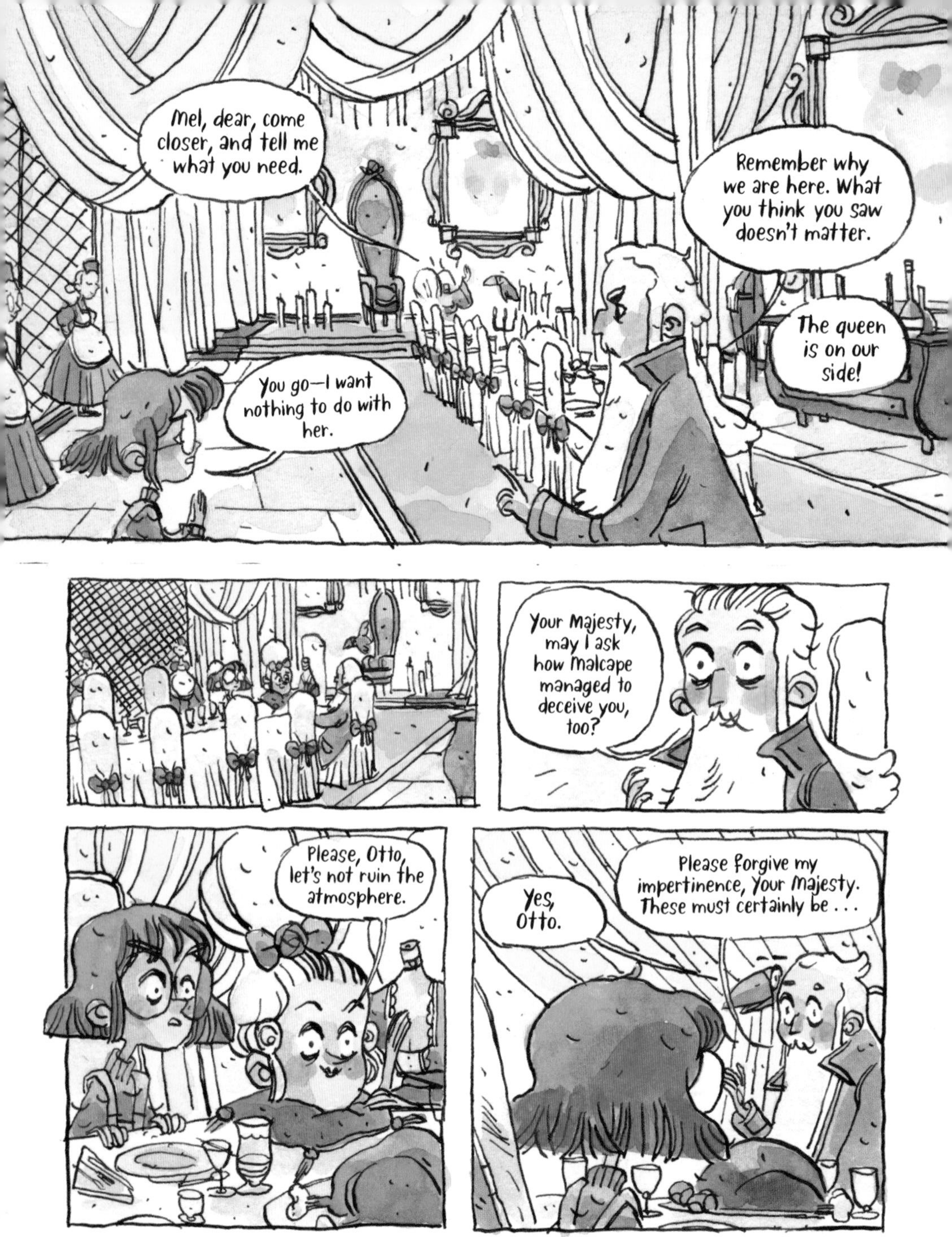
Mel, dear, come closer, and tell me what you need.
Remember why we are here. What you think you saw doesn't matter.
You go—I want nothing to do with her.
The queen is on our side!
Your Majesty, may I ask how Malcape managed to deceive you, too?
Please, Otto, let's not ruin the atmosphere.
Yes, Otto.
Please forgive my impertinence, Your Majesty. These must certainly be . . .

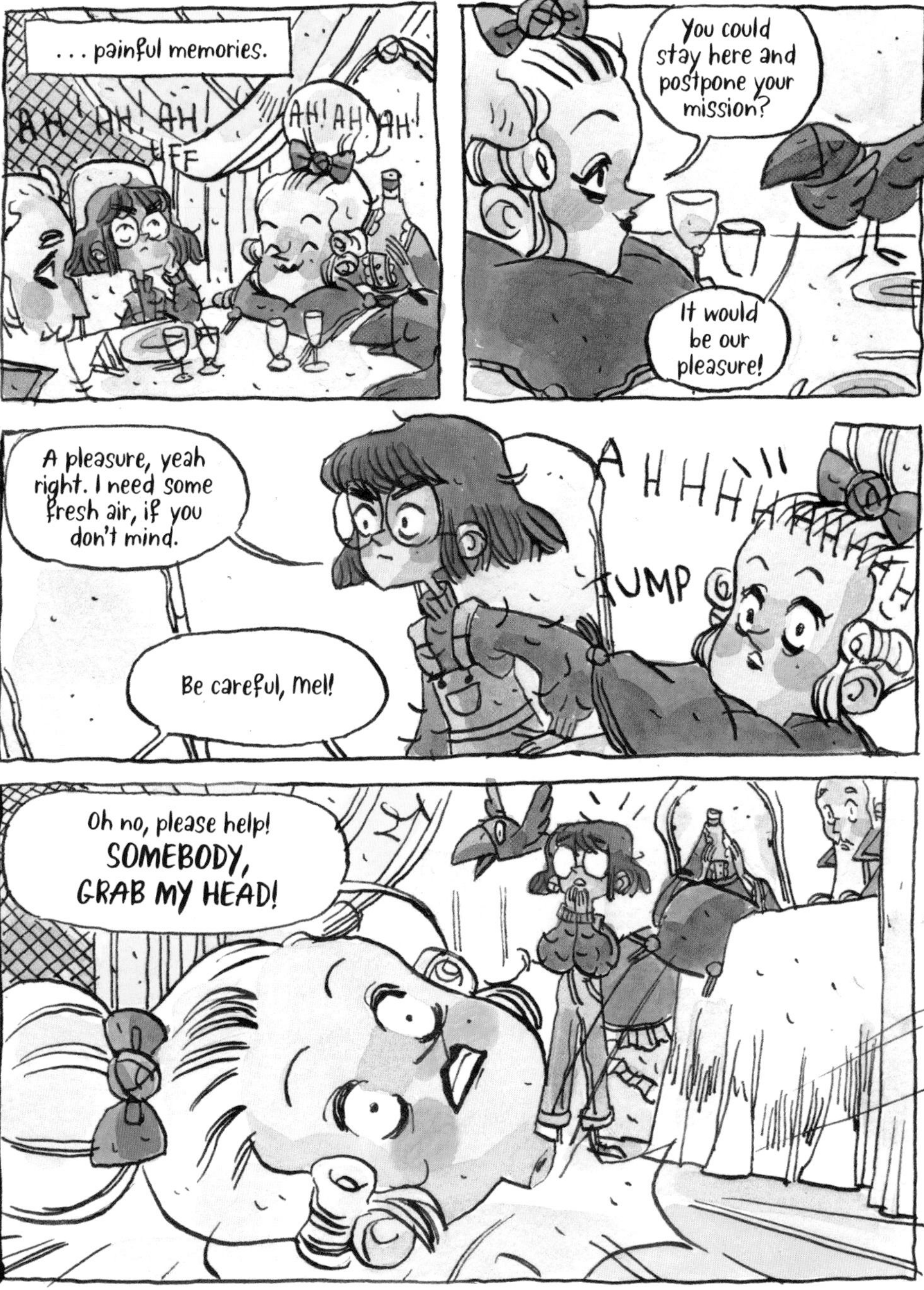

. . . painful memories.
AH! AH! AH!
UFF
AH! AH! AH!
You could stay here and postpone your mission?
It would be our pleasure!
A pleasure, yeah right. I need some fresh air, if you don't mind.
Be careful, mel!
AHHHH
TUMP
Oh no, please help!
SOMEBODY, GRAB MY HEAD!

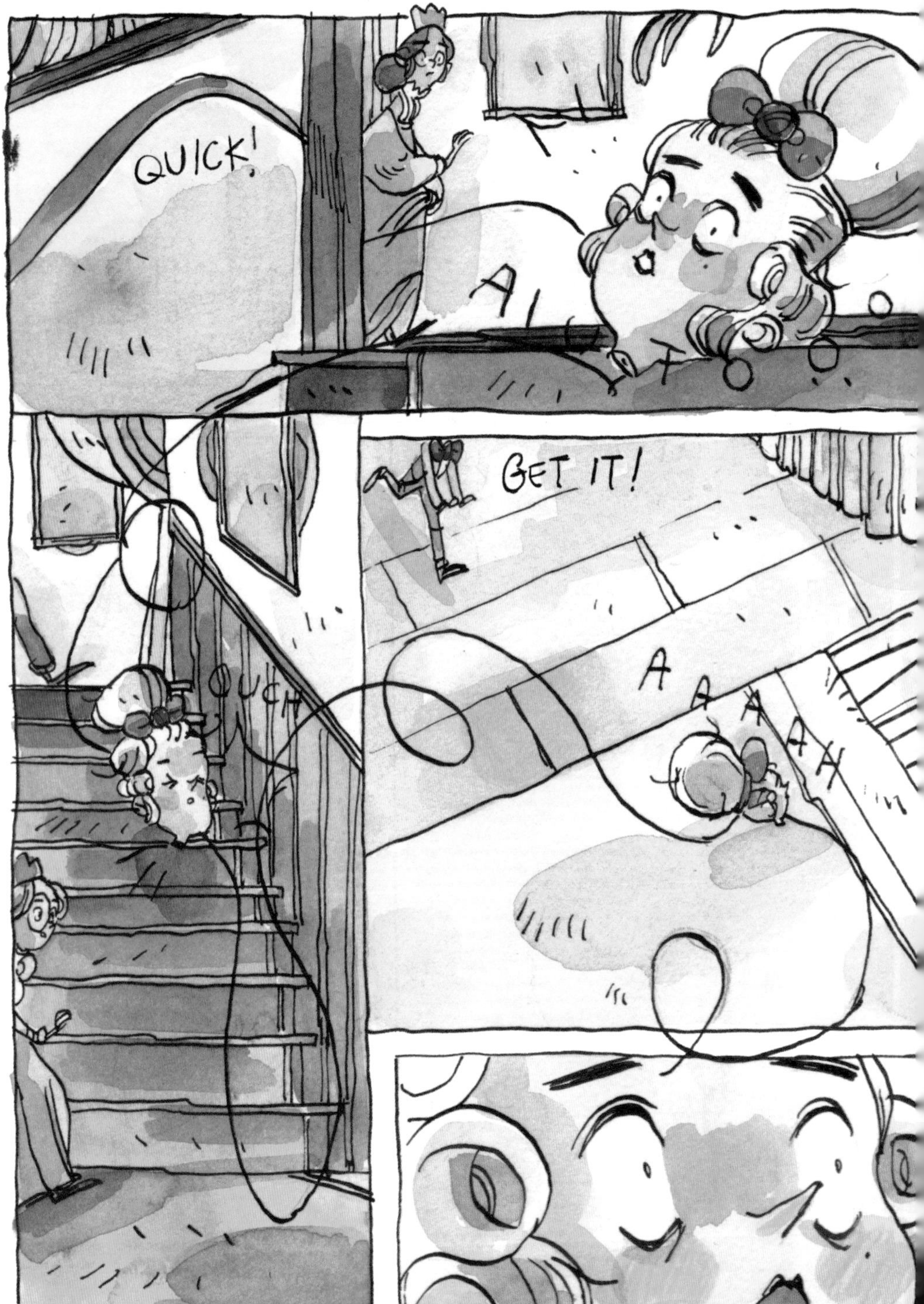
QUICK!
GET IT!
A A A A AH
OUCH

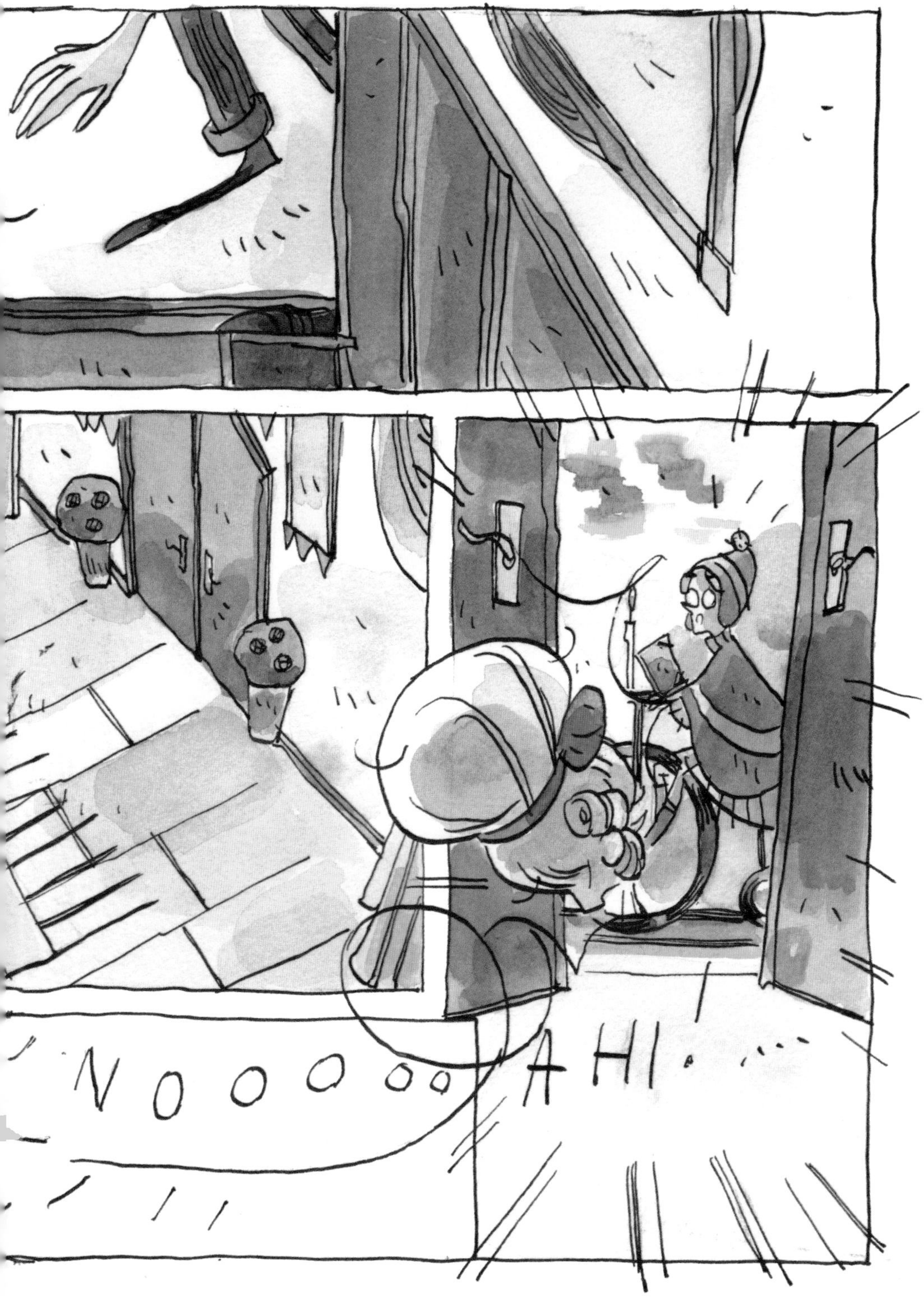
NOOOOOAH!...

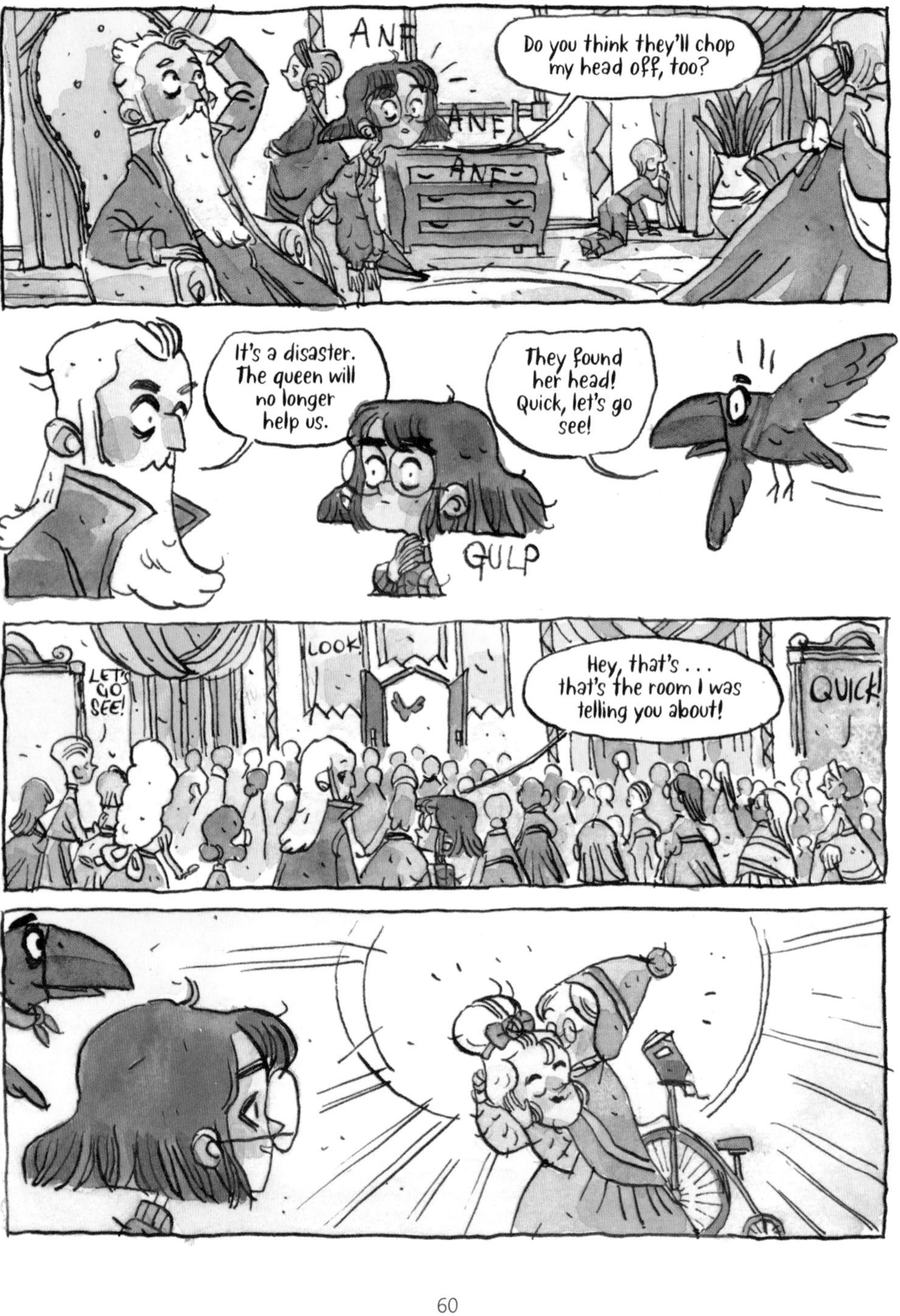
ANF
Do you think they'll chop my head off, too?
ANF
ANF
It's a disaster. The queen will no longer help us.
They found her head! Quick, let's go see!
GULP
LET'S GO SEE!
LOOK!
Hey, that's . . . that's the room I was telling you about!
QUICK!

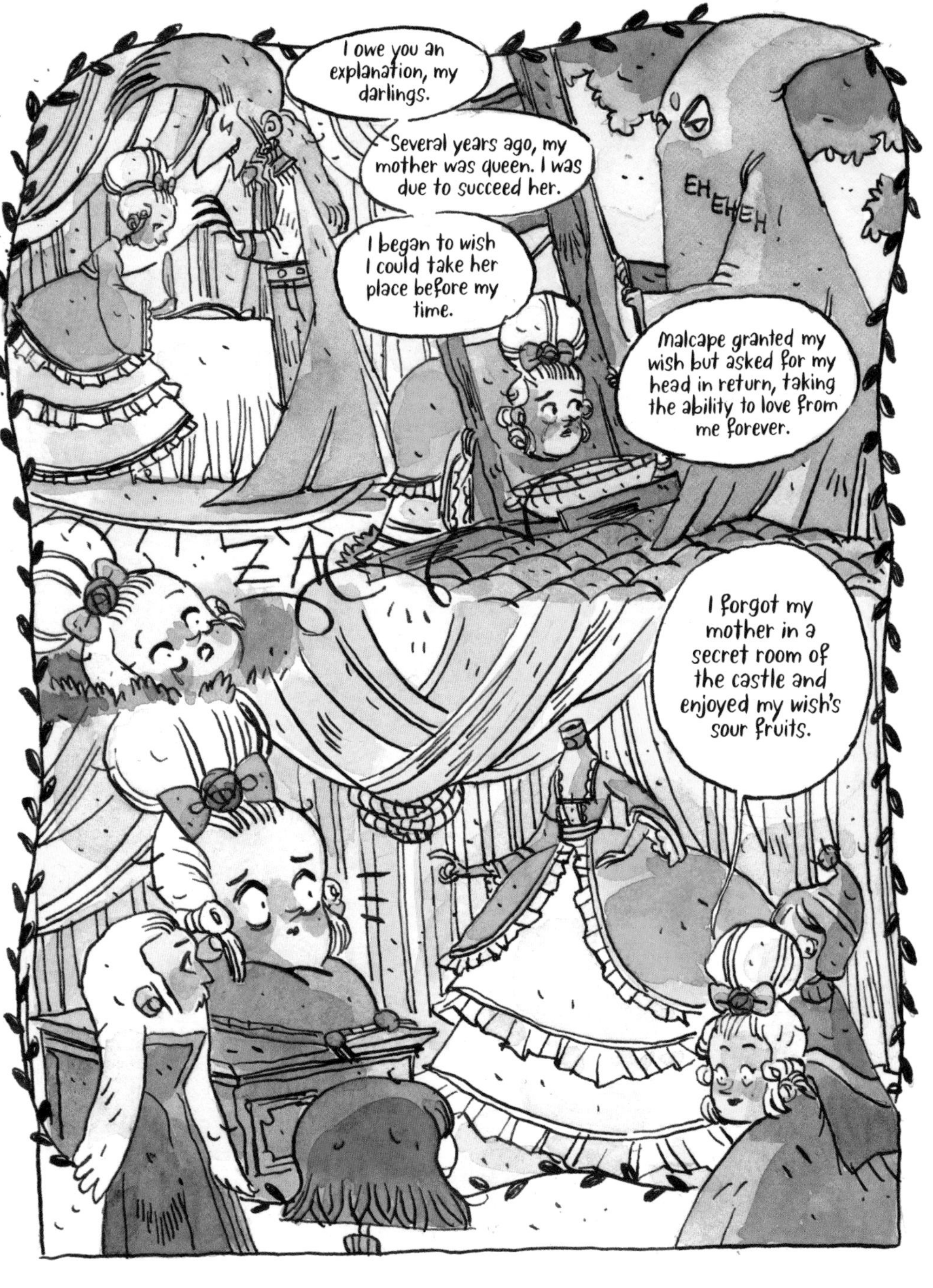
I owe you an explanation, my darlings.
Several years ago, my mother was queen. I was due to succeed her.
I began to wish I could take her place before my time.
EH EH EH EH!
Malcape granted my wish but asked for my head in return, taking the ability to love from me forever.
ZAC
I forgot my mother in a secret room of the castle and enjoyed my wish's sour fruits.

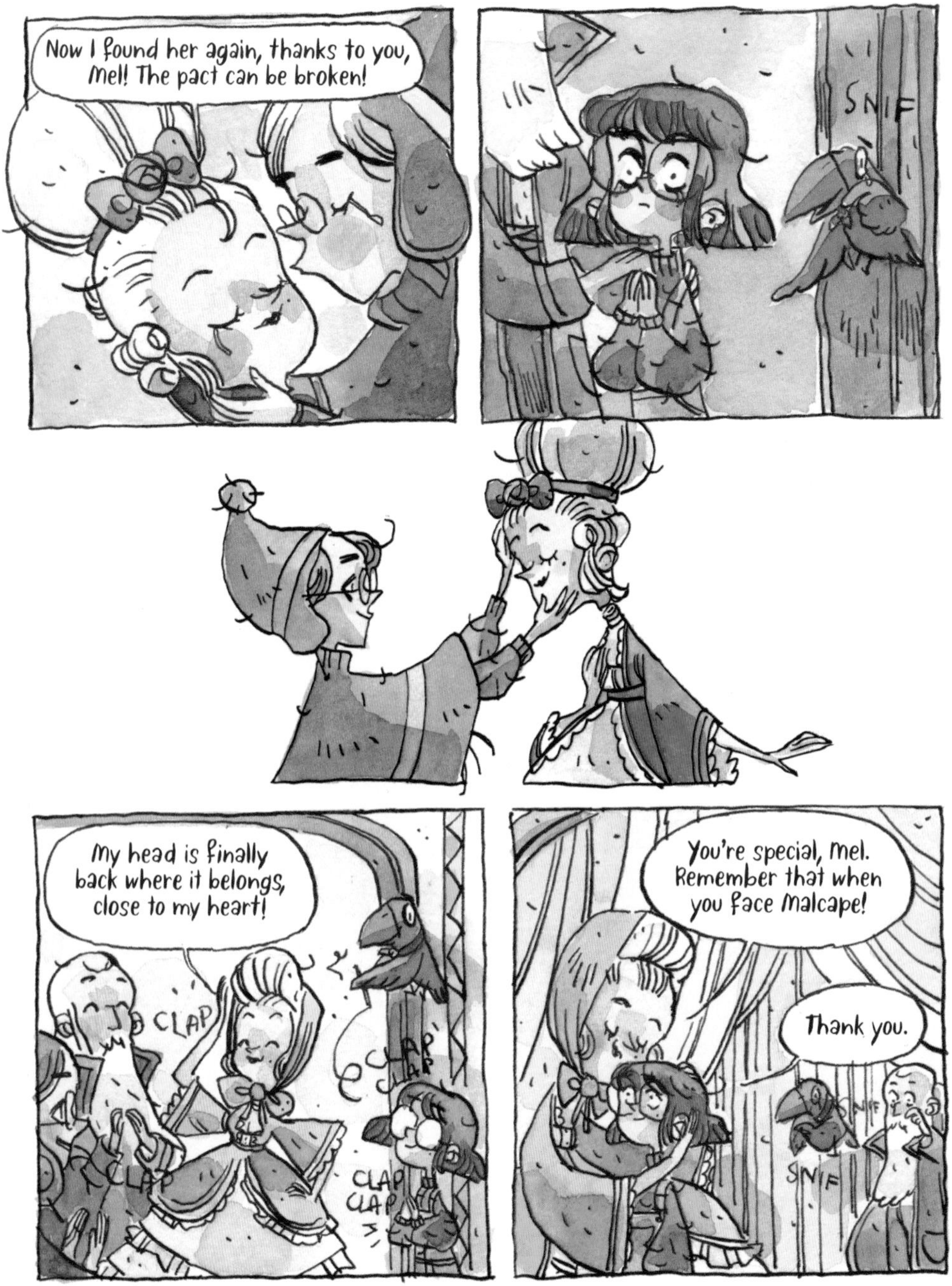
Now I found her again, thanks to you, Mel! The pact can be broken!
SNIF
My head is finally back where it belongs, close to my heart!
CLAP
CLAP
CLAP
CLAP
CLAP
CLAP
You're special, Mel. Remember that when you face Malcape!
Thank you.
SNIF
SNIF

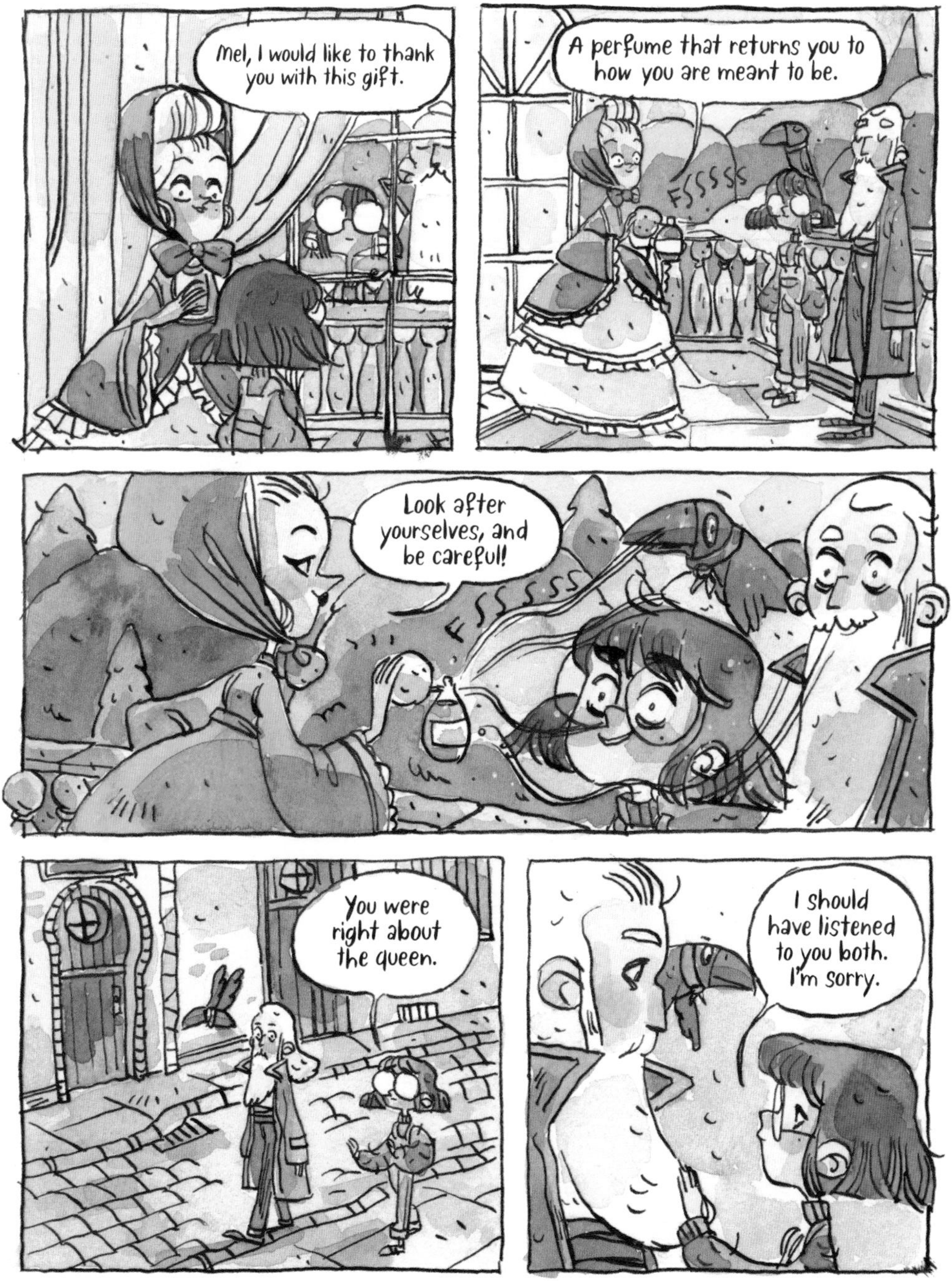
Mel, I would like to thank you with this gift.
A perfume that returns you to how you are meant to be.
FSSSSS
Look after yourselves, and be careful!
FSSSSS
You were right about the queen.
I should have listened to you both. I'm sorry.

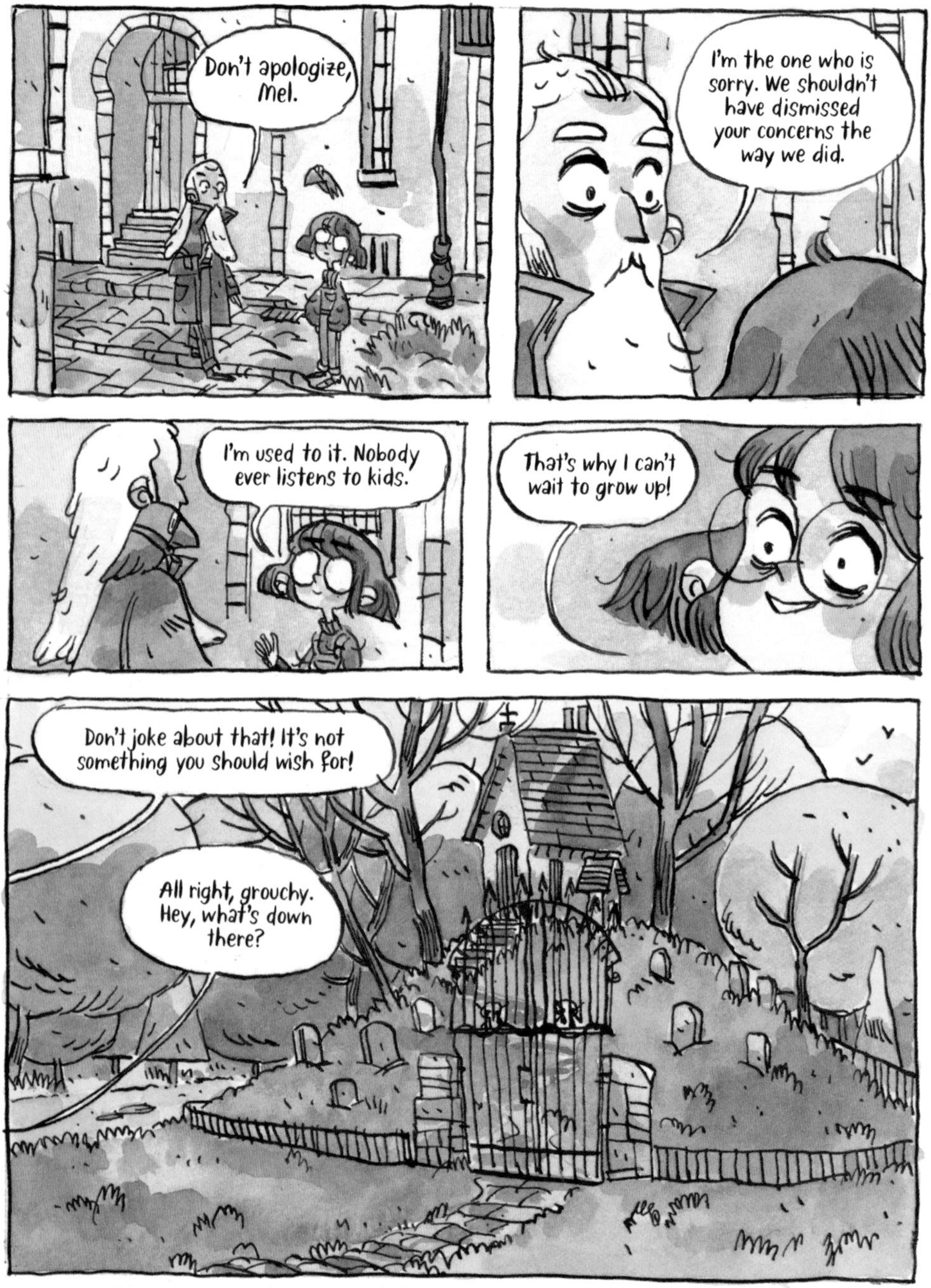

Don't apologize, Mel.
I'm the one who is sorry. We shouldn't have dismissed your concerns the way we did.
I'm used to it. Nobody ever listens to kids.
That's why I can't wait to grow up!
Don't joke about that! It's not something you should wish for!
All right, grouchy. Hey, what's down there?

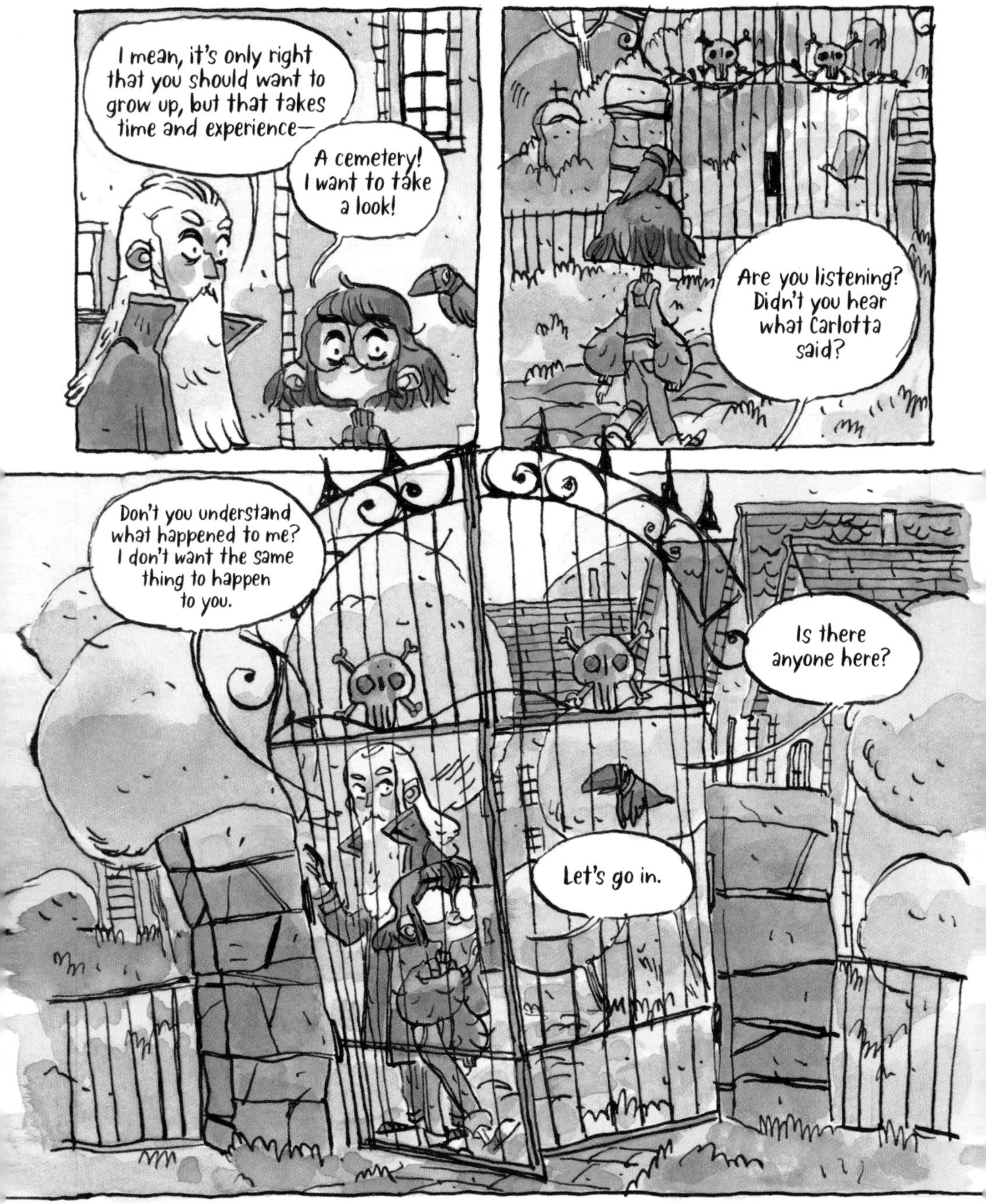
I mean, it's only right that you should want to grow up, but that takes time and experience—
A cemetery! I want to take a look!
Are you listening? Didn't you hear what Carlotta said?
Don't you understand what happened to me? I don't want the same thing to happen to you.
Is there anyone here?
Let's go in.

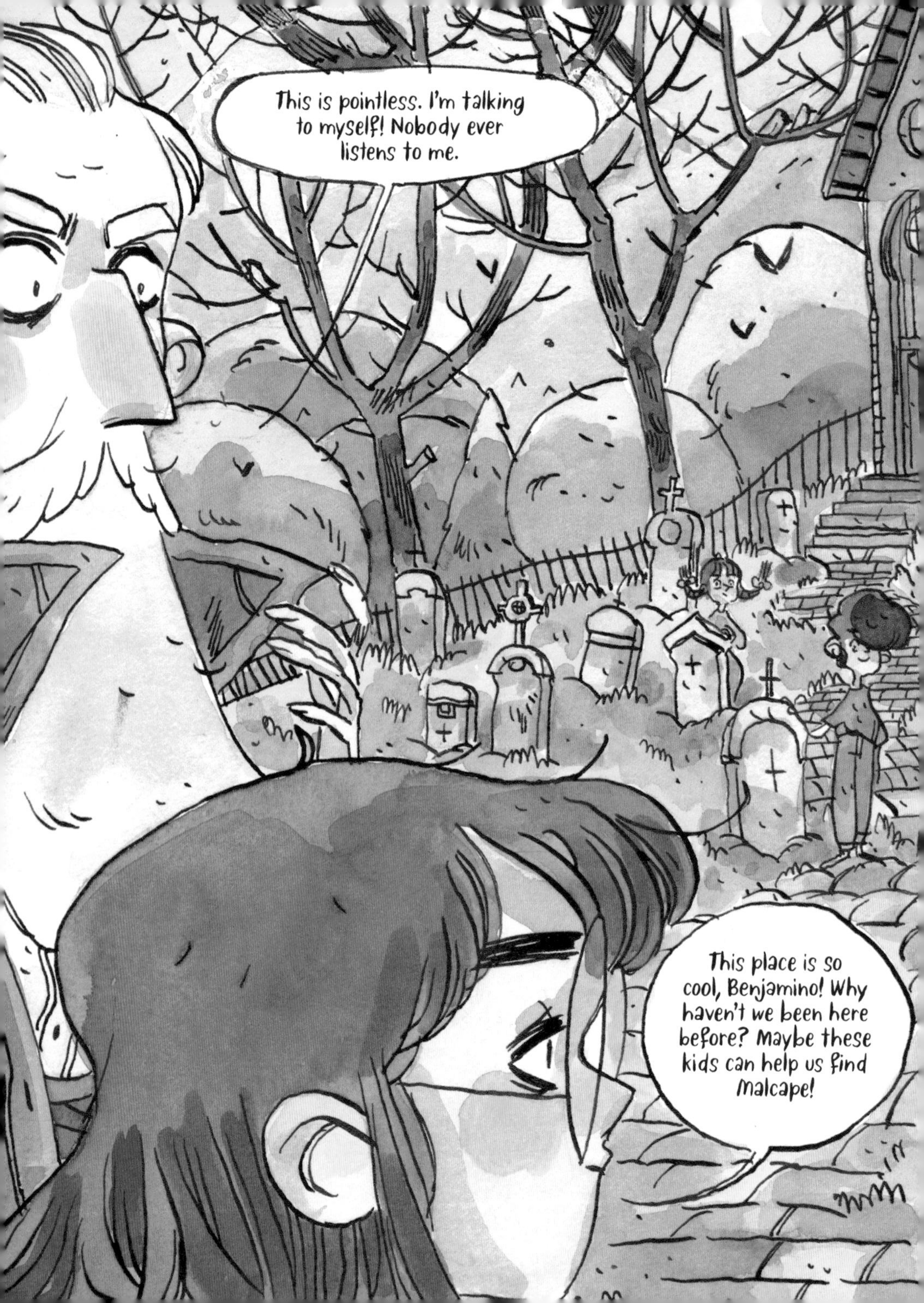
This is pointless. I'm talking to myself! Nobody ever listens to me.
This place is so cool, Benjamino! Why haven't we been here before? Maybe these kids can help us find Malcape!

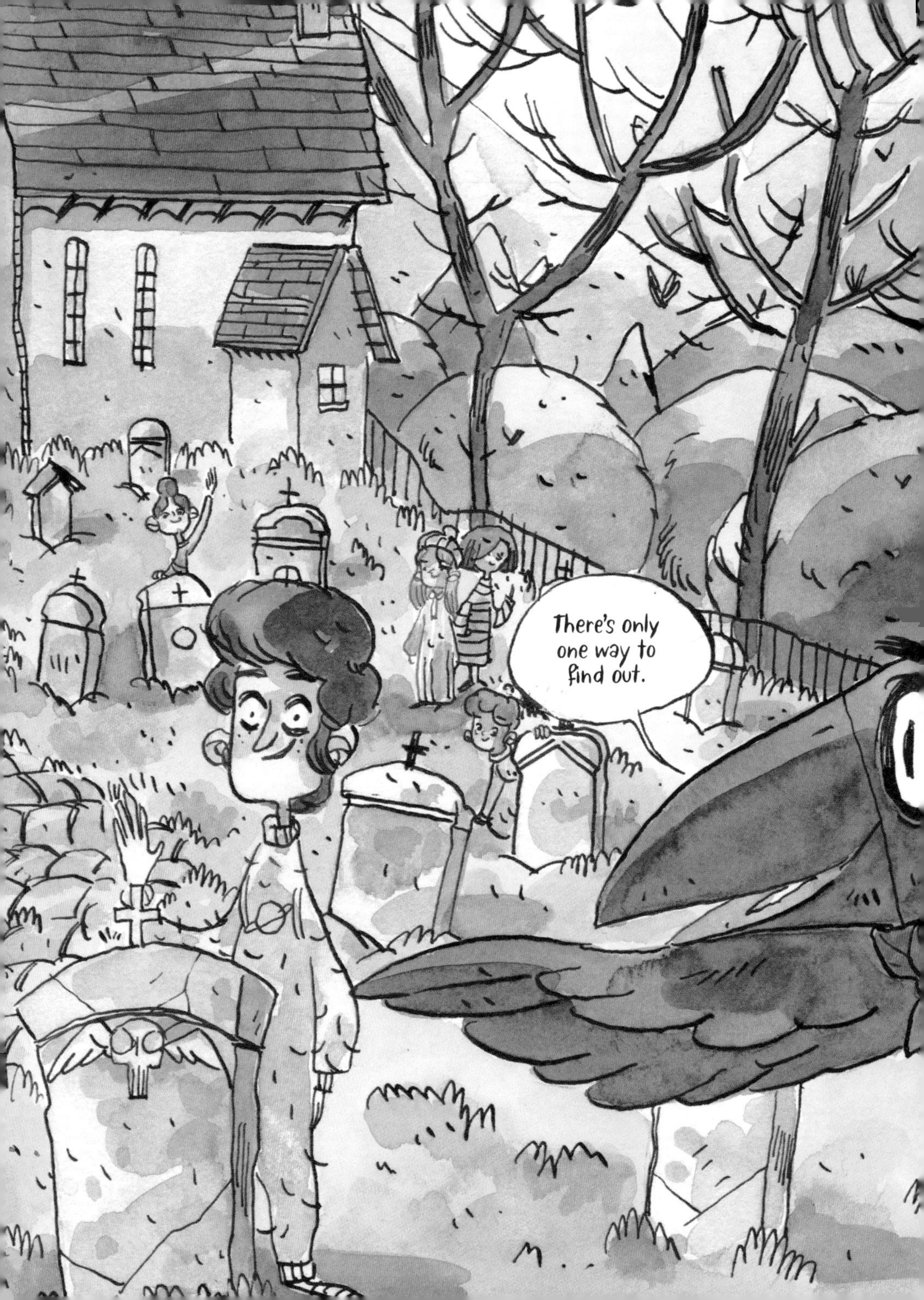
There's only one way to find out.

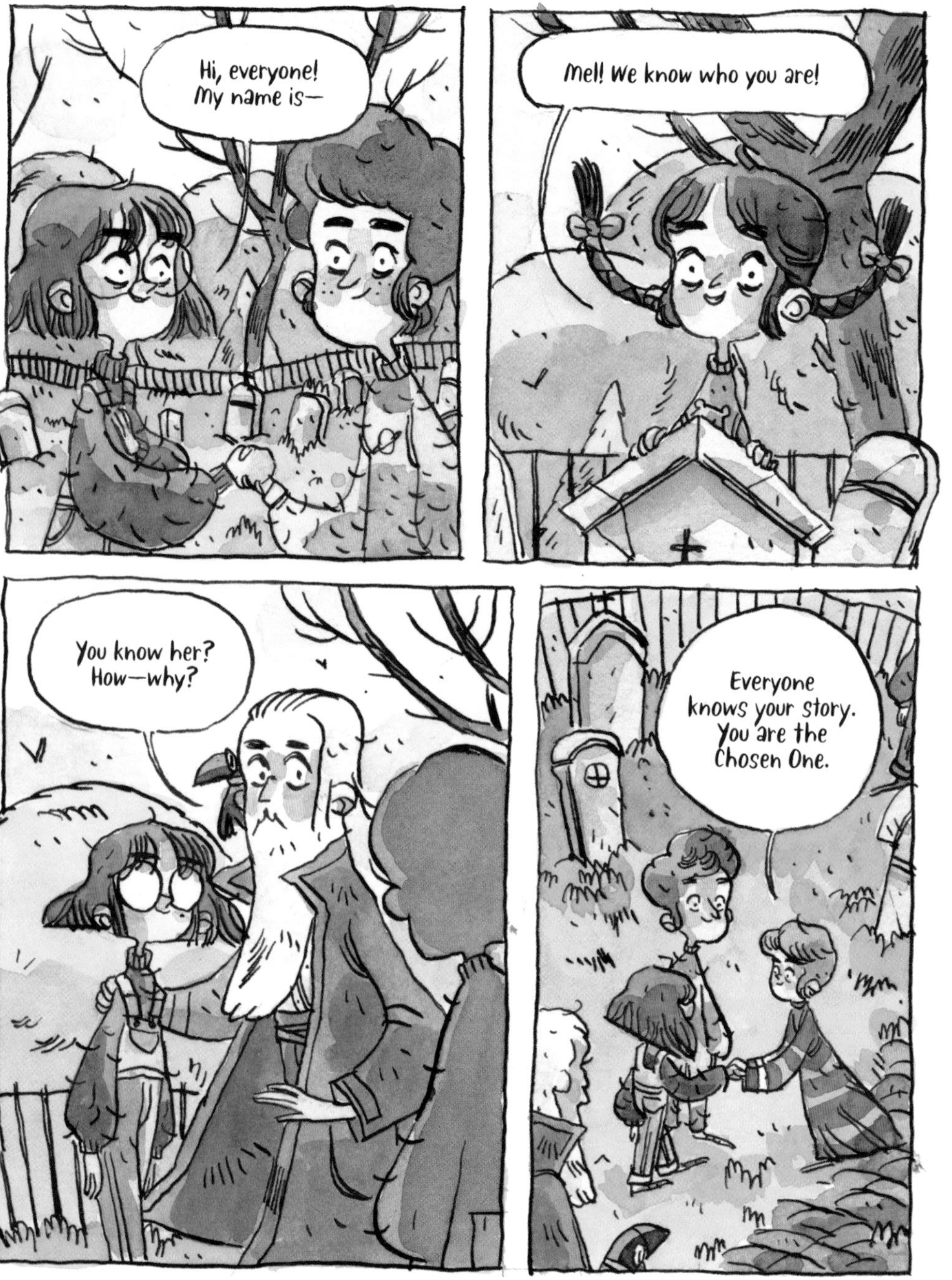
Hi, everyone! My name is—
Mel! We know who you are!
You know her? How—why?
Everyone knows your story. You are the Chosen One.

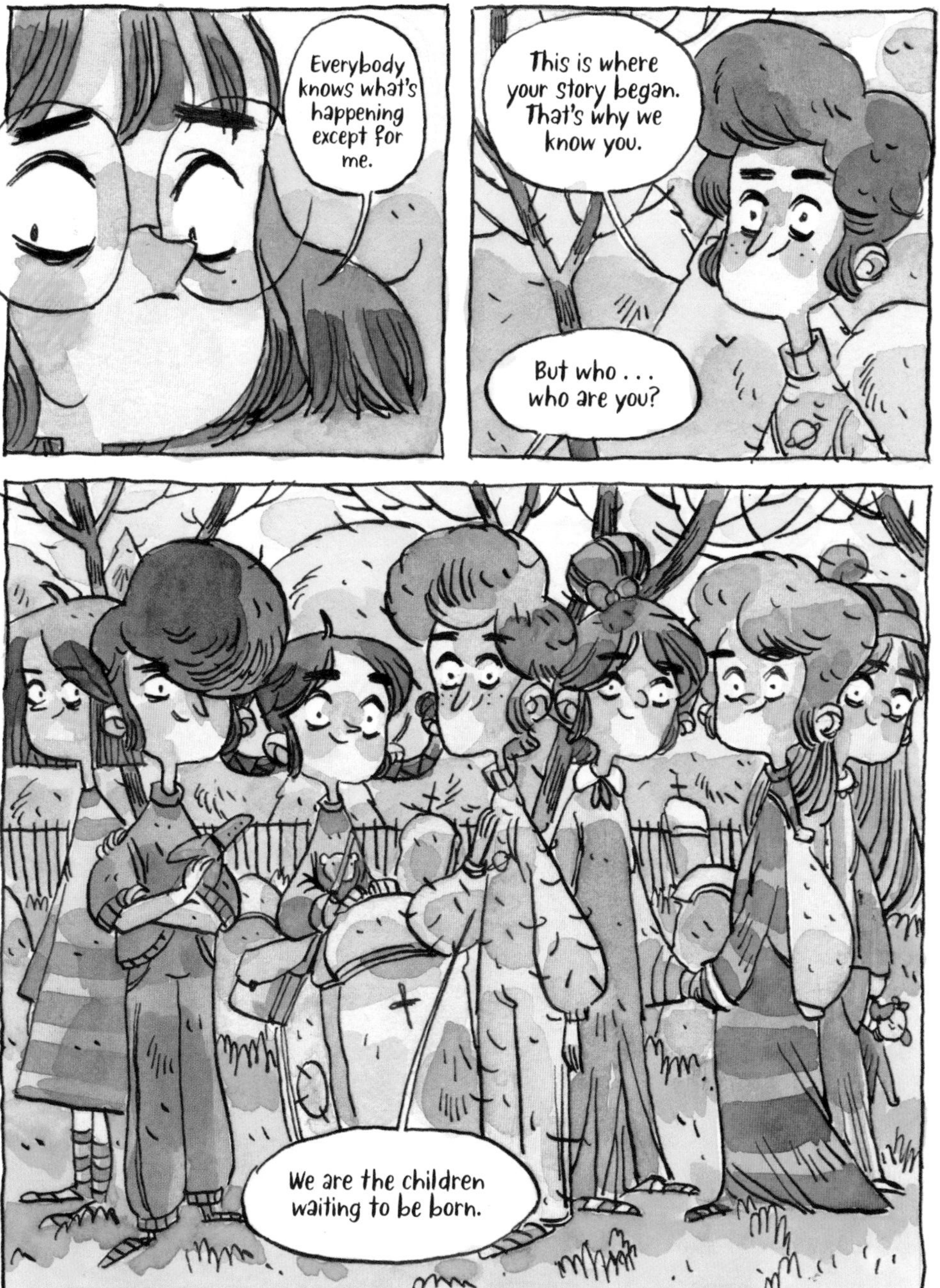
Everybody knows what's happening except for me.
This is where your story began. That's why we know you.
But who . . . who are you?
We are the children waiting to be born.

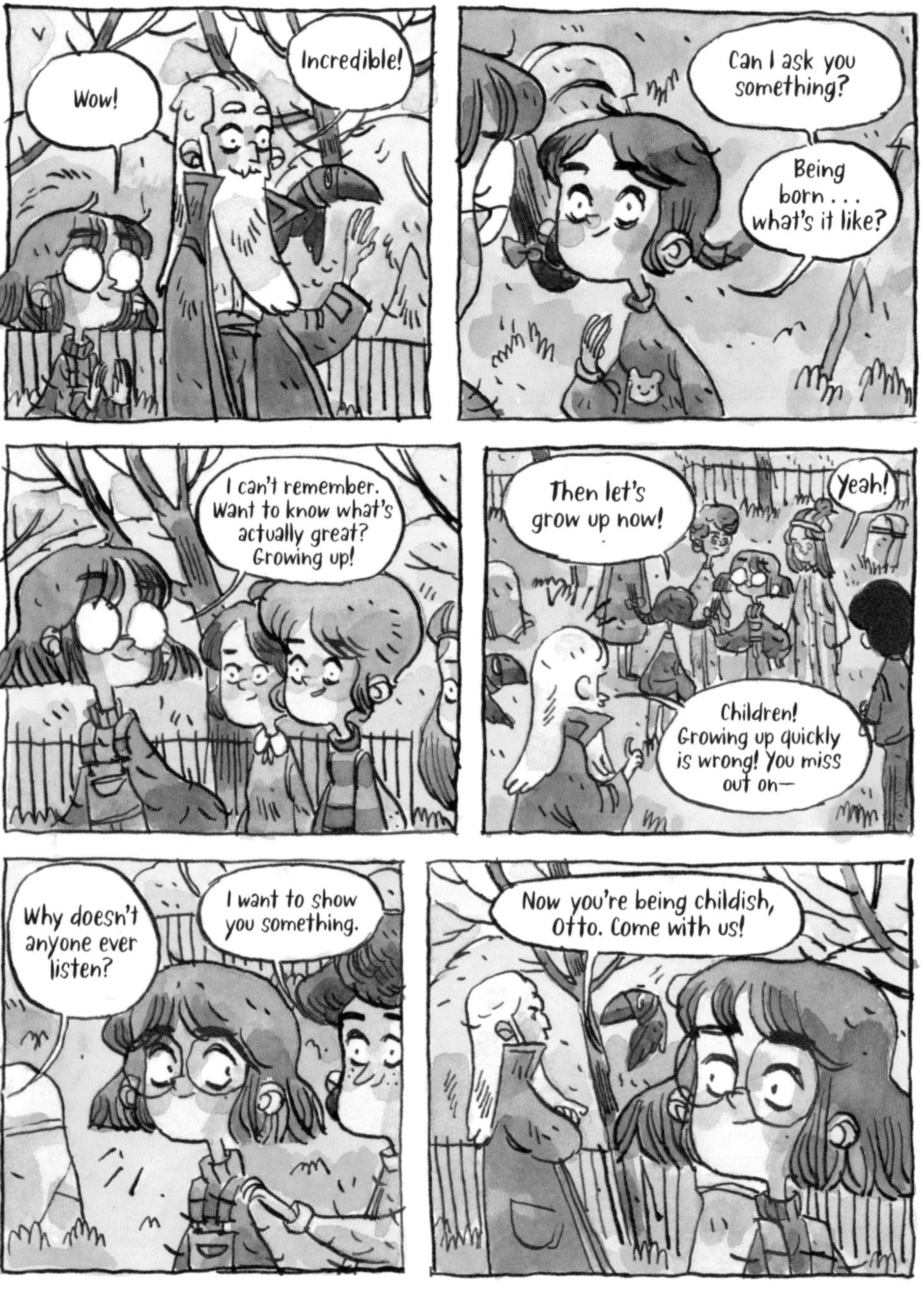
Wow!
Incredible!
Can I ask you something?
Being born . . . what's it like?
I can't remember. Want to know what's actually great? Growing up!
Then let's grow up now!
Yeah!
Children! Growing up quickly is wrong! You miss out on—
Why doesn't anyone ever listen?
I want to show you something.
Now you're being childish, Otto. Come with us!

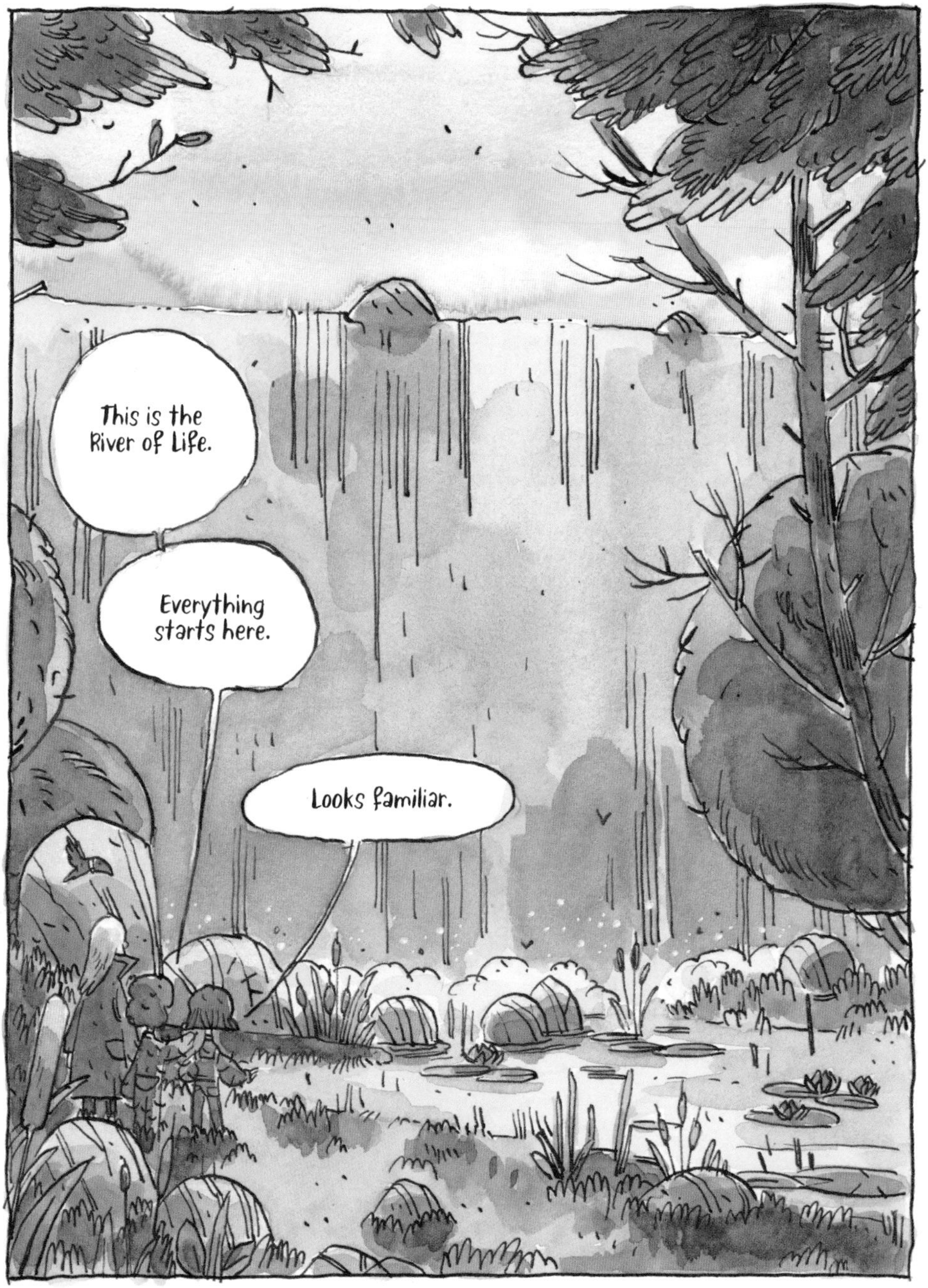
This is the River of Life.
Everything starts here.
Looks familiar.

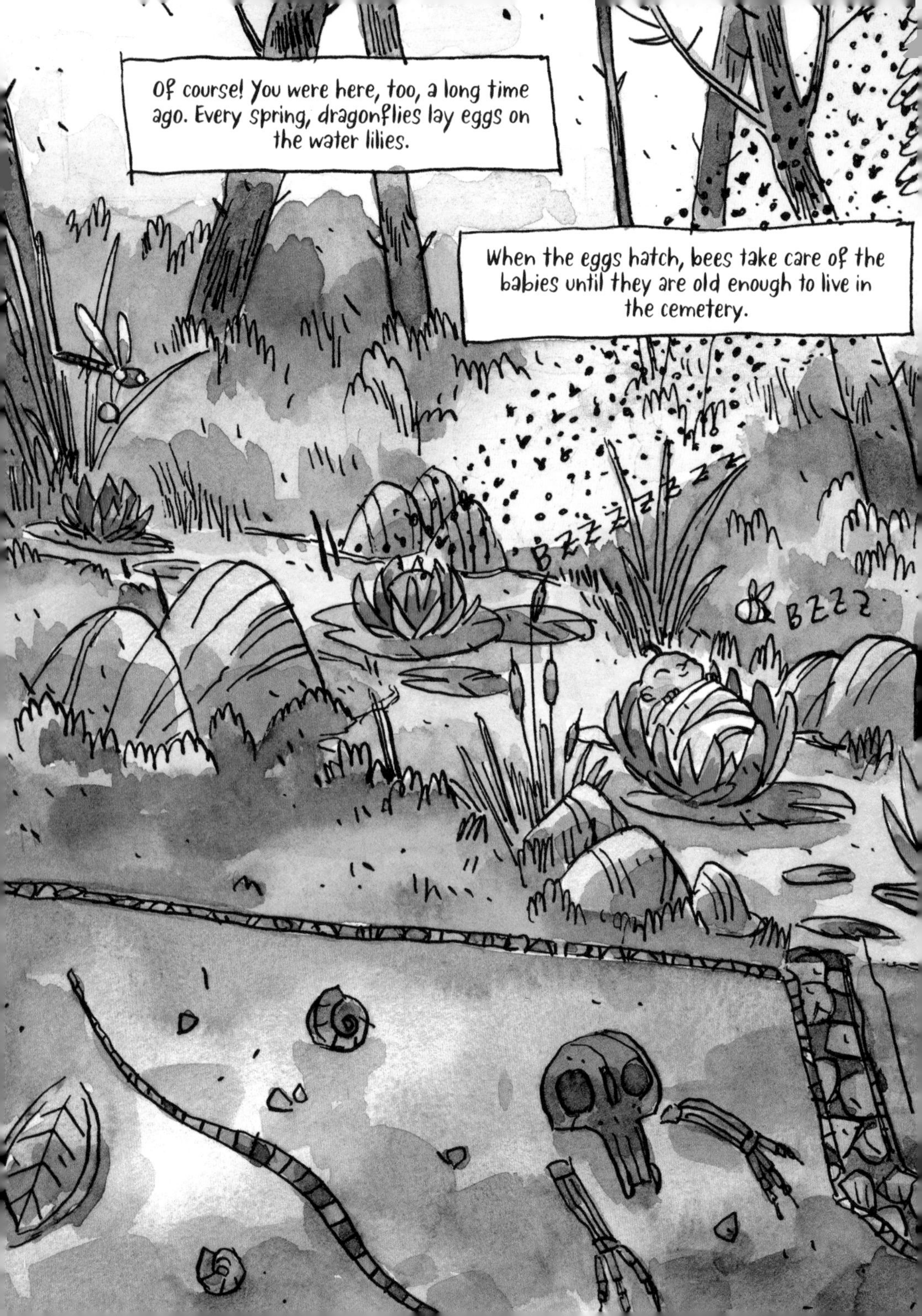
Of course! You were here, too, a long time ago. Every spring, dragonflies lay eggs on the water lilies.
When the eggs hatch, bees take care of the babies until they are old enough to live in the cemetery.
BZZZZ
BZZZ

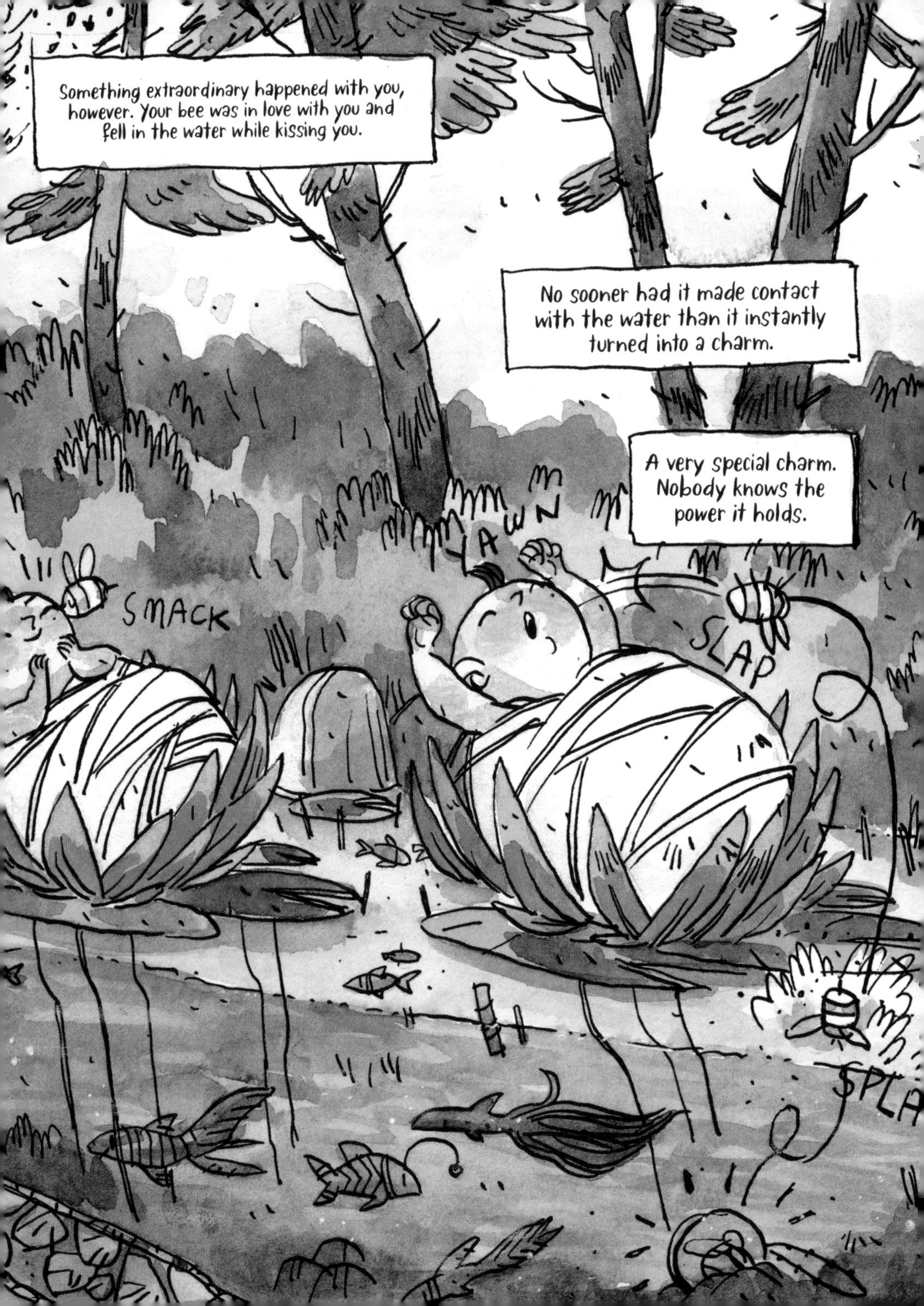

Something extraordinary happened with you, however. Your bee was in love with you and fell in the water while kissing you.
No sooner had it made contact with the water than it instantly turned into a charm.
A very special charm. Nobody knows the power it holds.
YAWN
SMACK
SLAP
SPLA

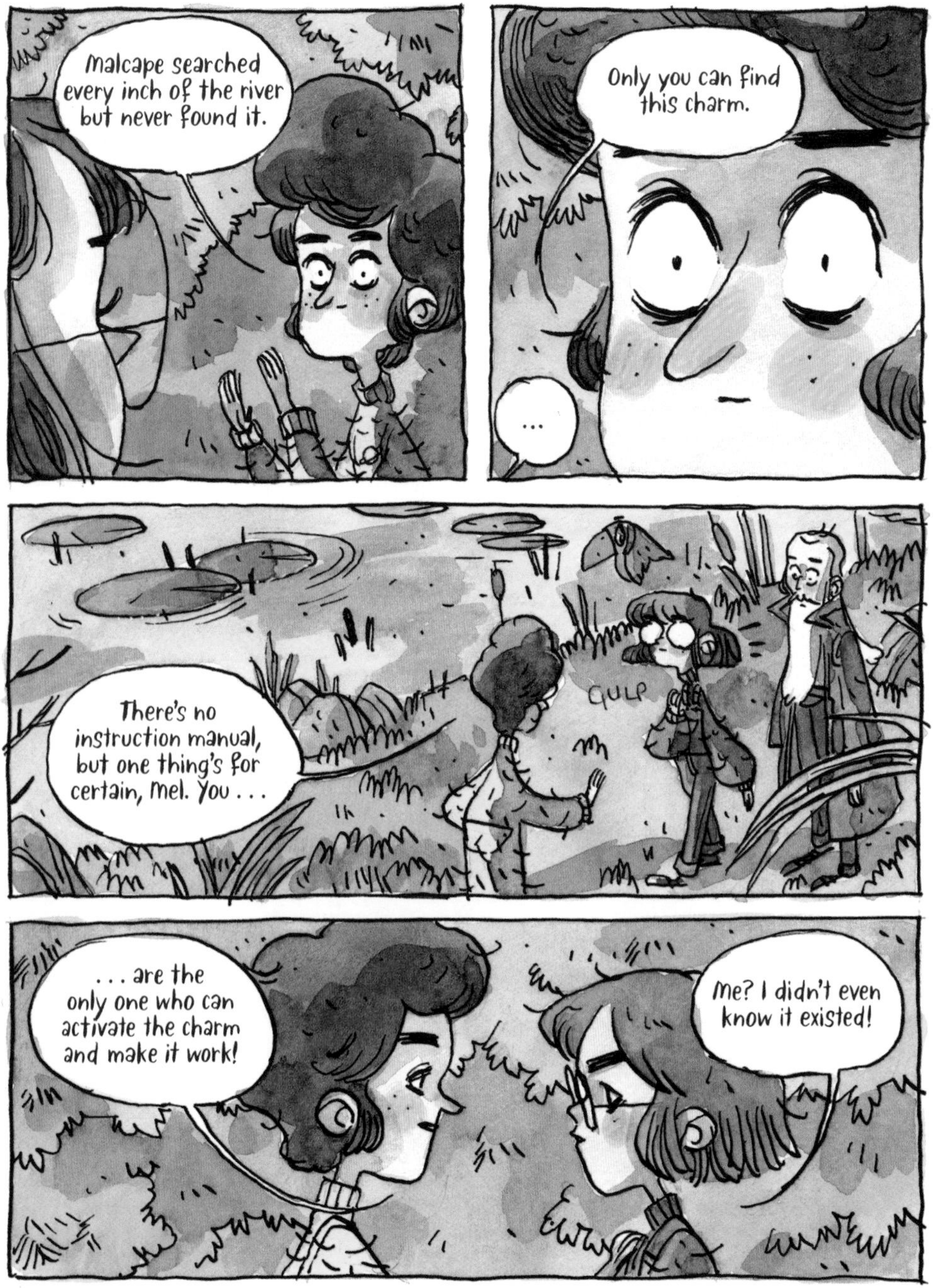
Malcape searched every inch of the river but never found it.
Only you can find this charm.
...
There's no instruction manual, but one thing's for certain, Mel. You . . .
GULP
. . . are the only one who can activate the charm and make it work!
Me? I didn't even know it existed!

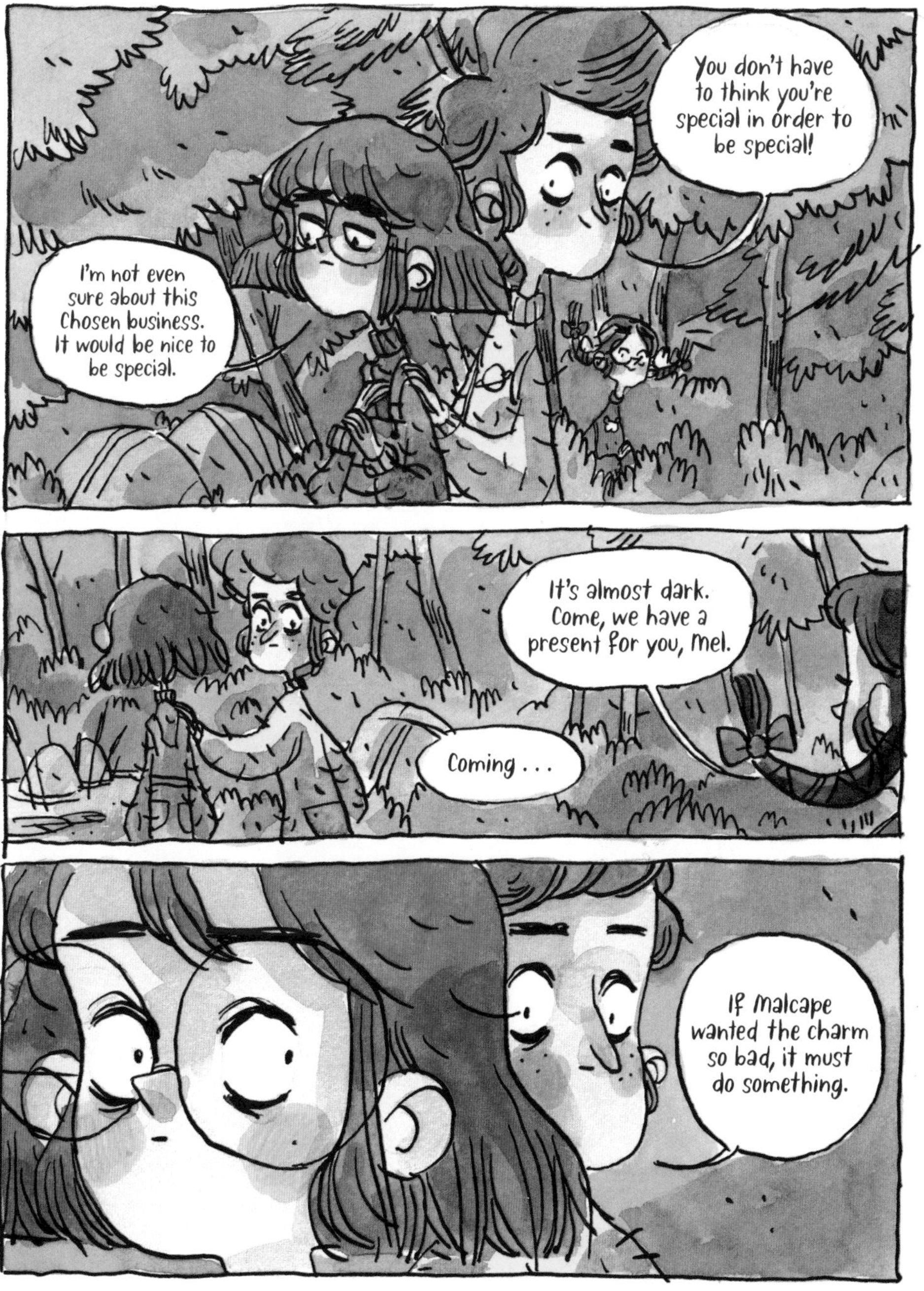
I'm not even sure about this Chosen business. It would be nice to be special.
You don't have to think you're special in order to be special!
It's almost dark. Come, we have a present for you, Mel.
Coming . . .
If Malcape wanted the charm so bad, it must do something.

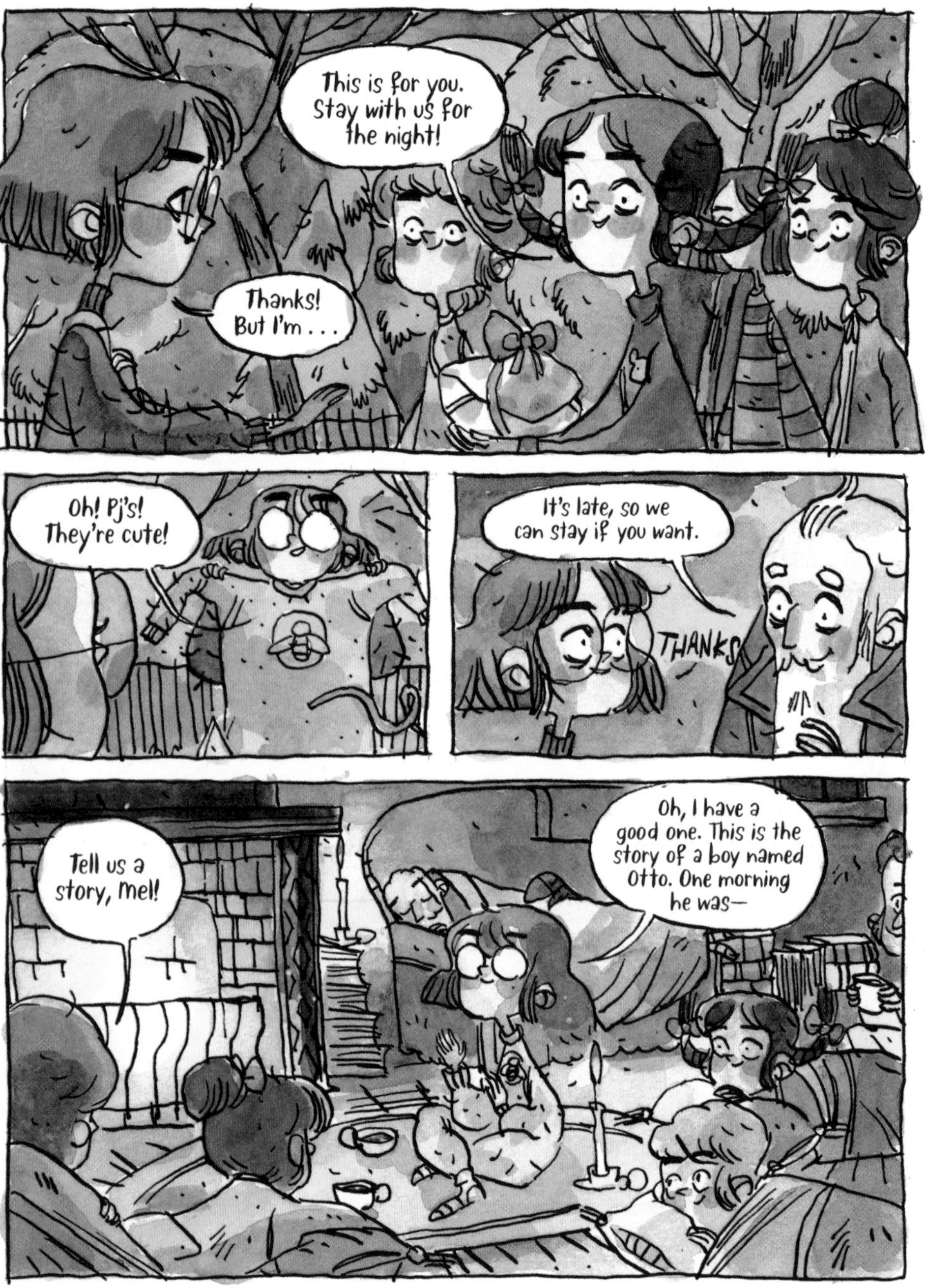
This is for you. Stay with us for the night!
Thanks! But I'm . . .
Oh! Pj's! They're cute!
It's late, so we can stay if you want.
THANKS
Tell us a story, Mel!
Oh, I have a good one. This is the story of a boy named Otto. One morning he was—

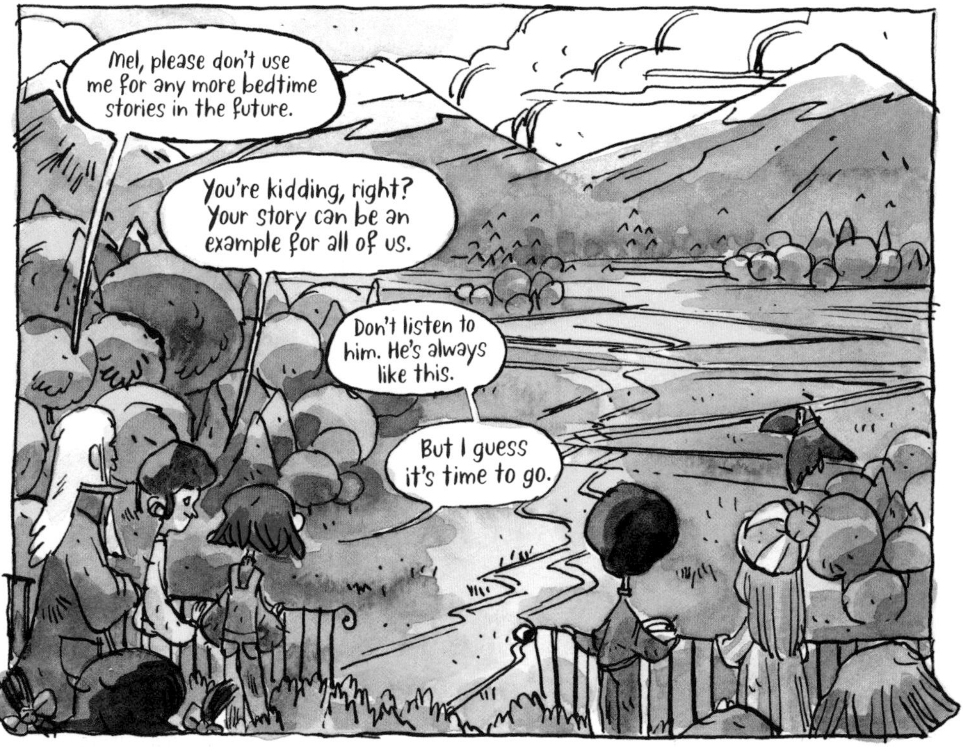
Mel, please don't use me for any more bedtime stories in the future.
You're kidding, right? Your story can be an example for all of us.
Don't listen to him. He's always like this.
But I guess it's time to go.

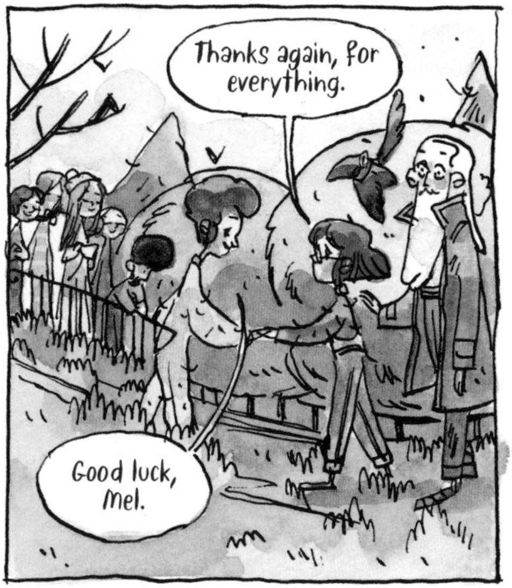
Thanks again, for everything.
Good luck, Mel.

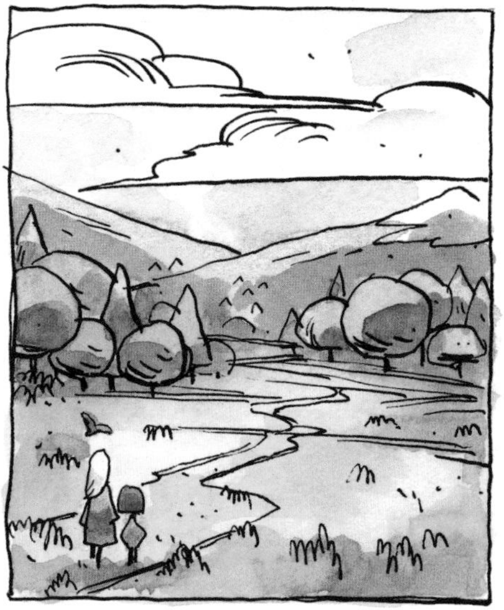

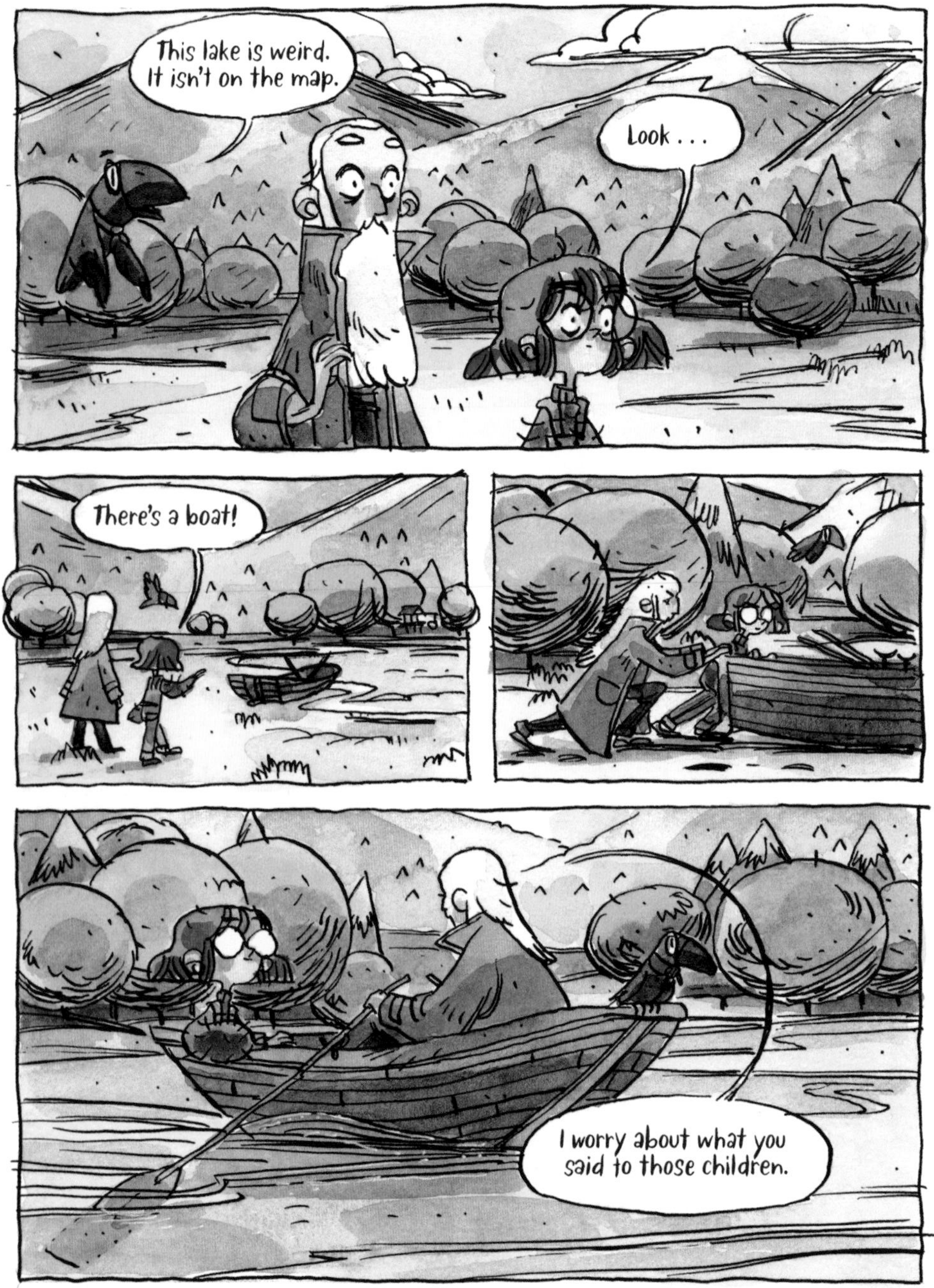
This lake is weird. It isn't on the map.
Look . . .
There's a boat!
I worry about what you said to those children.

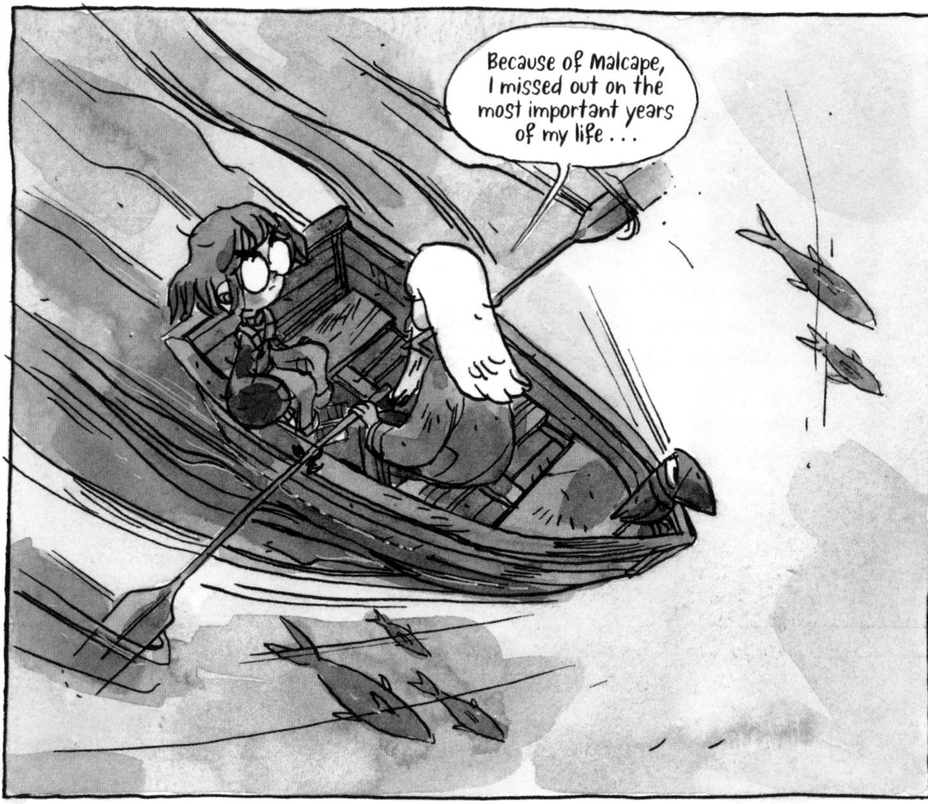
Because of Malcape, I missed out on the most important years of my life . . .

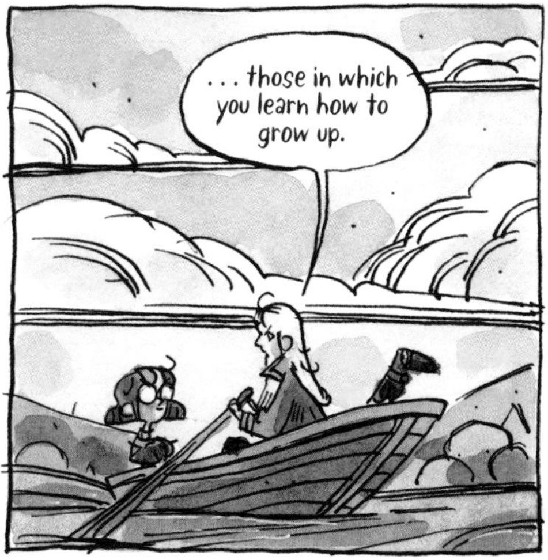
. . . those in which you learn how to grow up.

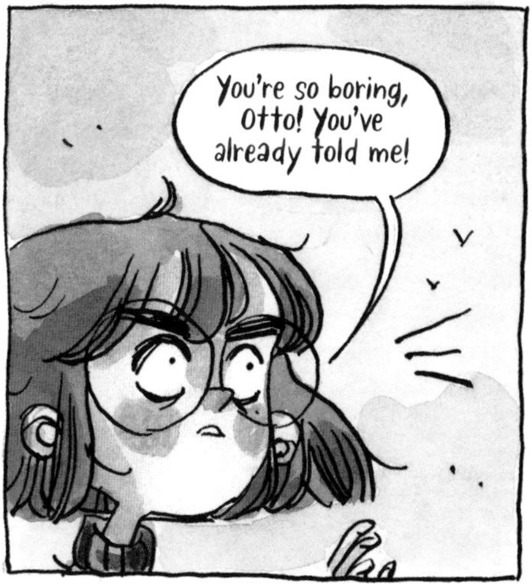
You're so boring, Otto! You've already told me!

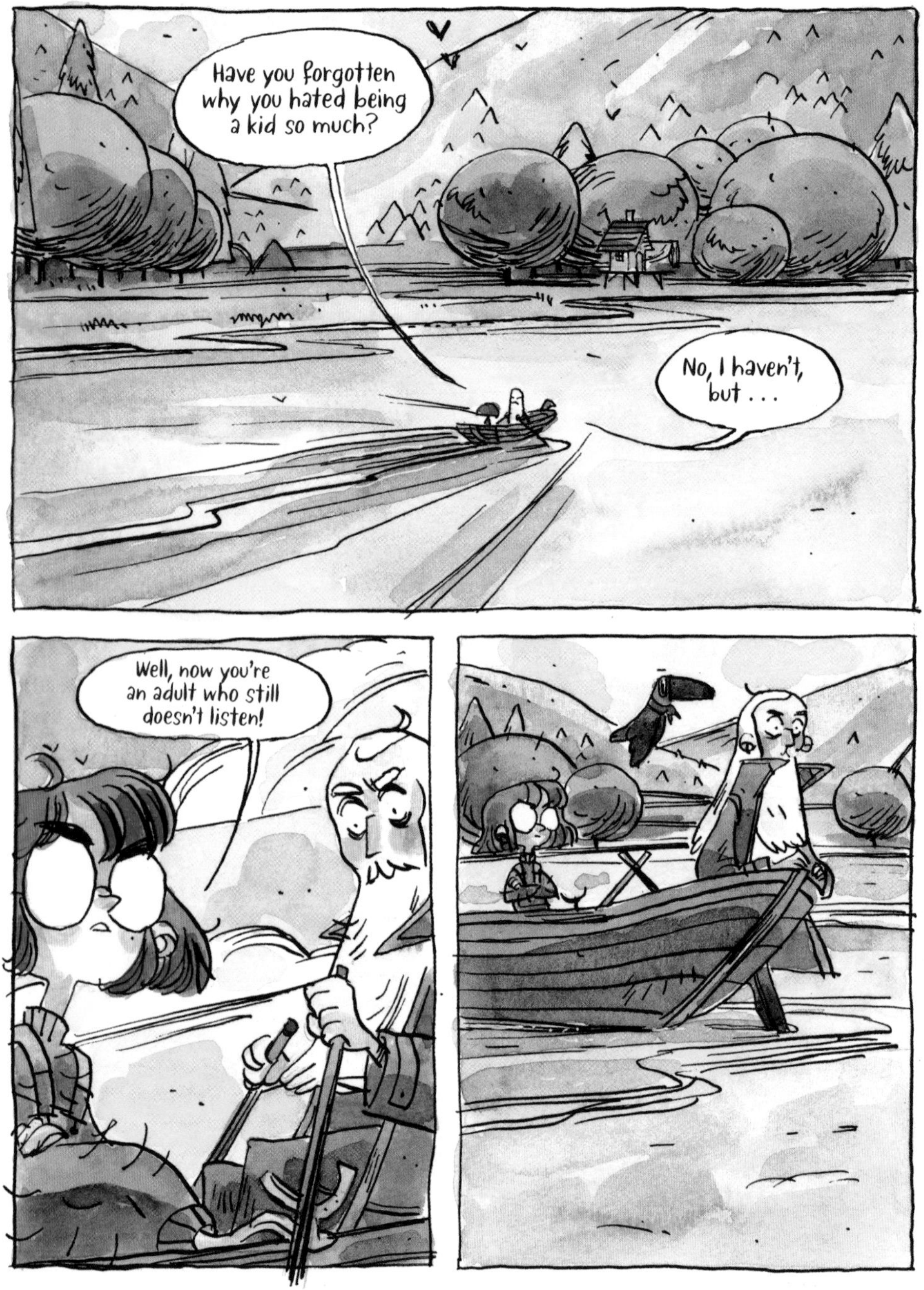
Have you forgotten why you hated being a kid so much?
No, I haven't, but . . .
Well, now you're an adult who still doesn't listen!

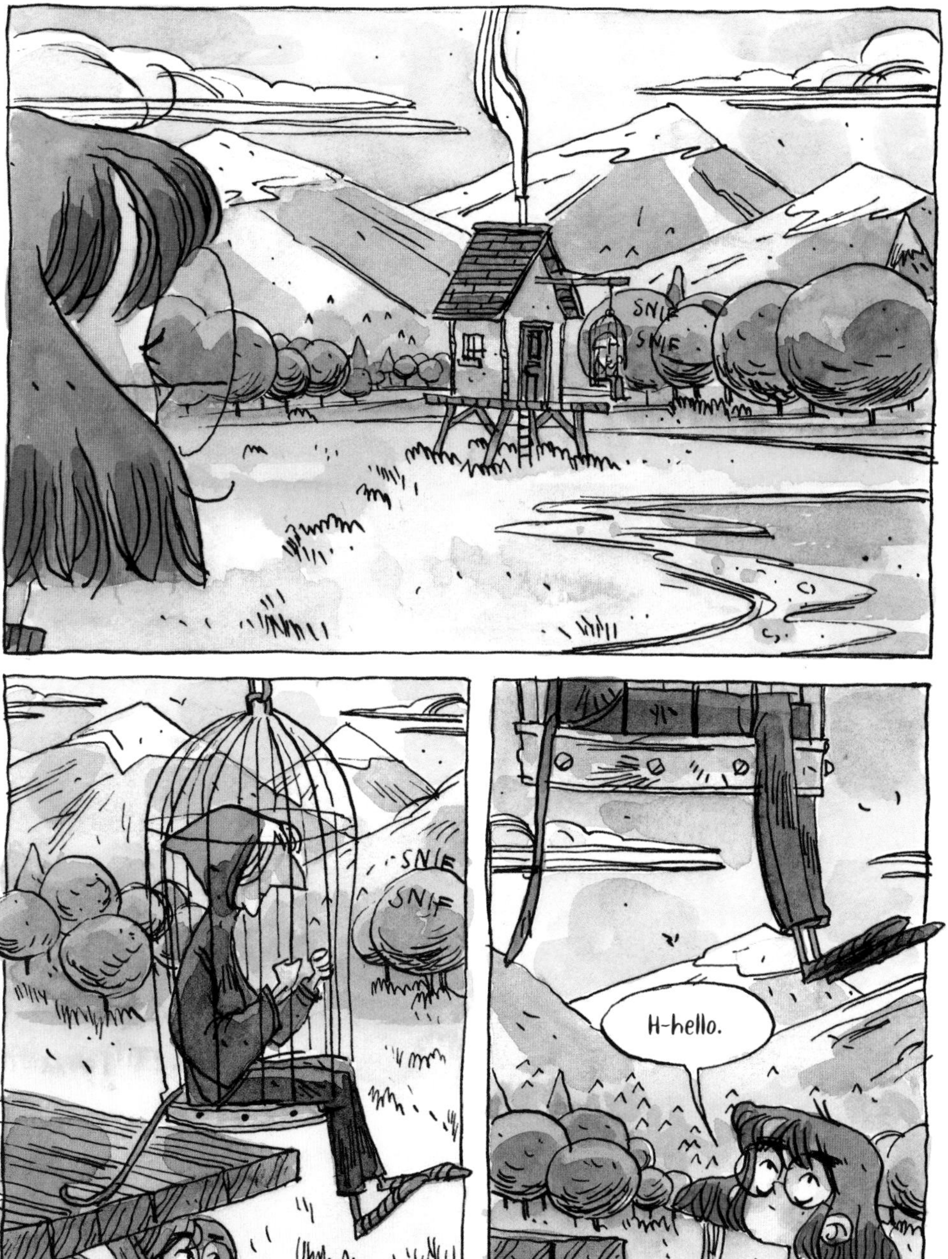
SNIF
SNIF
SNIF
SNIF
H-hello.

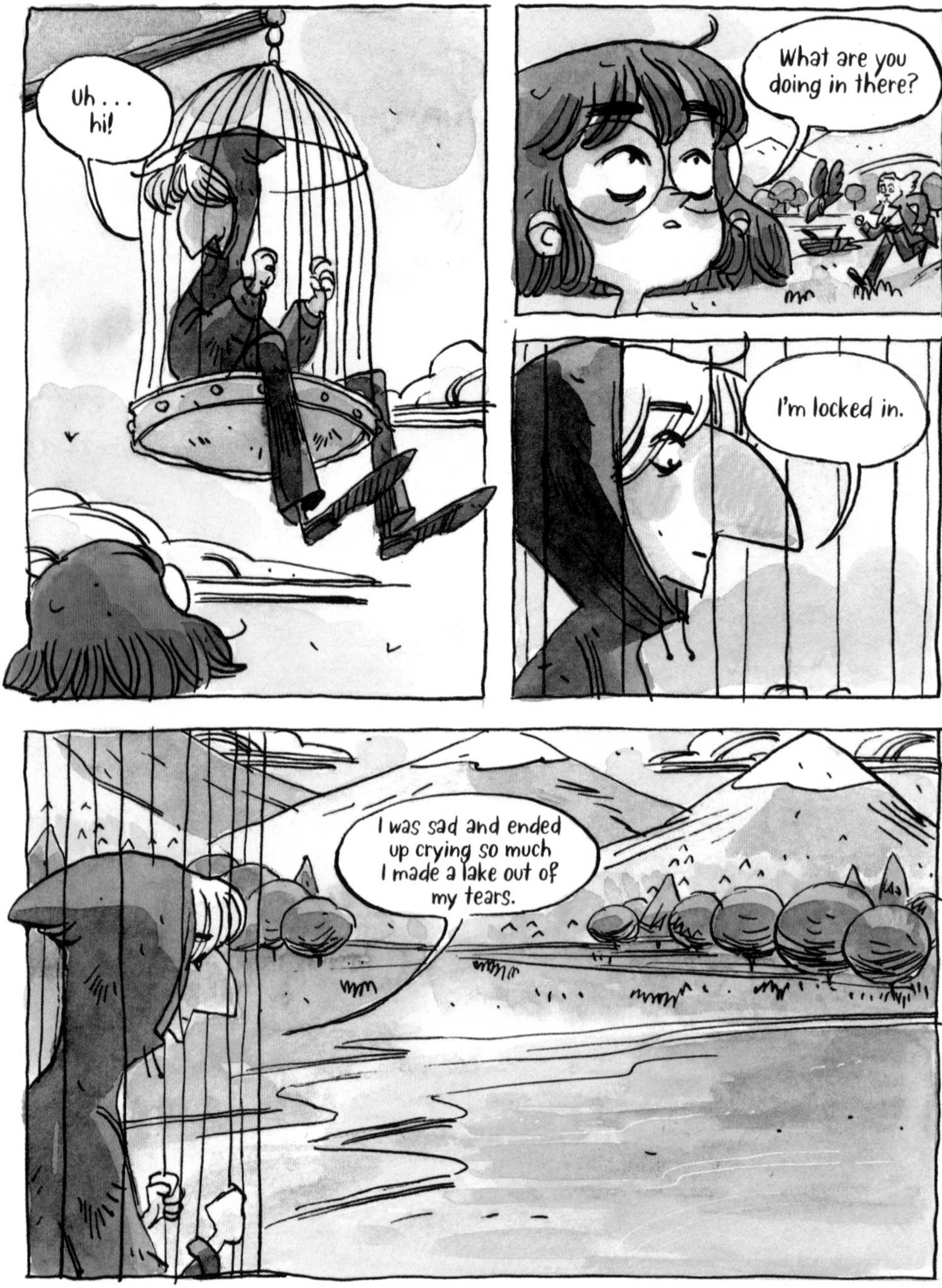
Uh . . . hi!
What are you doing in there?
I'm locked in.
I was sad and ended up crying so much I made a lake out of my tears.

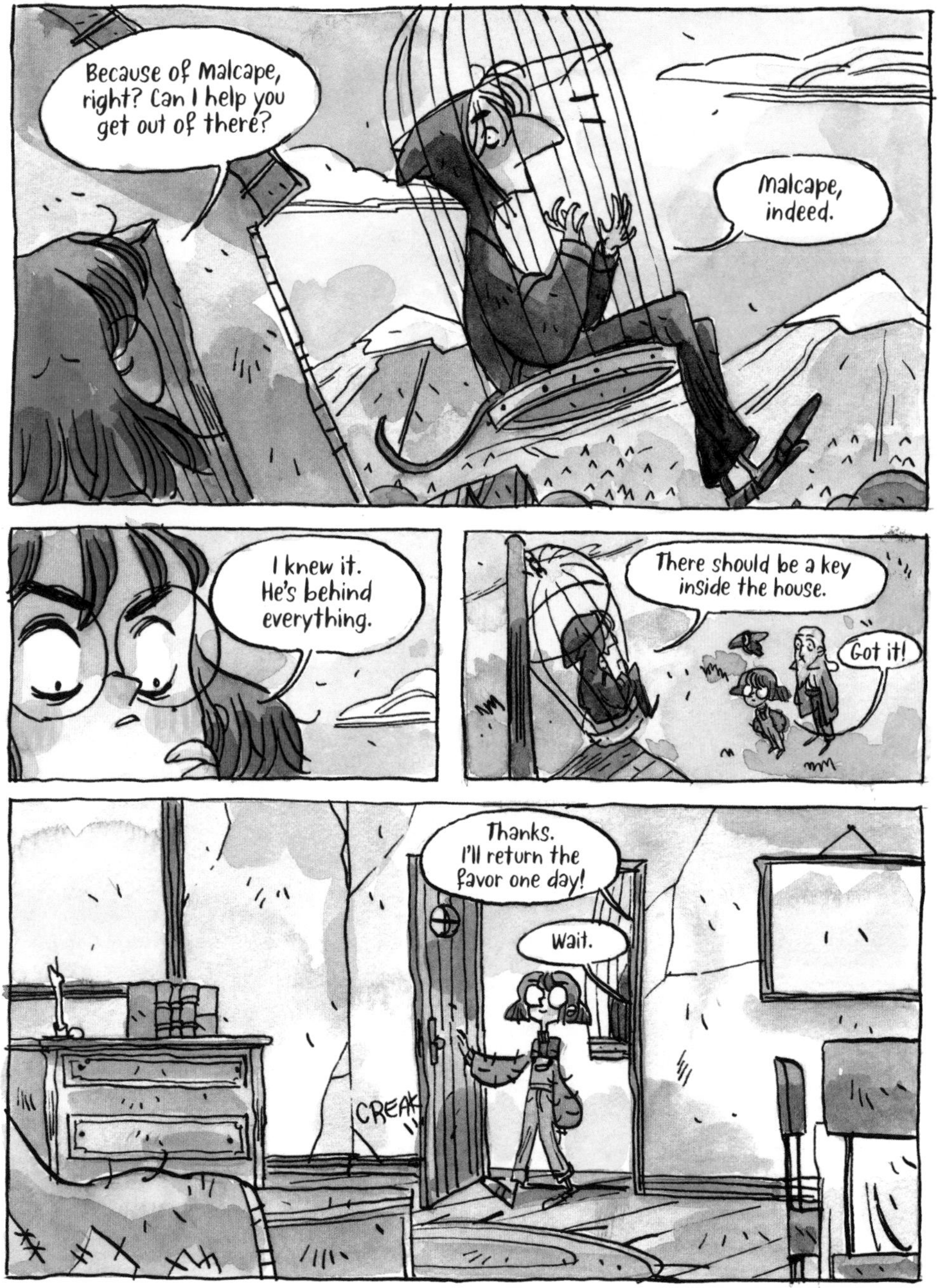
Because of Malcape, right? Can I help you get out of there?
Malcape, indeed.
I knew it. He's behind everything.
There should be a key inside the house.
Got it!
Thanks. I'll return the favor one day!
Wait.
CREAK

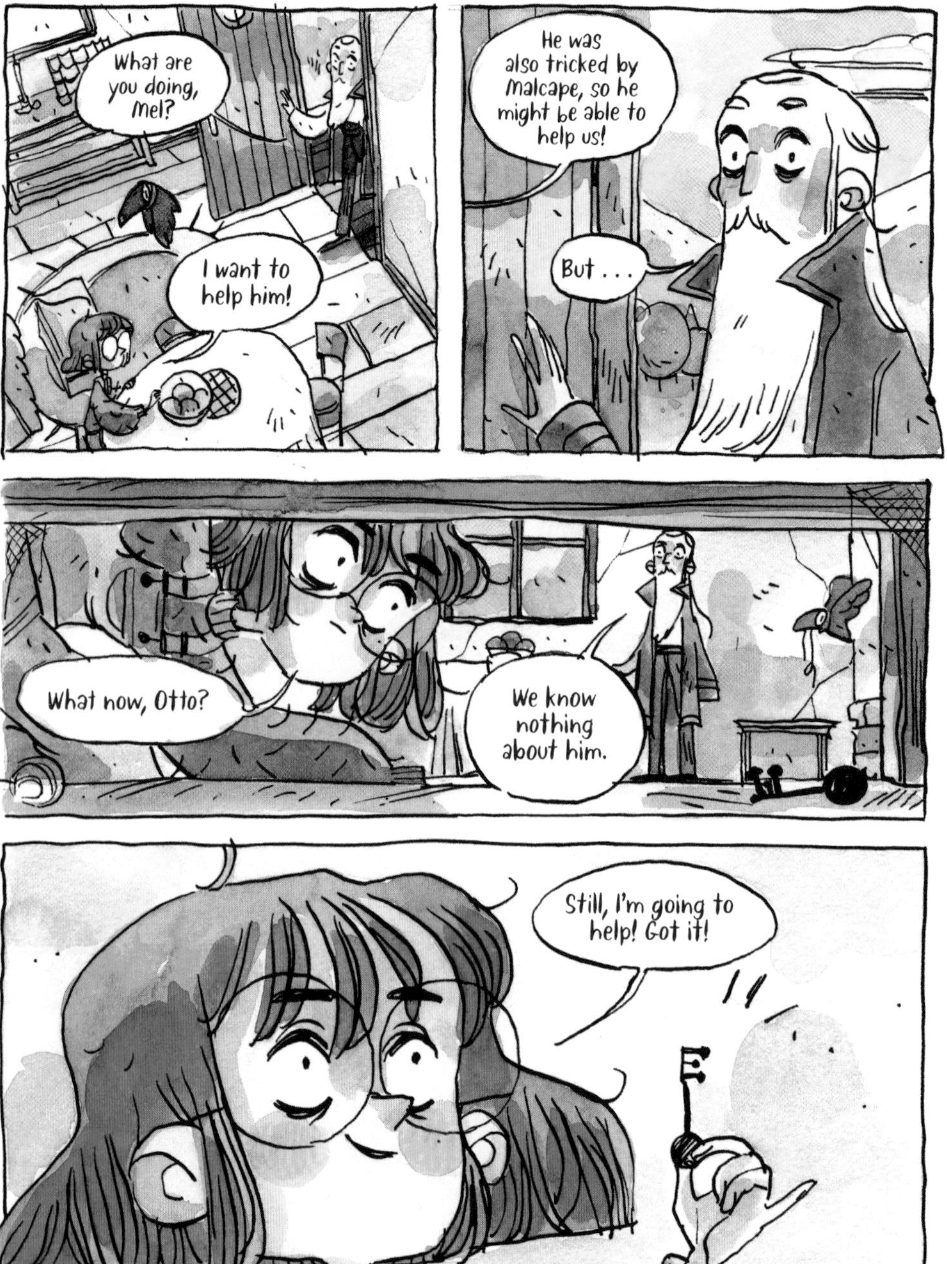
What are you doing, Mel?
I want to help him!
He was also tricked by Malcape, so he might be able to help us!
But . . .
What now, Otto?
We know nothing about him.
Still, I'm going to help! Got it!

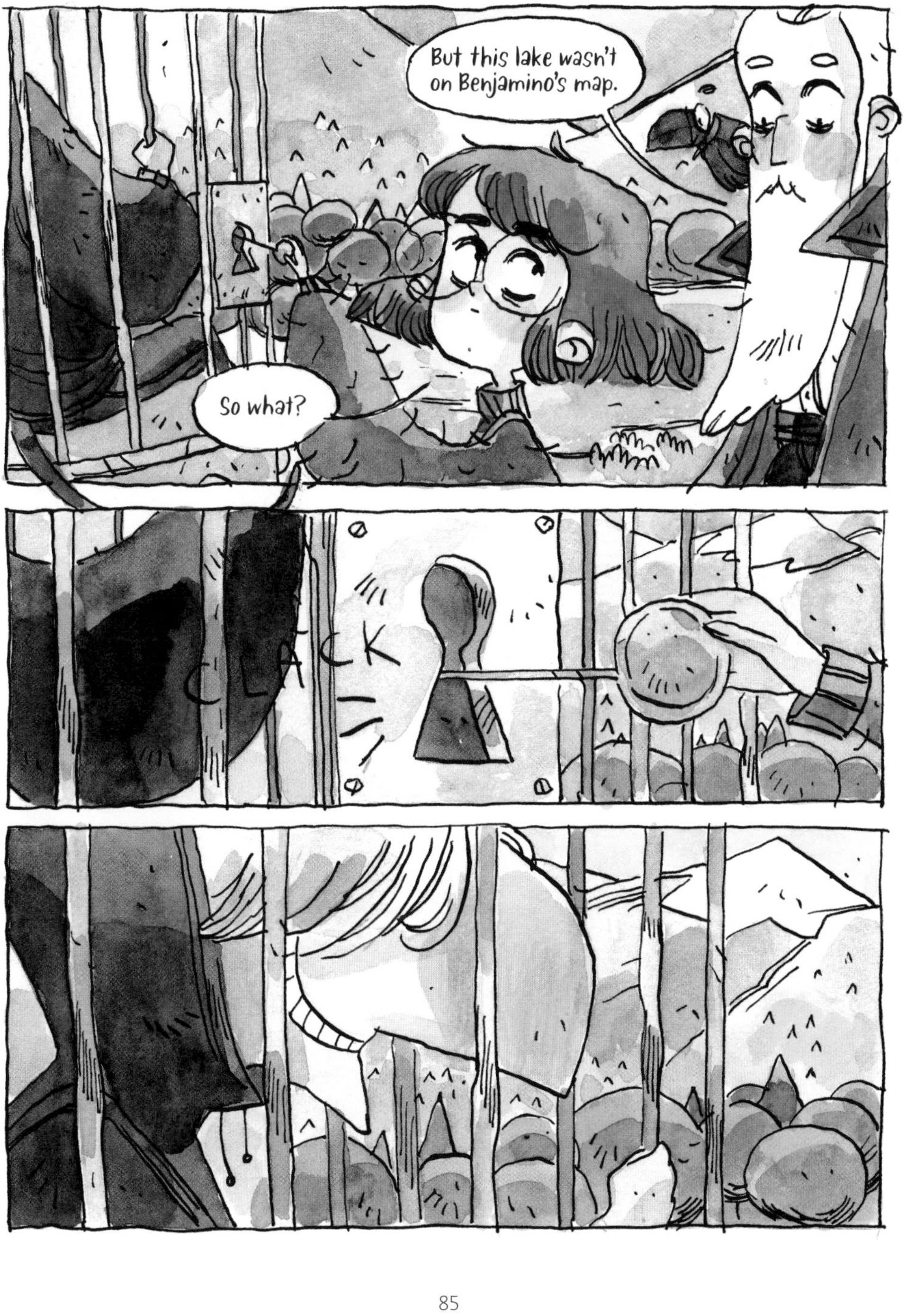
But this lake wasn't on Benjamino's map.
So what?
CLACK

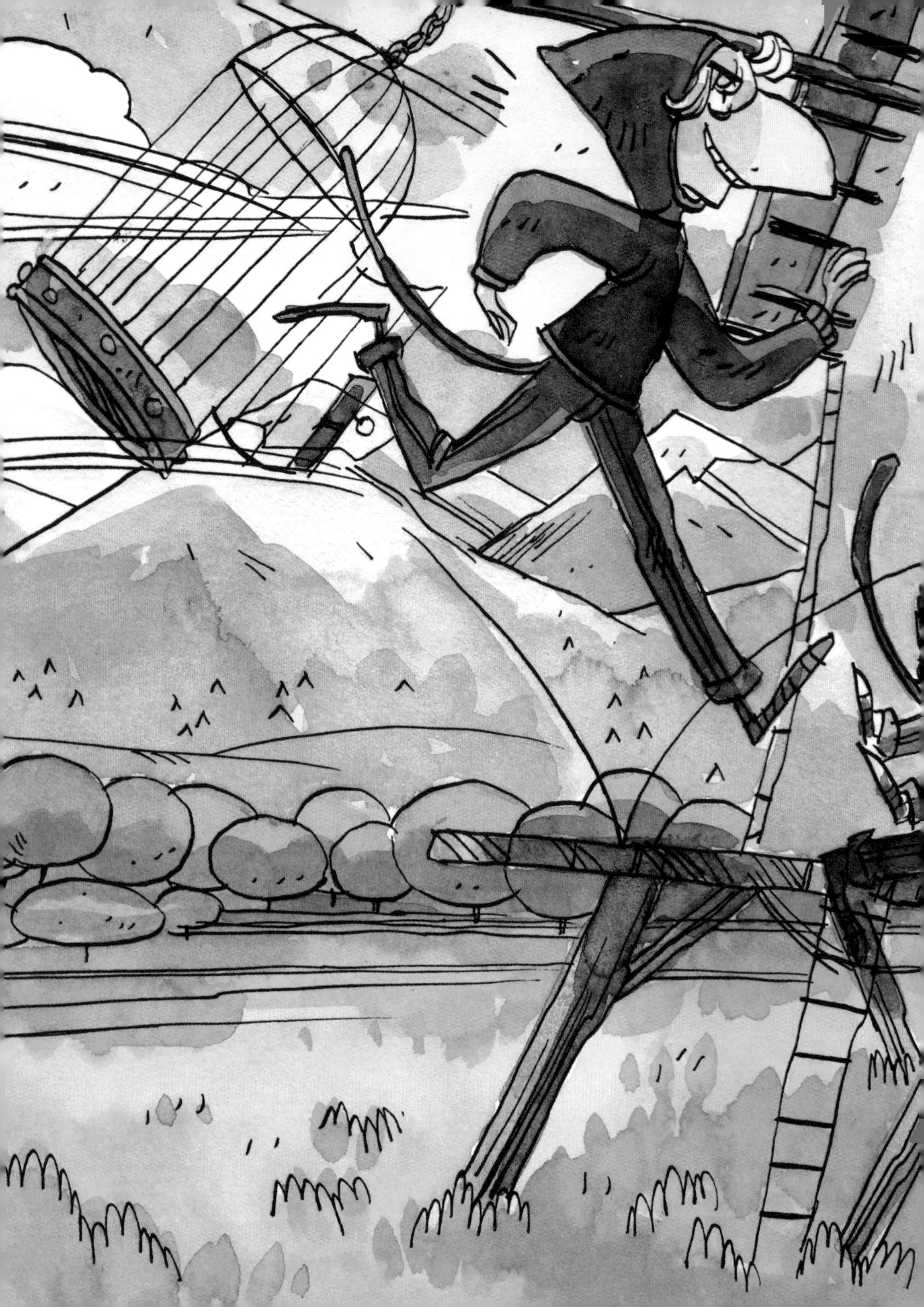

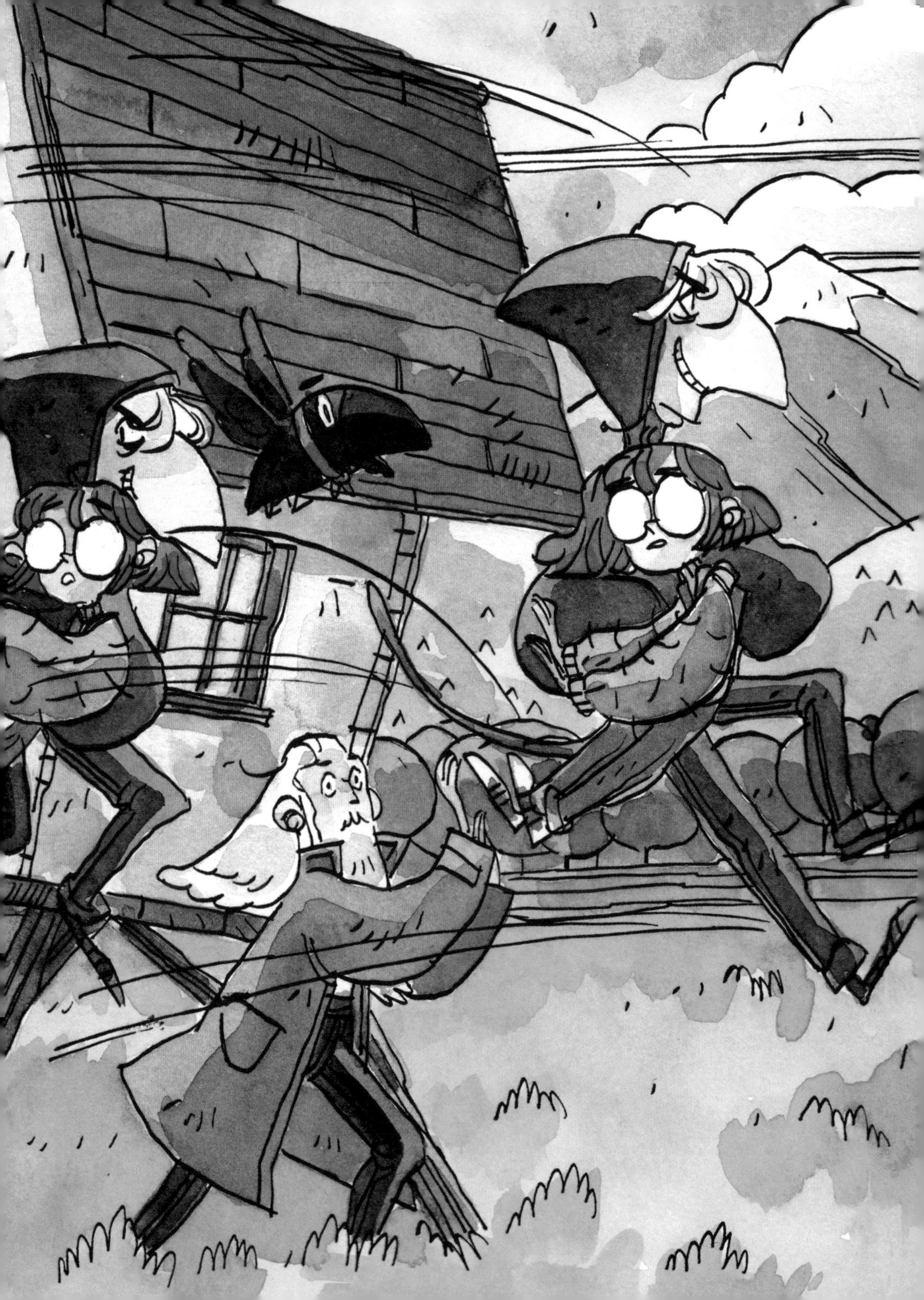

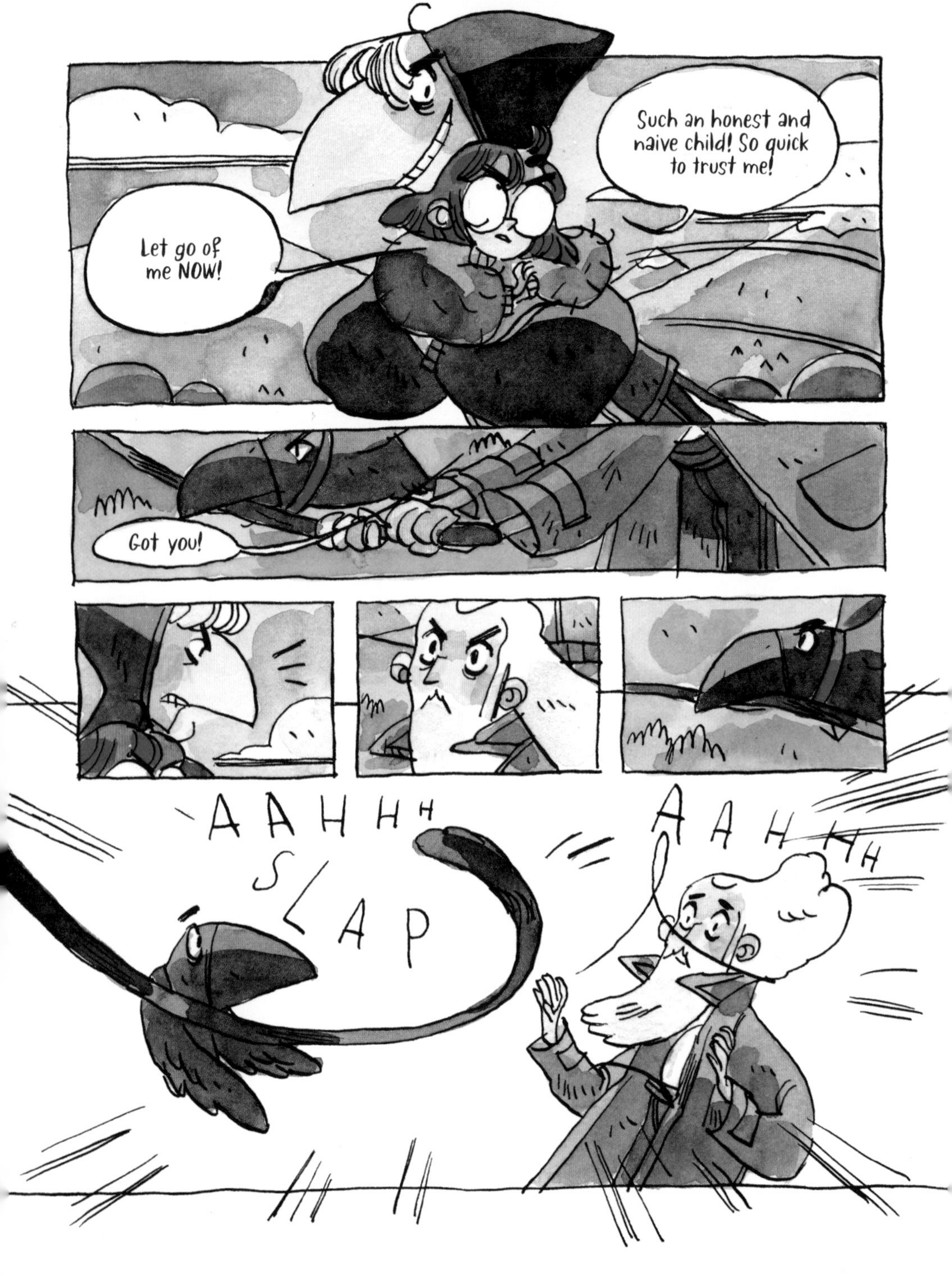

Let go of me NOW!
Such an honest and naive child! So quick to trust me!
Got you!
AAHHH
SLAP
AAHHH

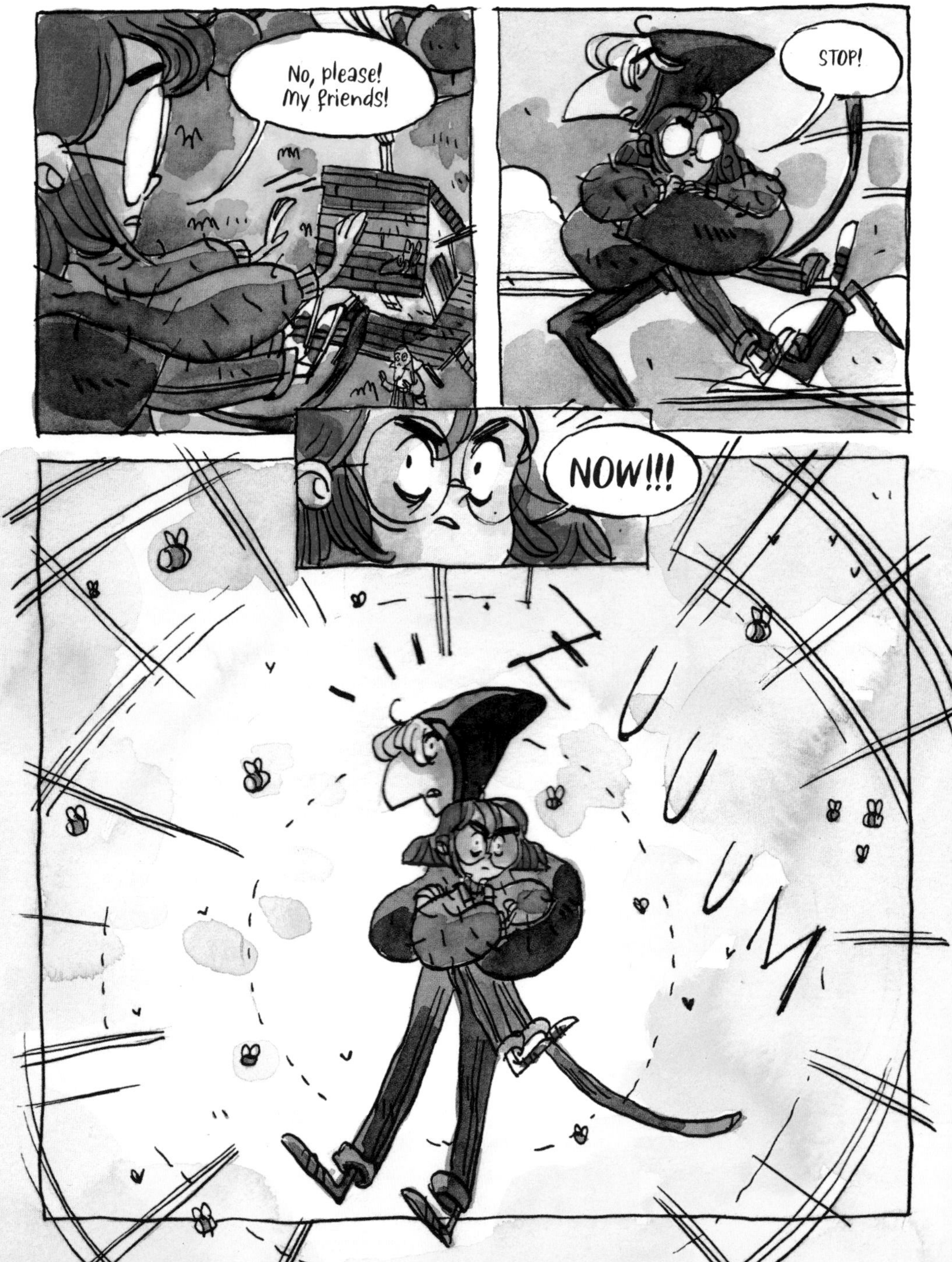
No, please! My friends!
STOP!
NOW!!!
THUUM

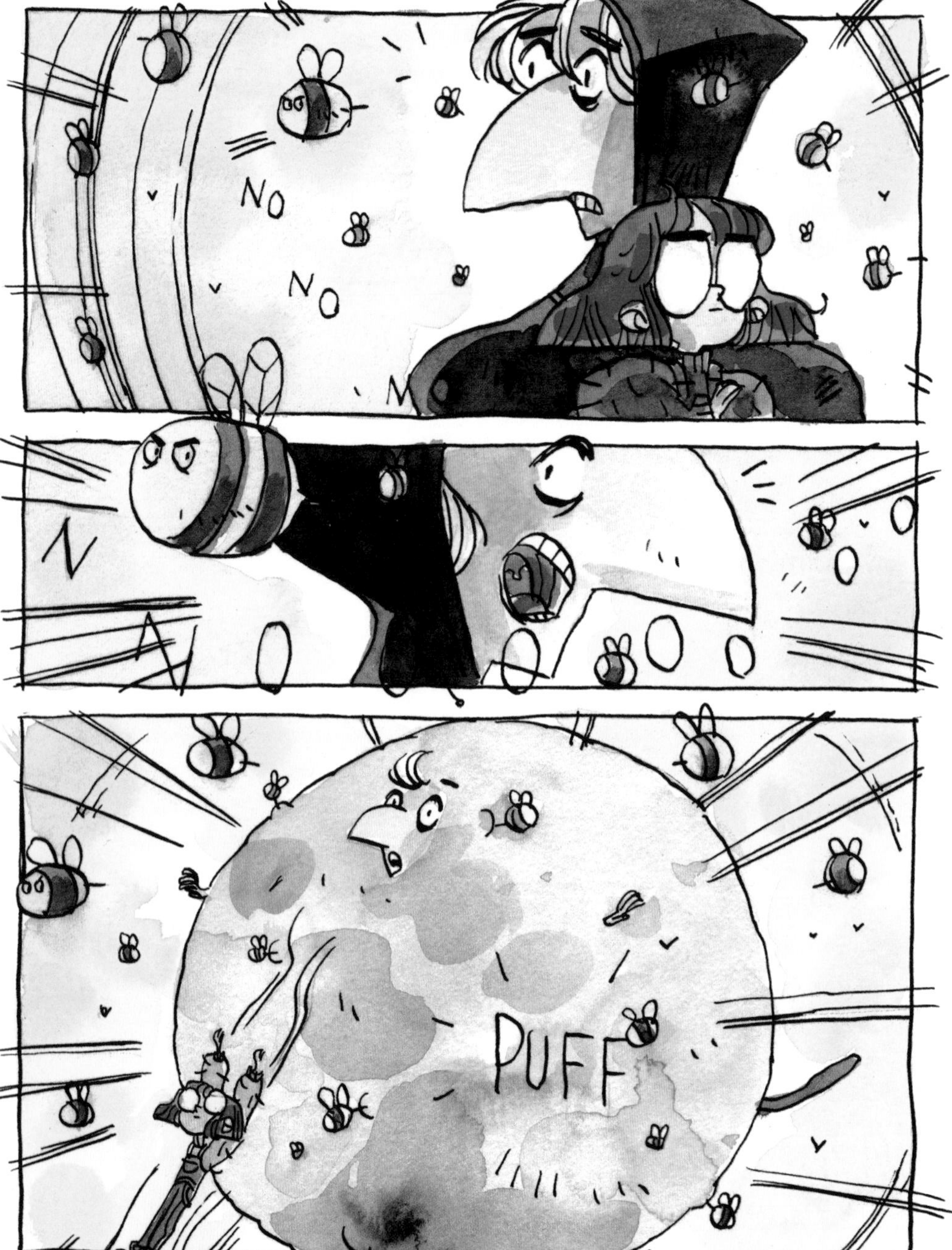
NO
NO
PUFF

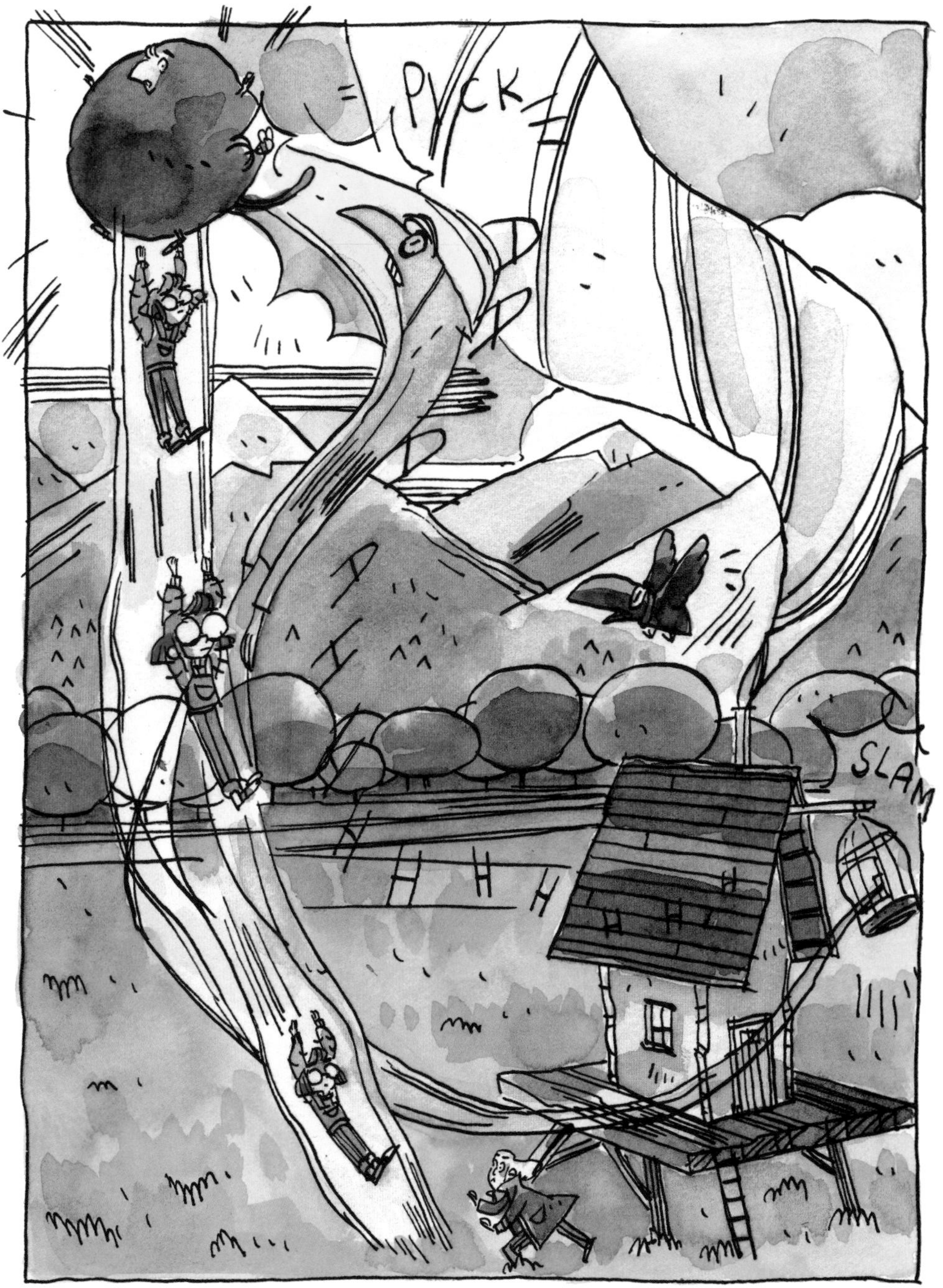
PYCK
SLAM

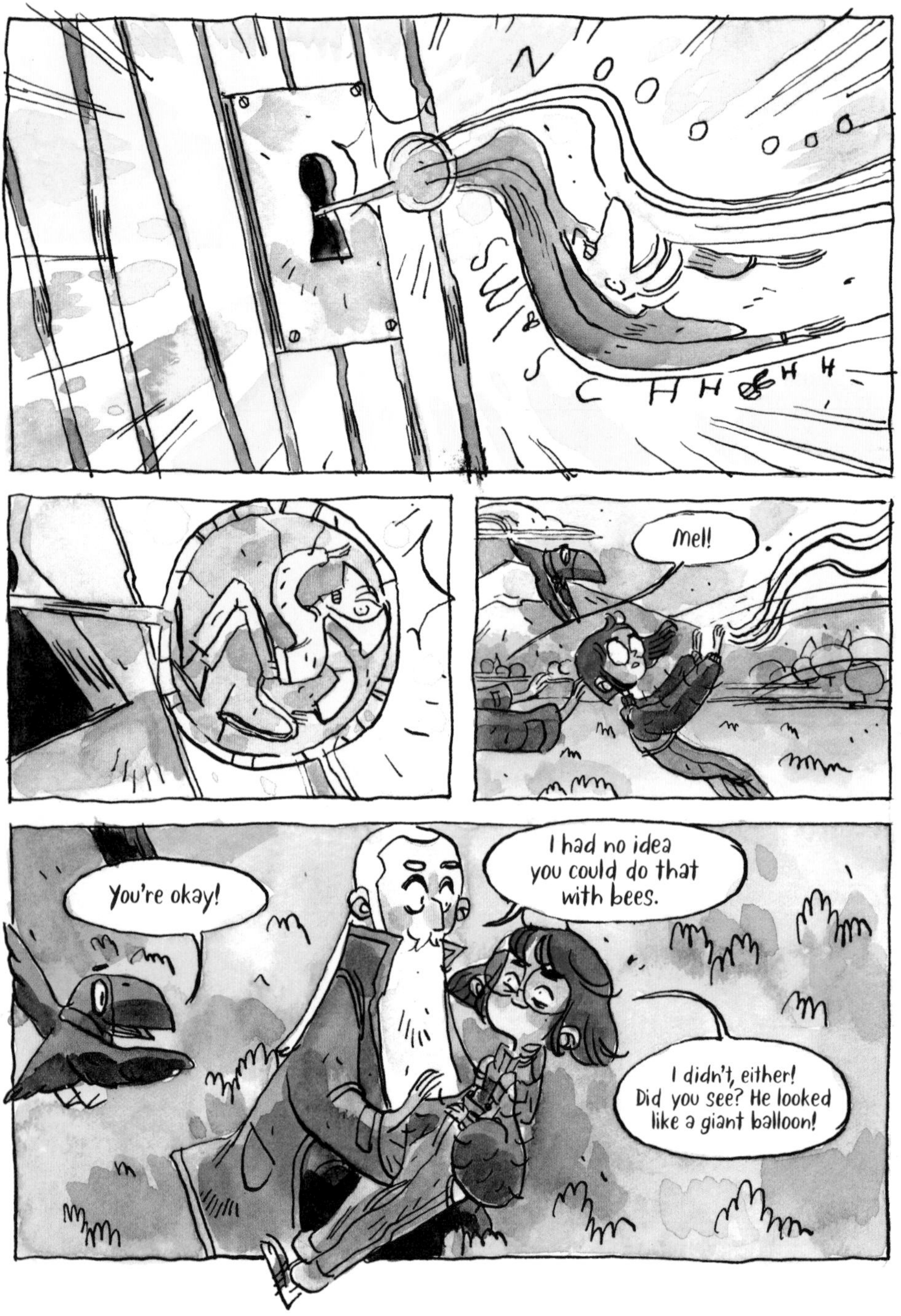
NOOOOOOO
SWISCHHHH
Mel!
You're okay!
I had no idea you could do that with bees.
I didn't, either! Did you see? He looked like a giant balloon!

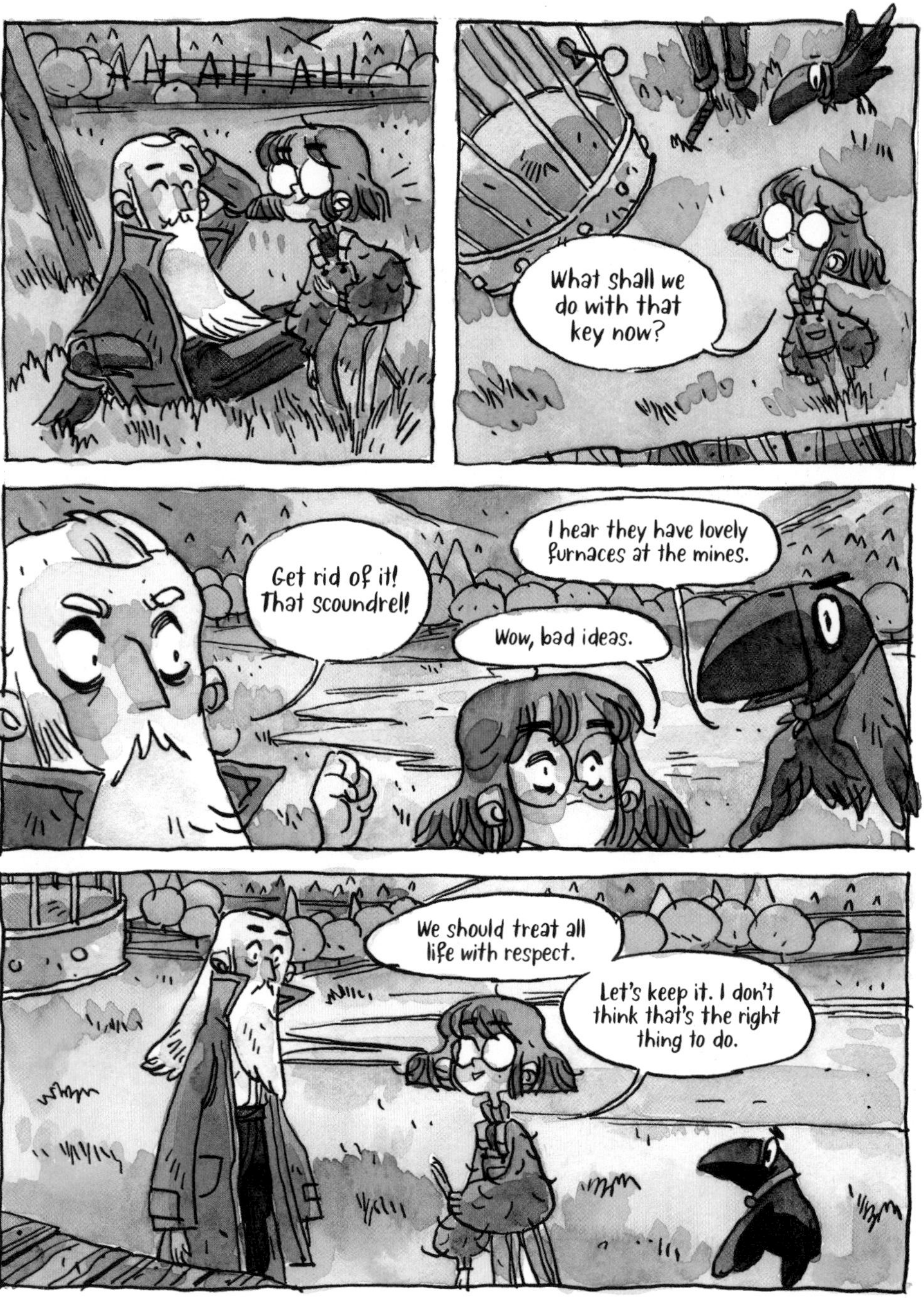
AH! AH! AH!
What shall we do with that key now?
Get rid of it! That scoundrel!
I hear they have lovely furnaces at the mines.
Wow, bad ideas.
We should treat all life with respect.
Let's keep it. I don't think that's the right thing to do.

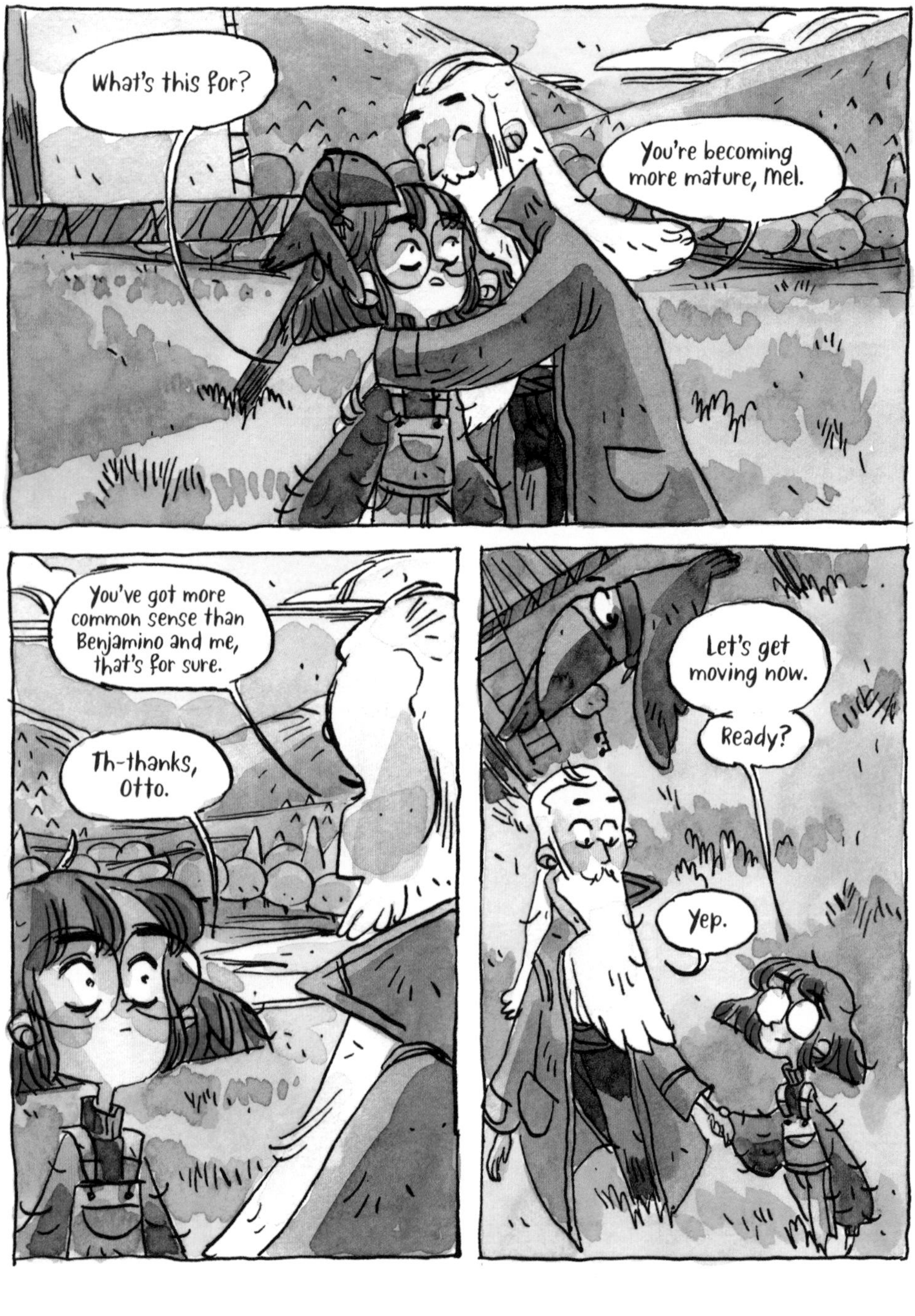
What's this for?
You're becoming more mature, Mel.
You've got more common sense than Benjamino and me, that's for sure.
Th-thanks, Otto.
Let's get moving now.
Ready?
Yep.

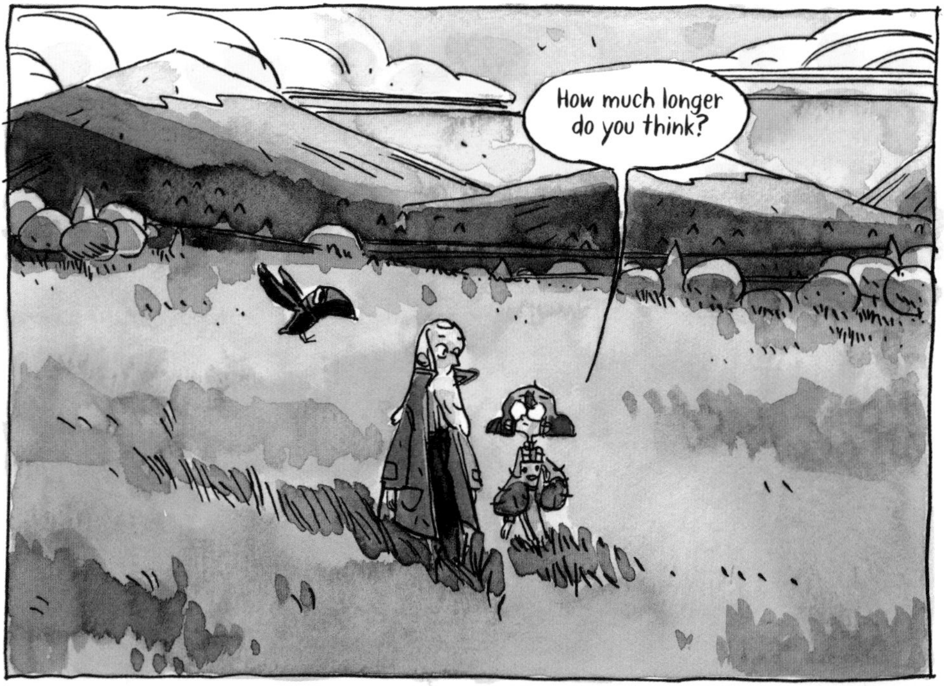
How much longer do you think?

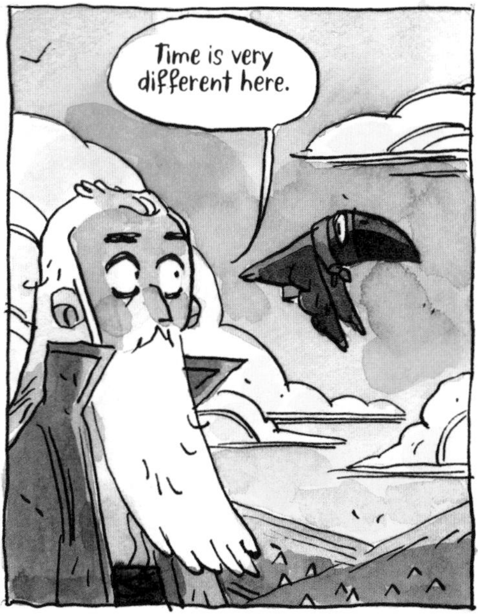
Time is very different here.

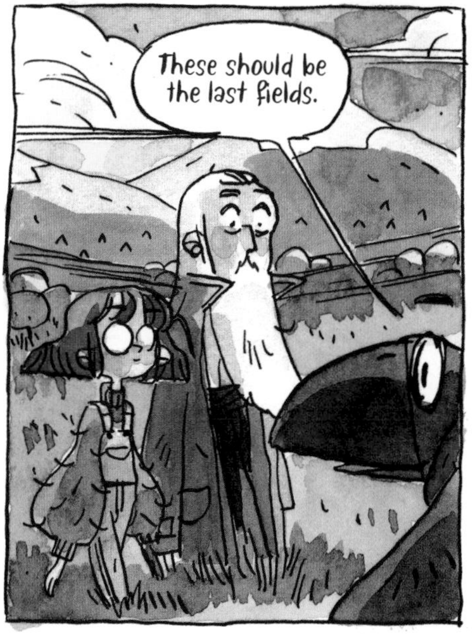
These should be the last fields.

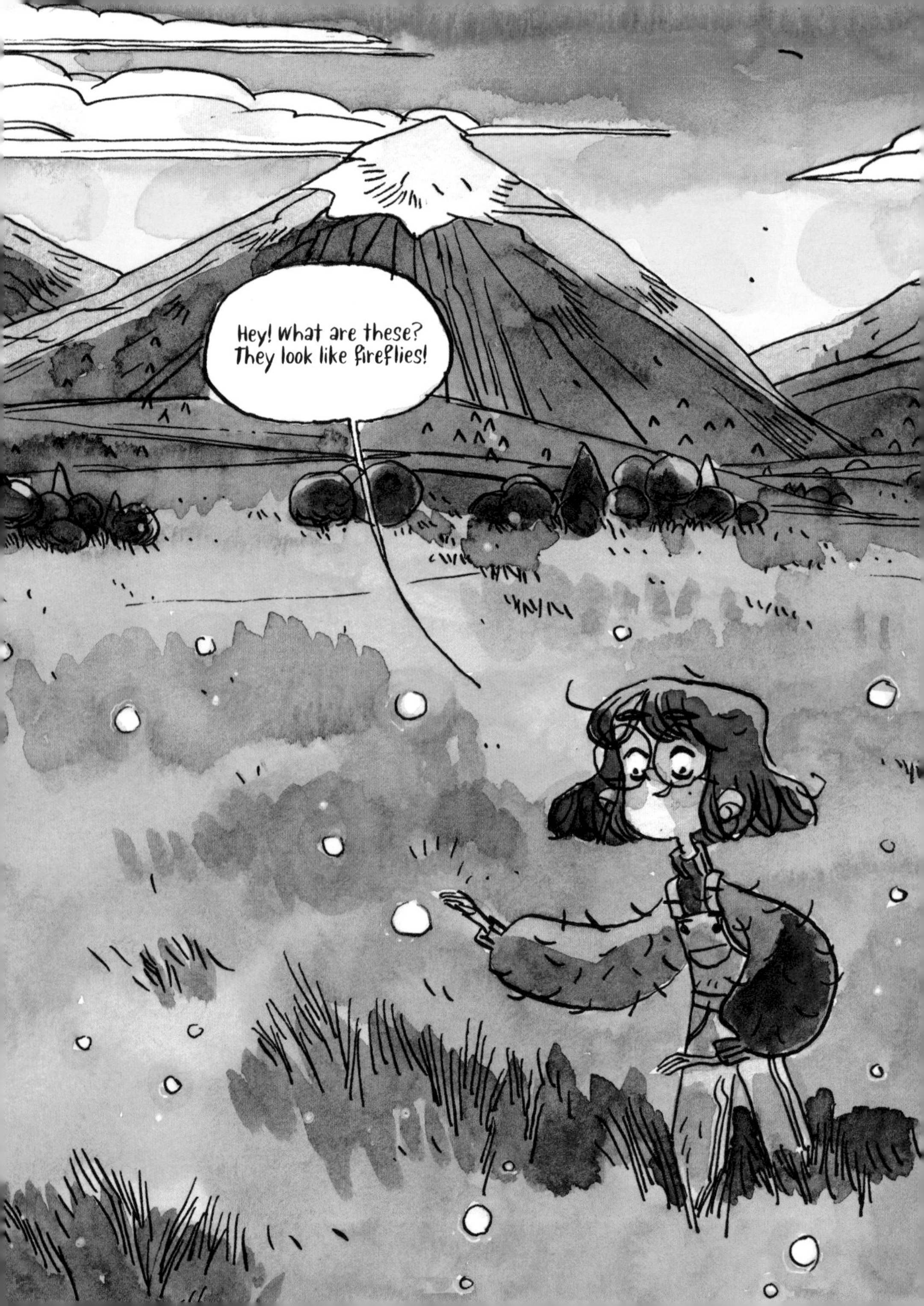
Hey! What are these? They look like fireflies!

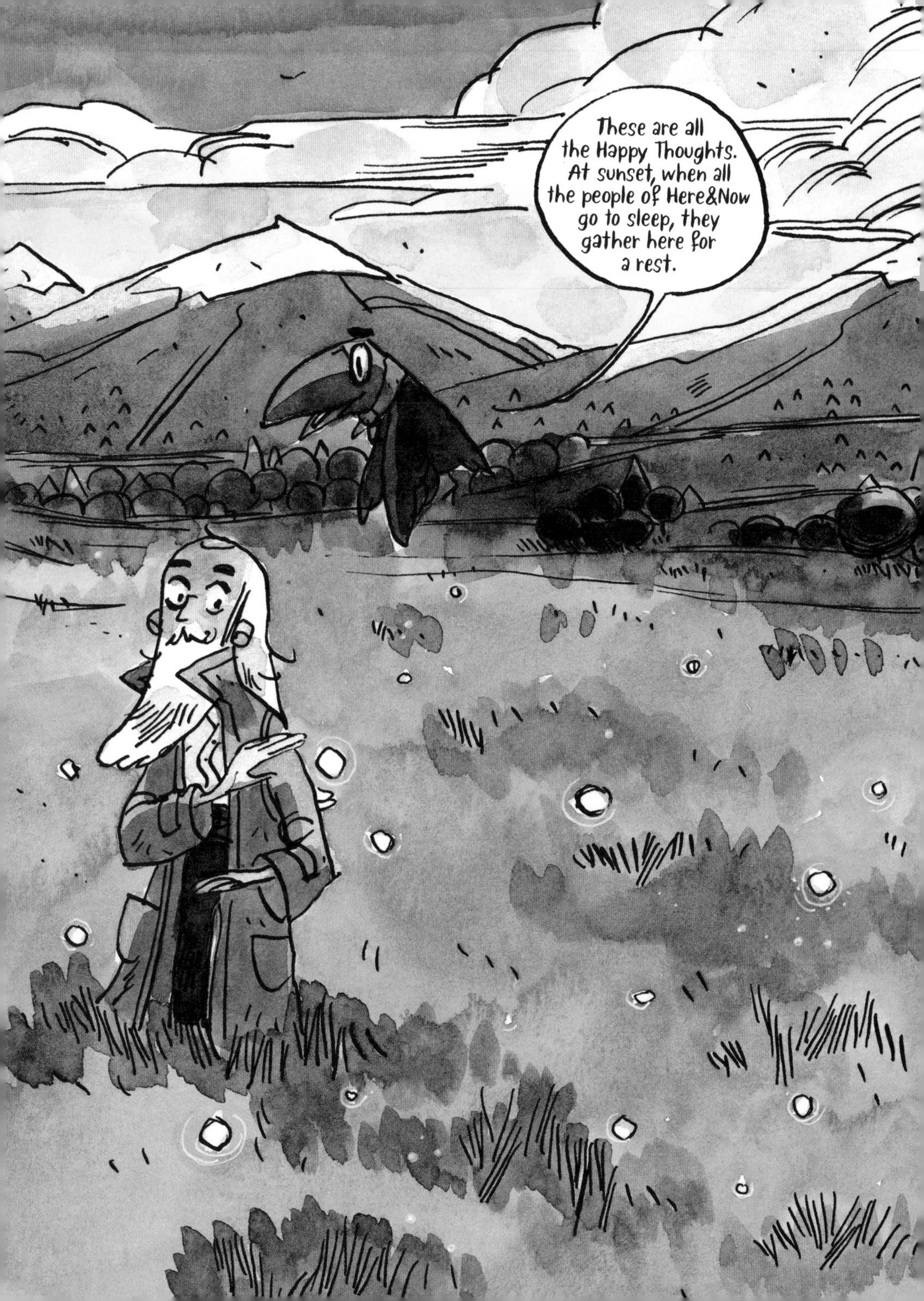
These are all the Happy Thoughts. At sunset, when all the people of Here&Now go to sleep, they gather here for a rest.

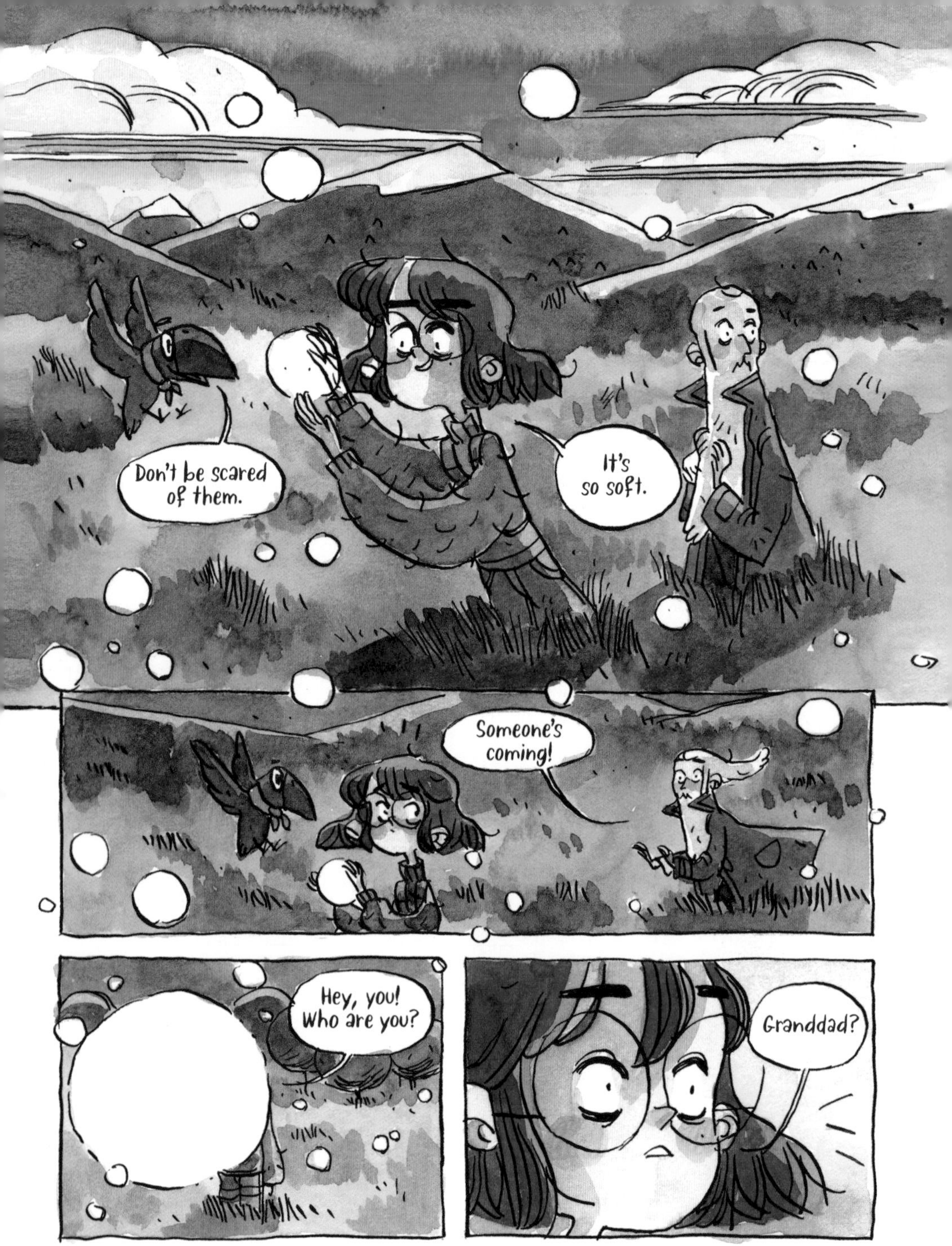
Don't be scared of them.
It's so soft.
Someone's coming!
Hey, you! Who are you?
Granddad?

GRANDPA!
MEL?!
The Happy Thoughts told me you were here, but I couldn't believe them.

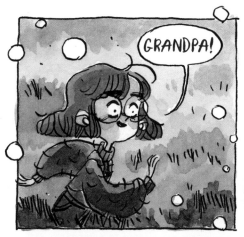

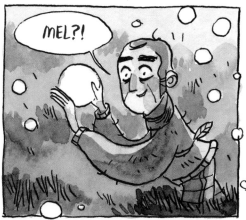

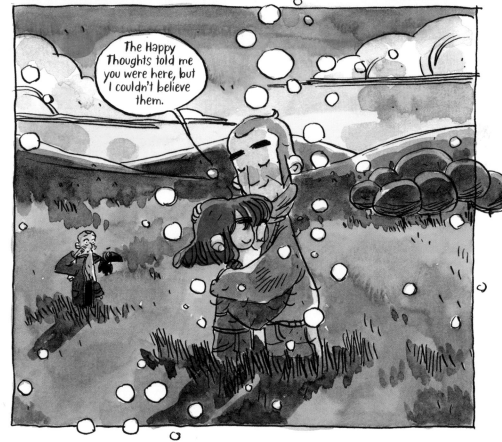

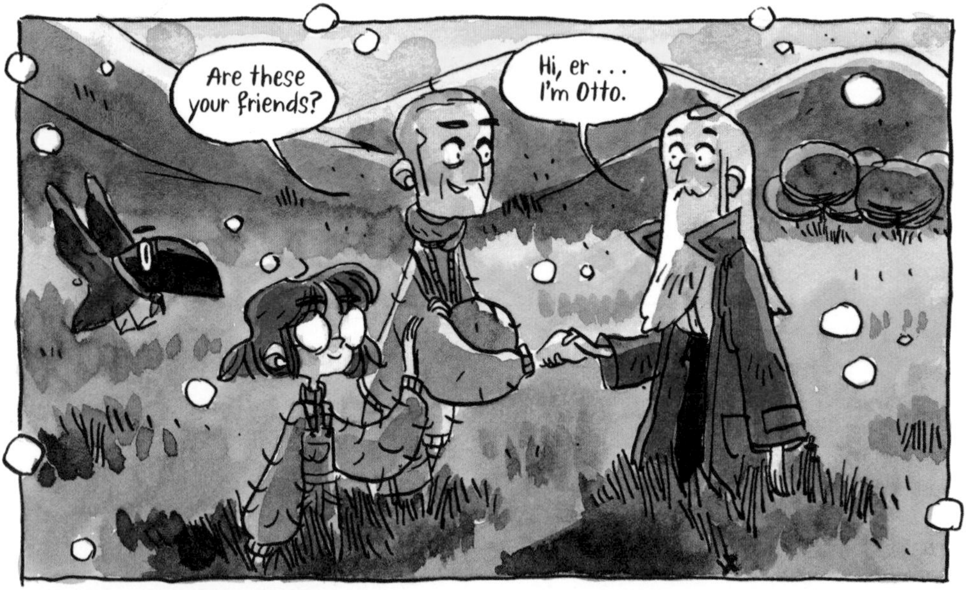
Are these your friends?
Hi, er . . . I'm Otto.

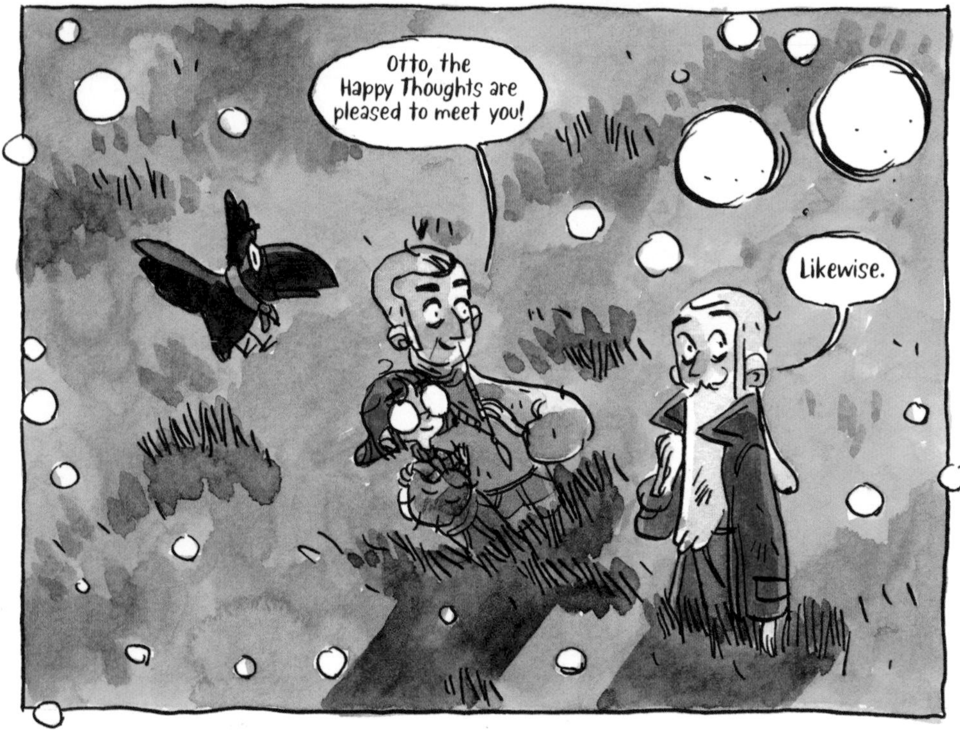
Otto, the Happy Thoughts are pleased to meet you!
Likewise.

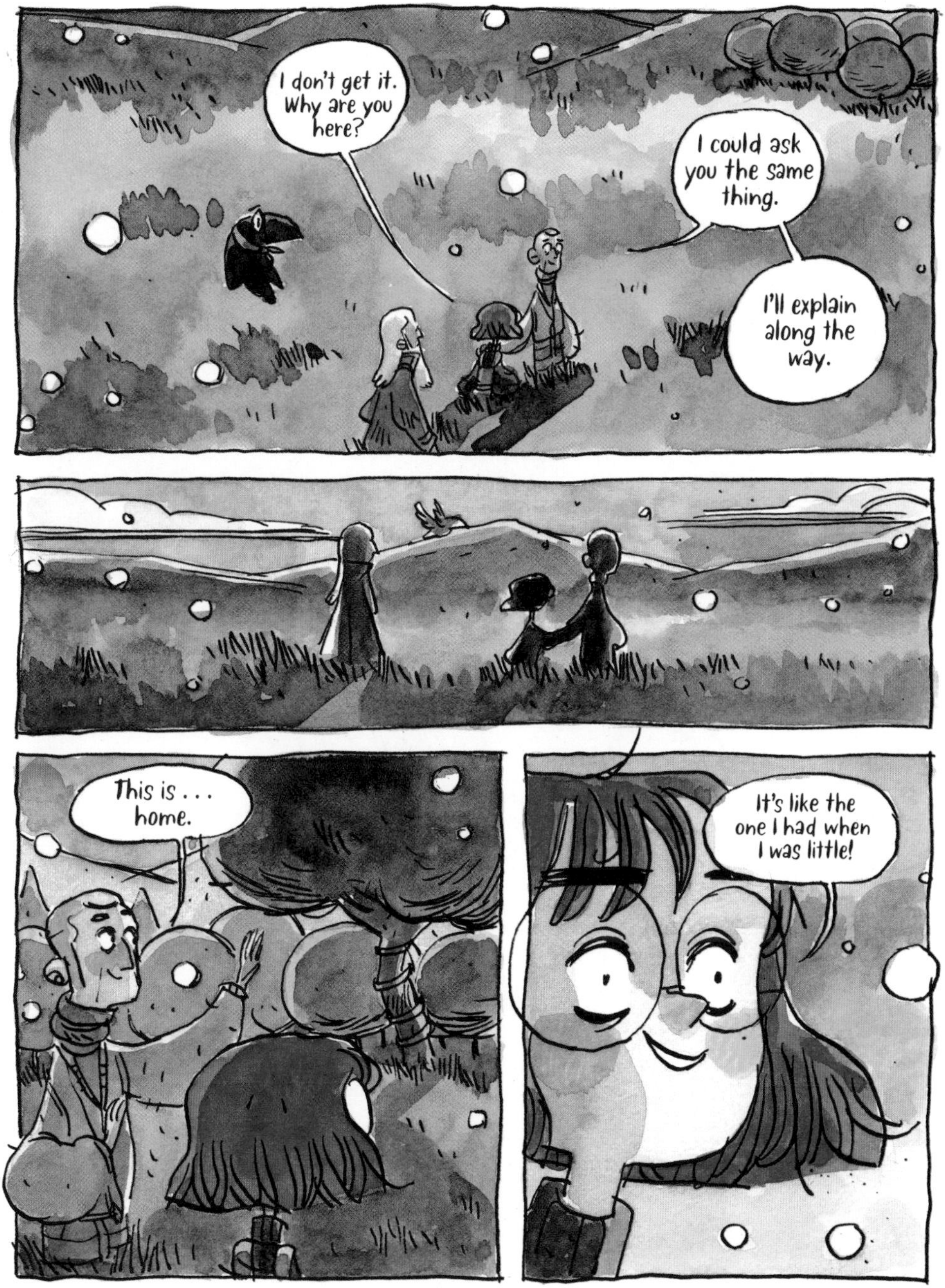
I don't get it. Why are you here?
I could ask you the same thing.
I'll explain along the way.
This is . . . home.
It's like the one I had when I was little!

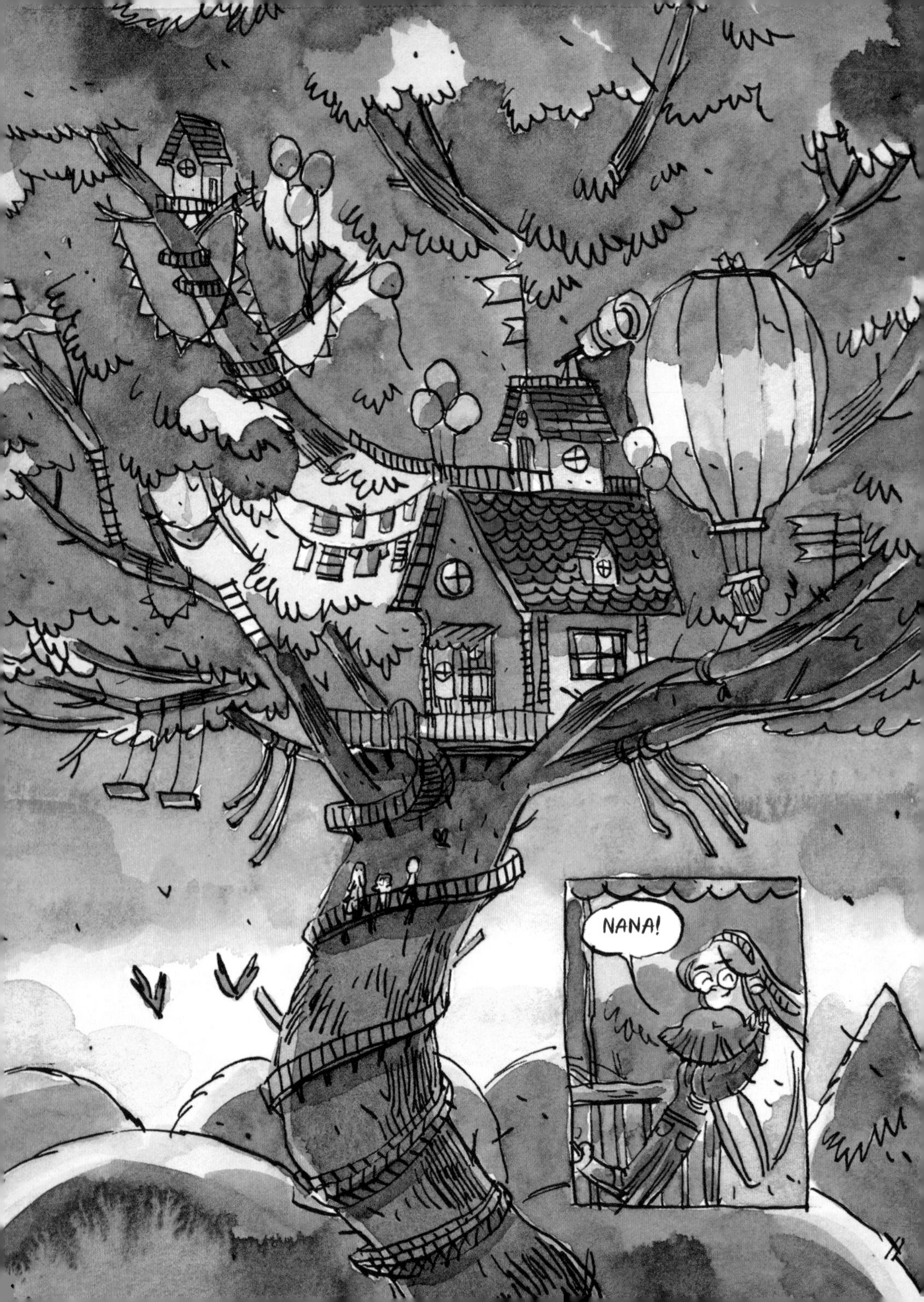
NANA!

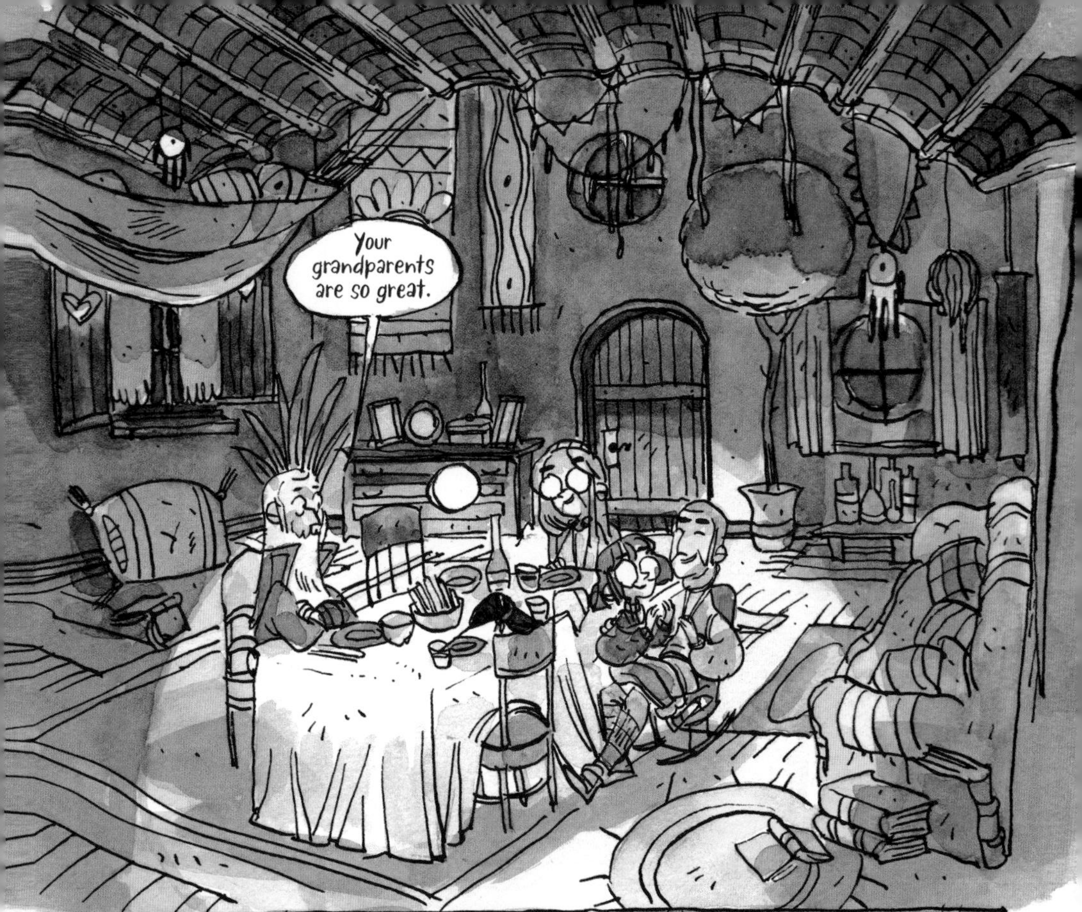
Your grandparents are so great.

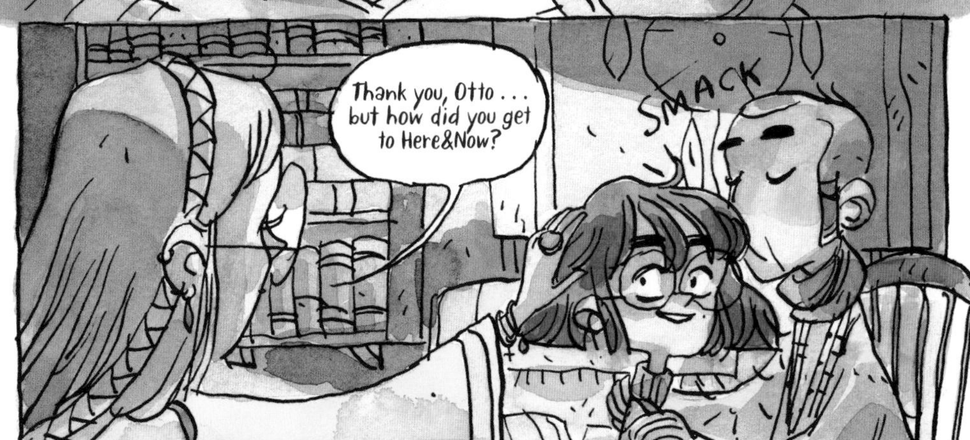
Thank you, Otto . . . but how did you get to Here&Now?
SMACK

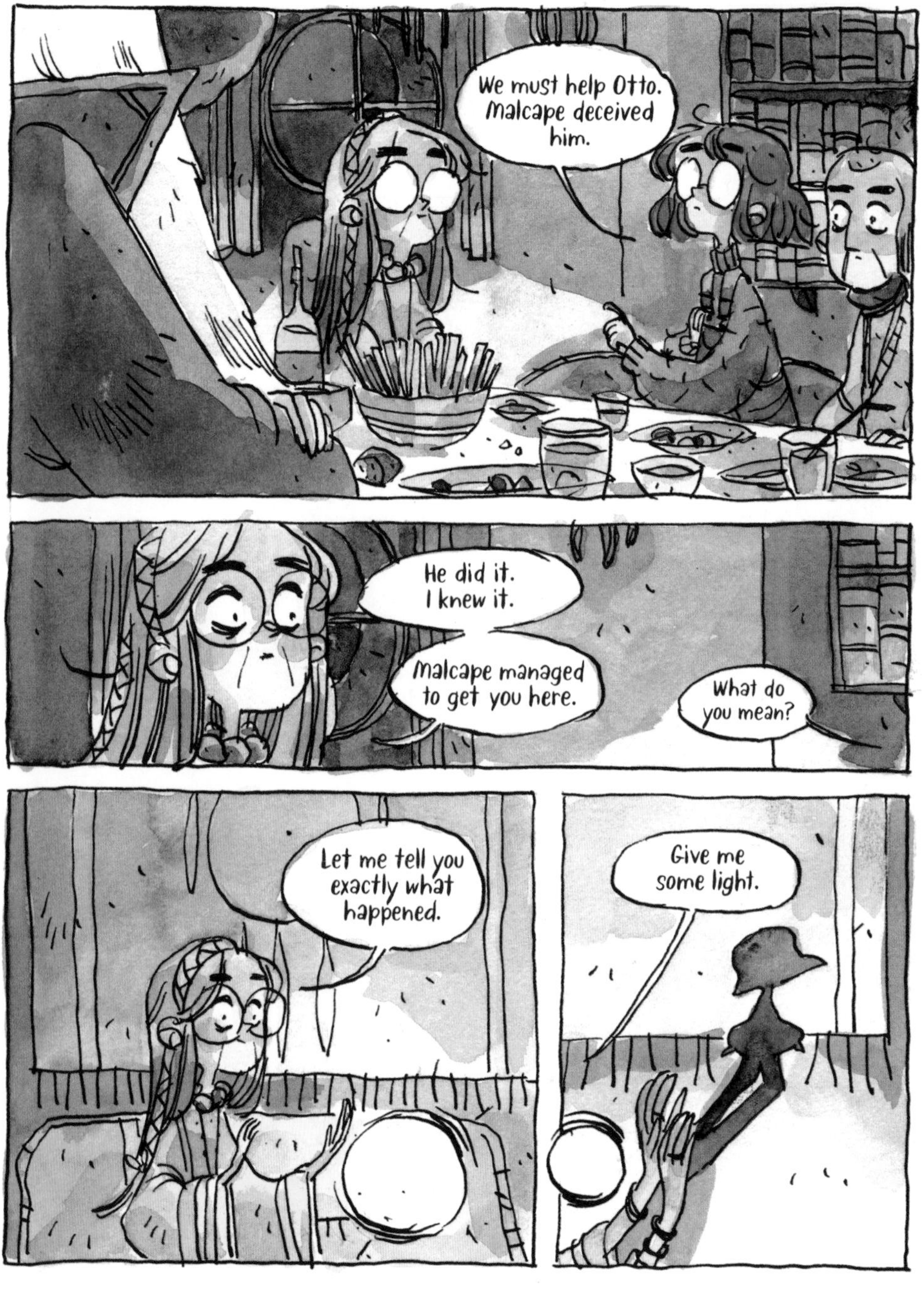
We must help Otto. Malcape deceived him.
He did it. I knew it.
Malcape managed to get you here.
What do you mean?
Let me tell you exactly what happened.
Give me some light.

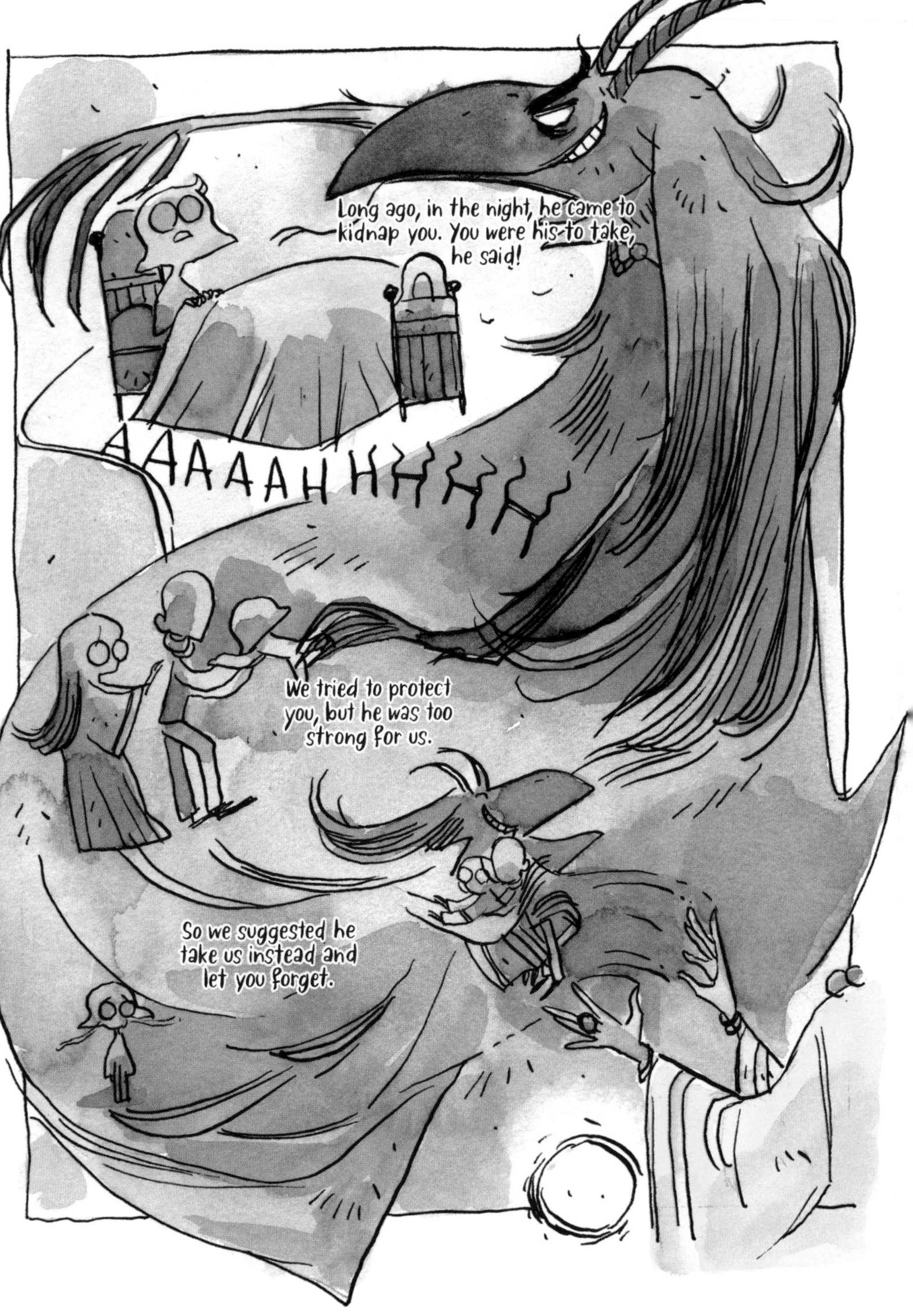
Long ago, in the night, he came to kidnap you. You were his to take, he said!
AAAAAAHHHHHH
We tried to protect you, but he was too strong for us.
So we suggested he take us instead and let you forget.

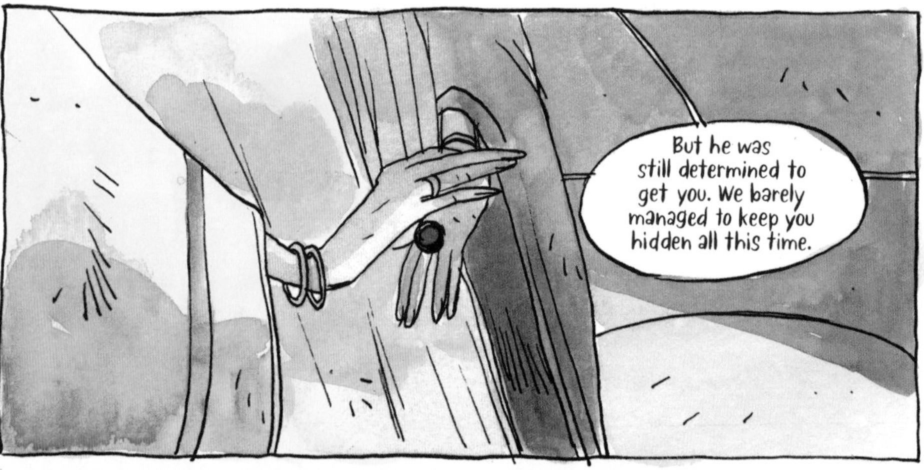
But he was still determined to get you. We barely managed to keep you hidden all this time.

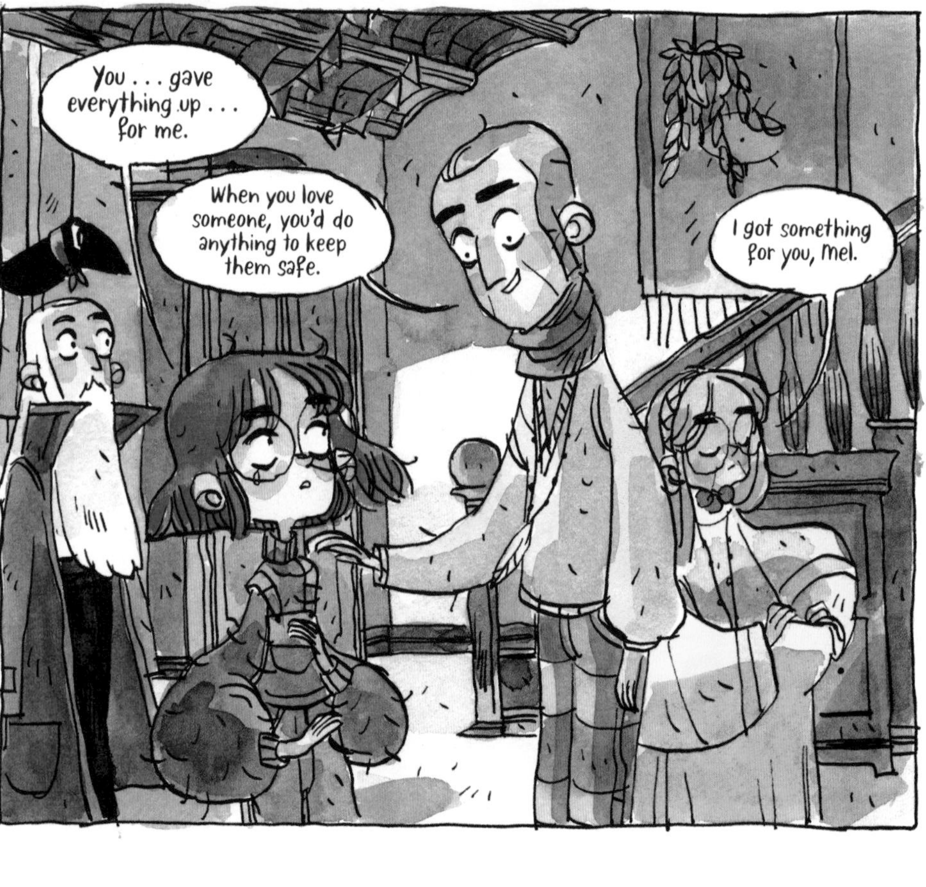
You . . . gave everything up . . . for me.
When you love someone, you'd do anything to keep them safe.
I got something for you, Mel.

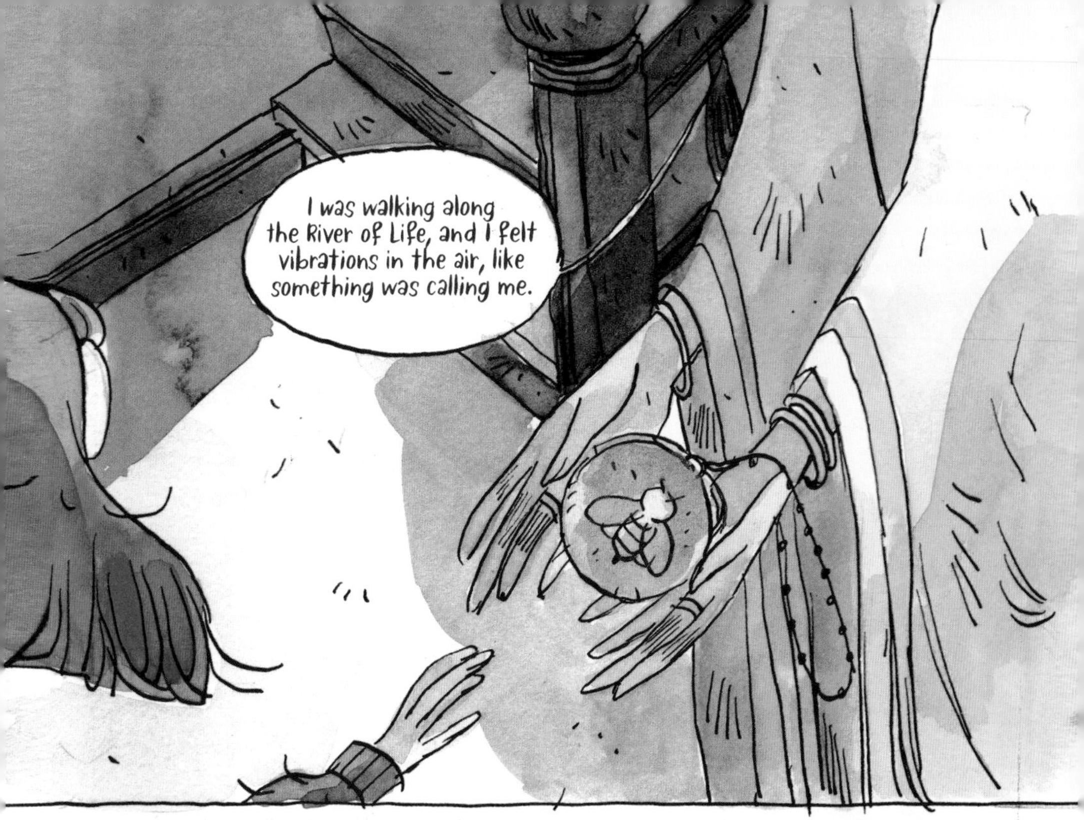
I was walking along the River of Life, and I felt vibrations in the air, like something was calling me.

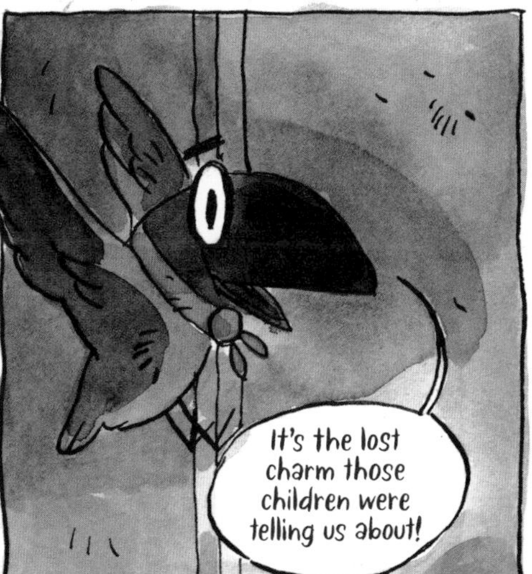
It's the lost charm those children were telling us about!

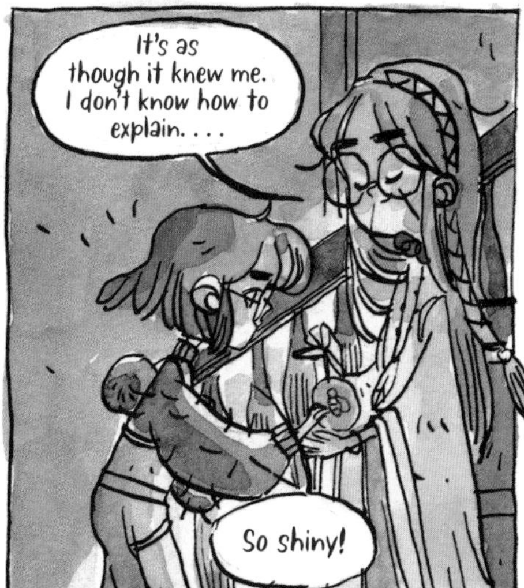
It's as though it knew me. I don't know how to explain. . . .
So shiny!

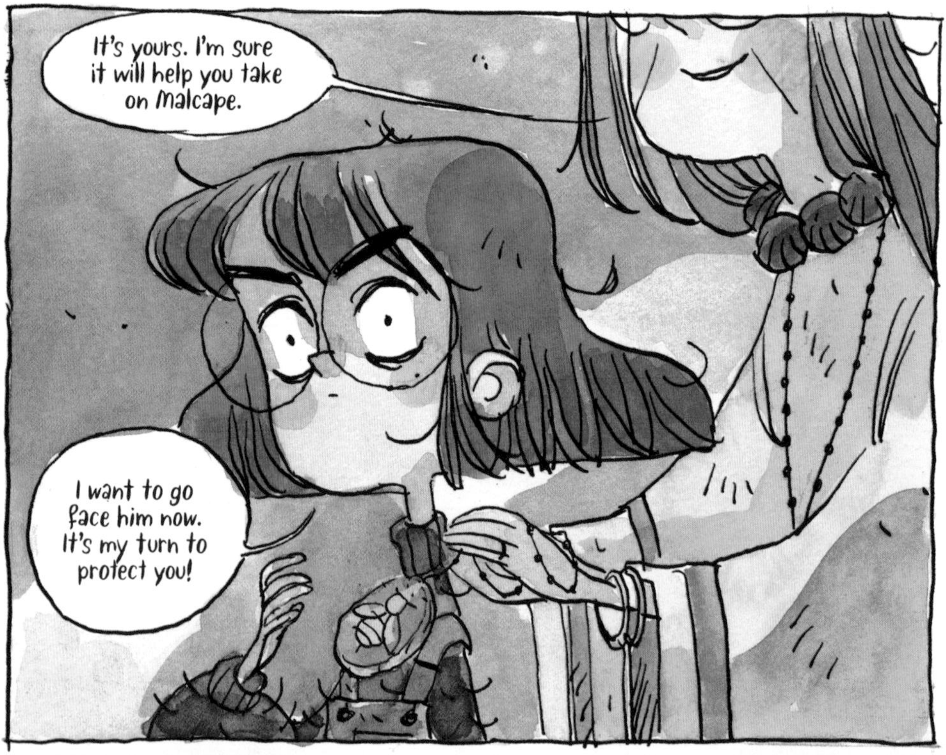
It's yours. I'm sure it will help you take on Malcape.
I want to go face him now. It's my turn to protect you!

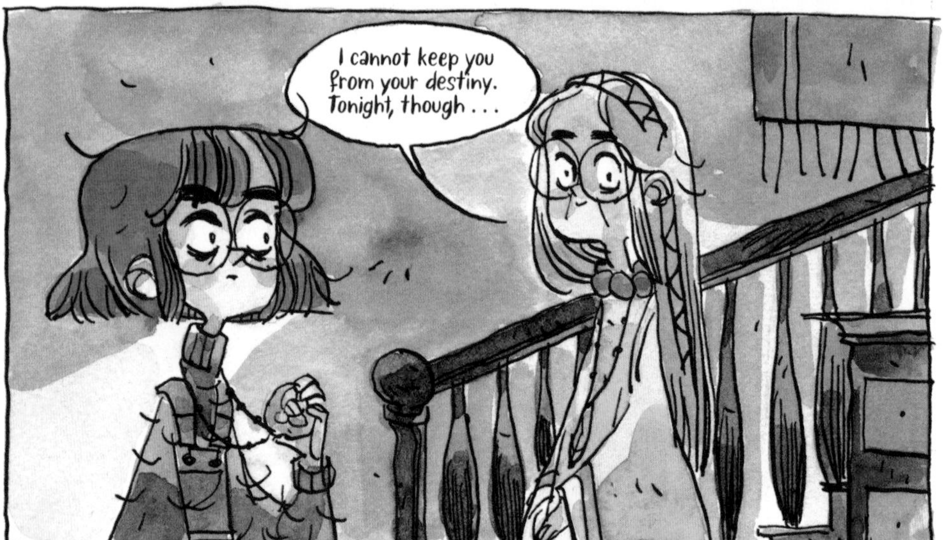
I cannot keep you from your destiny. Tonight, though . . .

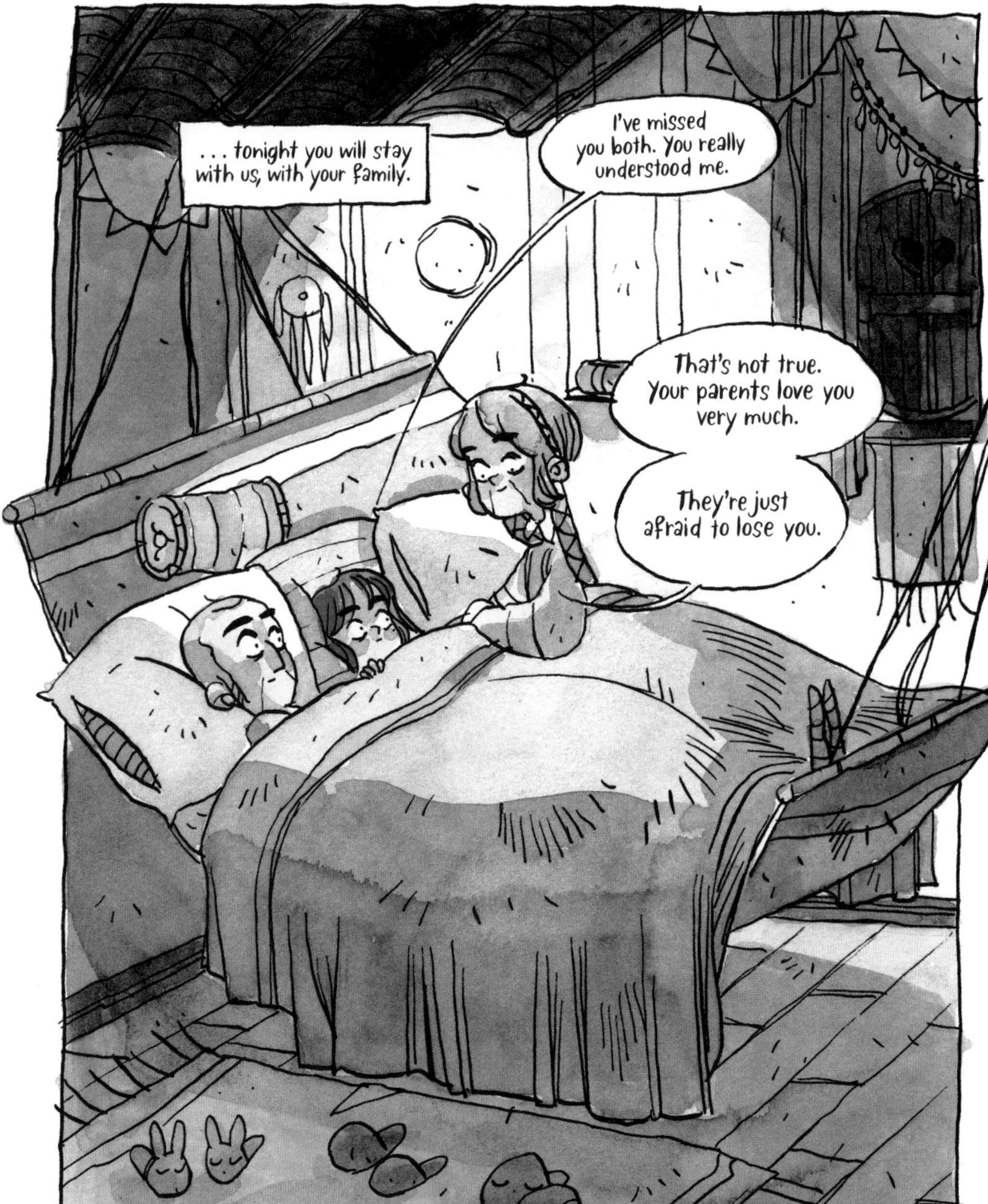
. . . tonight you will stay with us, with your family.
I've missed you both. You really understood me.
That's not true. Your parents love you very much.
They're just afraid to lose you.

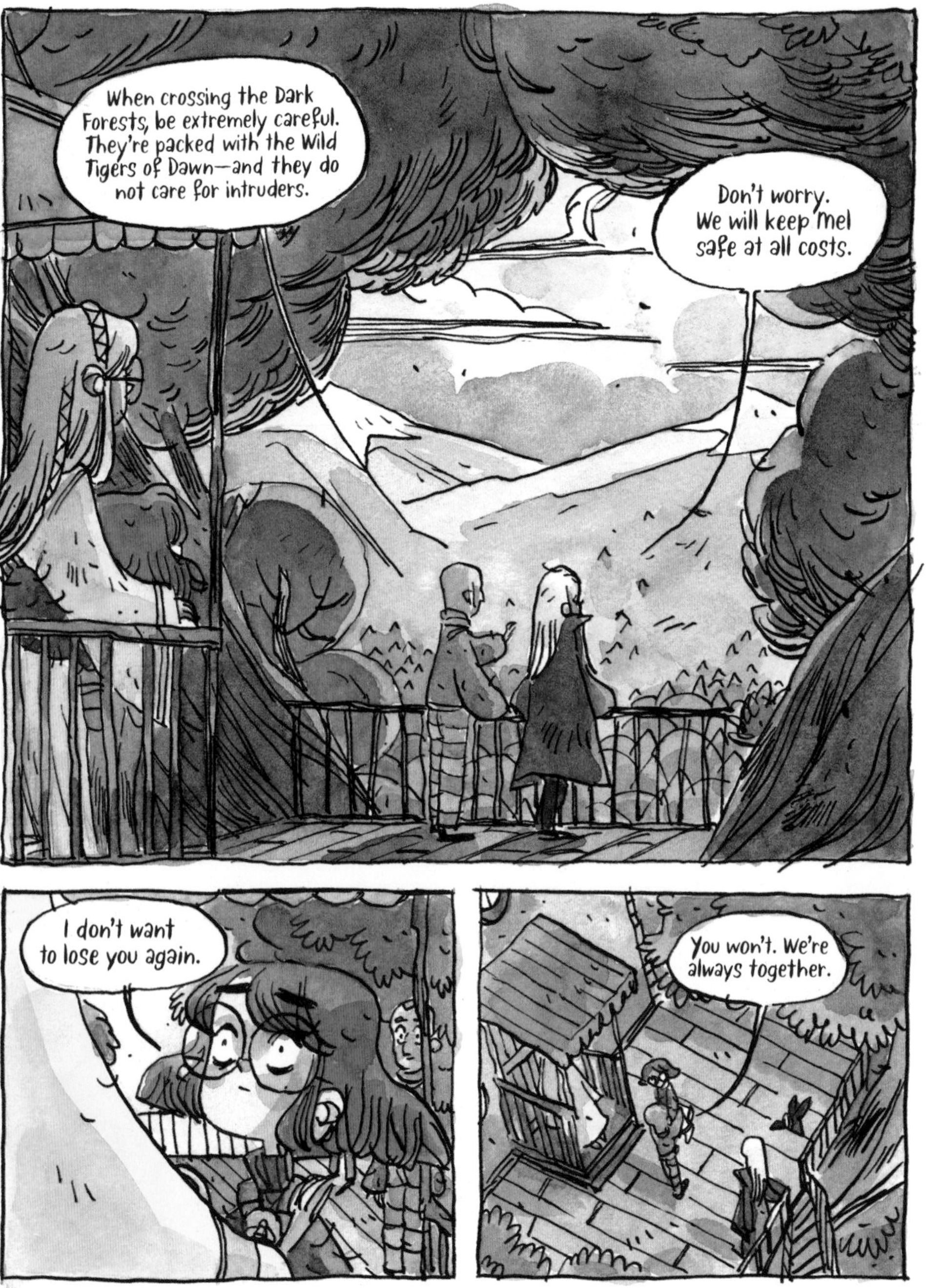
When crossing the Dark Forests, be extremely careful. They're packed with the Wild Tigers of Dawn—and they do not care for intruders.
Don't worry. We will keep Mel safe at all costs.
I don't want to lose you again.
You won't. We're always together.

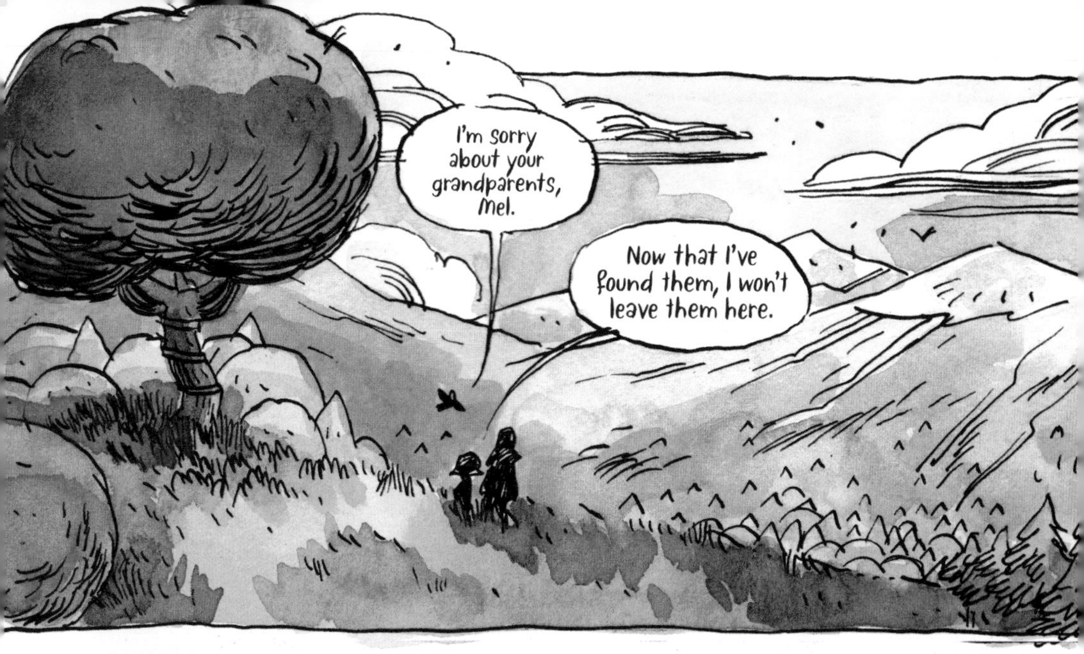
I'm sorry about your grandparents, Mel.
Now that I've found them, I won't leave them here.

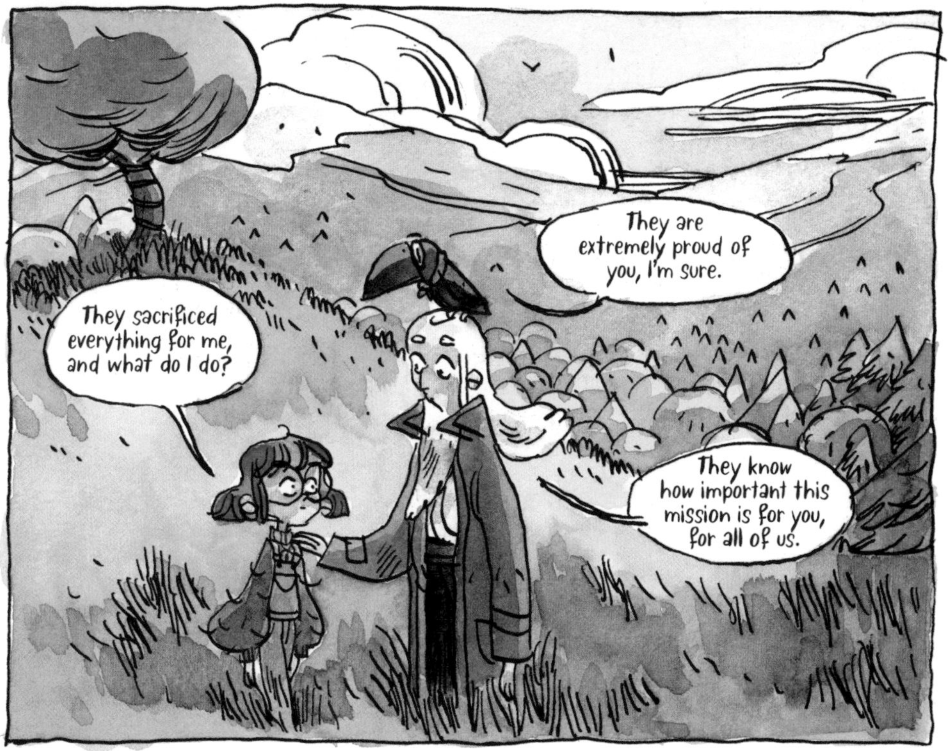
They are extremely proud of you, I'm sure.
They sacrificed everything for me, and what do I do?
They know how important this mission is for you, for all of us.

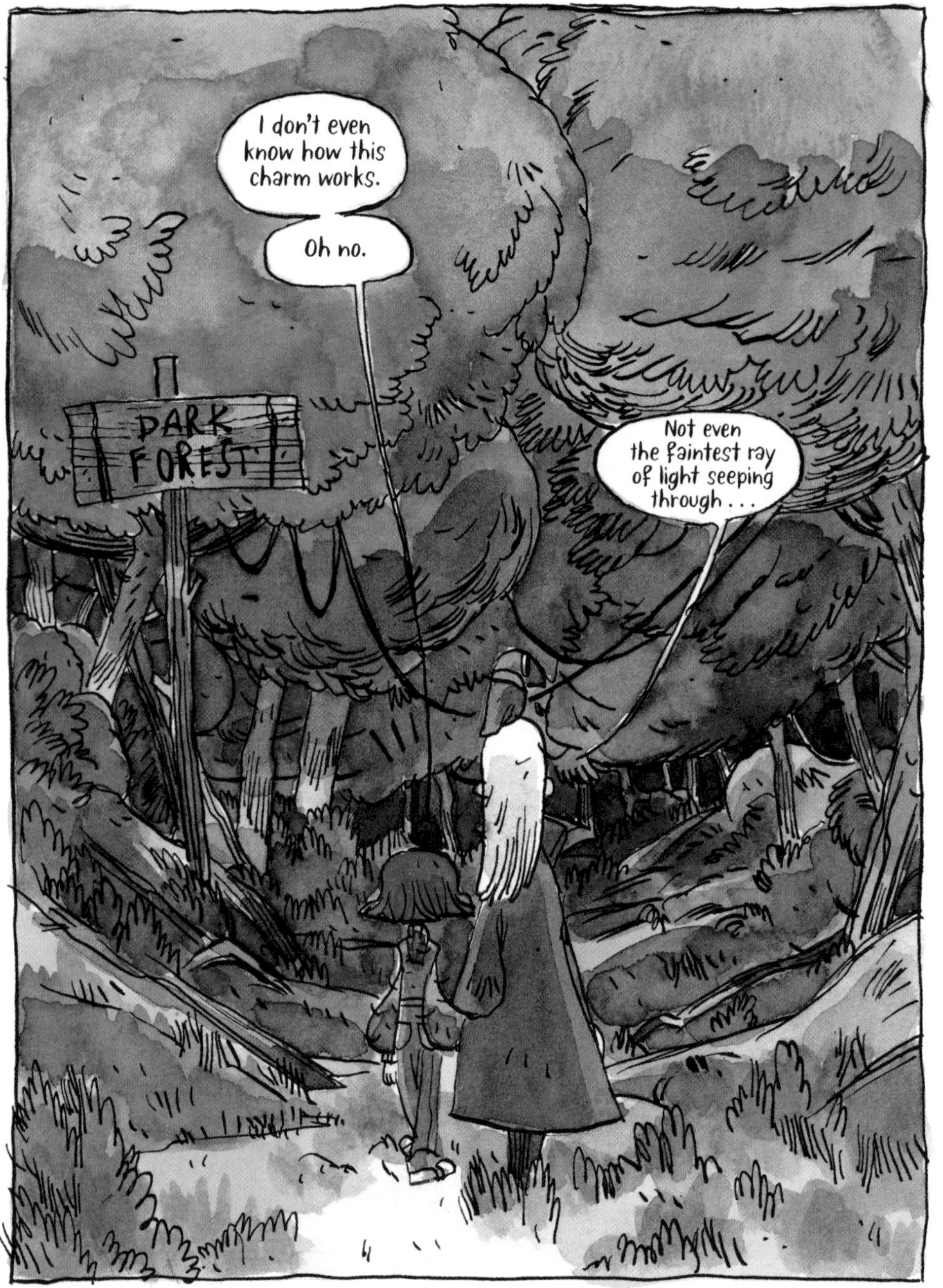
DARK FOREST
I don't even know how this charm works.
Oh no.
Not even the faintest ray of light seeping through . . .

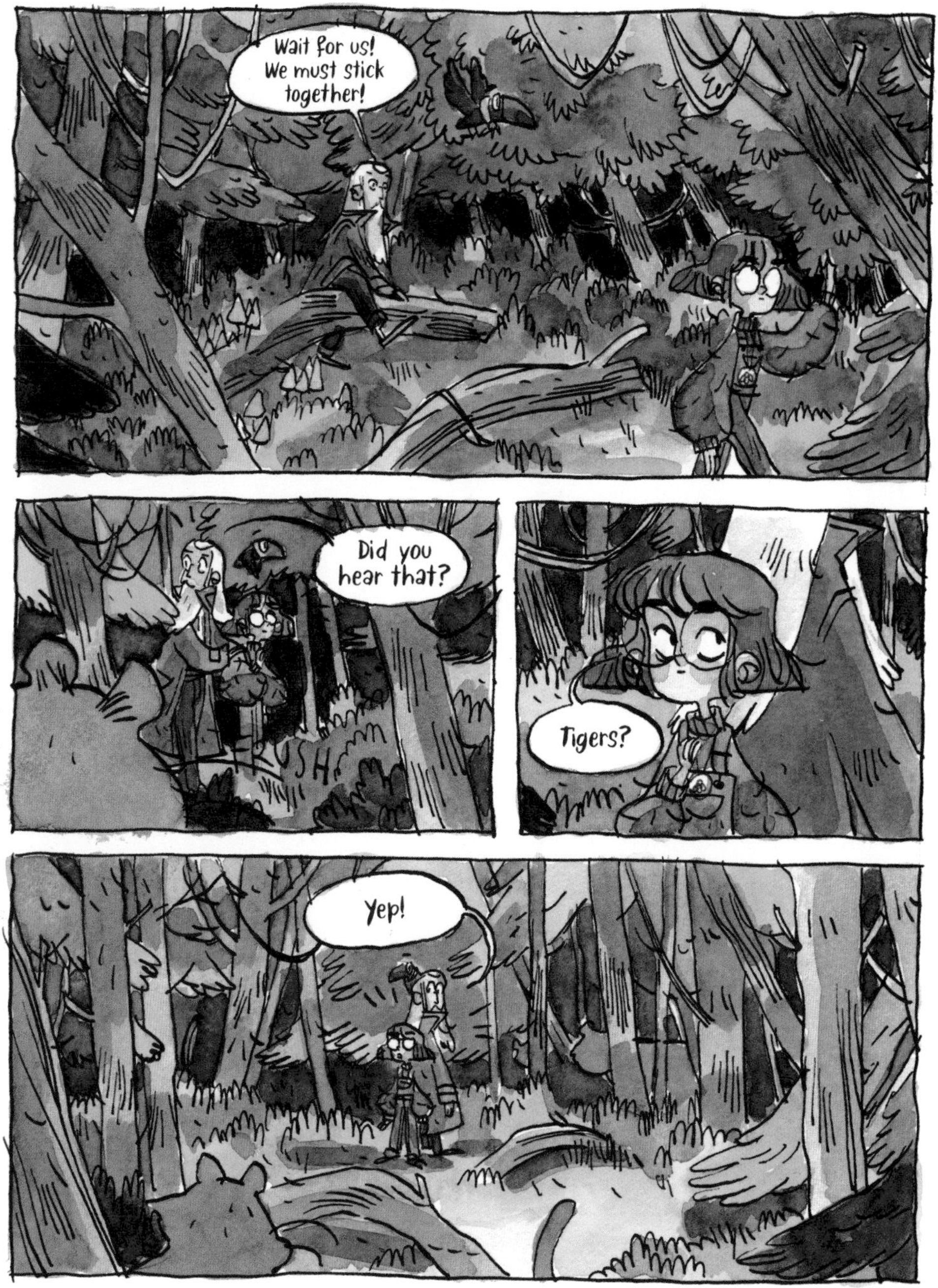
Wait for us! We must stick together!
Did you hear that?
Tigers?
Yep!

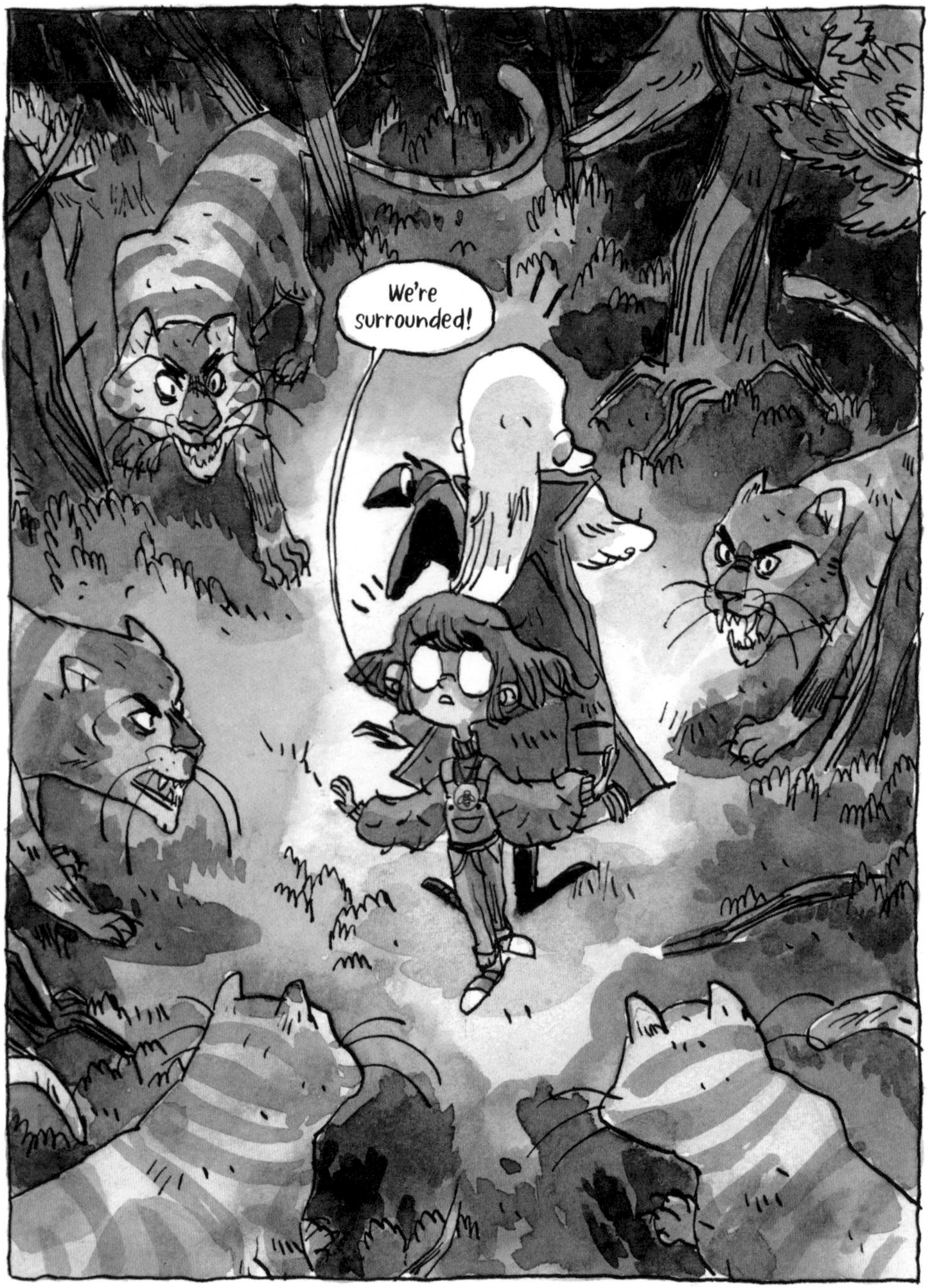
We're surrounded!

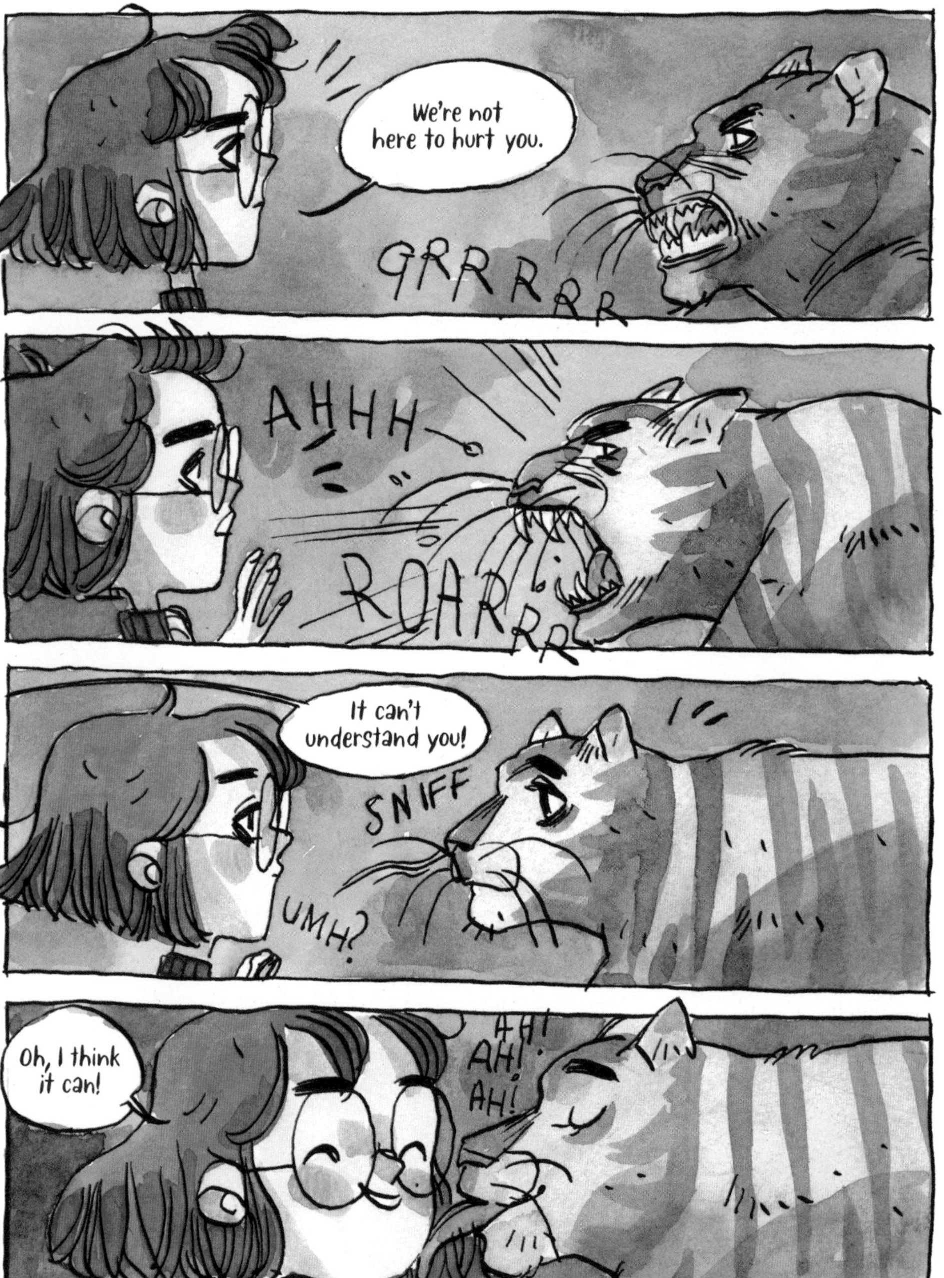

We're not here to hurt you.
GRRRRRR
AHHH
ROARRR
It can't understand you!
SNIFF
UMH?
Oh, I think it can!
AH! AH! AH!

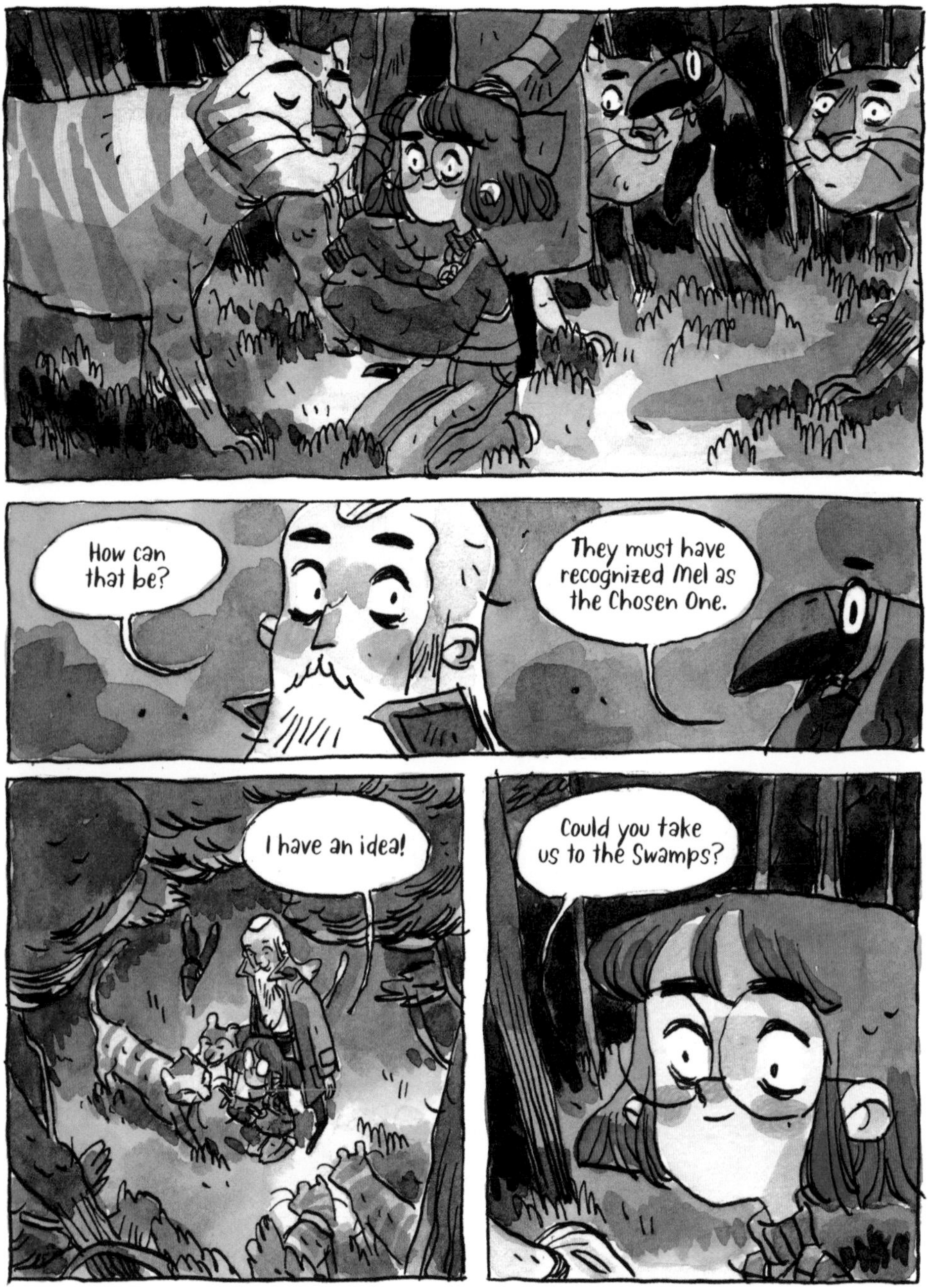
How can that be?
They must have recognized Mel as the Chosen One.
I have an idea!
Could you take us to the Swamps?

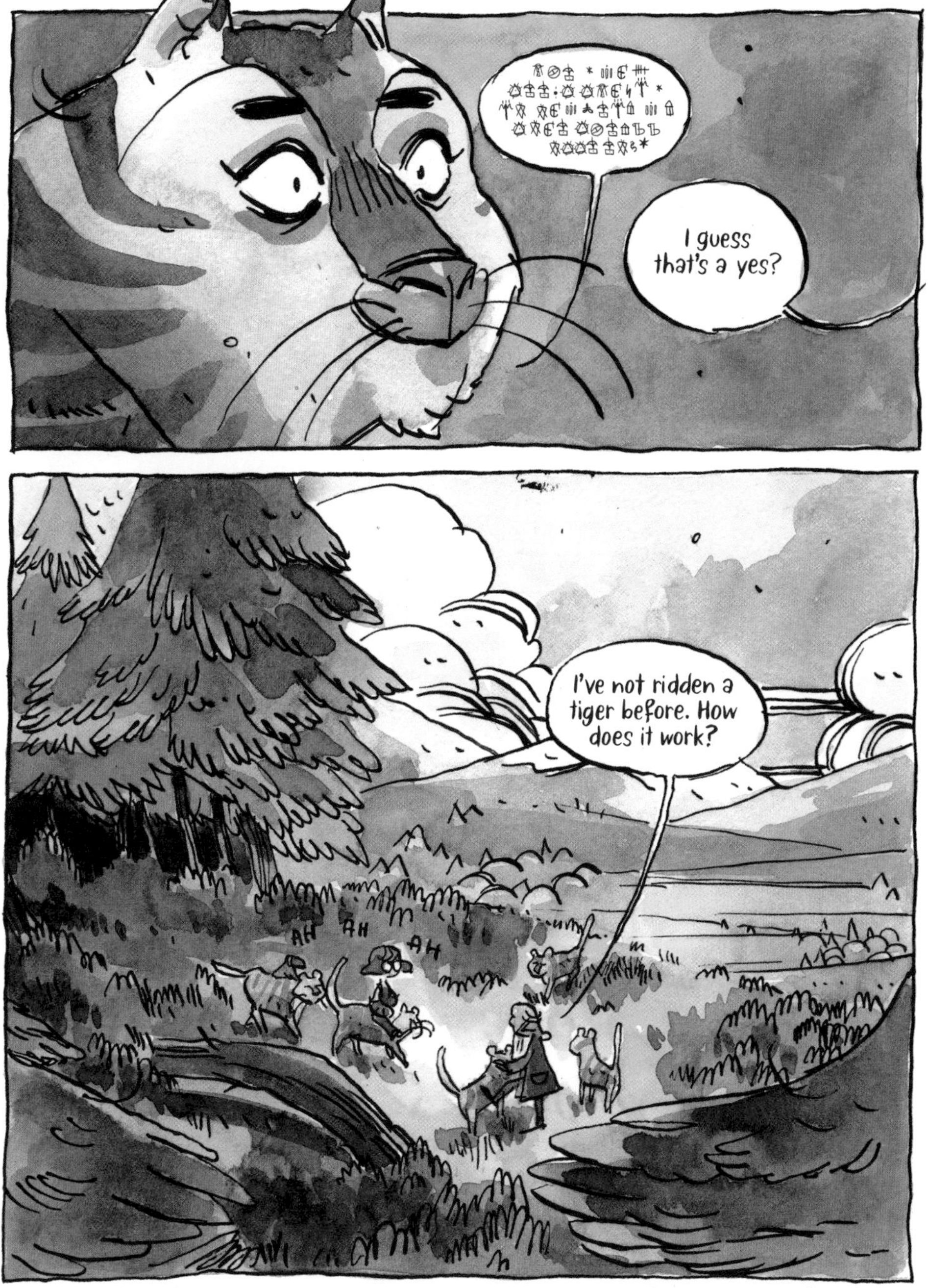
I guess that's a yes?
I've not ridden a tiger before. How does it work?
AH AH AH

*We've been waiting for this moment for so long!

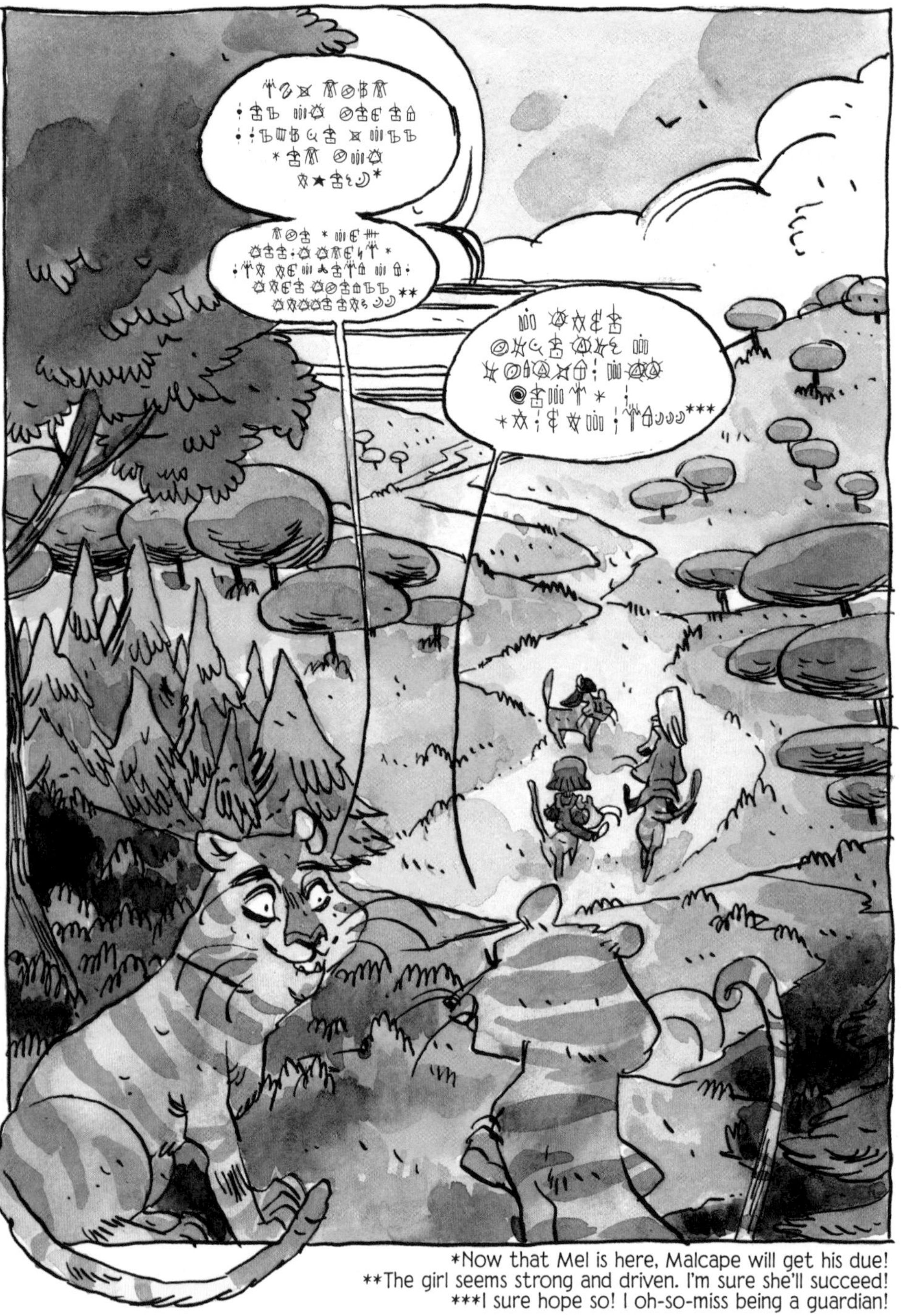

*Now that Mel is here, Malcape will get his due!
**The girl seems strong and driven. I'm sure she'll succeed!
***I sure hope so! I oh-so-miss being a guardian!

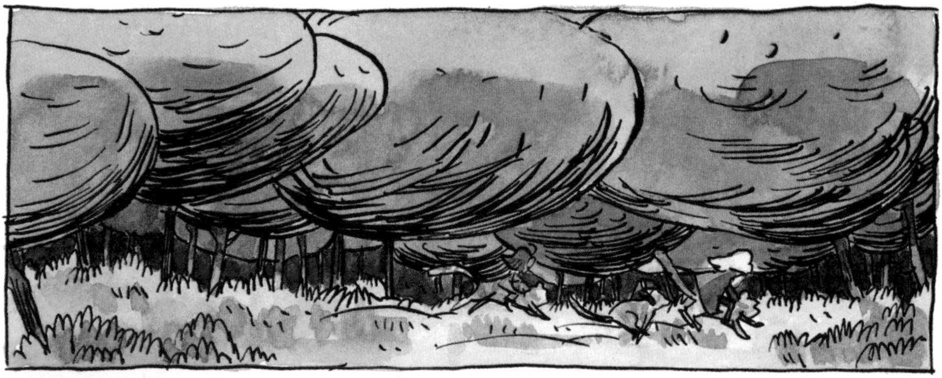

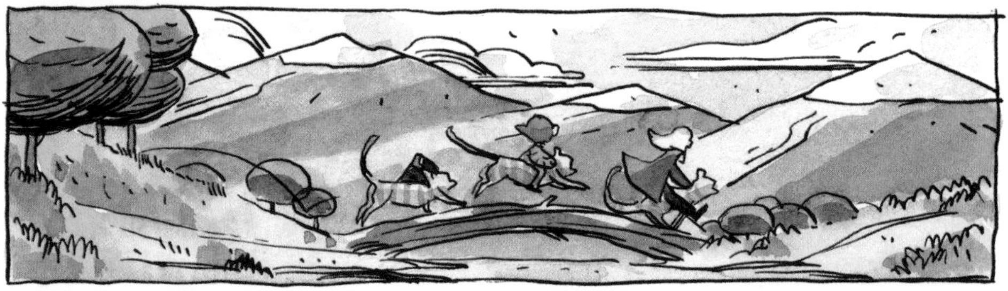

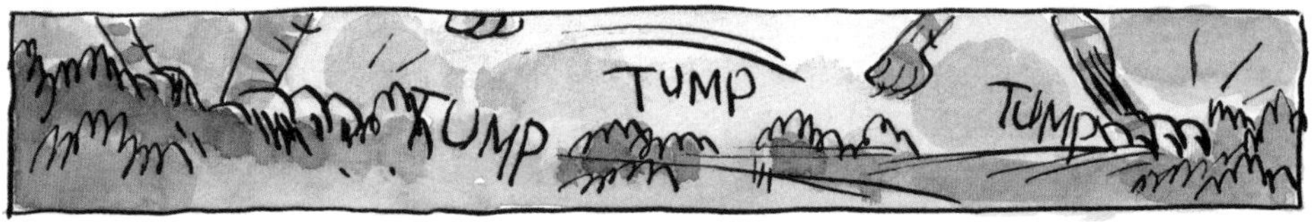
TUMP
TUMP
TUMP

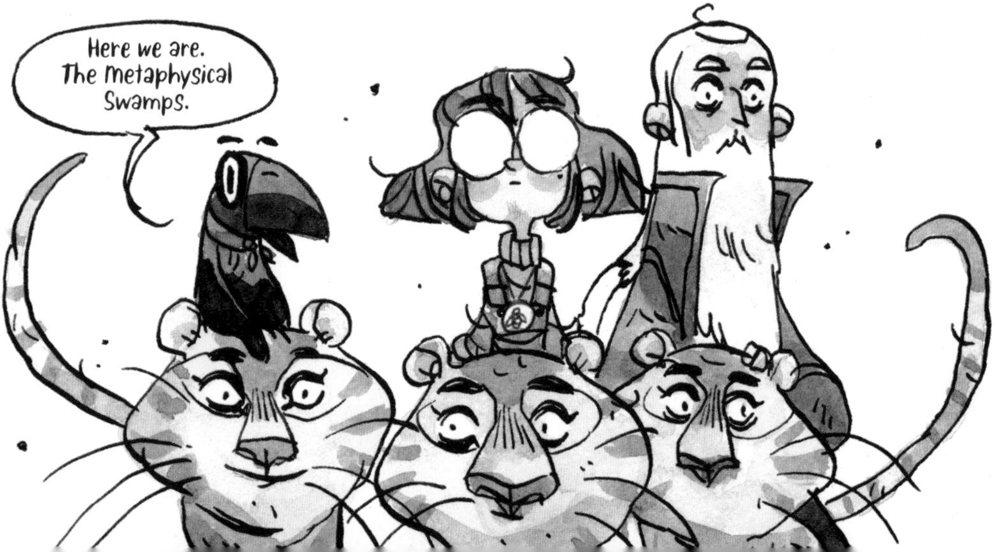
Here we are. The Metaphysical Swamps.

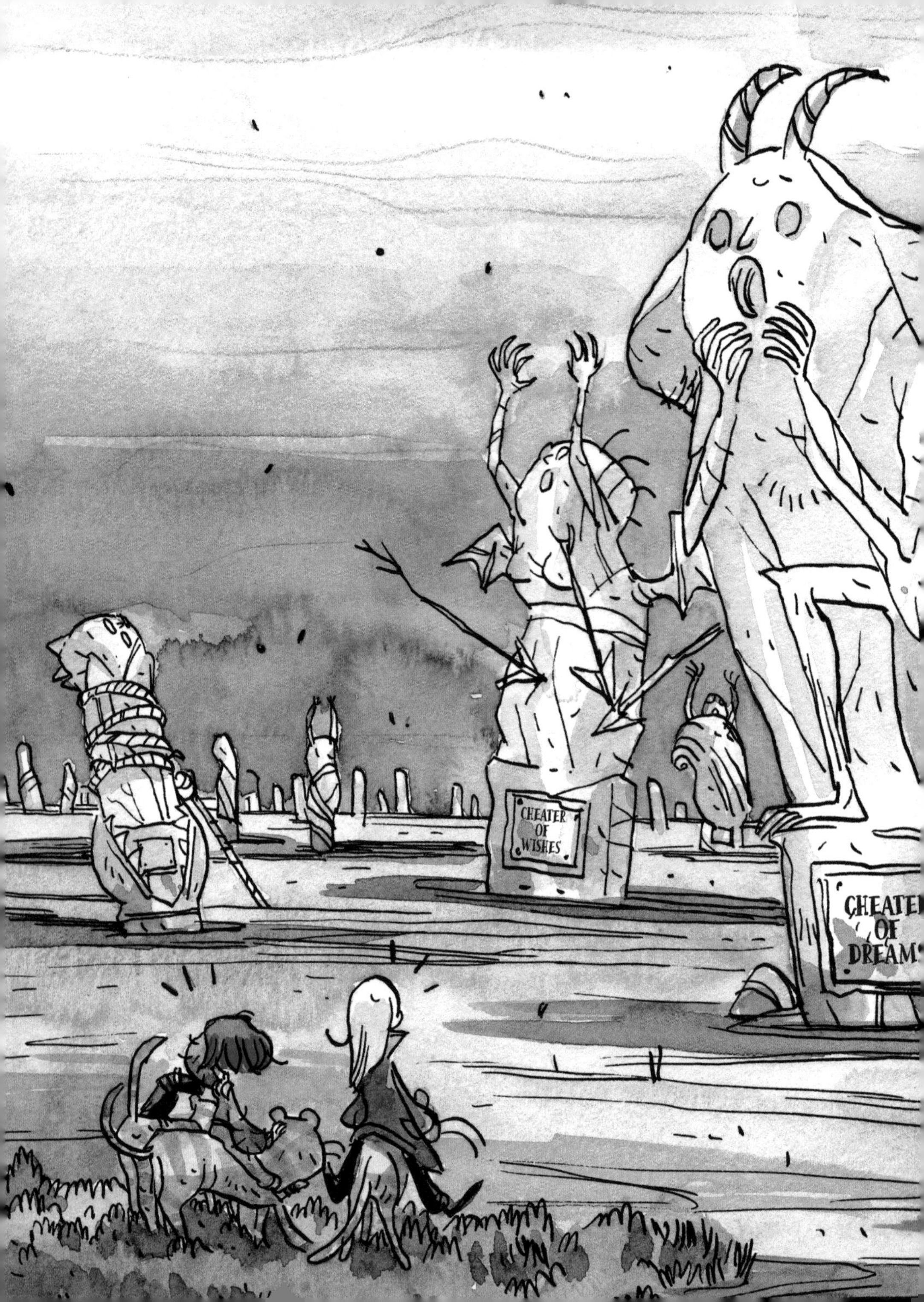
CHEATER OF WISHES
CHEATER OF DREAMS

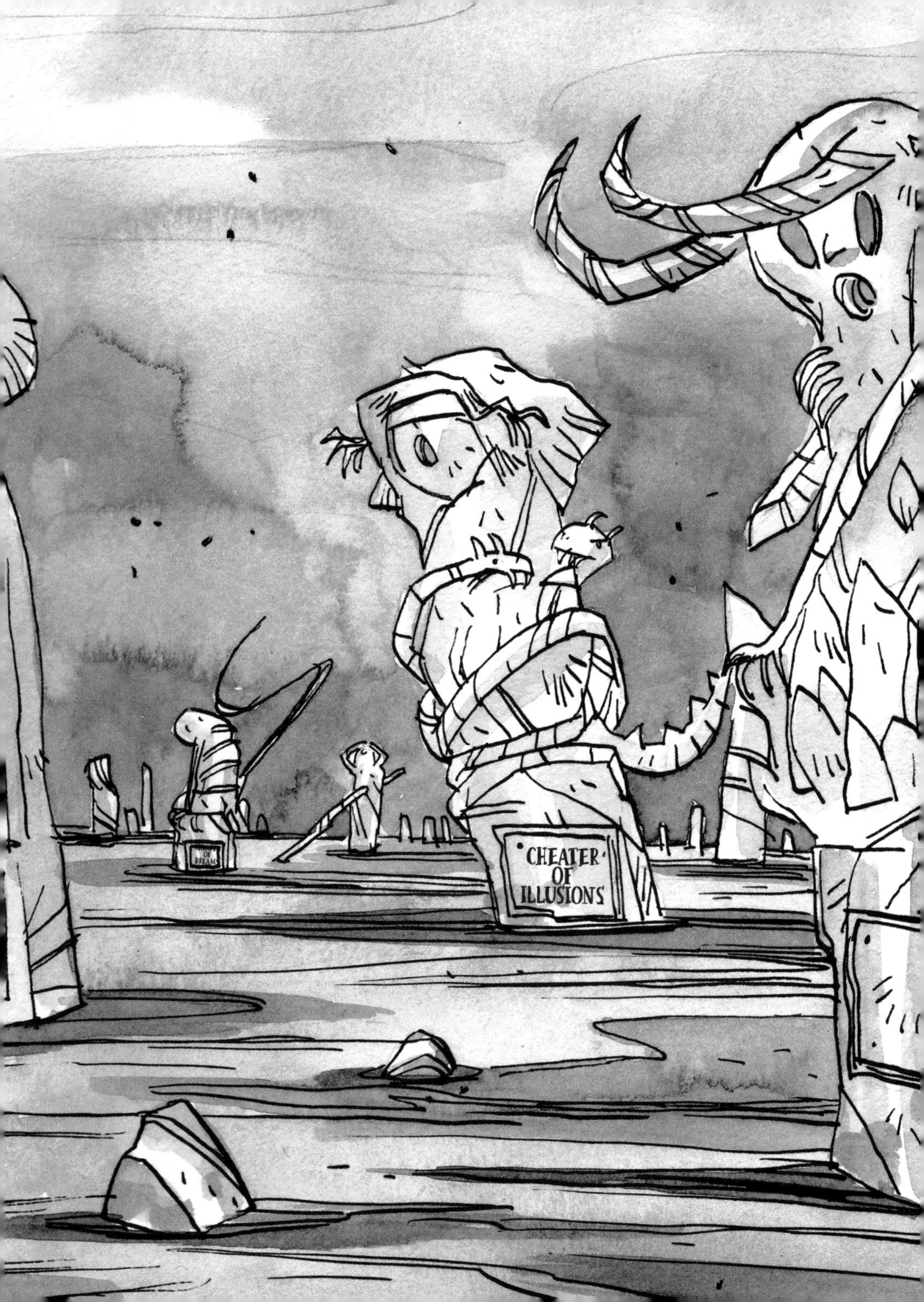
CHEATER OF ILLUSIONS

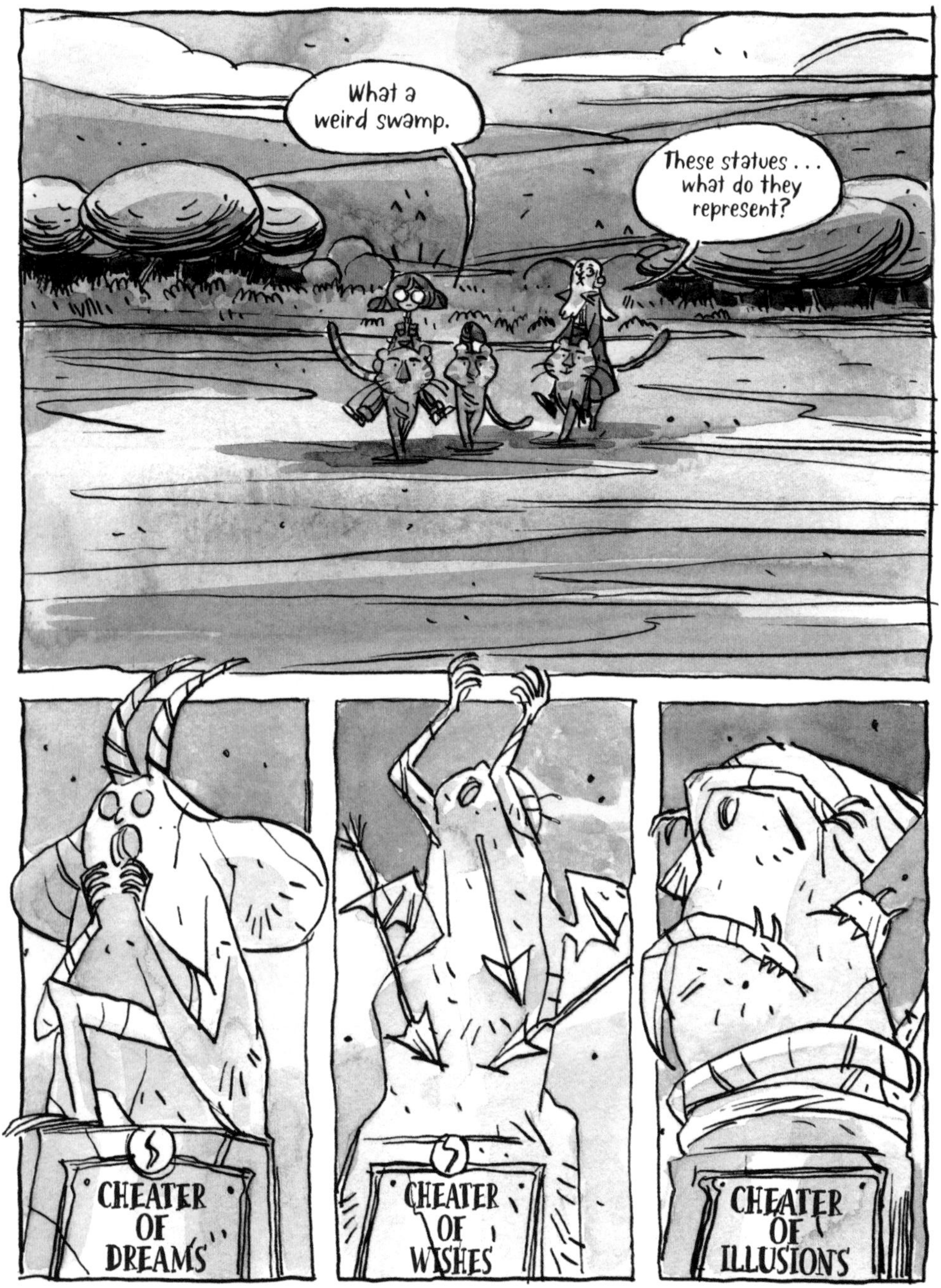
What a weird swamp.
These statues . . . what do they represent?
CHEATER OF DREAMS
CHEATER OF WISHES
CHEATER OF ILLUSIONS

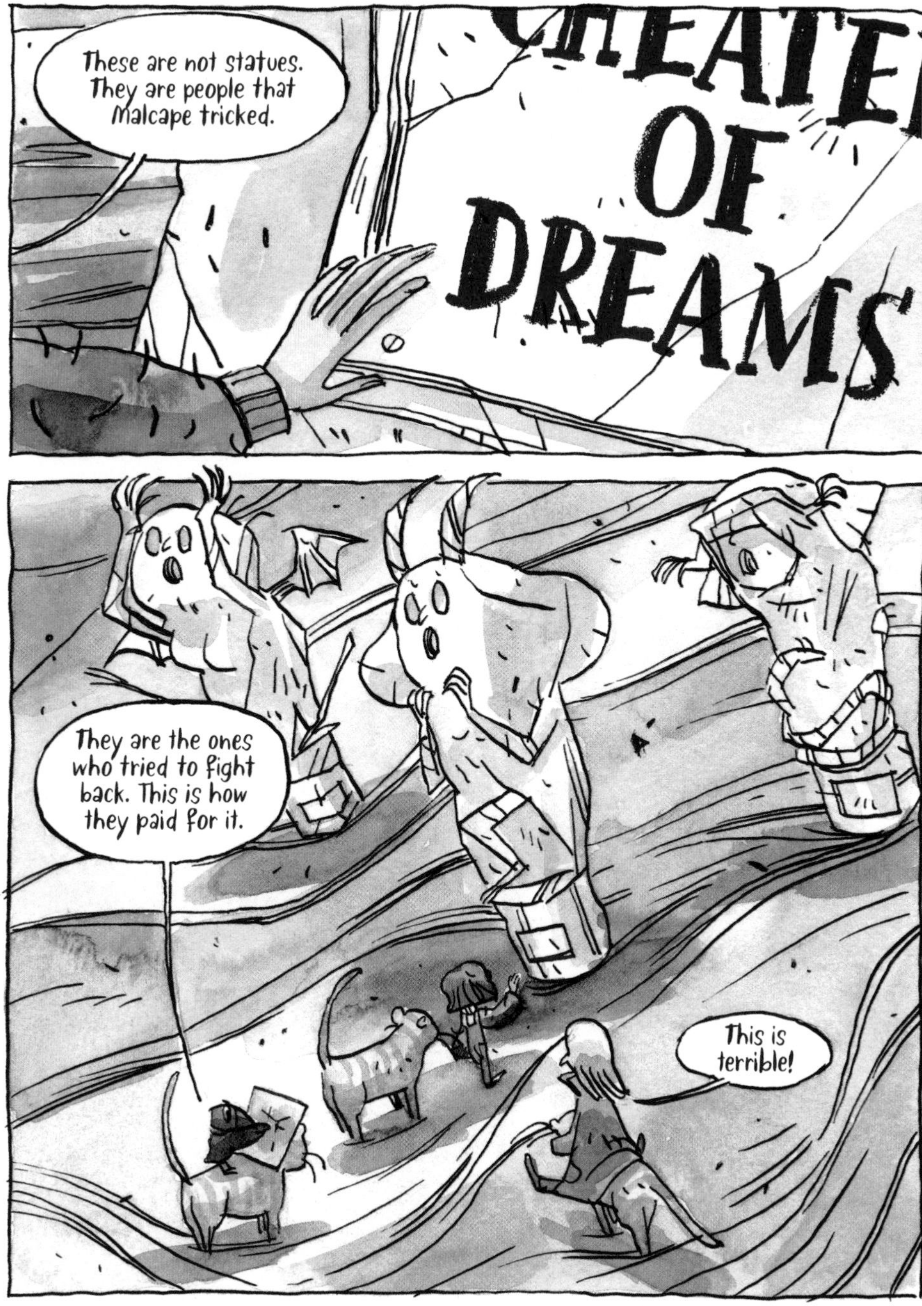
These are not statues. They are people that Malcape tricked.
OF
DREAMS
They are the ones who tried to fight back. This is how they paid for it.
This is terrible!

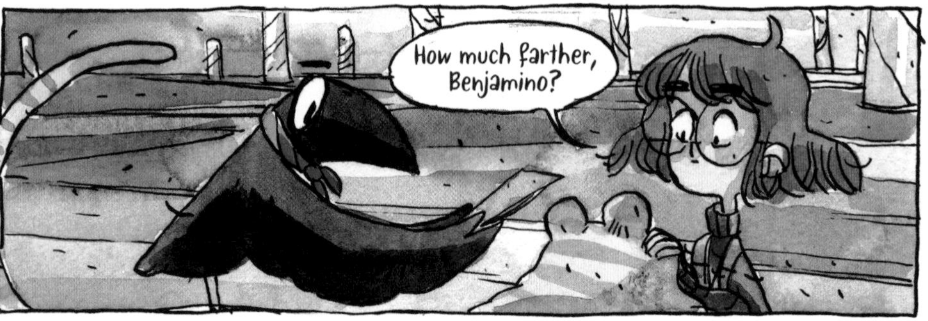
How much farther, Benjamino?

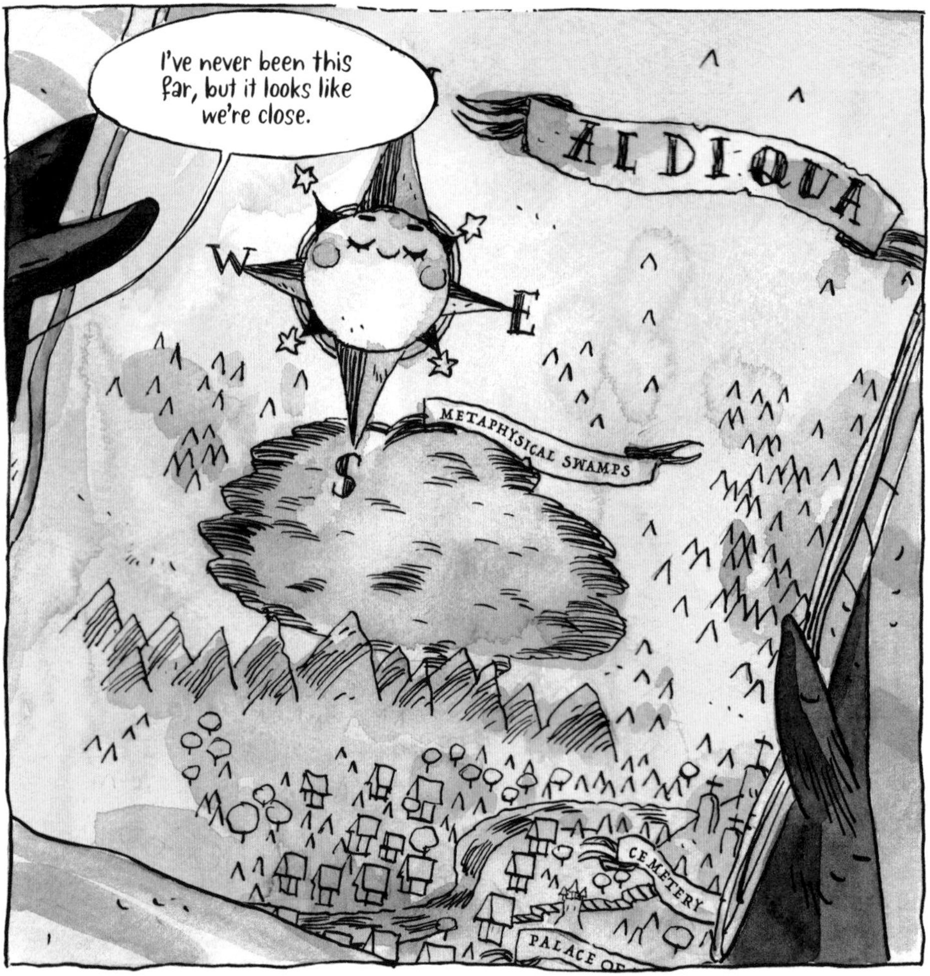
I've never been this far, but it looks like we're close.
ALDIQUA
W
E
S
METAPHYSICAL SWAMPS
CEMETERY
PALACE OF

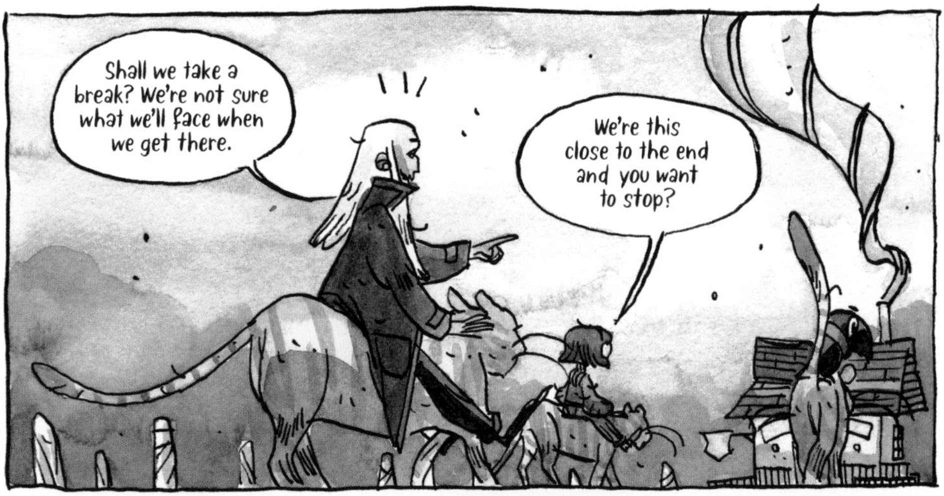
Shall we take a break? We're not sure what we'll face when we get there.
We're this close to the end and you want to stop?

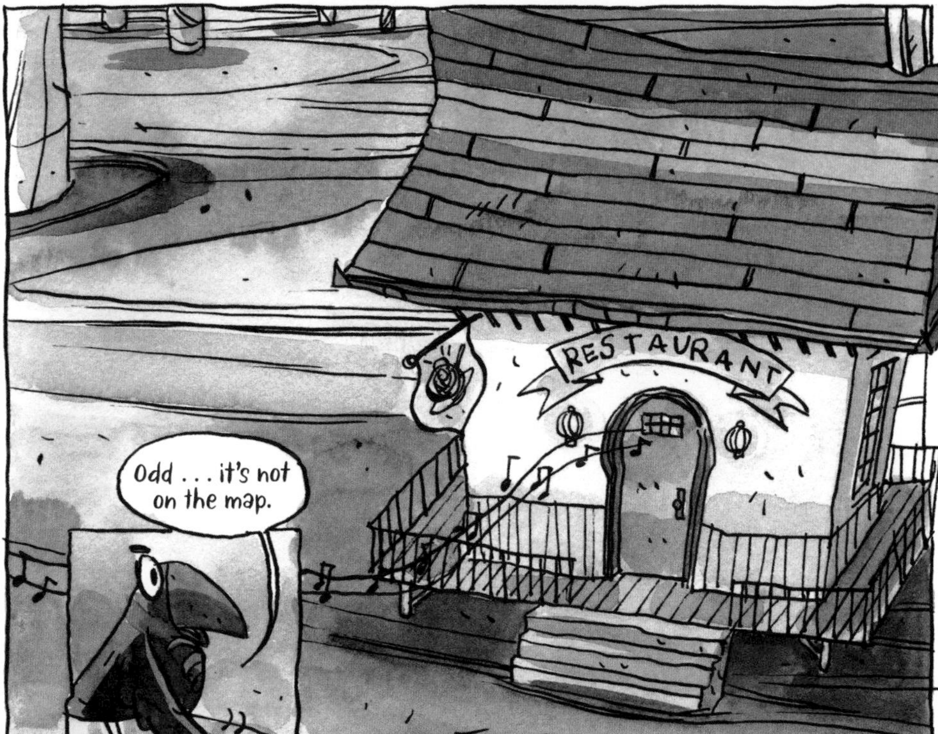
RESTAURANT
Odd . . . it's not on the map.

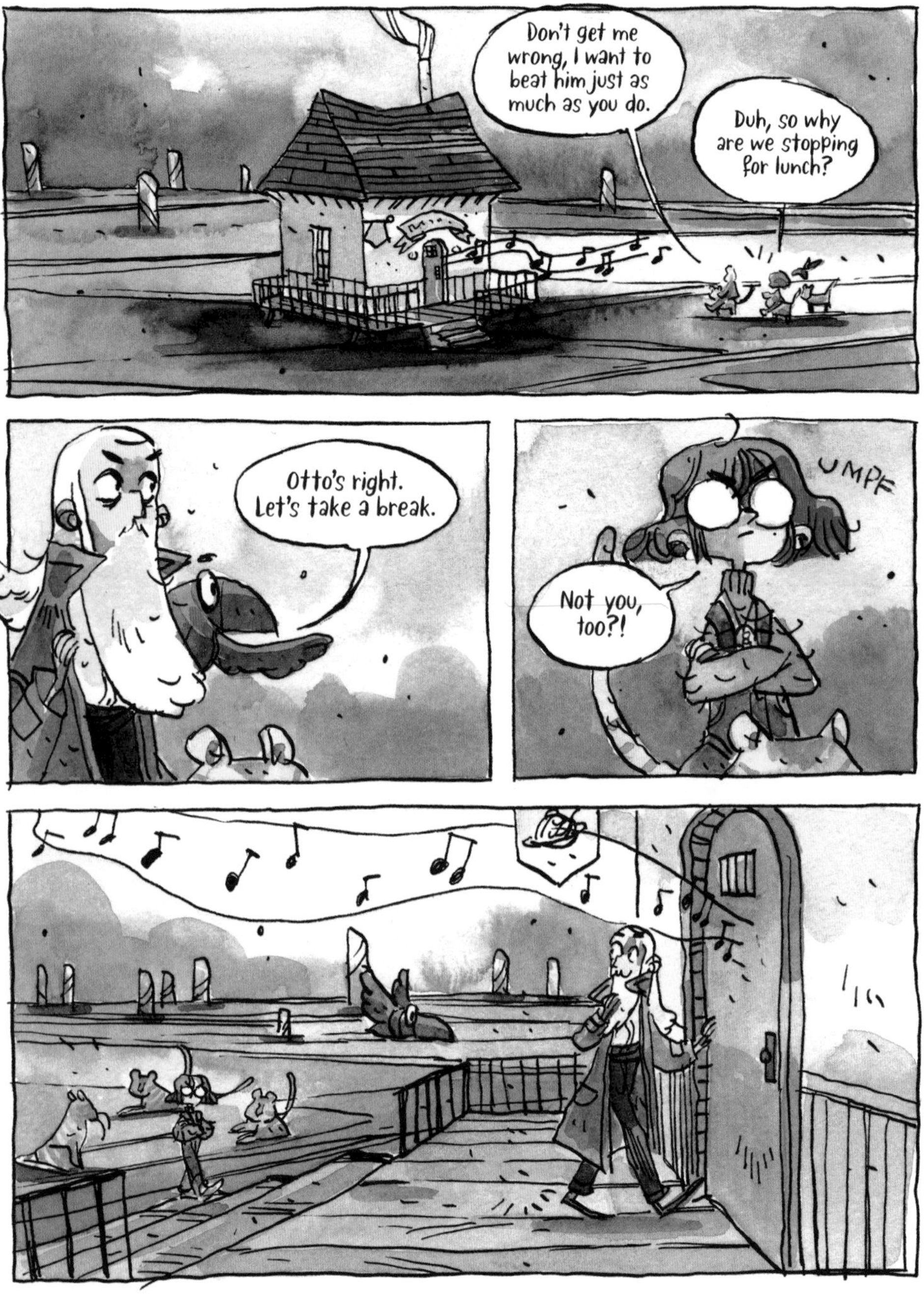

Don't get me wrong, I want to beat him just as much as you do.
Duh, so why are we stopping for lunch?
Otto's right. Let's take a break.
UMPF
Not you, too?!

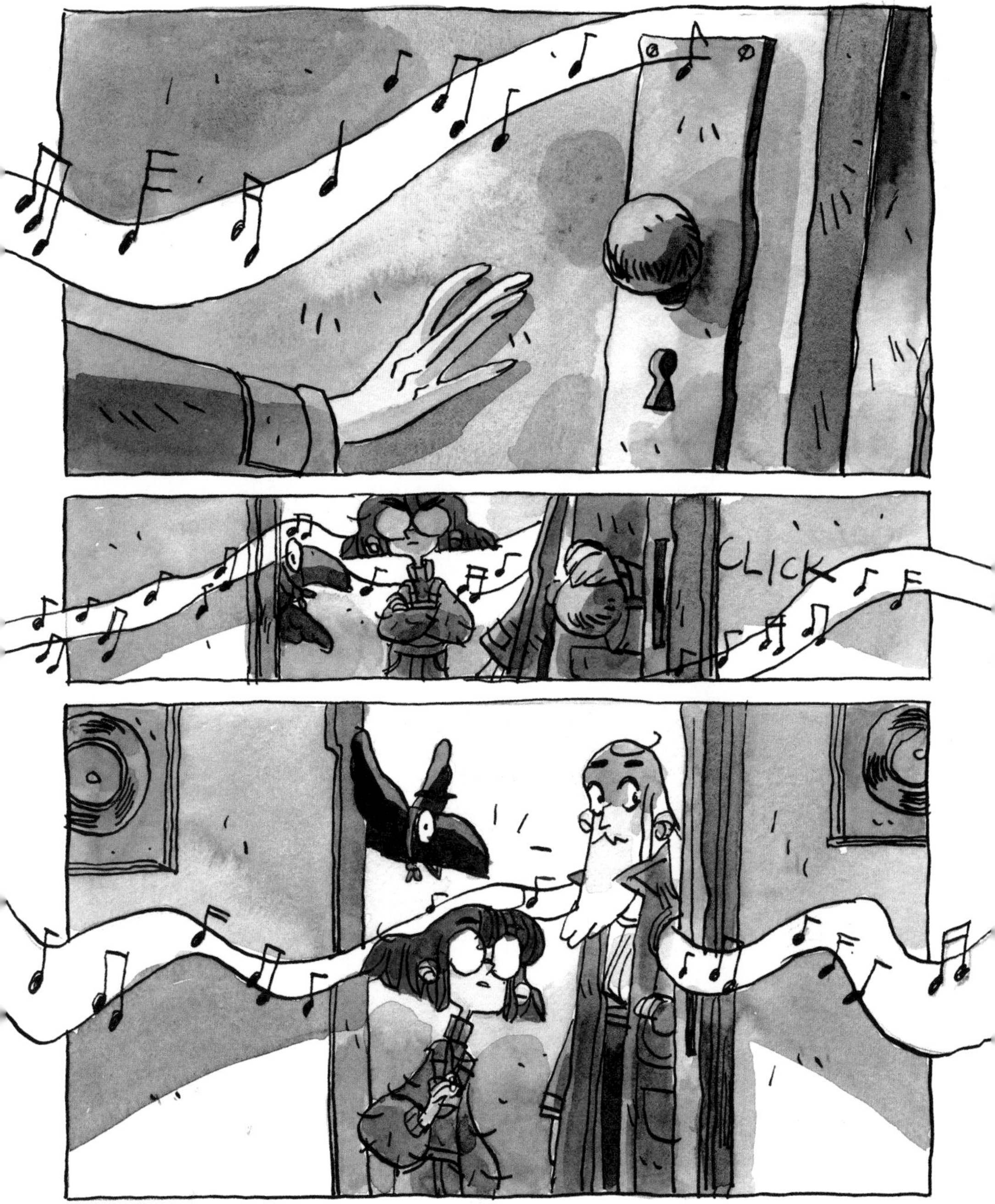
CLICK

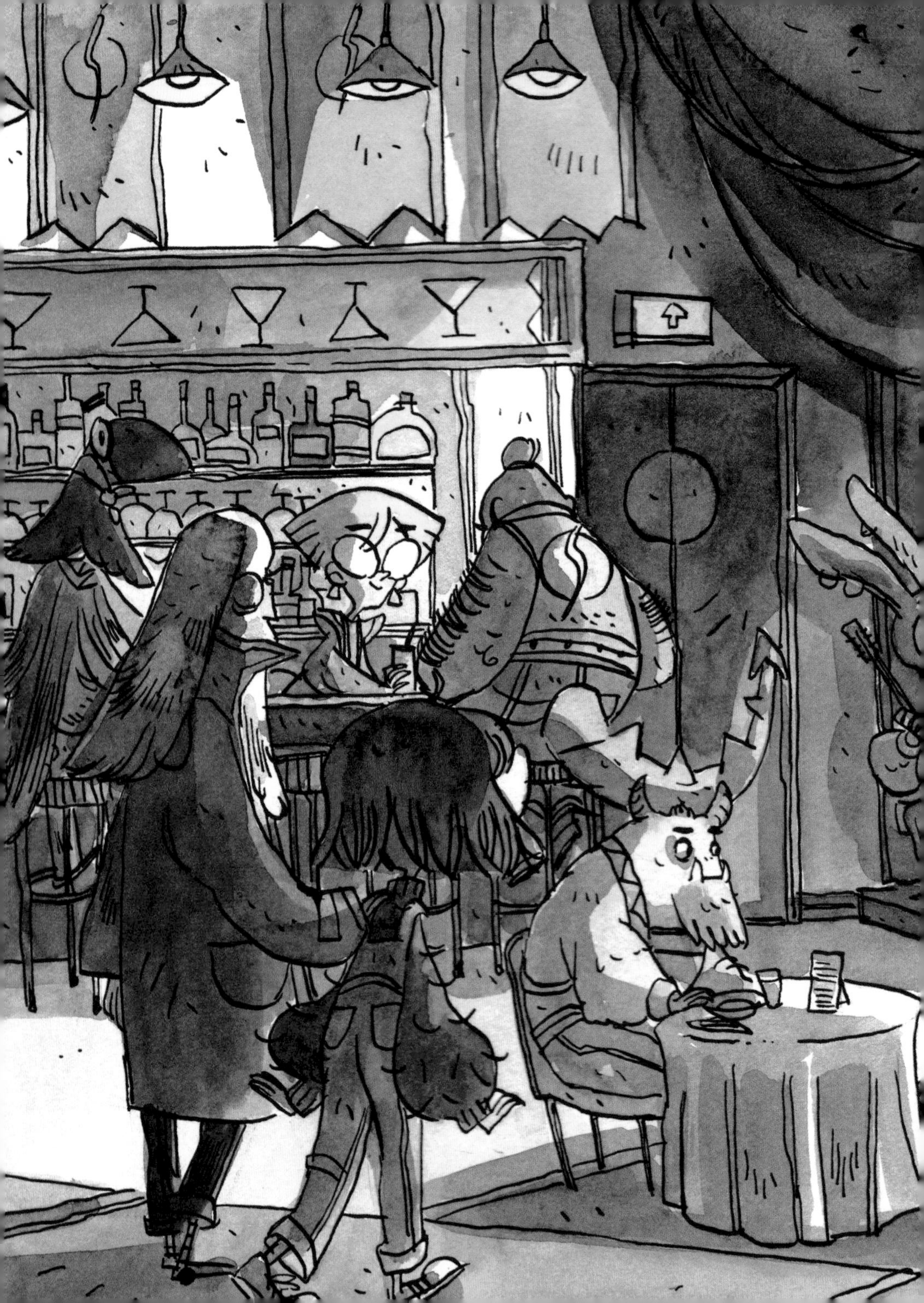

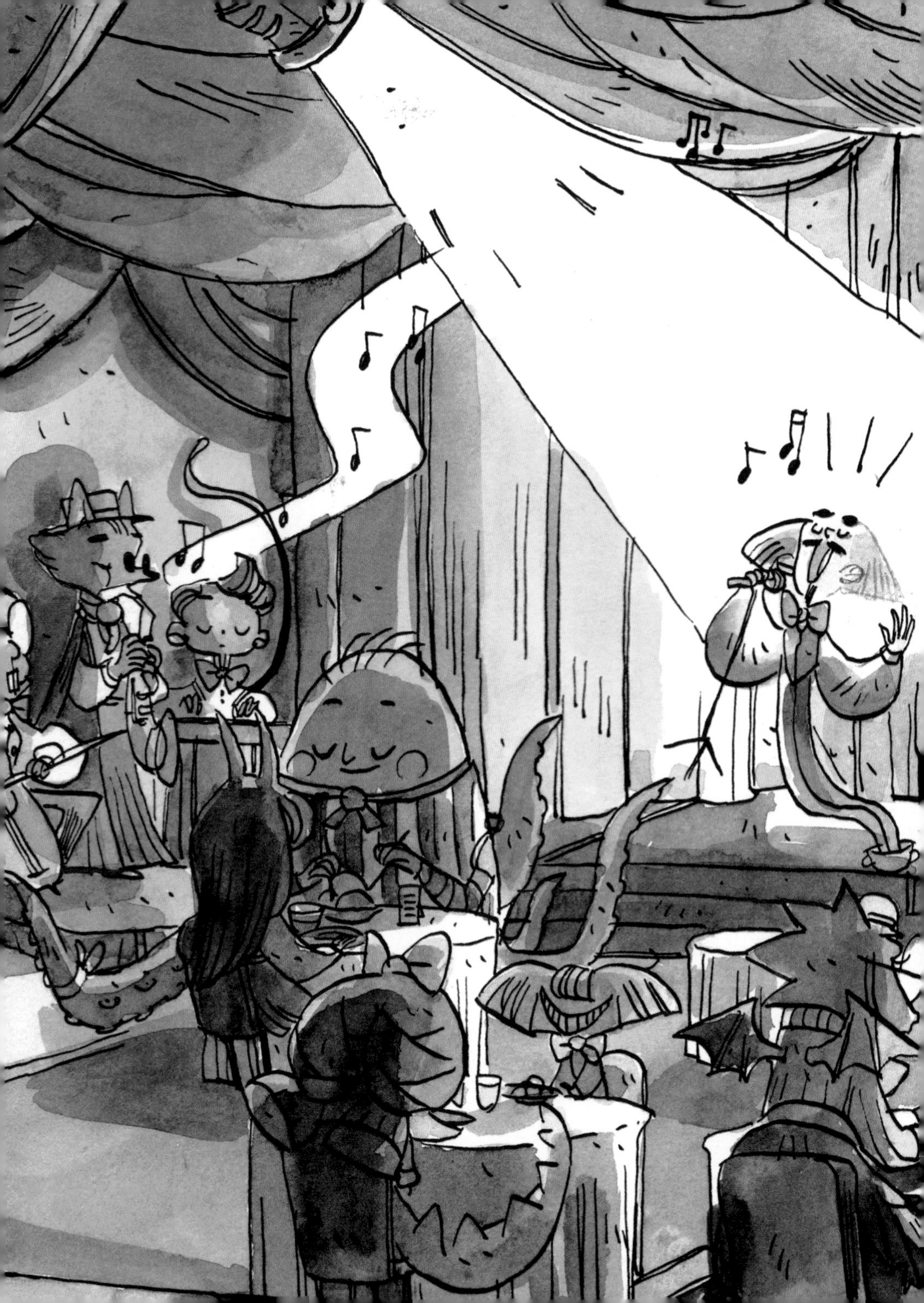

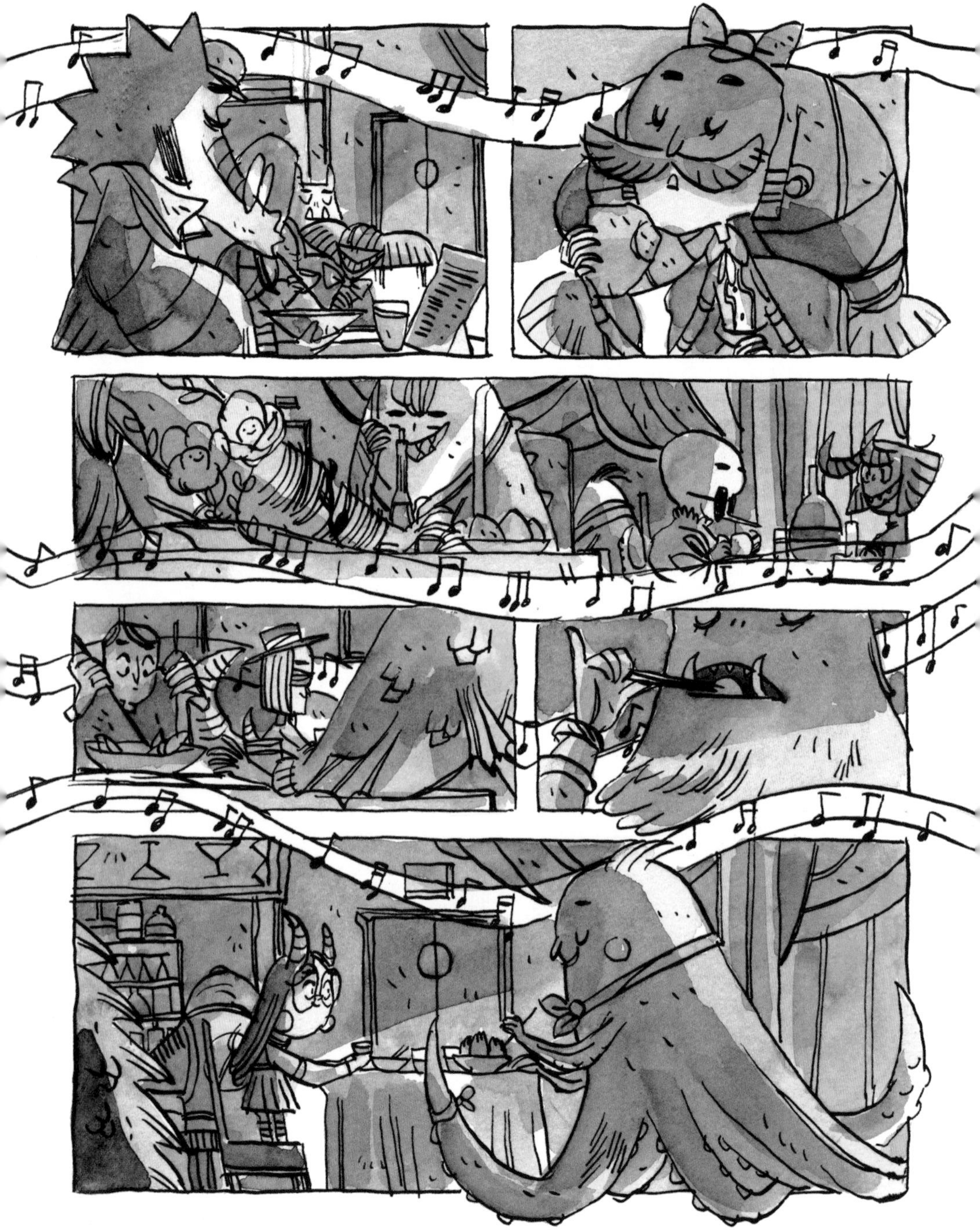

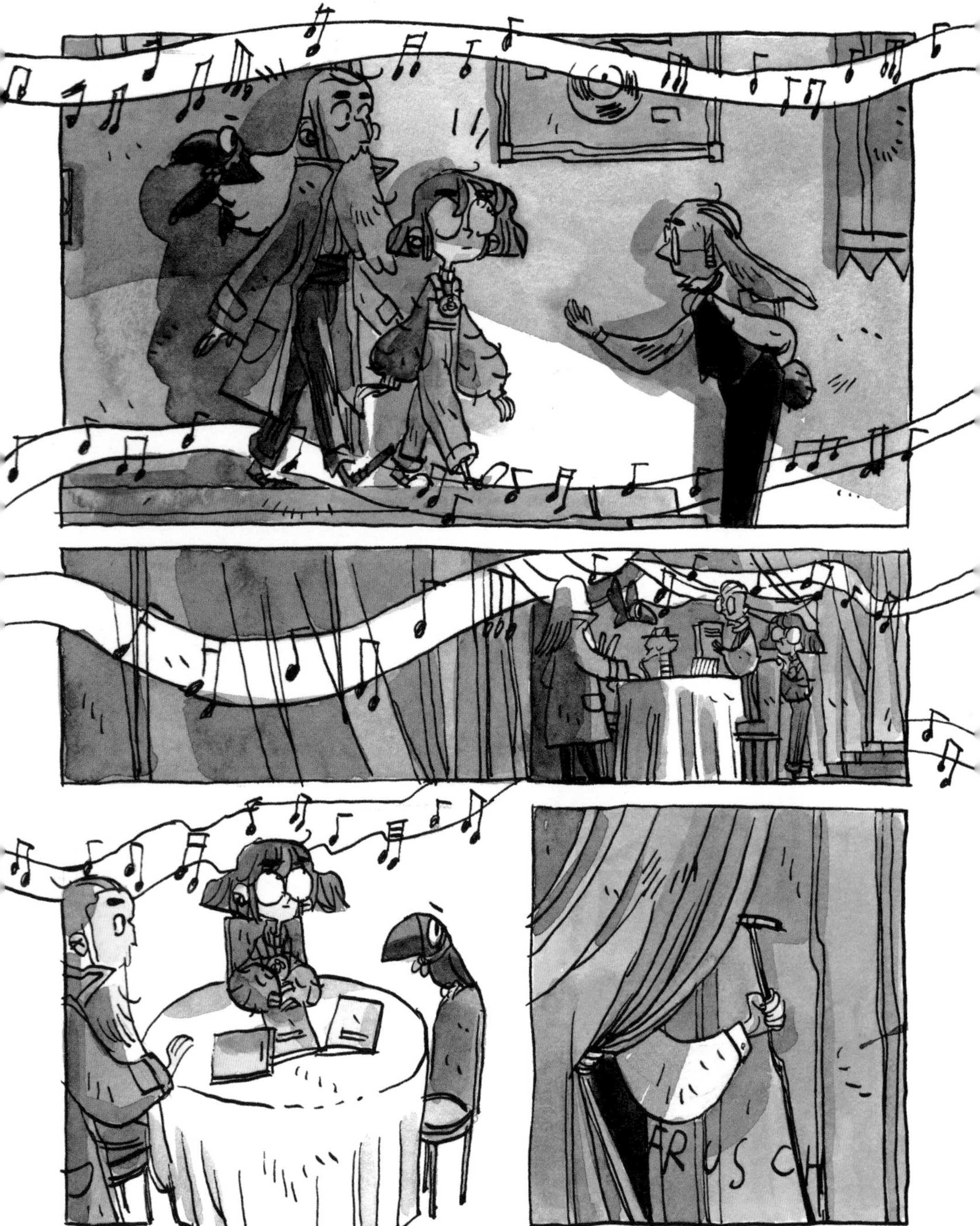

FRUSCH

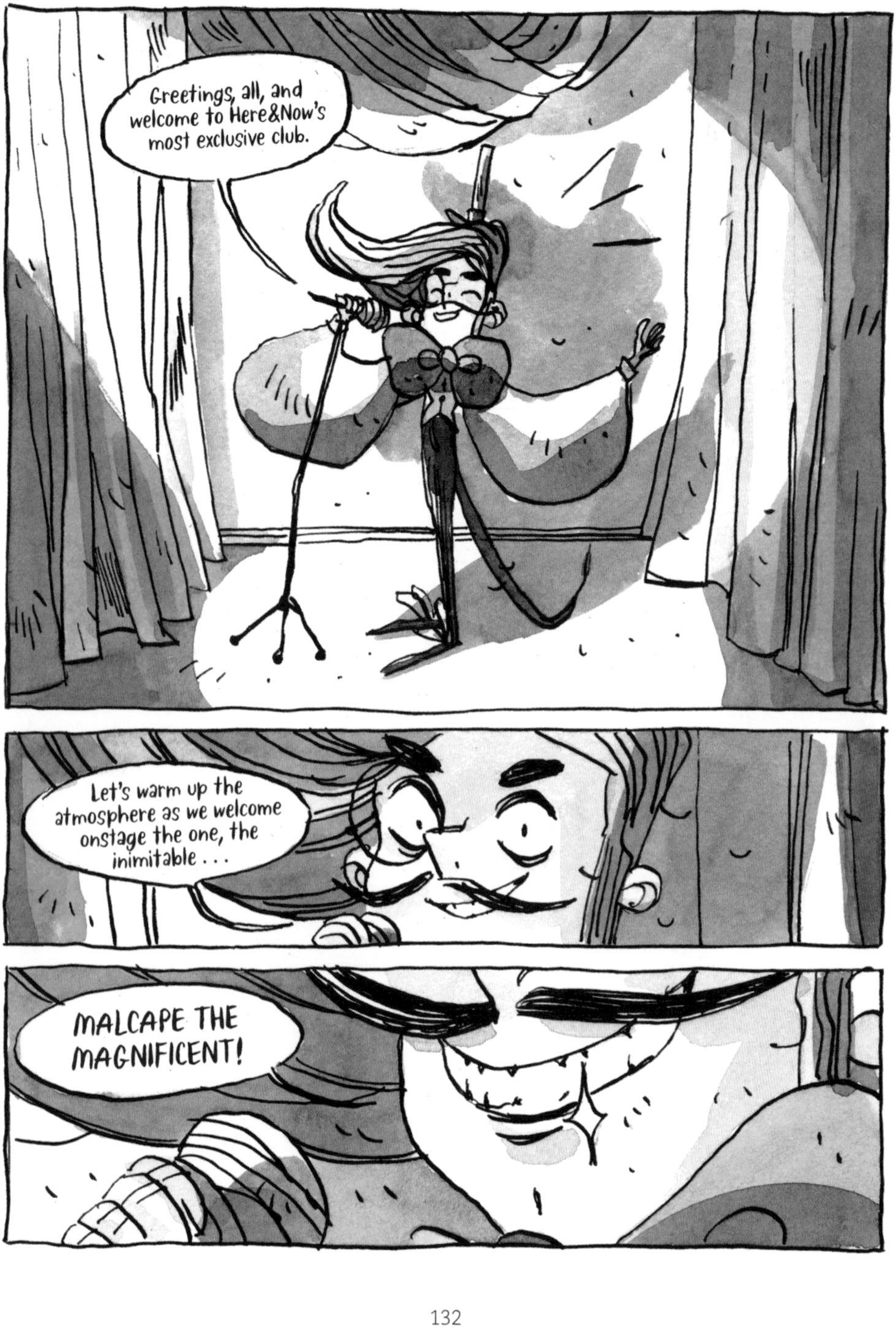
Greetings, all, and welcome to Here&Now's most exclusive club.
Let's warm up the atmosphere as we welcome onstage the one, the inimitable . . .
MALCAPE THE MAGNIFICENT!

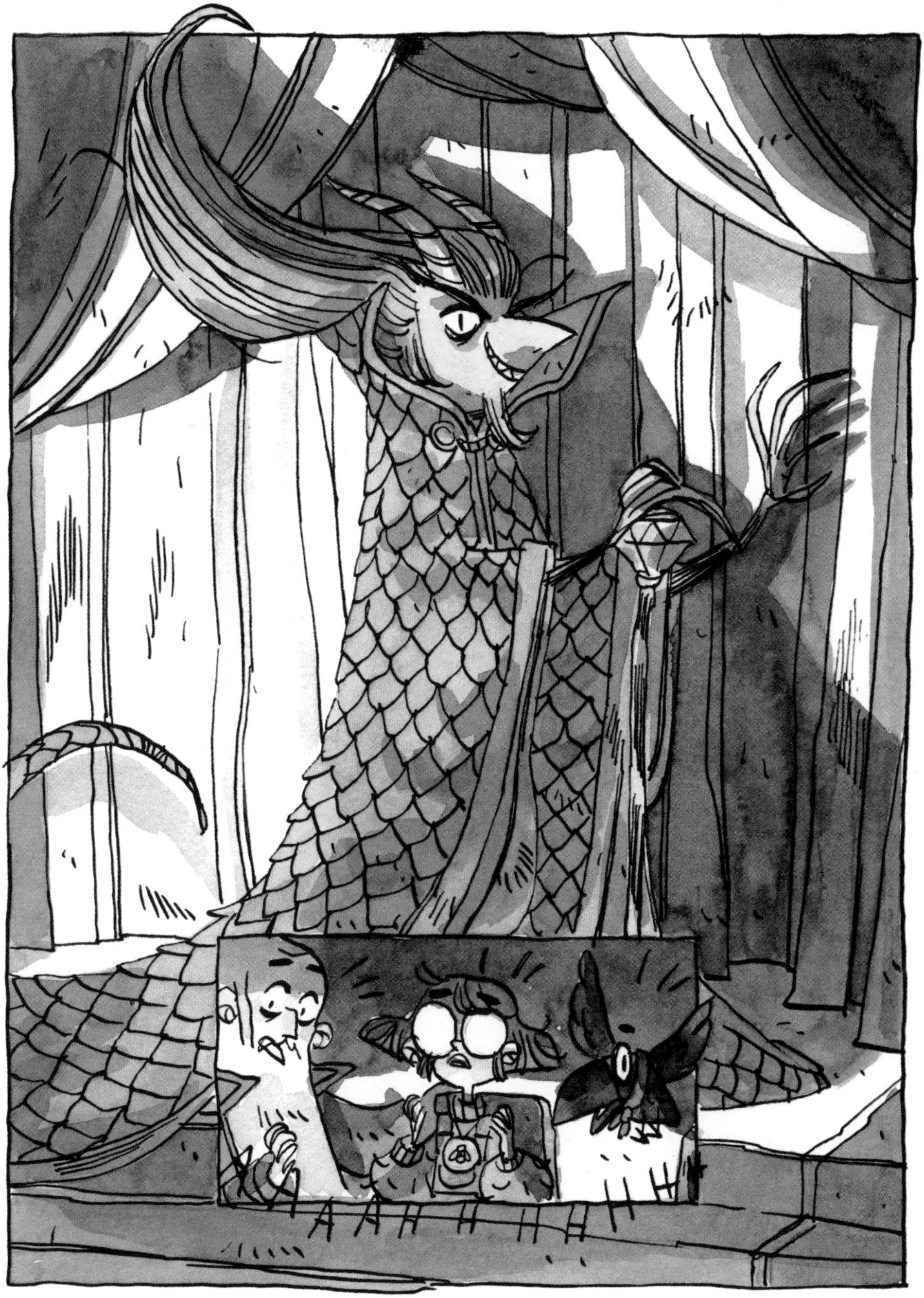
AAAAHHHHHH

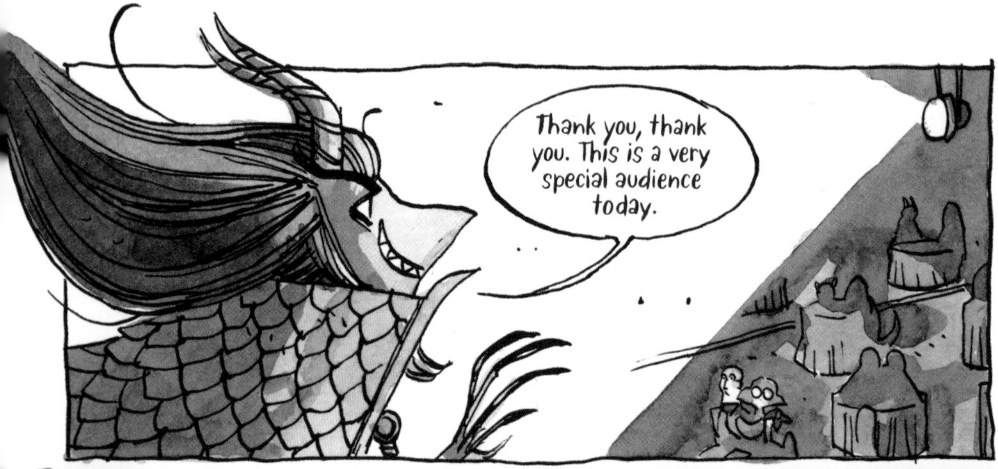
Thank you, thank you. This is a very special audience today.

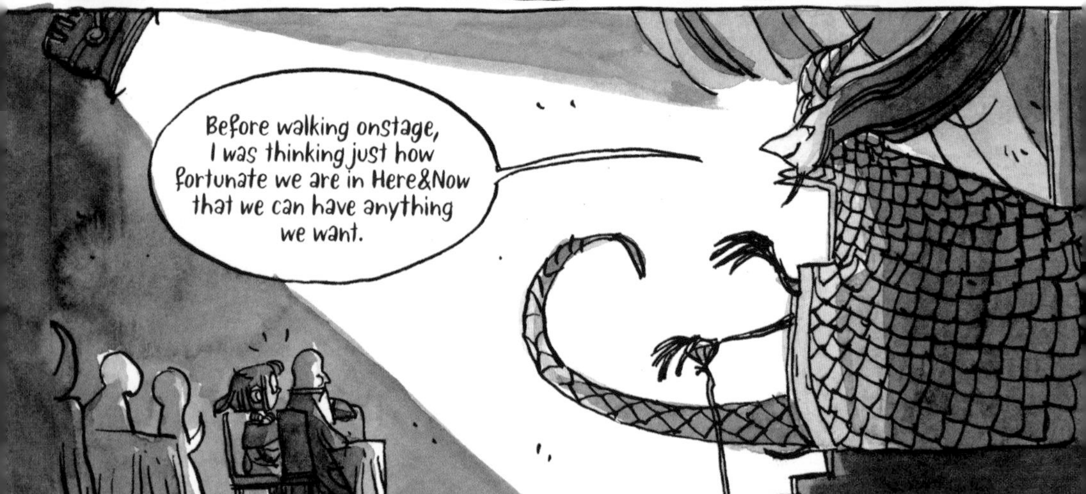
Before walking onstage, I was thinking just how fortunate we are in Here&Now that we can have anything we want.

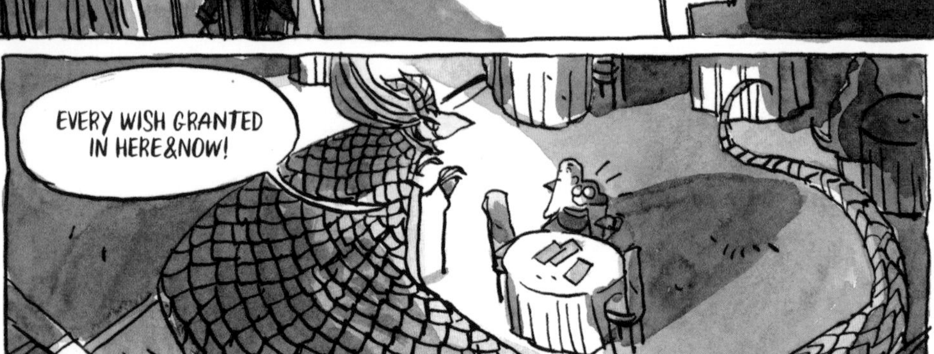
EVERY WISH GRANTED IN HERE&NOW!

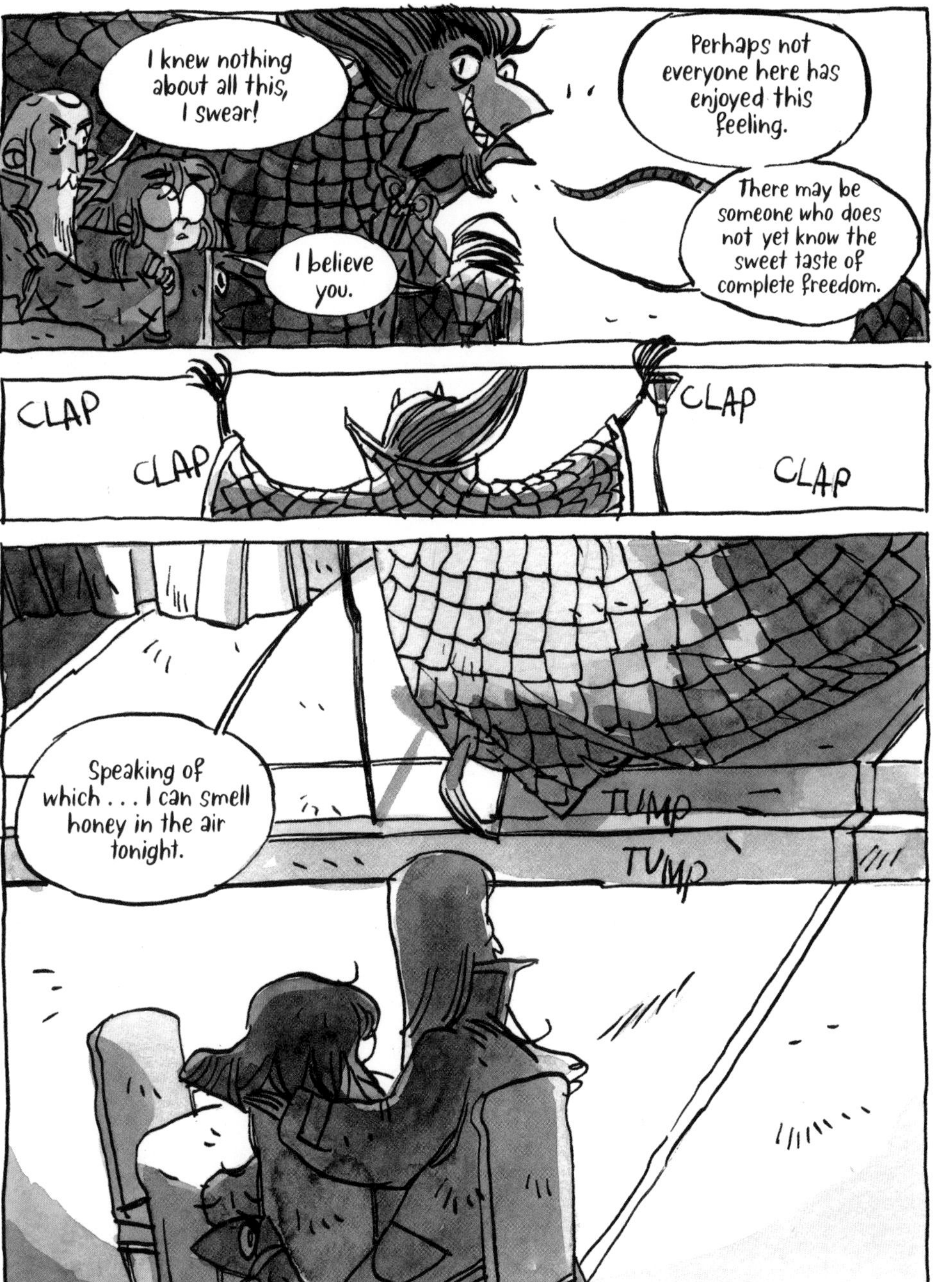
I knew nothing about all this, I swear!
I believe you.
Perhaps not everyone here has enjoyed this feeling.
There may be someone who does not yet know the sweet taste of complete freedom.
CLAP
CLAP
CLAP
CLAP
Speaking of which . . . I can smell honey in the air tonight.
TUMP
TUMP

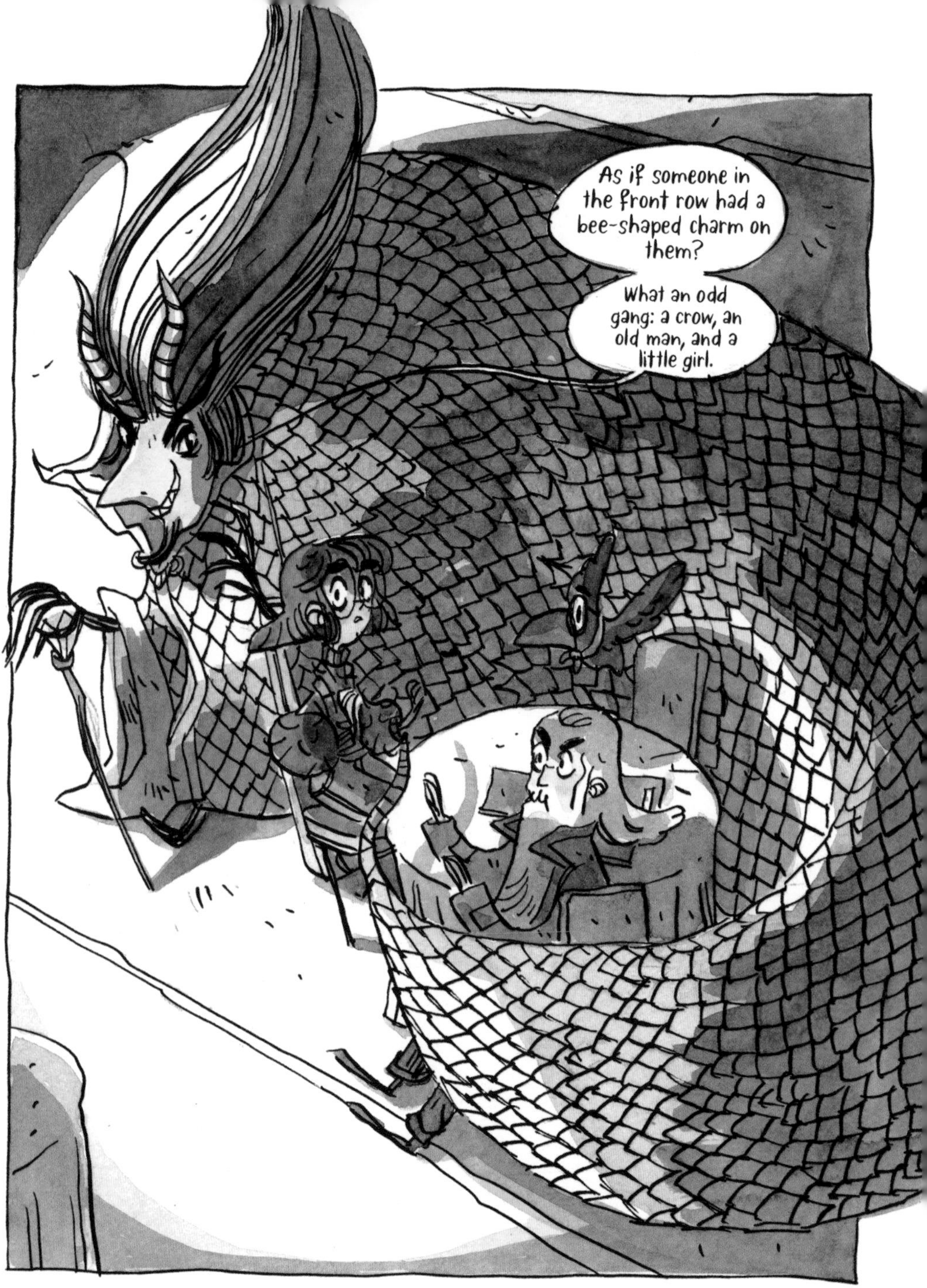
As if someone in the front row had a bee-shaped charm on them?
What an odd gang: a crow, an old man, and a little girl.

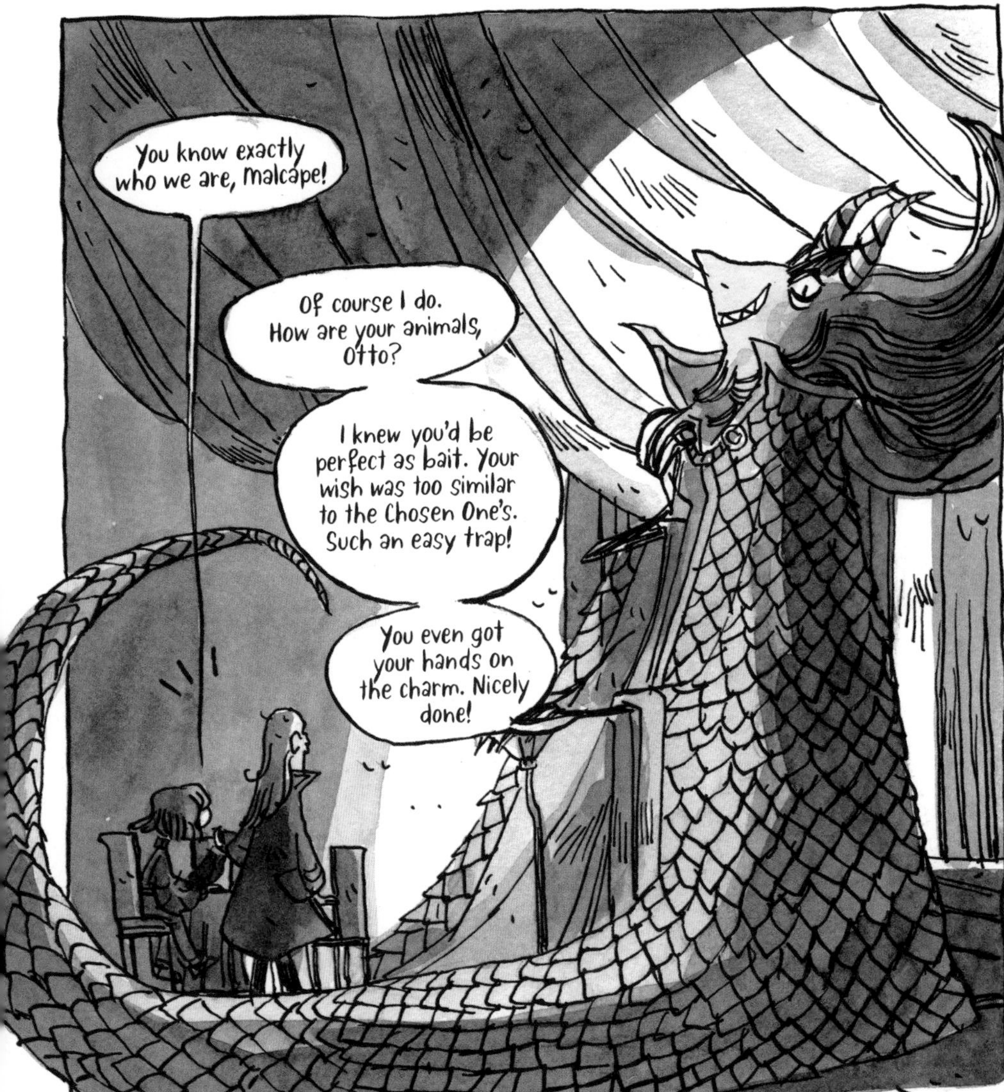
You know exactly who we are, Malcape!
Of course I do. How are your animals, Otto?
I knew you'd be perfect as bait. Your wish was too similar to the Chosen One's. Such an easy trap!
You even got your hands on the charm. Nicely done!

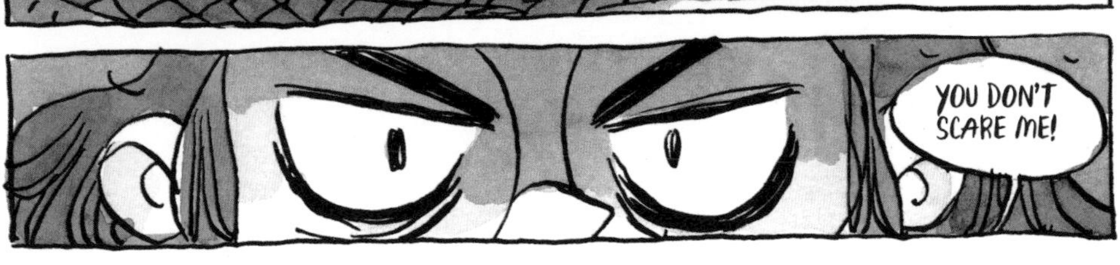
YOU DON'T SCARE ME!

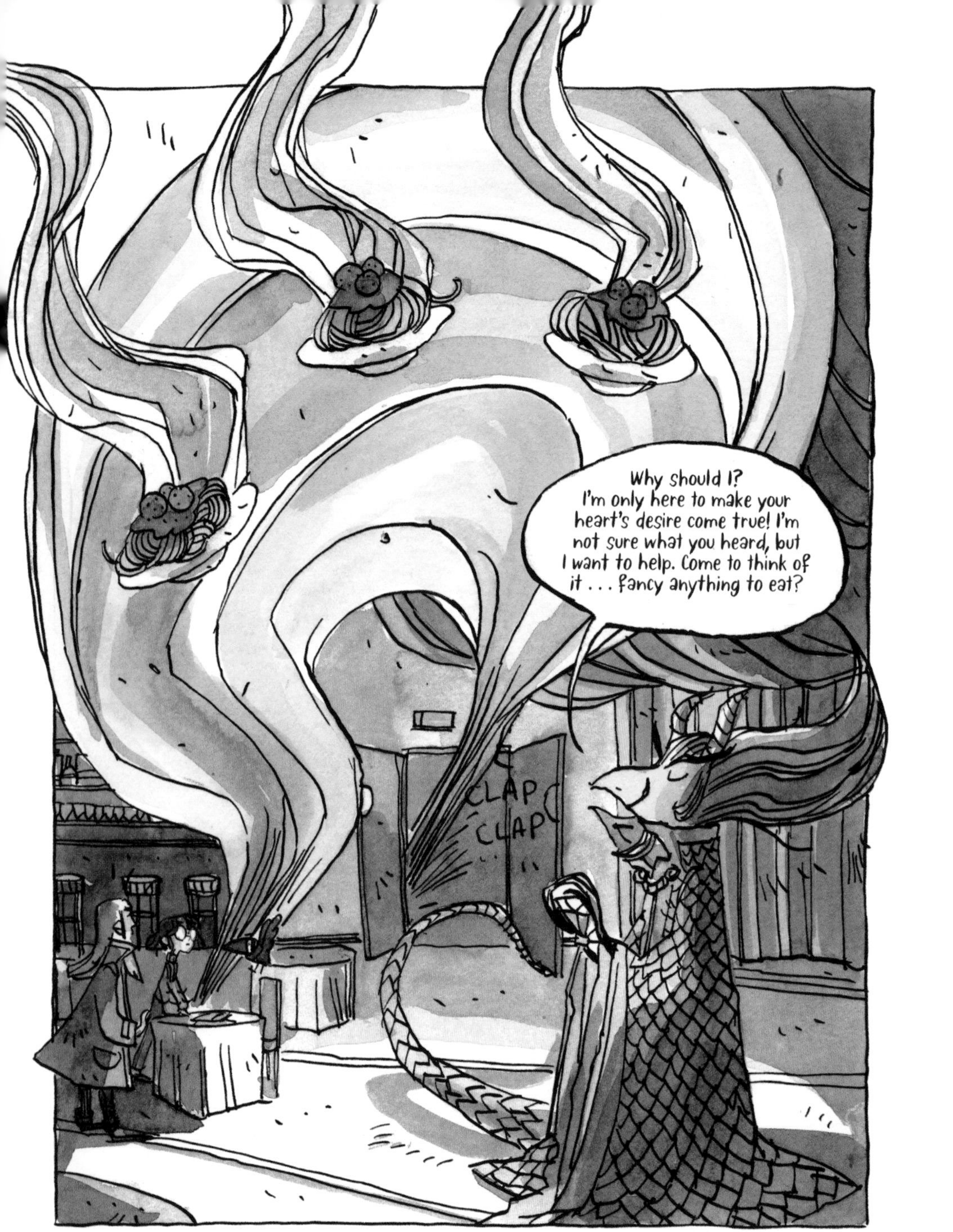
Why should I? I'm only here to make your heart's desire come true! I'm not sure what you heard, but I want to help. Come to think of it . . . fancy anything to eat?
CLAP
CLAP

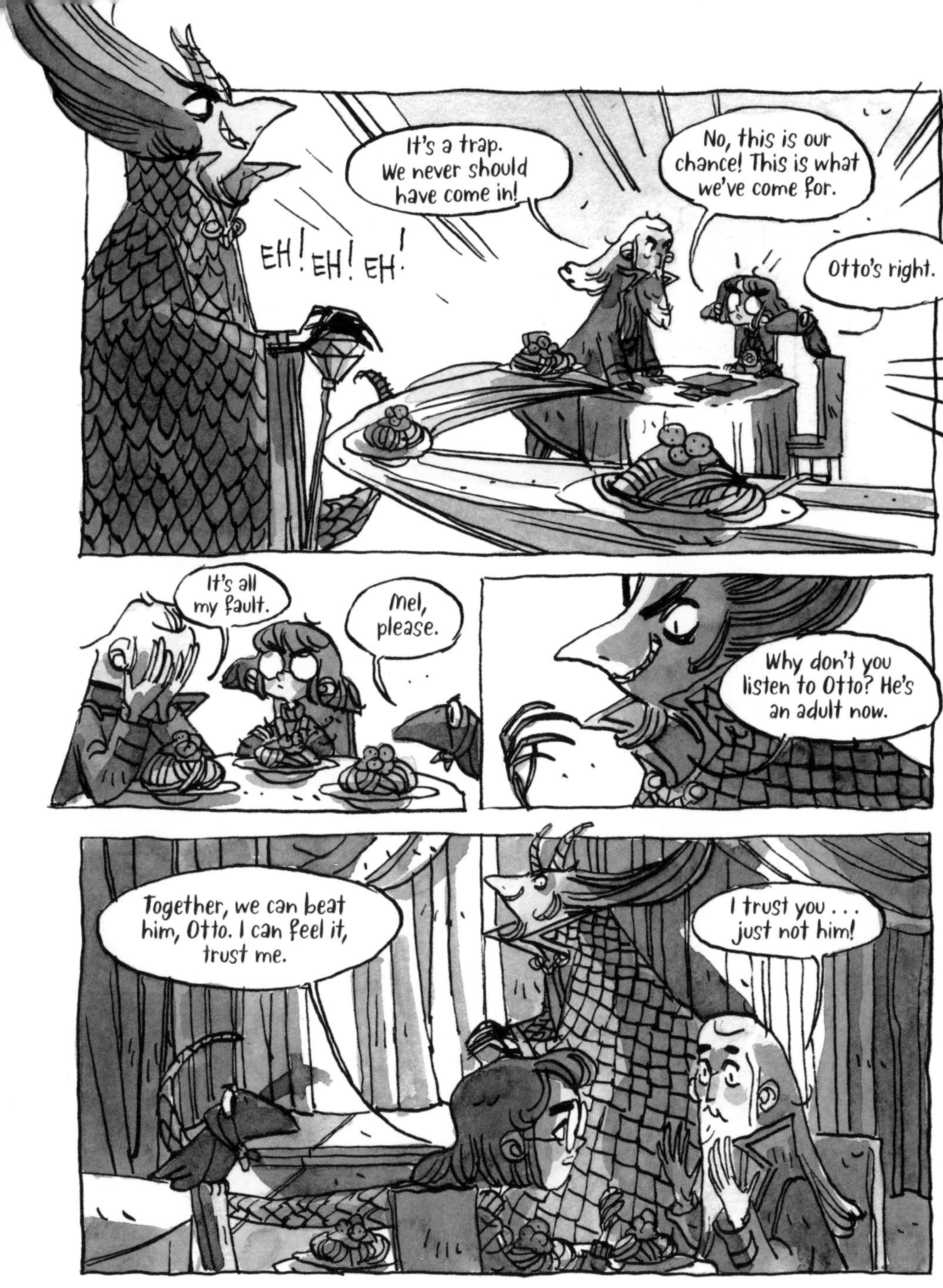
EH! EH! EH!
It's a trap. We never should have come in!
No, this is our chance! This is what we've come for.
Otto's right.
It's all my fault.
Mel, please.
Why don't you listen to Otto? He's an adult now.
Together, we can beat him, Otto. I can feel it, trust me.
I trust you . . . just not him!

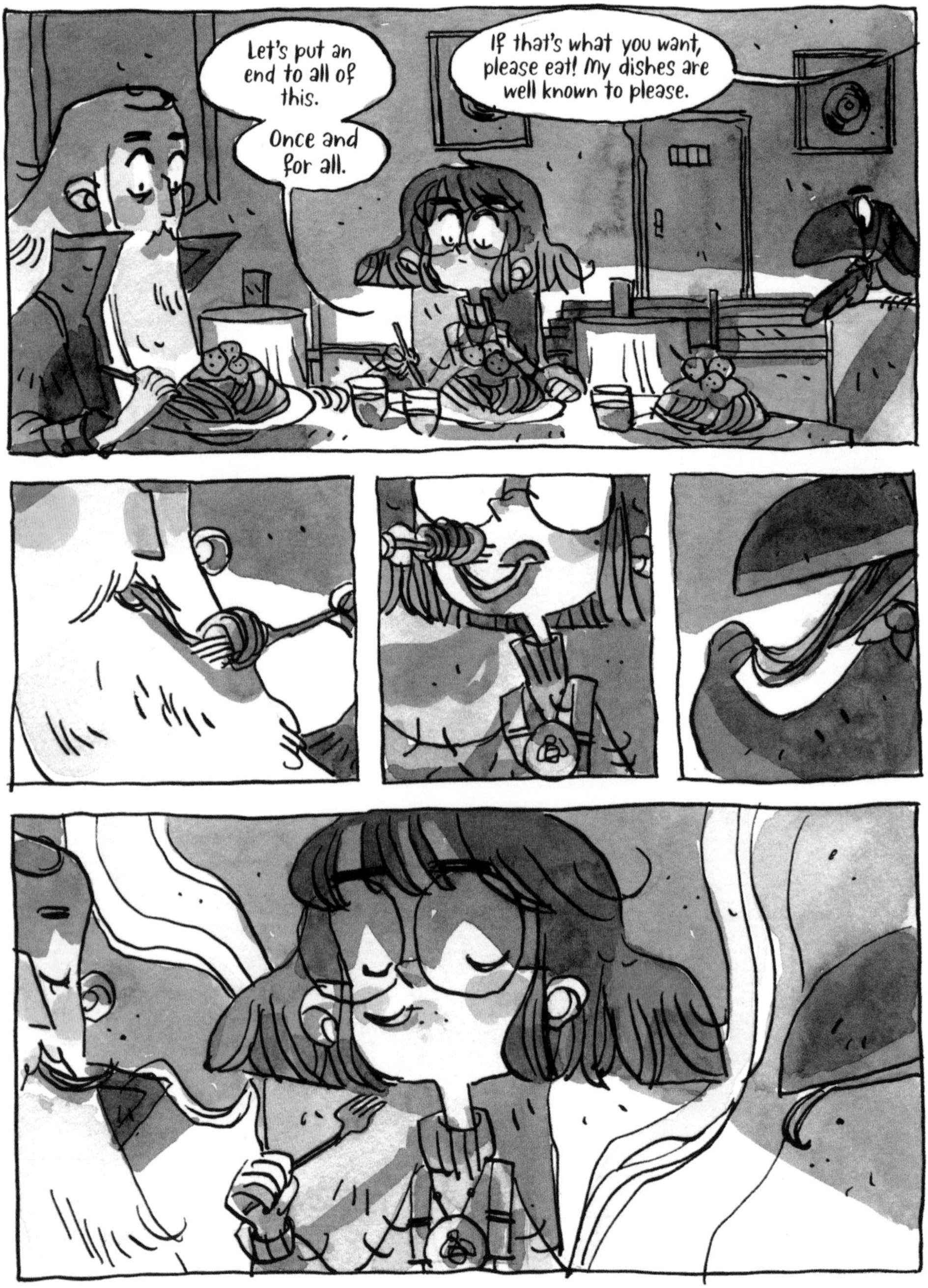

Let's put an end to all of this.
Once and for all.
If that's what you want, please eat! My dishes are well known to please.

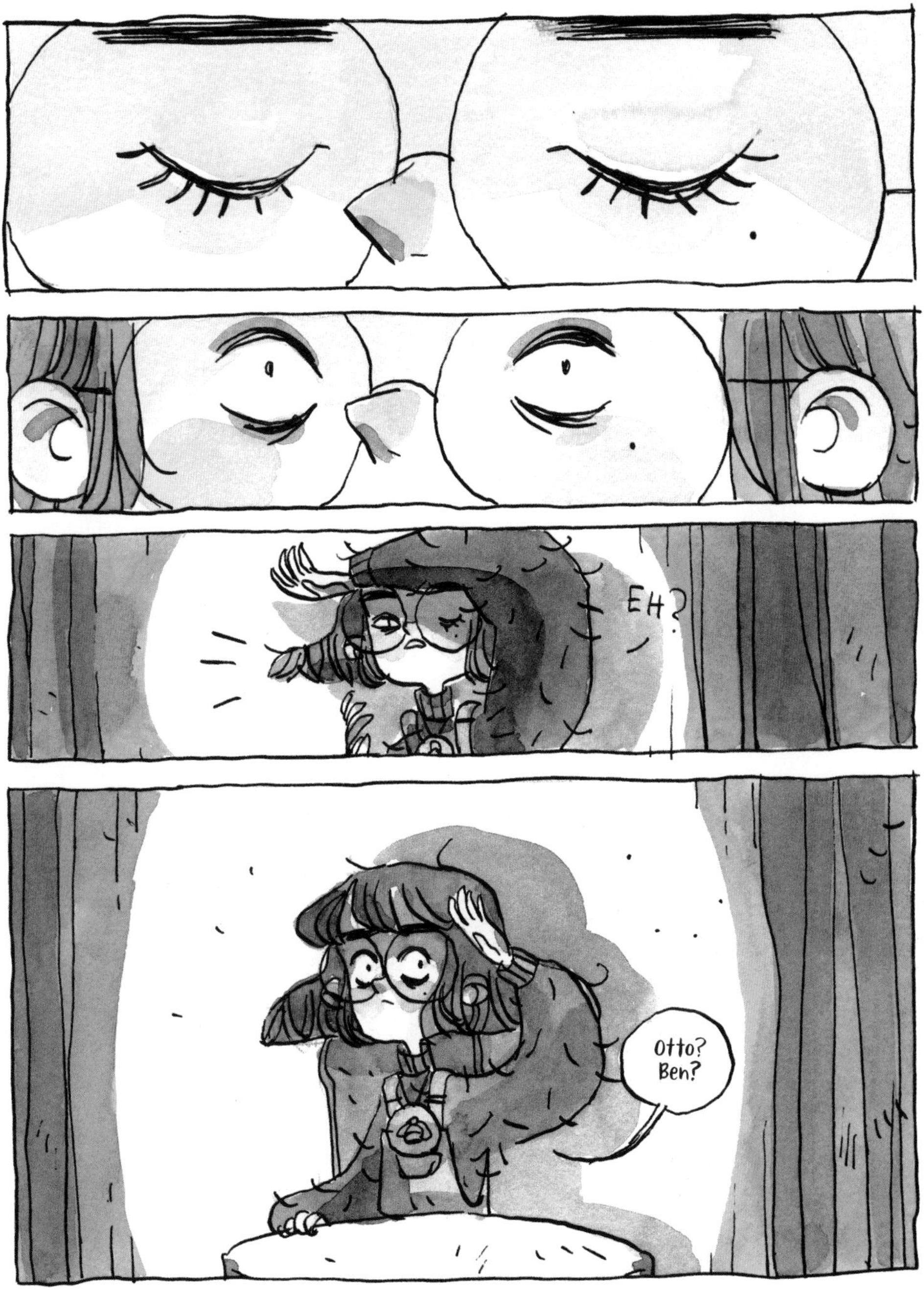
EH?
Otto?
Ben?

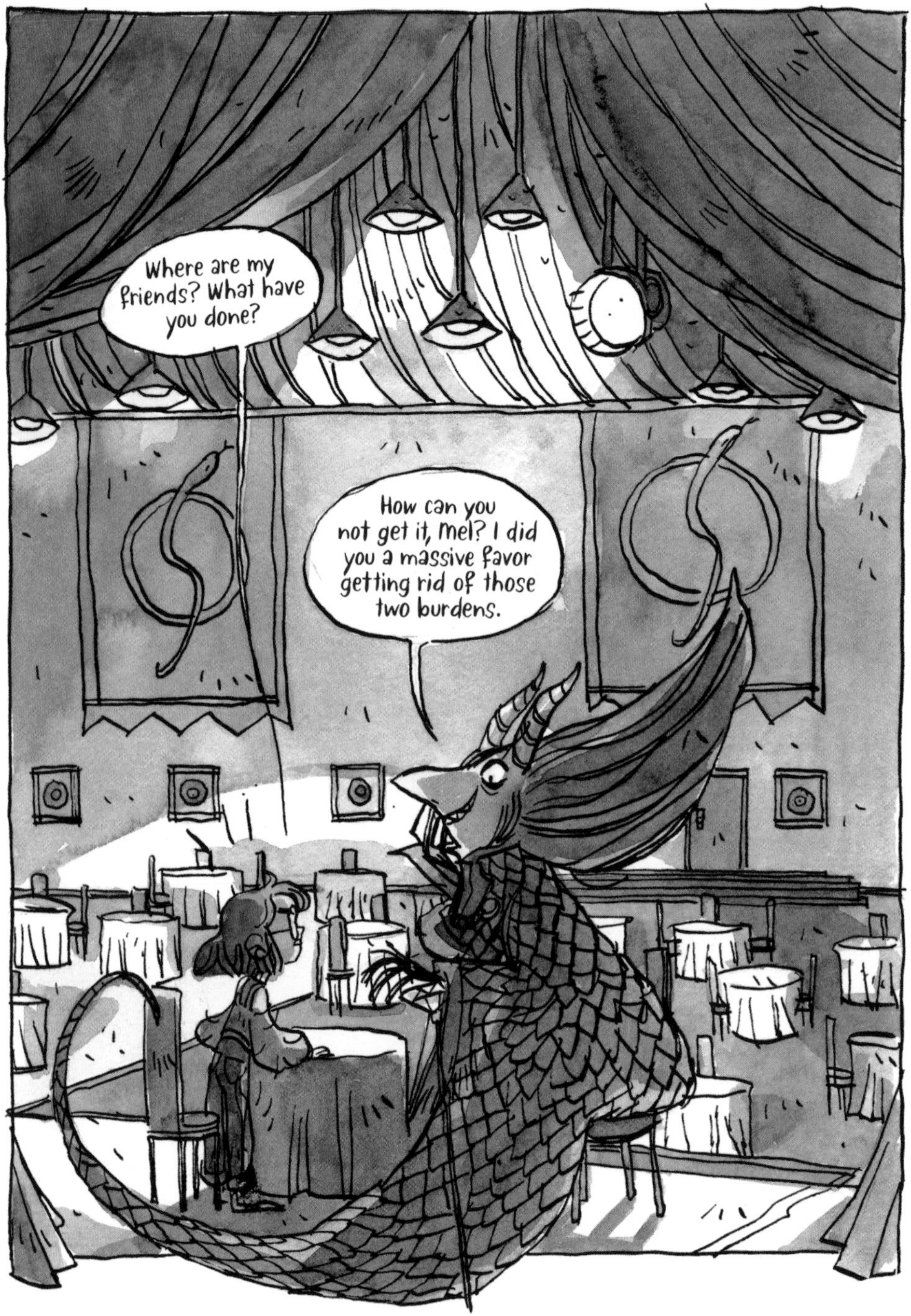
Where are my friends? What have you done?
How can you not get it, Mel? I did you a massive favor getting rid of those two burdens.

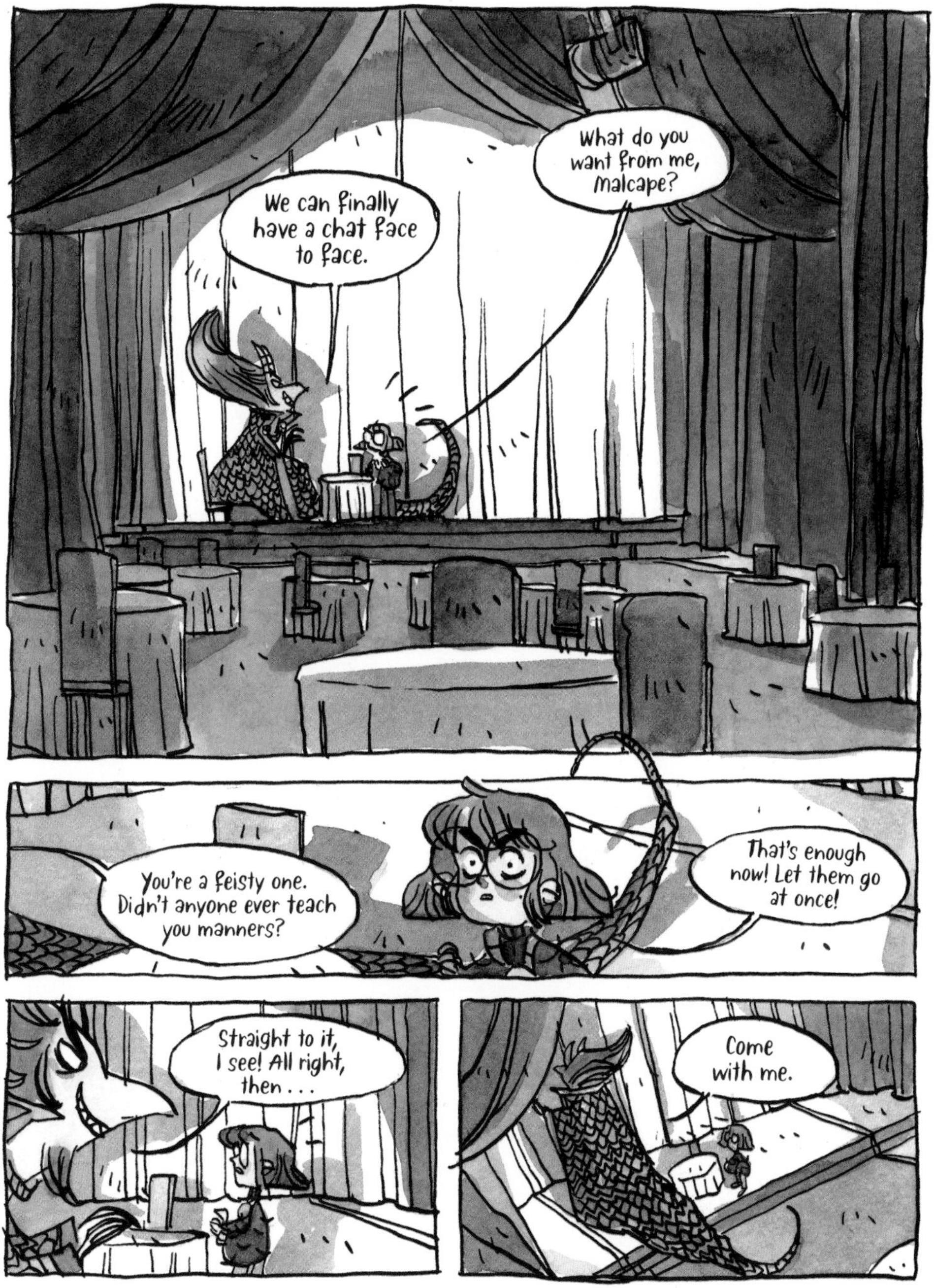
We can finally have a chat face to face.
What do you want from me, Malcape?
You're a feisty one. Didn't anyone ever teach you manners?
That's enough now! Let them go at once!
Straight to it, I see! All right, then . . .
Come with me.

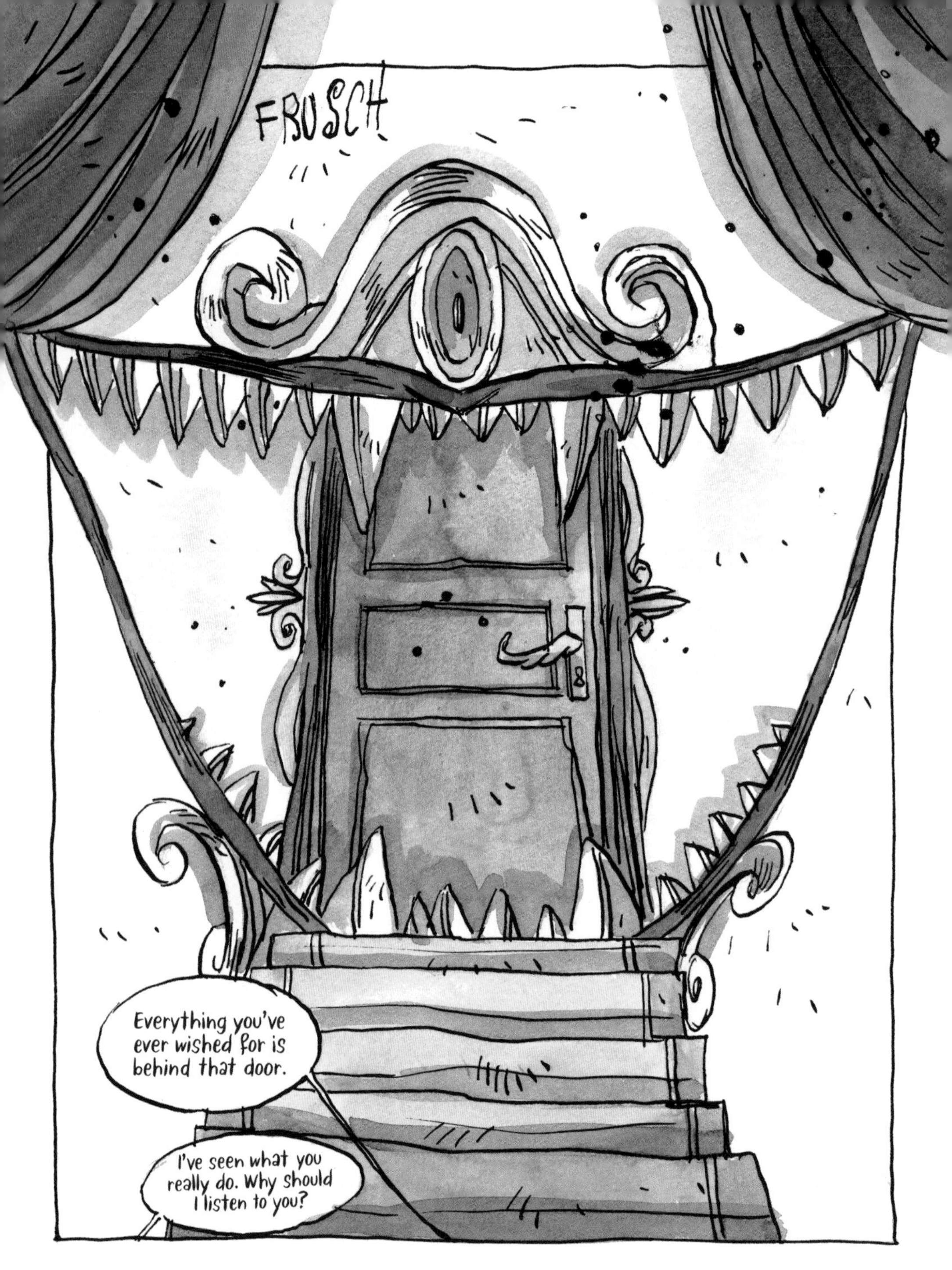
FRUSCH
Everything you've ever wished for is behind that door.
I've seen what you really do. Why should I listen to you?

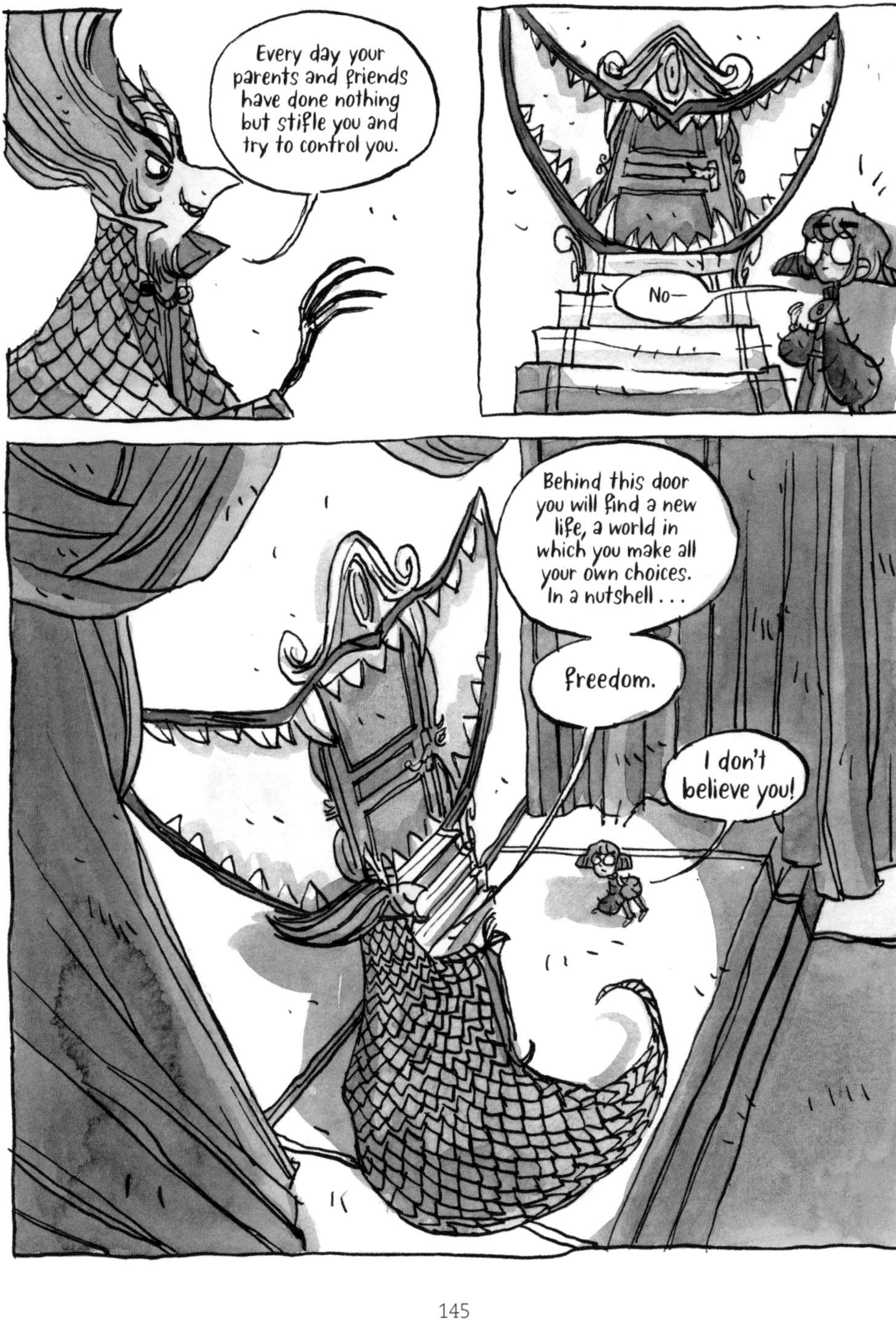
Every day your parents and friends have done nothing but stifle you and try to control you.
No—
Behind this door you will find a new life, a world in which you make all your own choices. In a nutshell . . .
freedom.
I don't believe you!

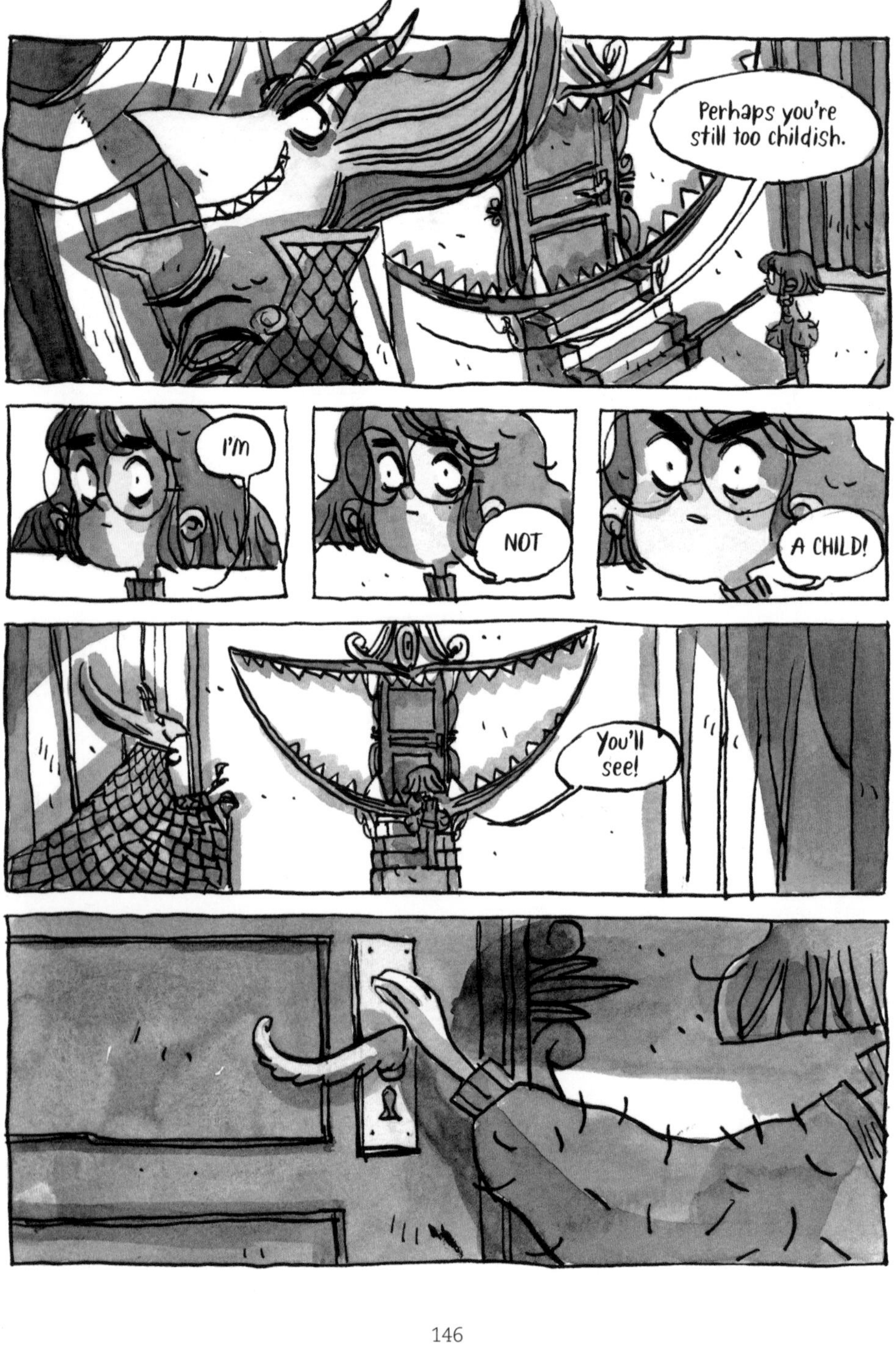
Perhaps you're still too childish.
I'M
NOT
A CHILD!
You'll see!

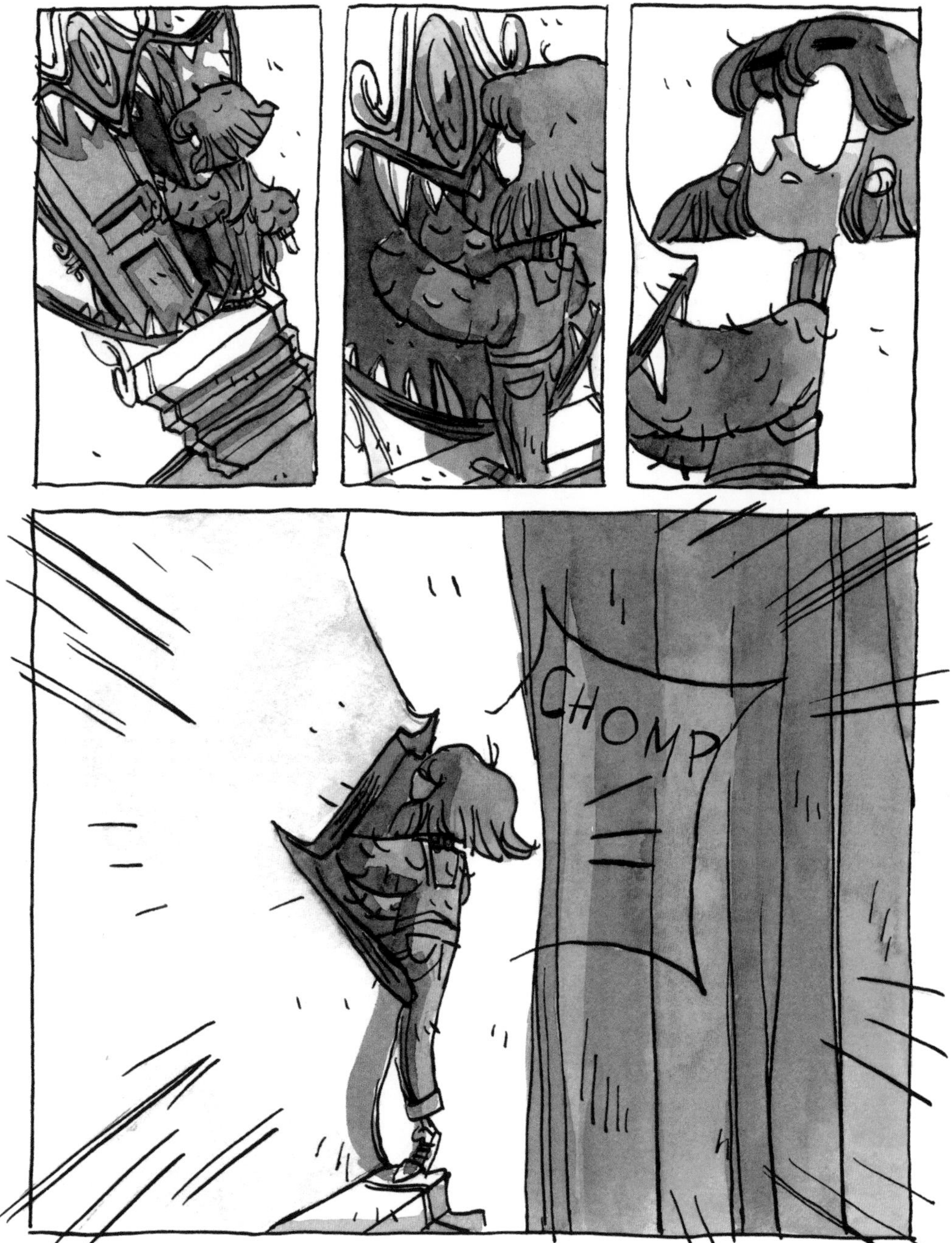
CHOMP

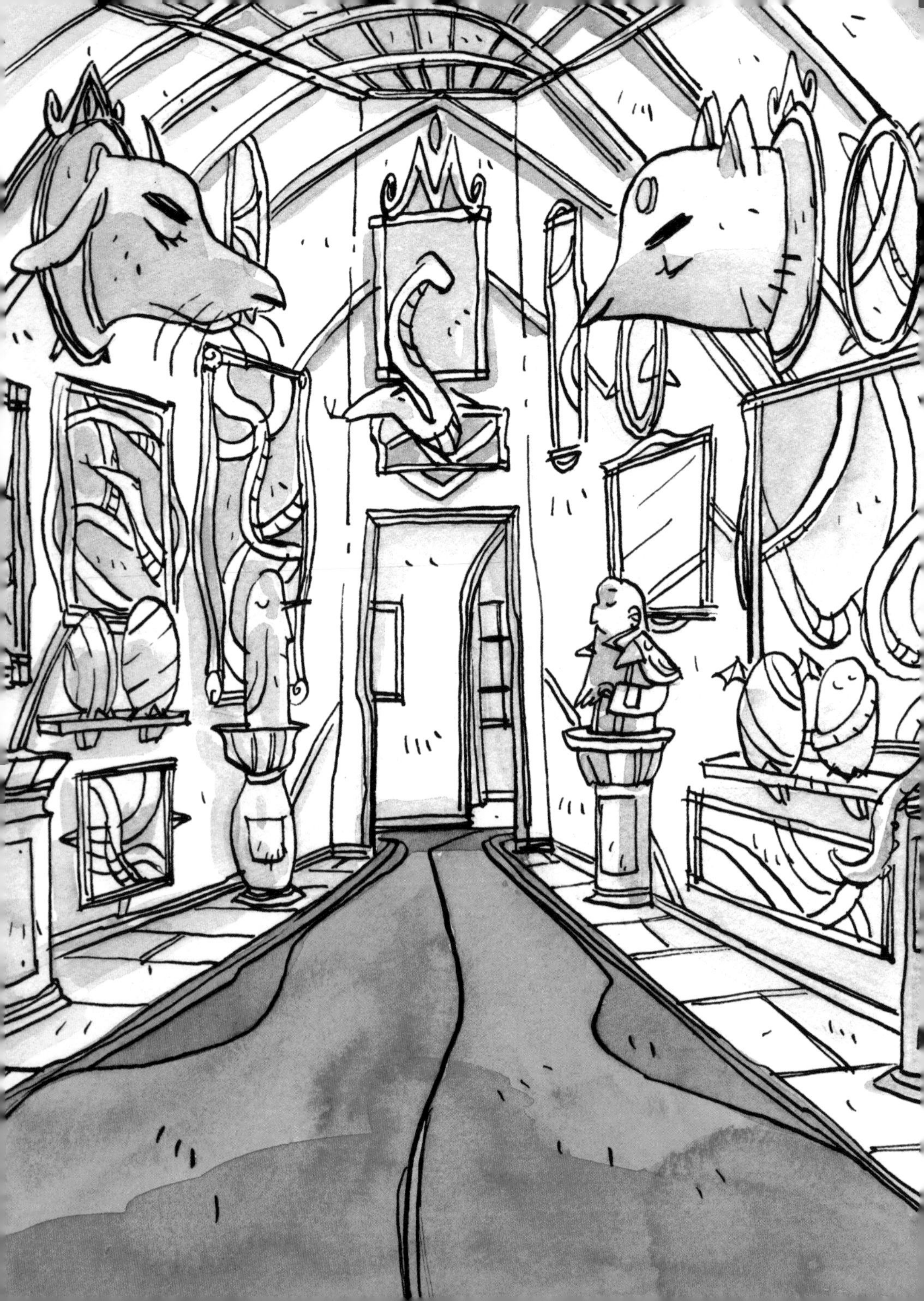

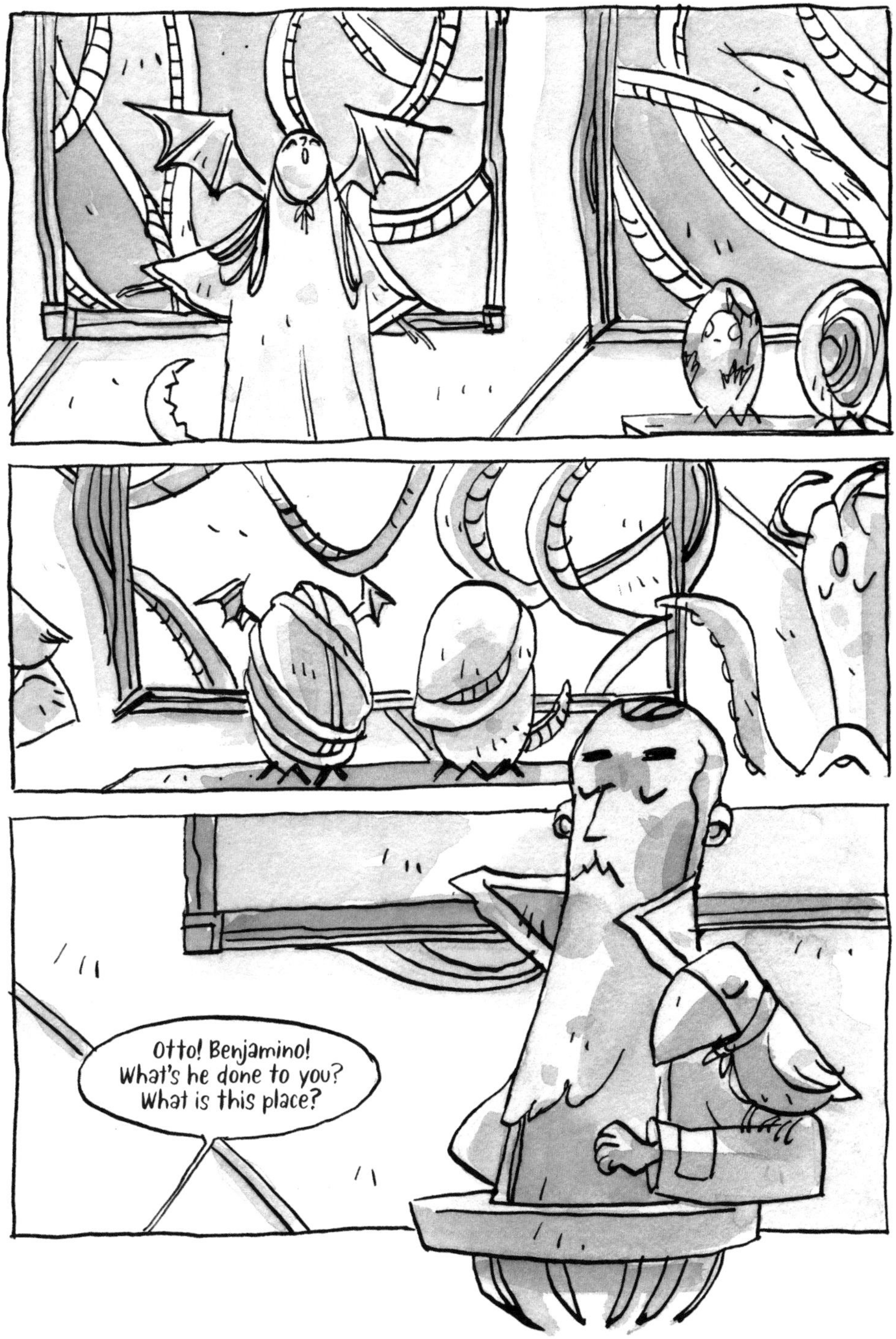
Otto! Benjamino! What's he done to you? What is this place?

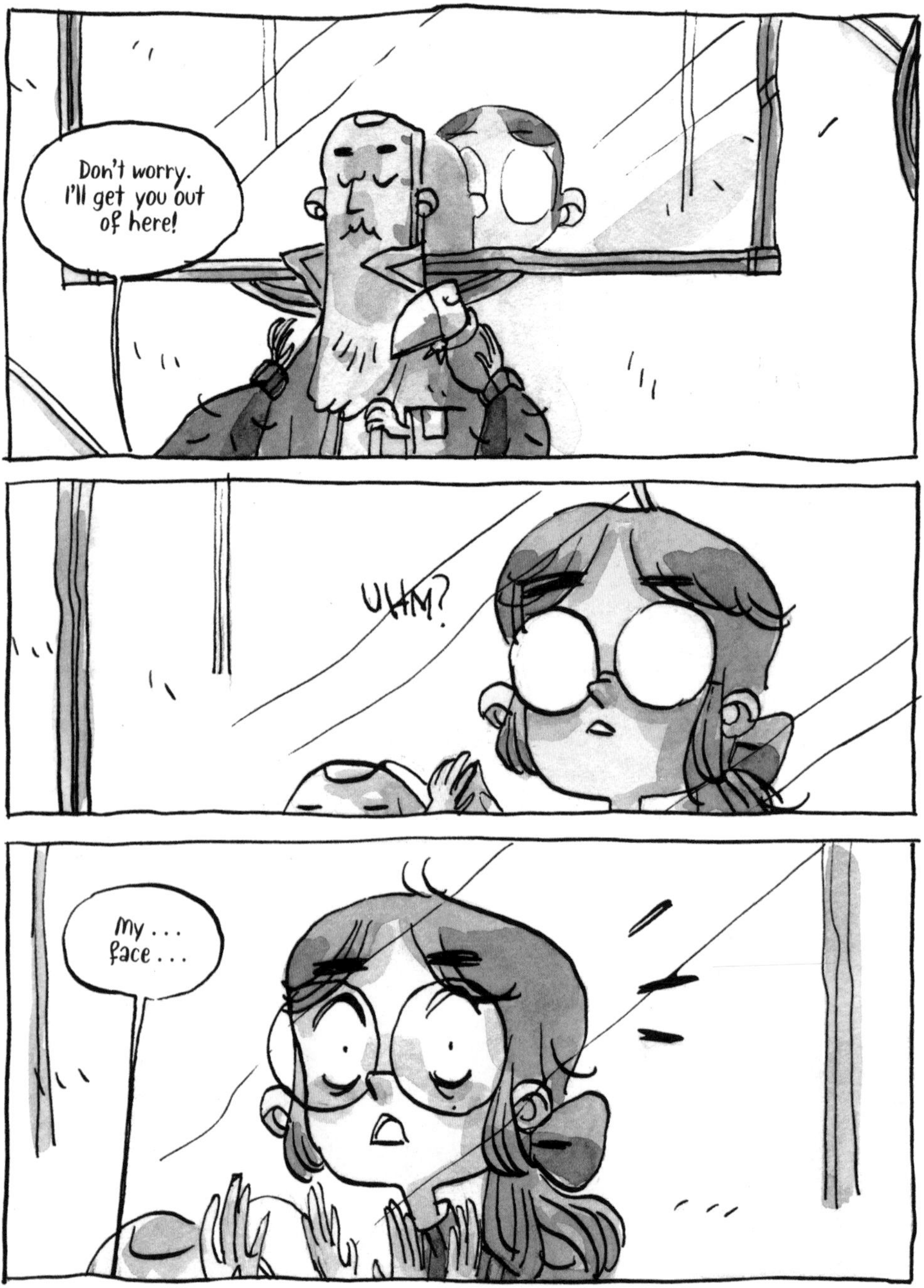
Don't worry. I'll get you out of here!
UHM?
my . . . face . . .

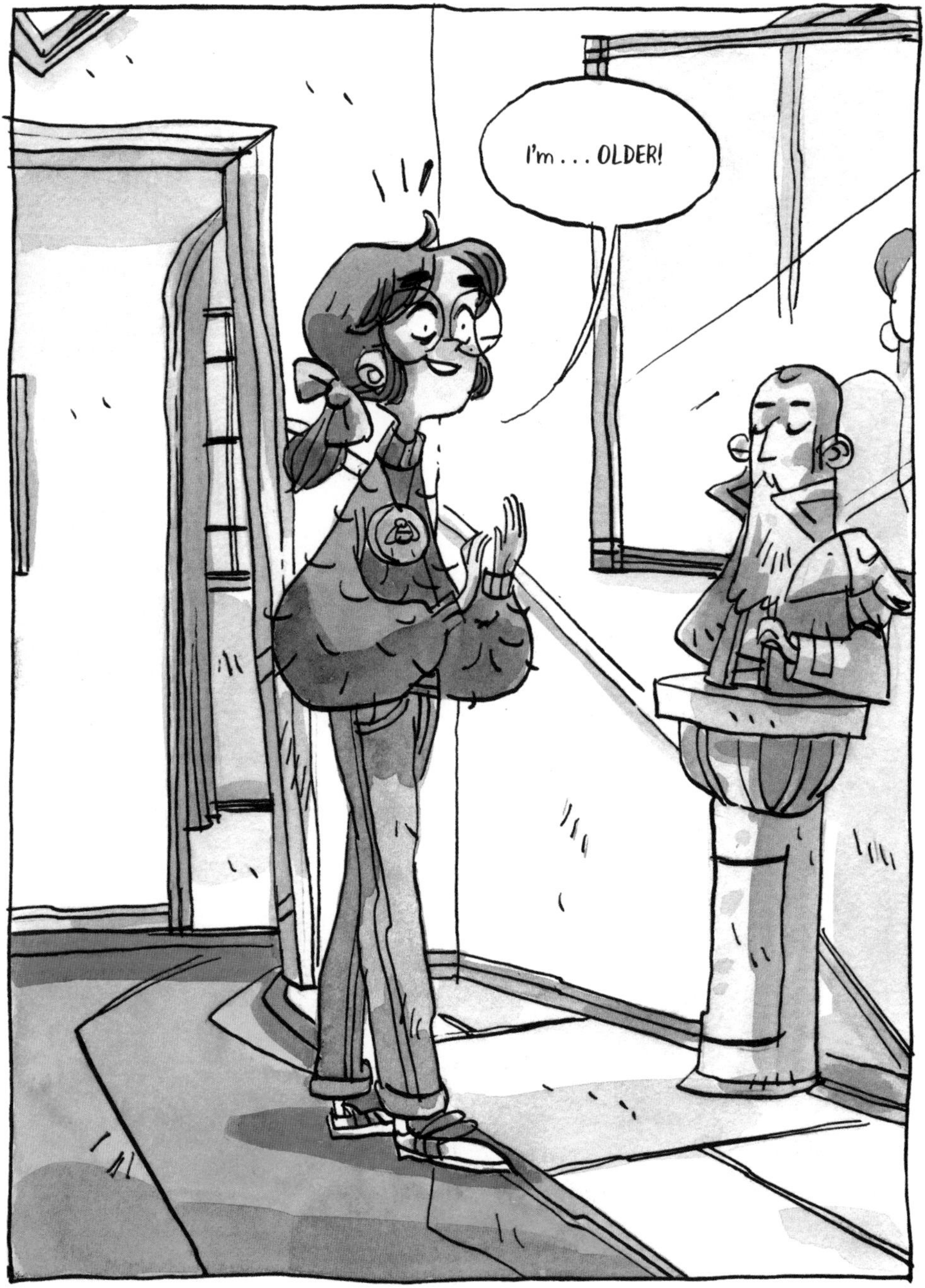
I'm . . . OLDER!

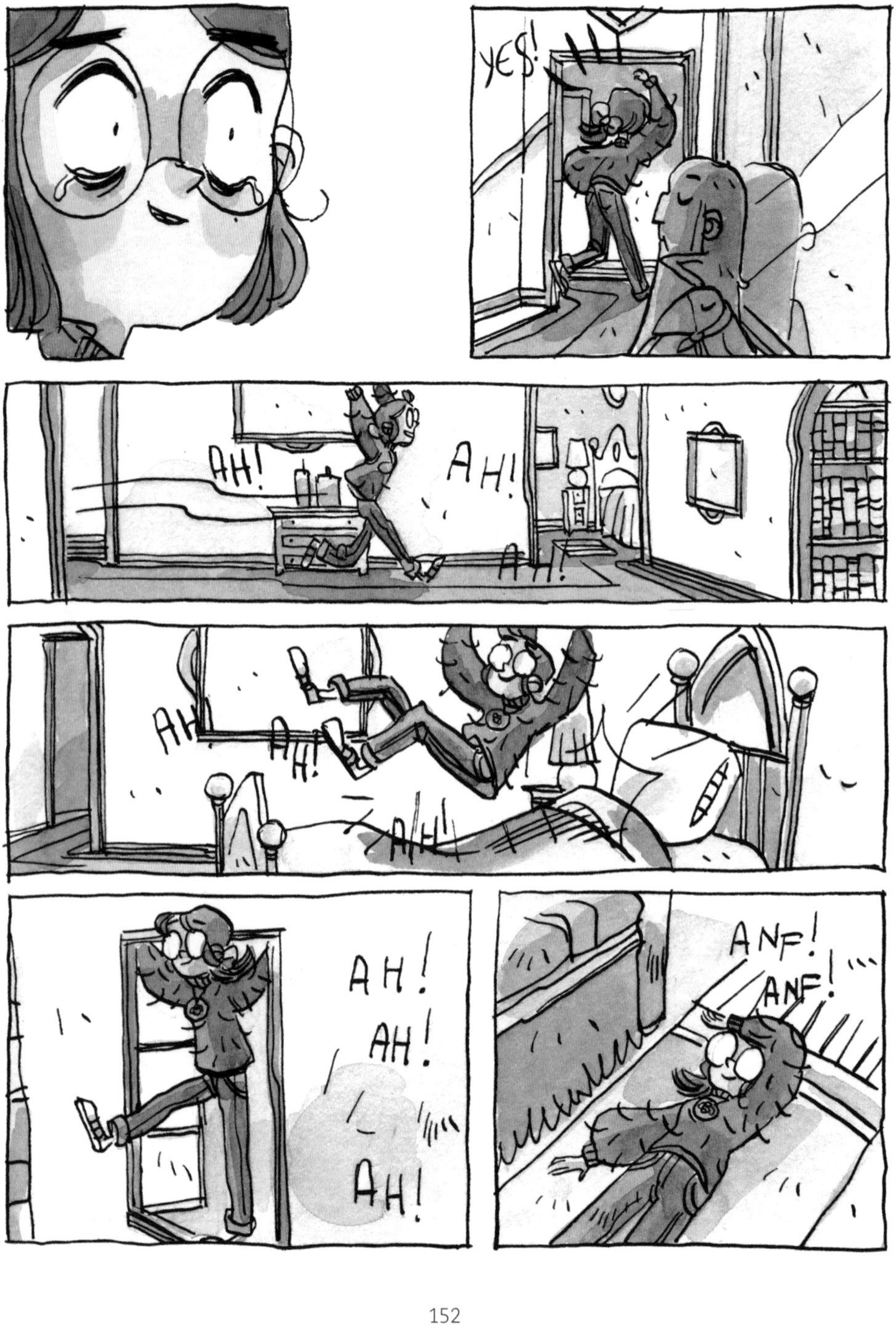
YES!
AH!
AH!
AH!
AH!
AH!
AH!
AH!
AH!
AH!
ANF!
ANF!

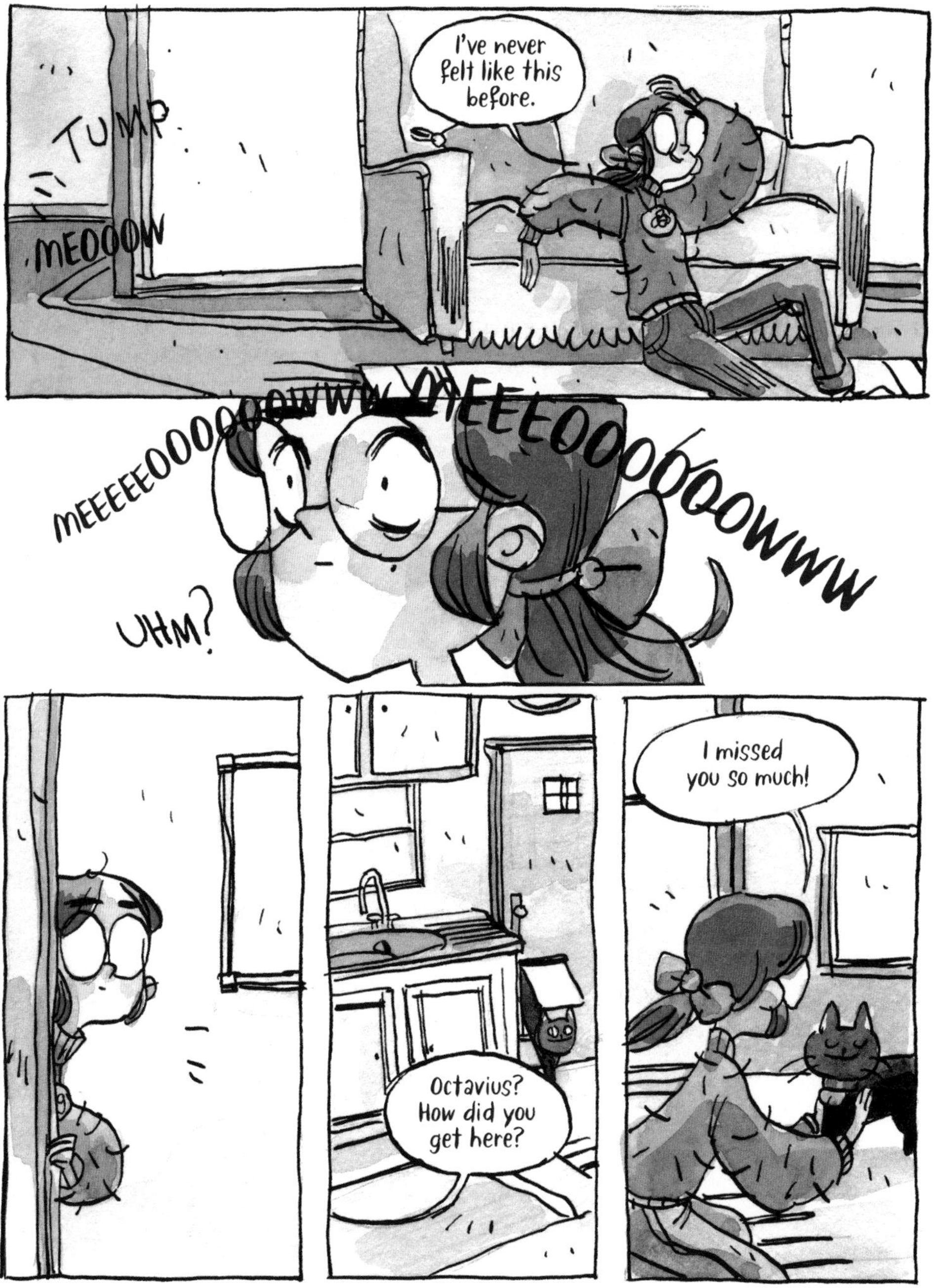
I've never felt like this before.
TUMP
MEOOOW
MEEEEEOOOOOOWWW
MEEEOOOOOOOOWWWW
UHM?
Octavius? How did you get here?
I missed you so much!

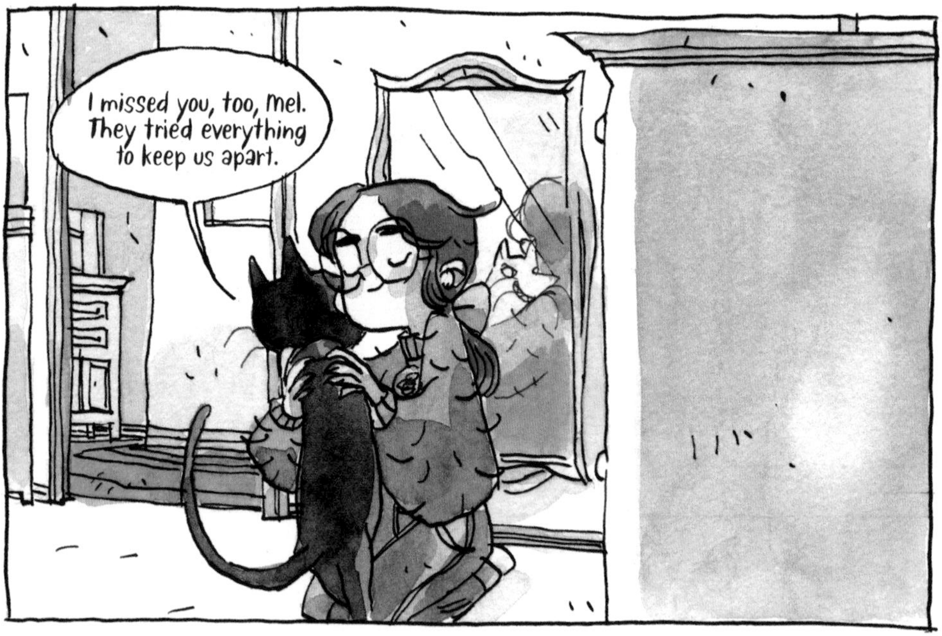
I missed you, too, mel. They tried everything to keep us apart.

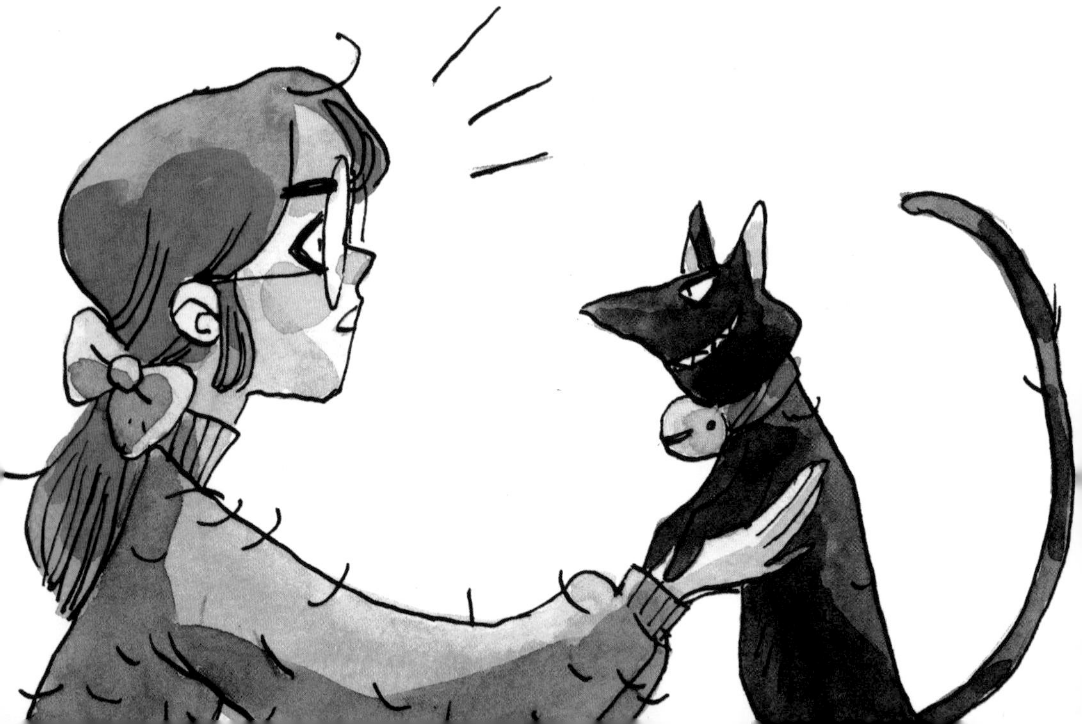

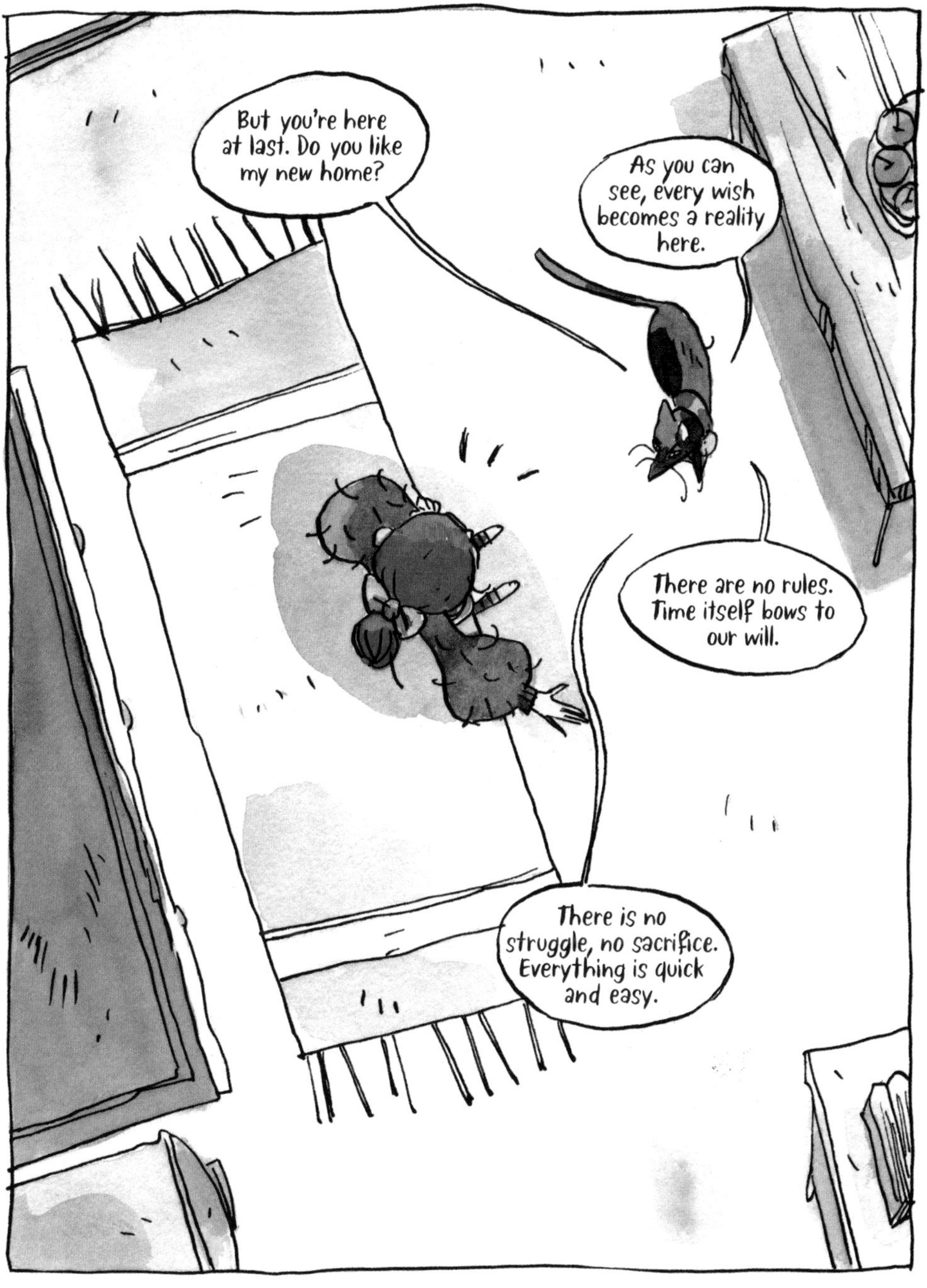
But you're here at last. Do you like my new home?
As you can see, every wish becomes a reality here.
There are no rules. Time itself bows to our will.
There is no struggle, no sacrifice. Everything is quick and easy.

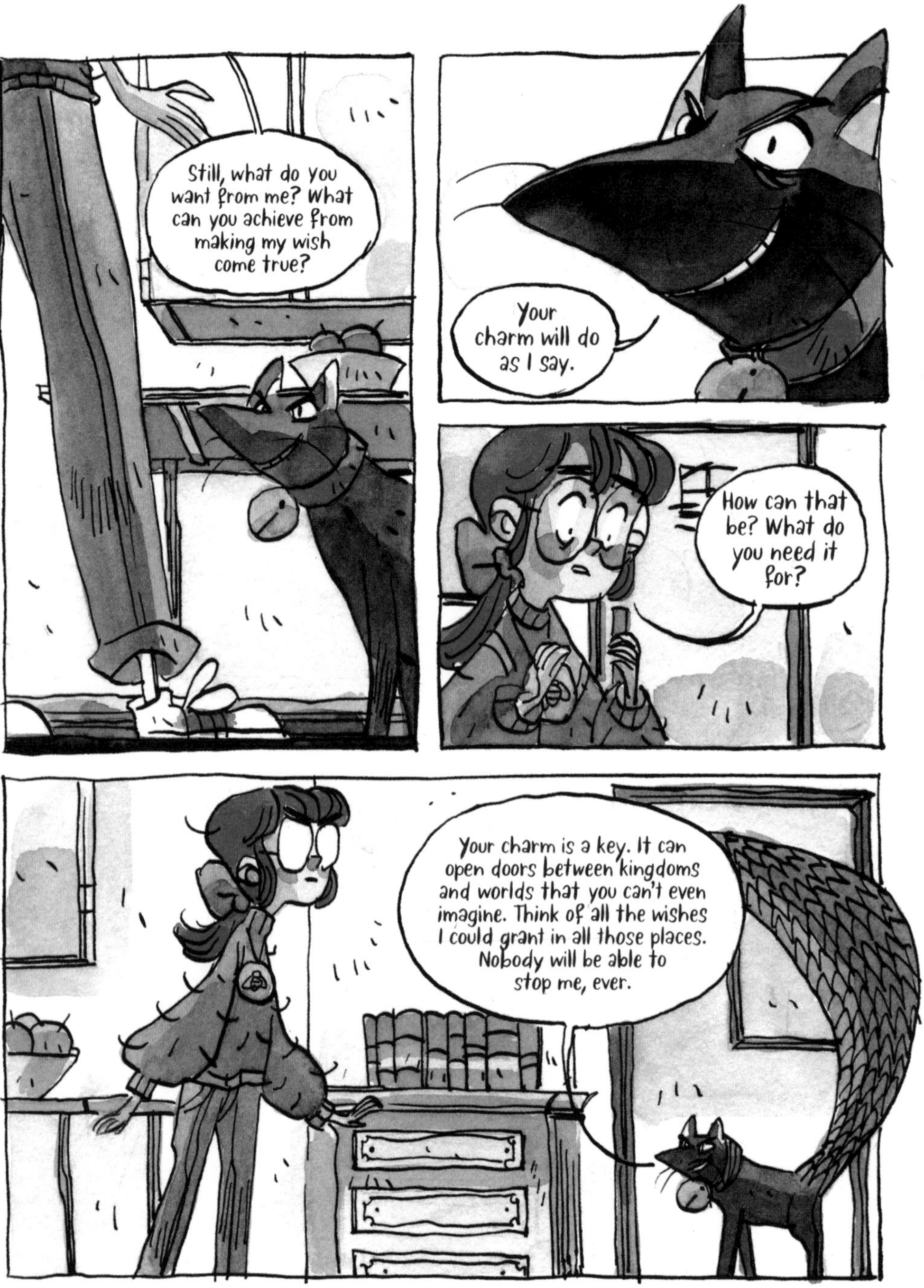
Still, what do you want from me? What can you achieve from making my wish come true?
Your charm will do as I say.
How can that be? What do you need it for?
Your charm is a key. It can open doors between kingdoms and worlds that you can't even imagine. Think of all the wishes I could grant in all those places. Nobody will be able to stop me, ever.

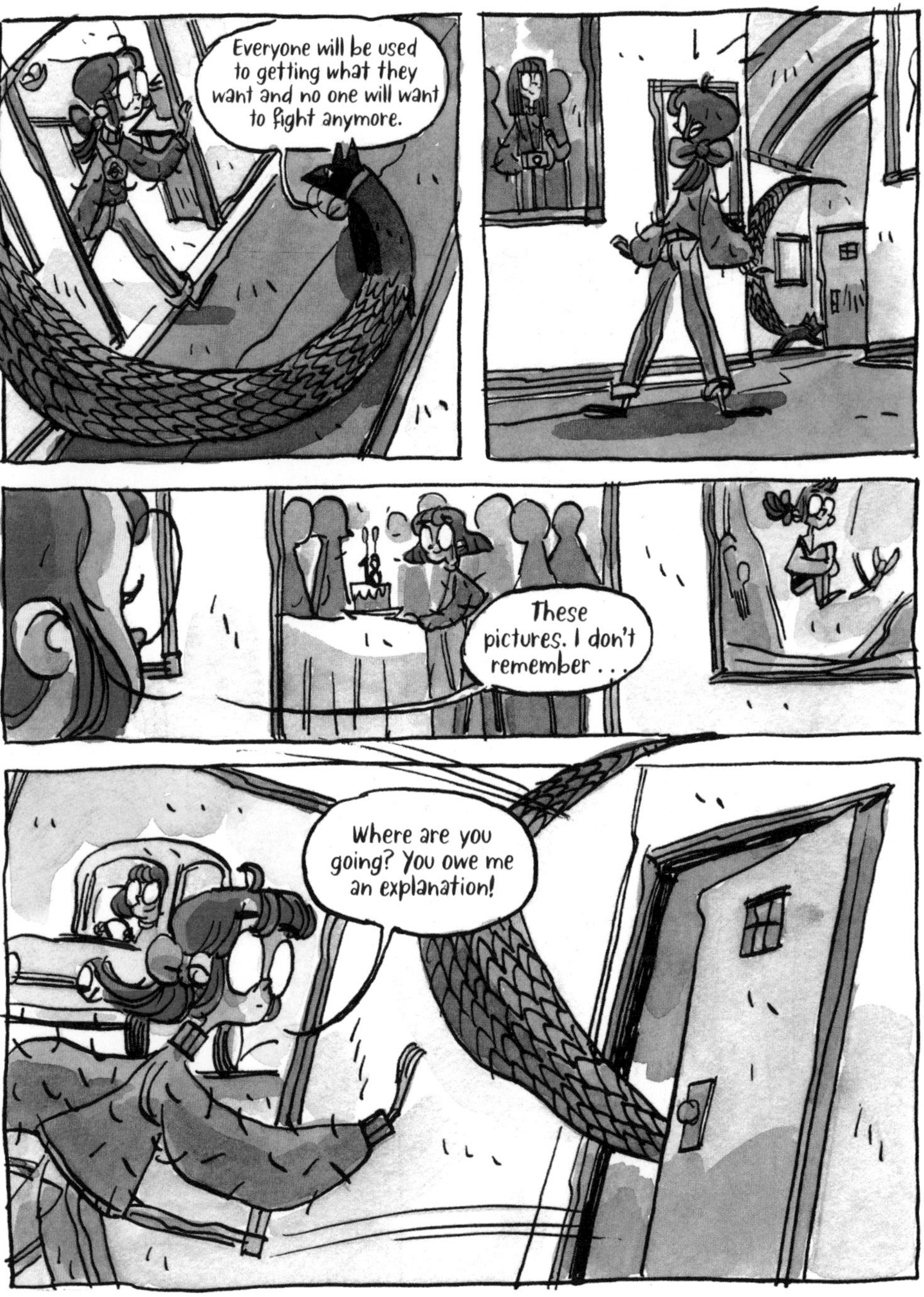
Everyone will be used to getting what they want and no one will want to fight anymore.
These pictures. I don't remember . . .
Where are you going? You owe me an explanation!

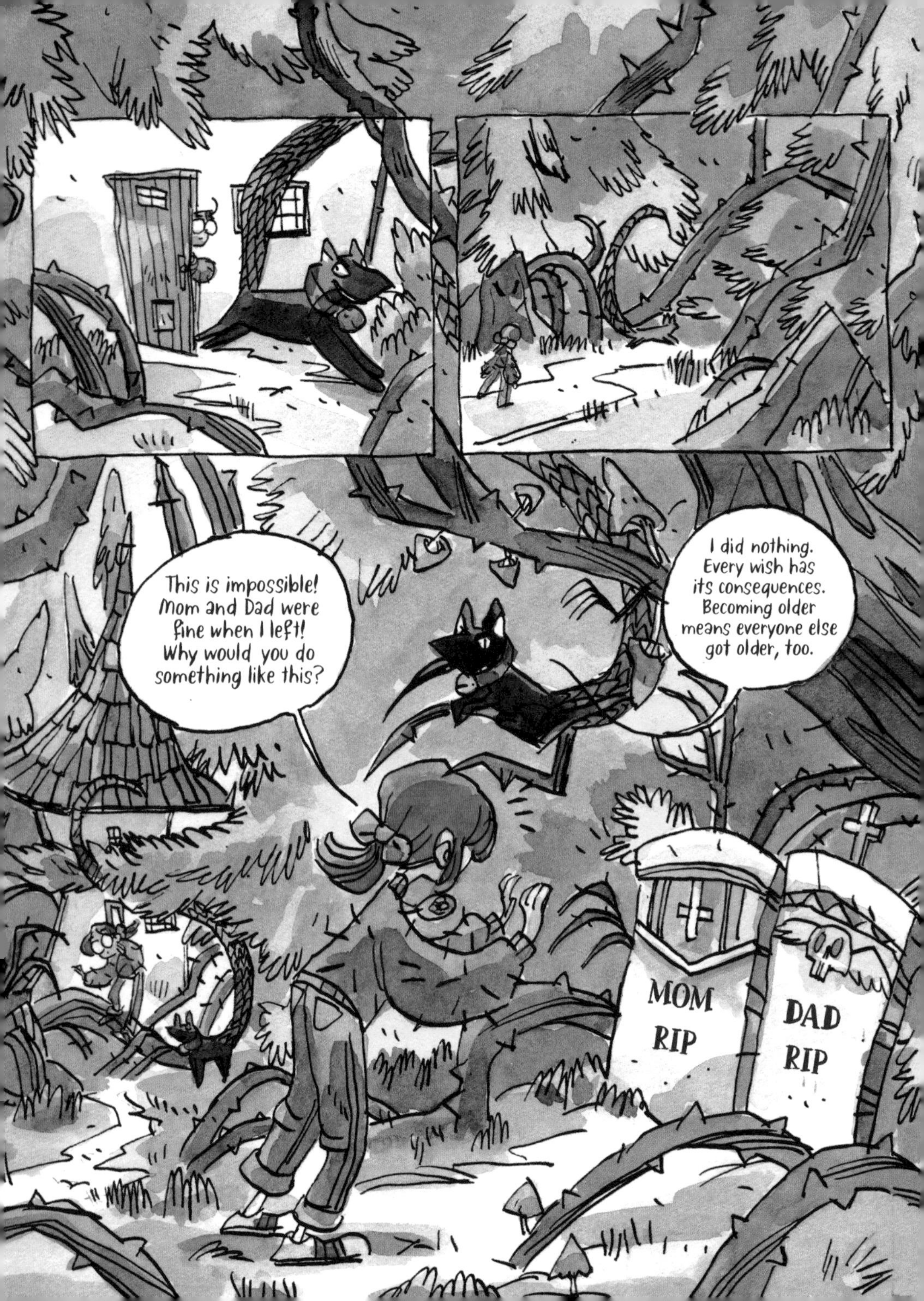
This is impossible! Mom and Dad were fine when I left! Why would you do something like this?
I did nothing. Every wish has its consequences. Becoming older means everyone else got older, too.
MOM RIP
DAD RIP

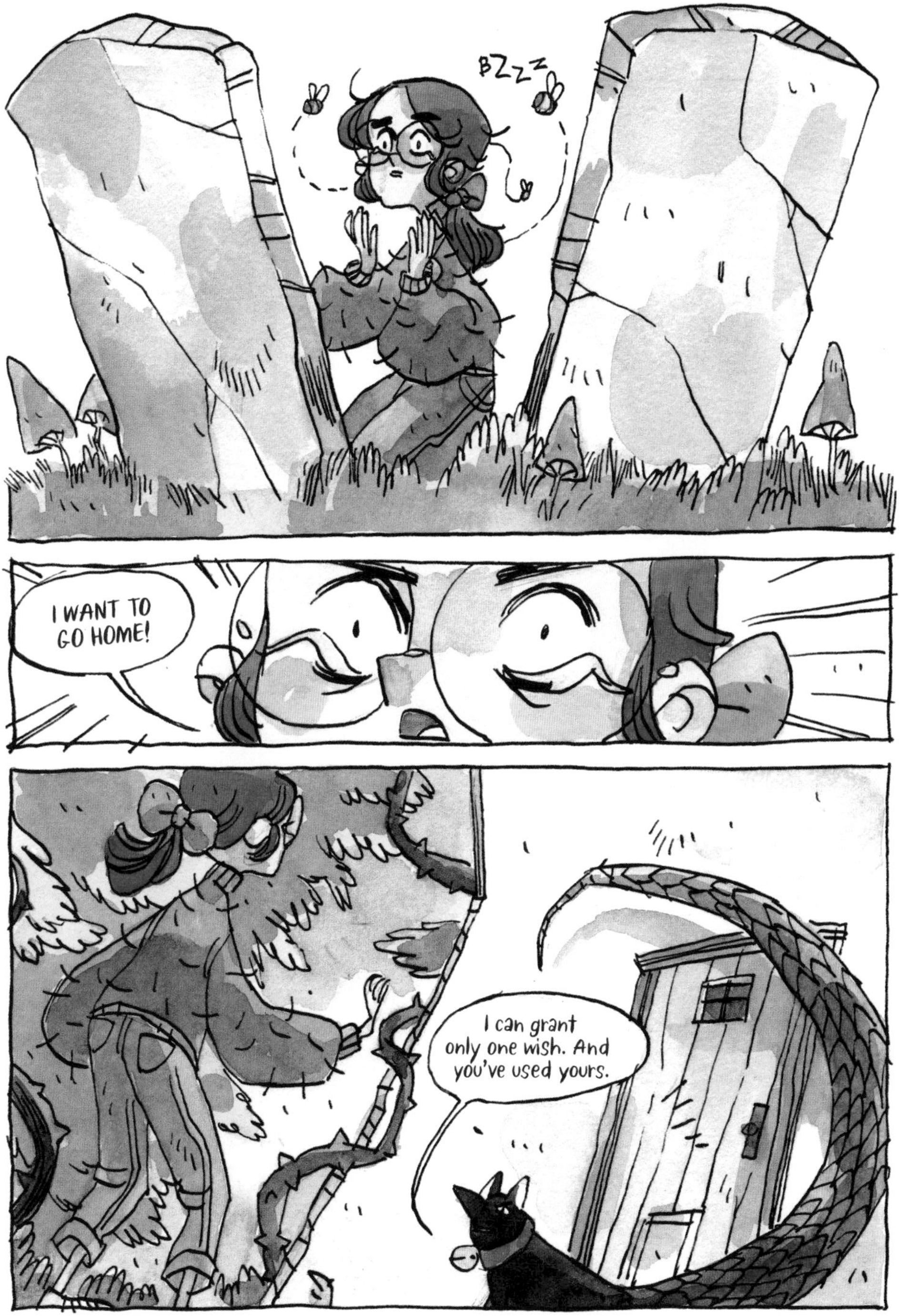
BZZZ
I WANT TO GO HOME!
I can grant only one wish. And you've used yours.

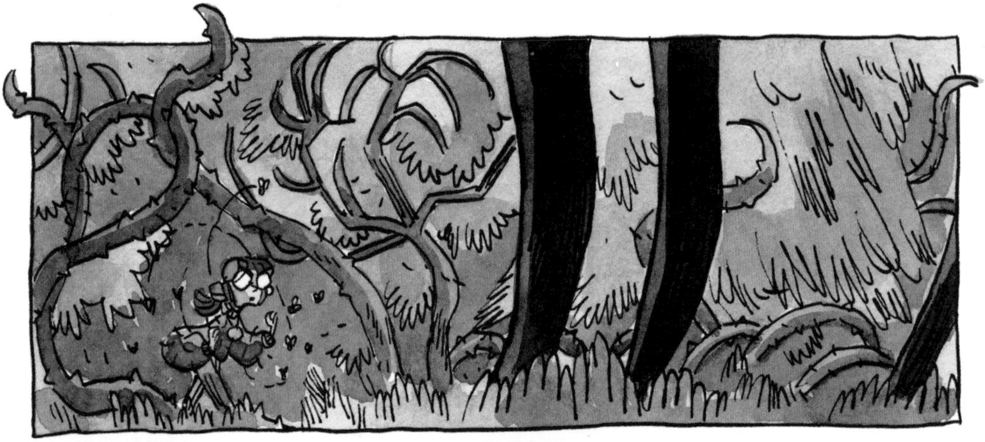

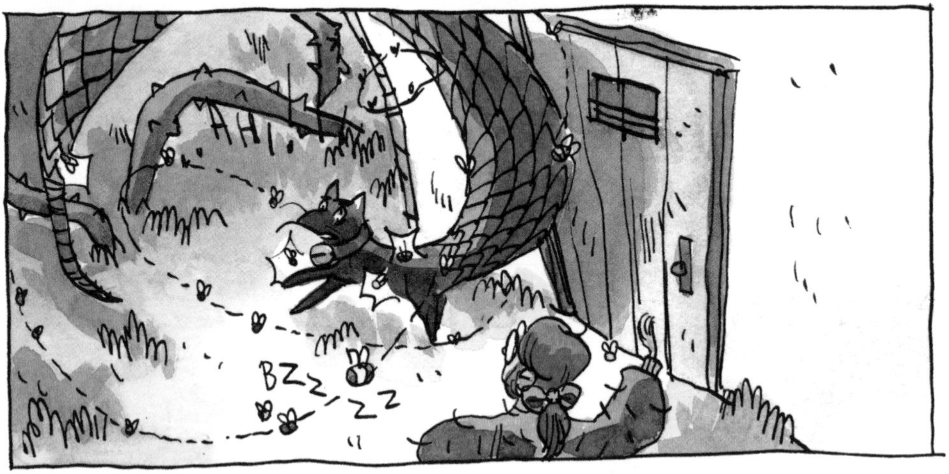
AH!
BZZZZZ

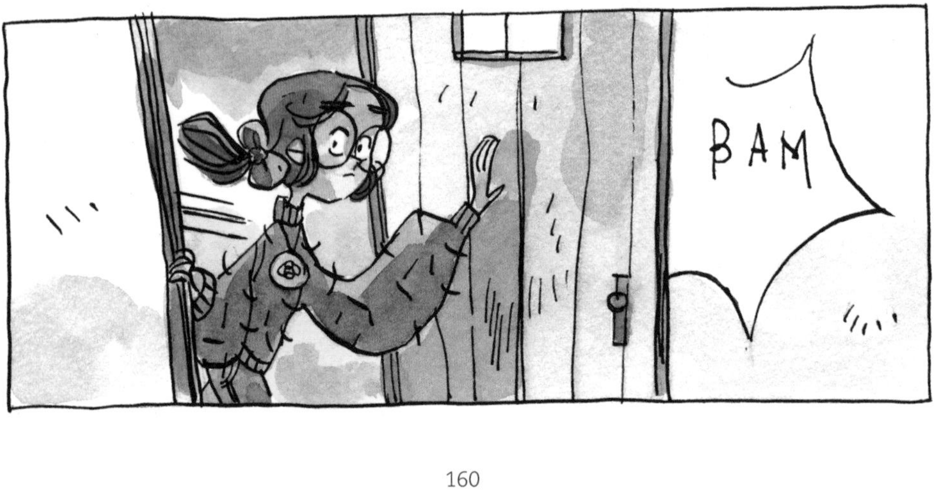
BAM

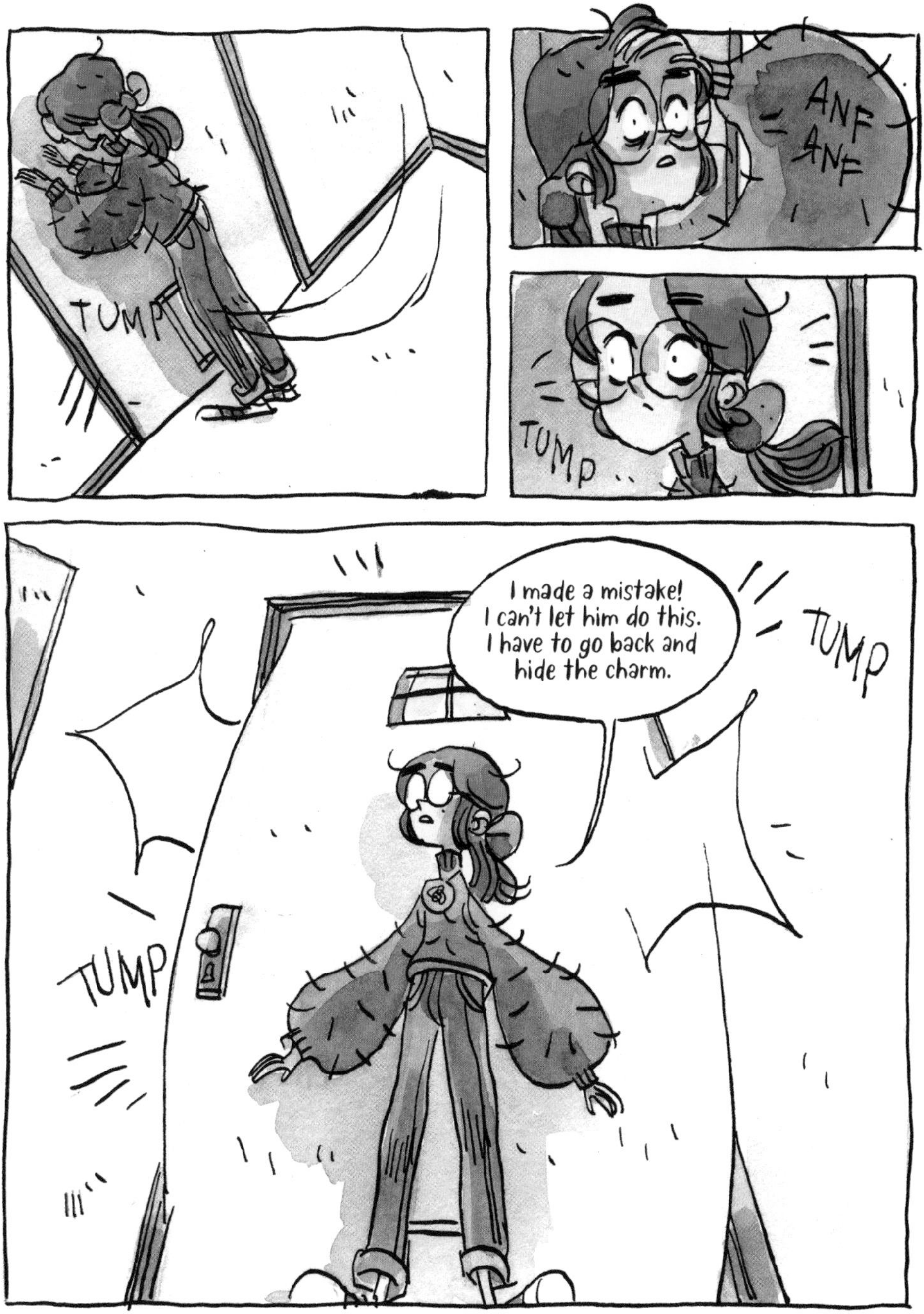
TUMP
ANF ANF
TUMP...
I made a mistake! I can't let him do this. I have to go back and hide the charm.
TUMP
TUMP

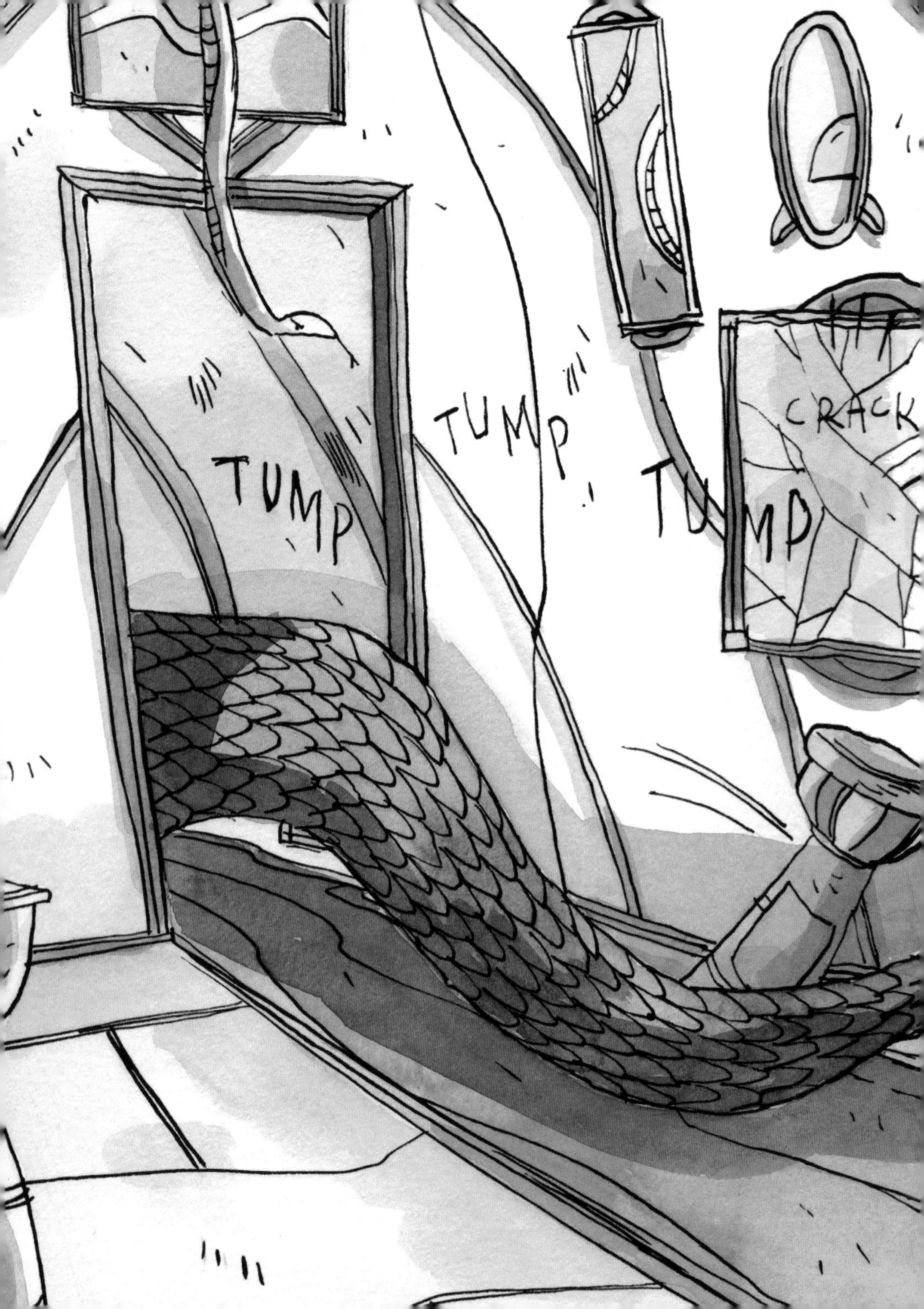
TUMP
TUMP
TUMP
TUMP
CRACK

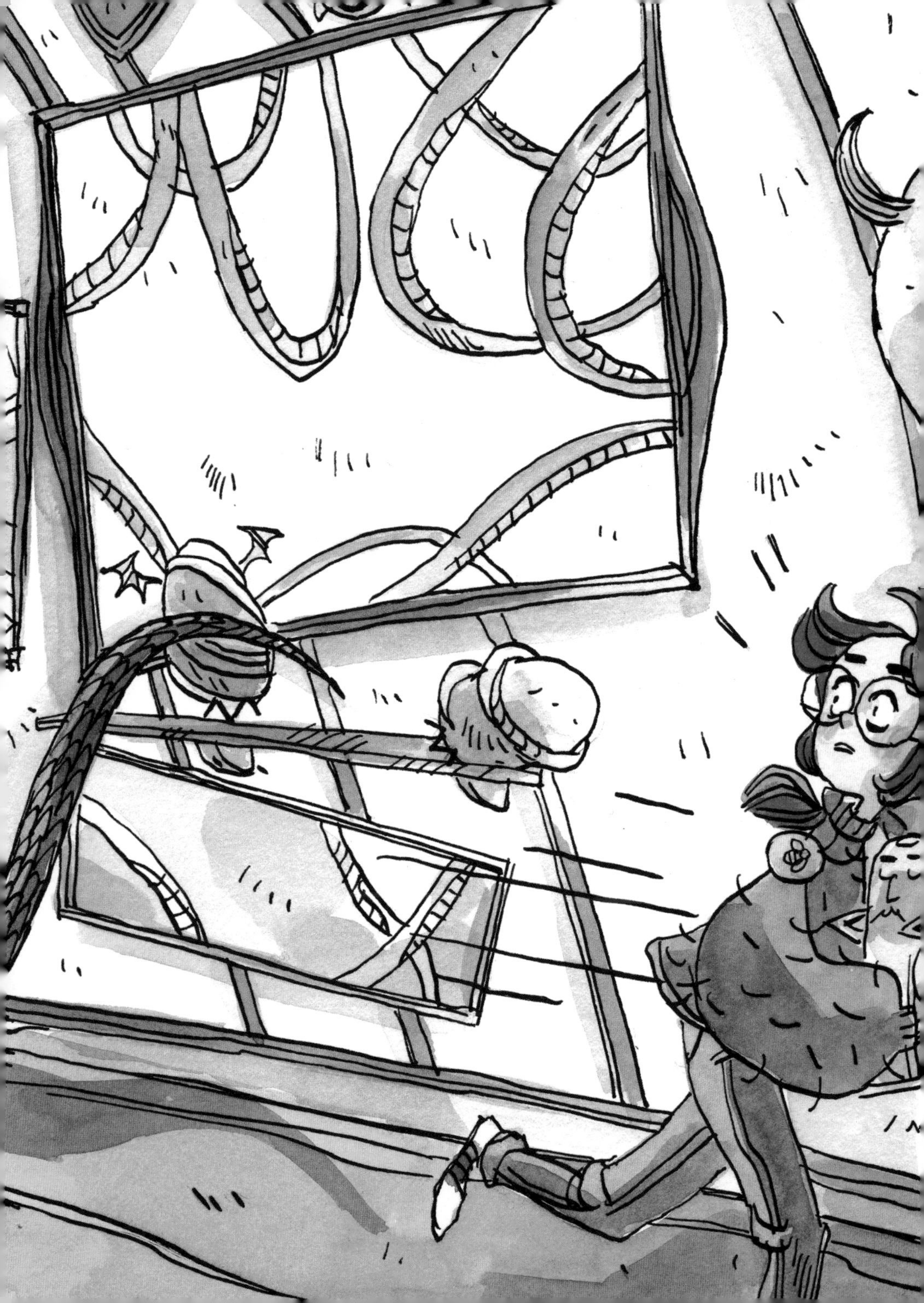

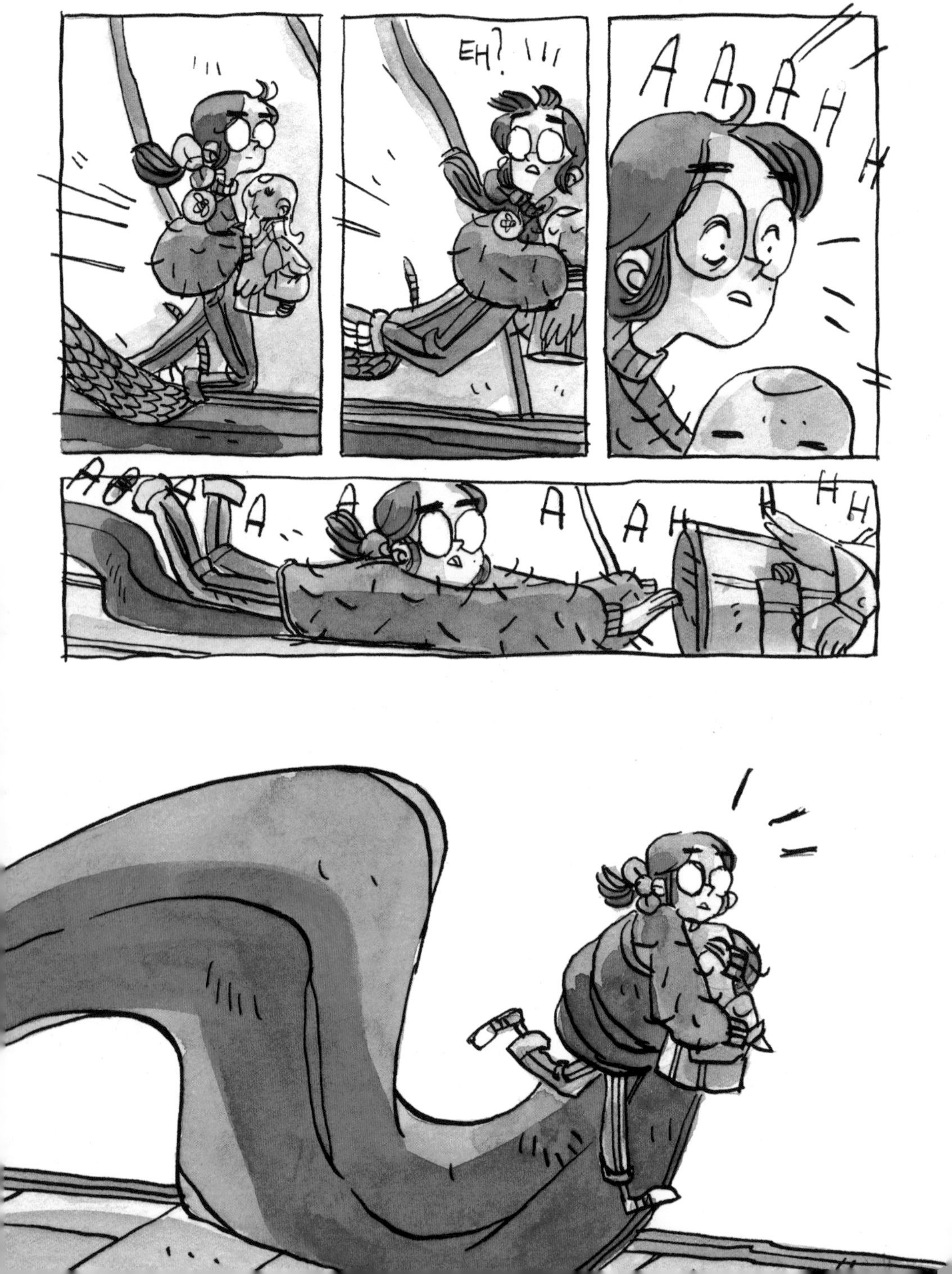
EH?
AAAHH
AAAAAAAAHHH

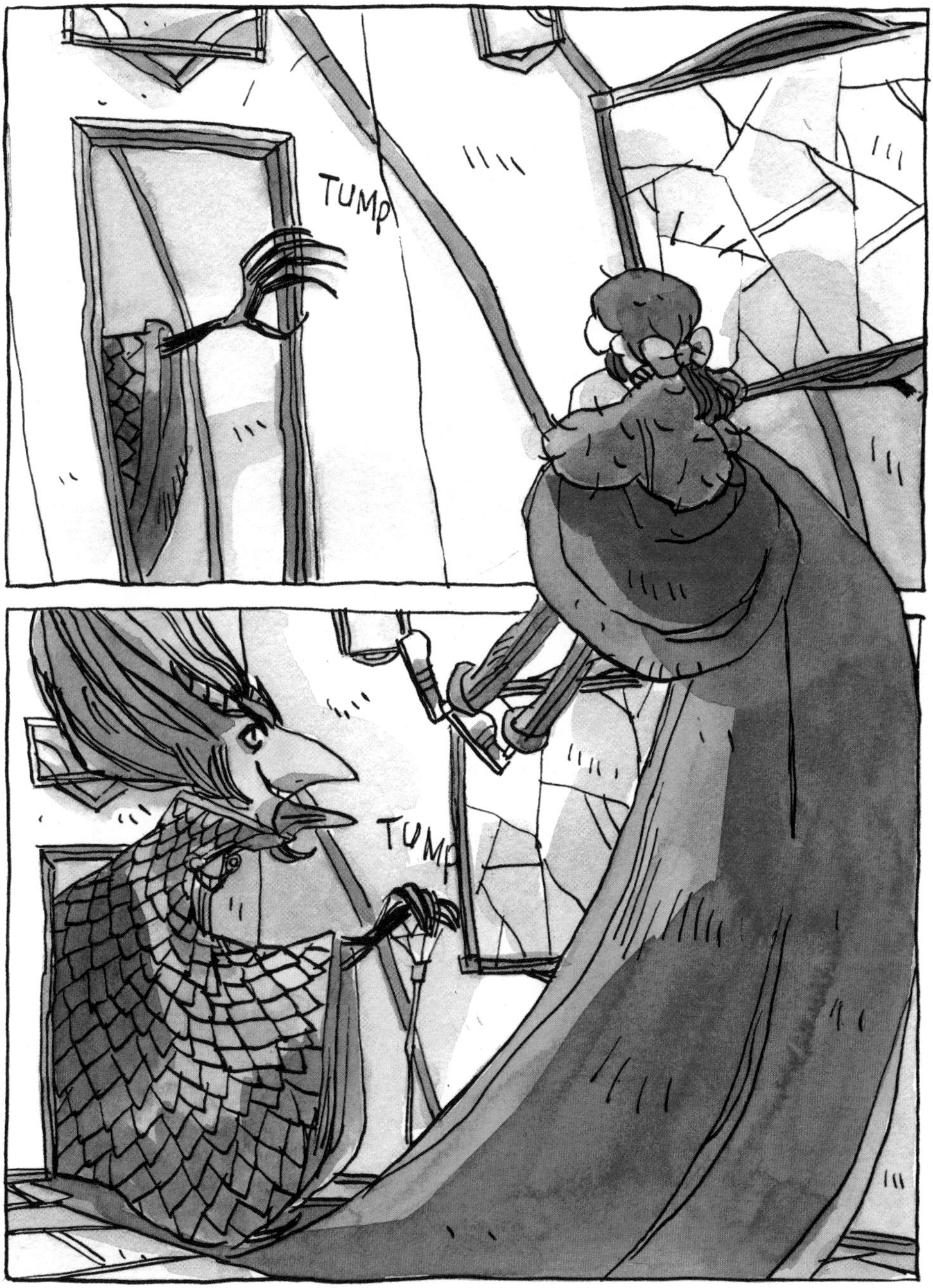
TUMP
TUMP

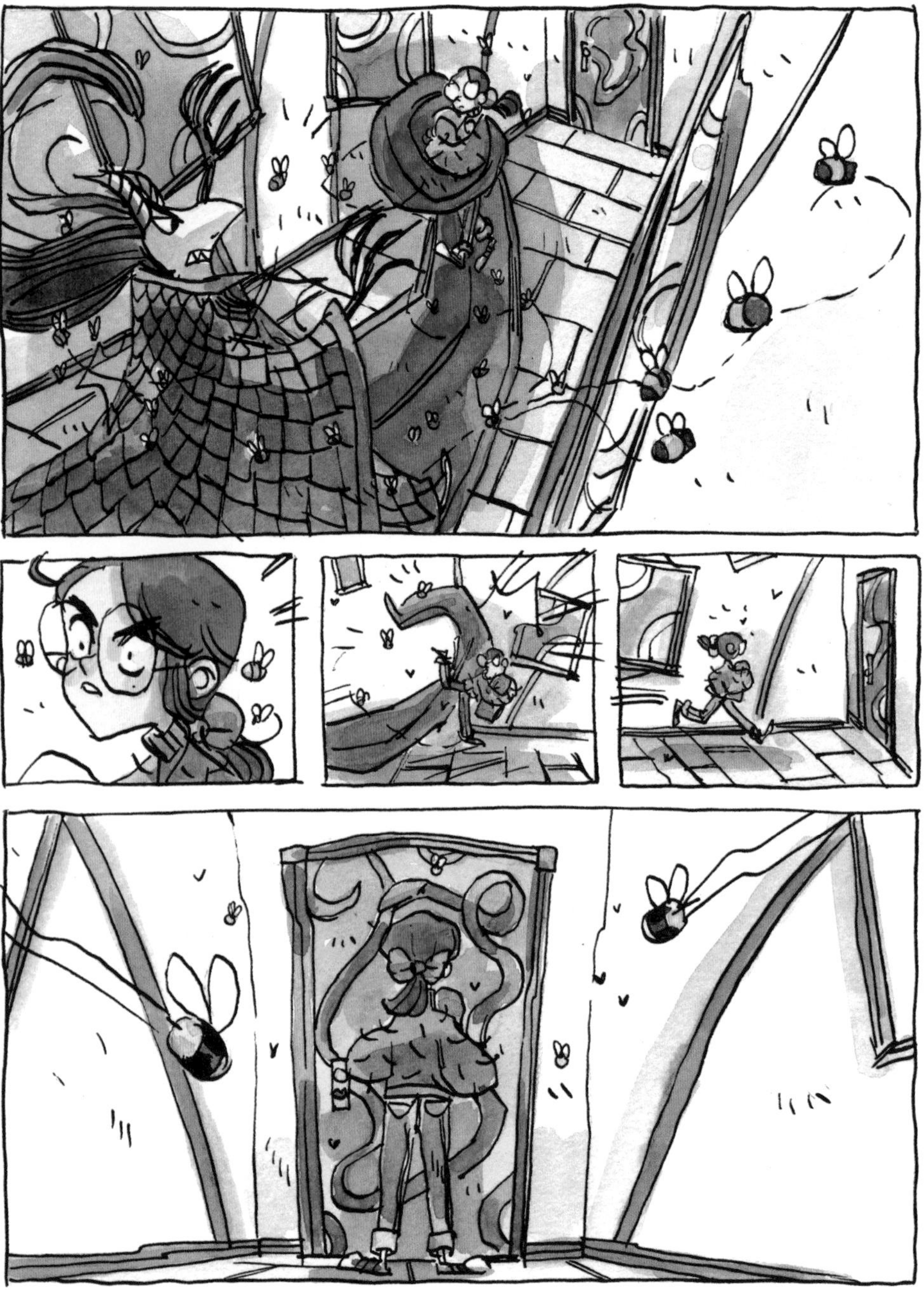

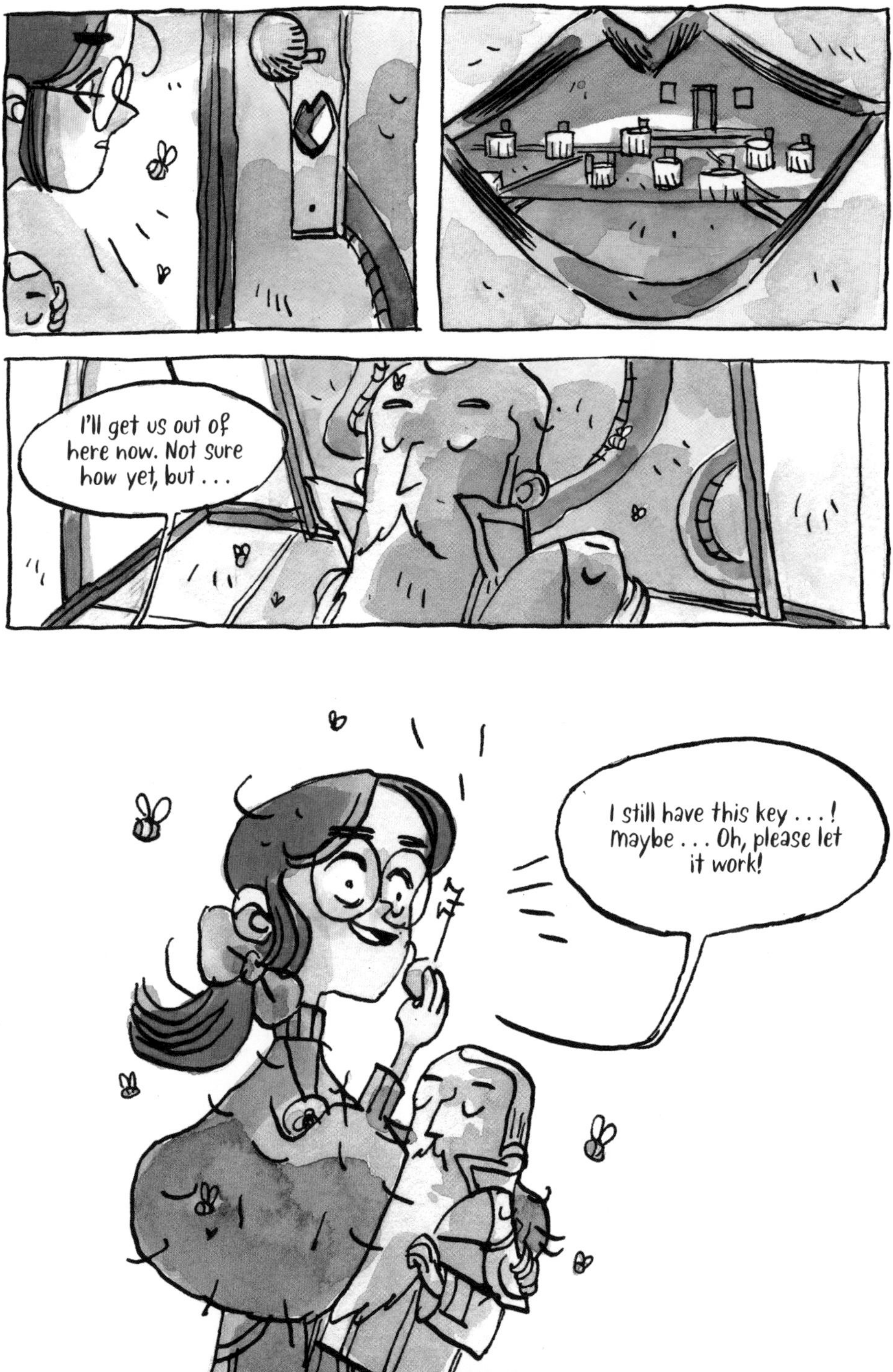
I'll get us out of here now. Not sure how yet, but . . .
I still have this key . . . ! maybe . . . Oh, please let it work!

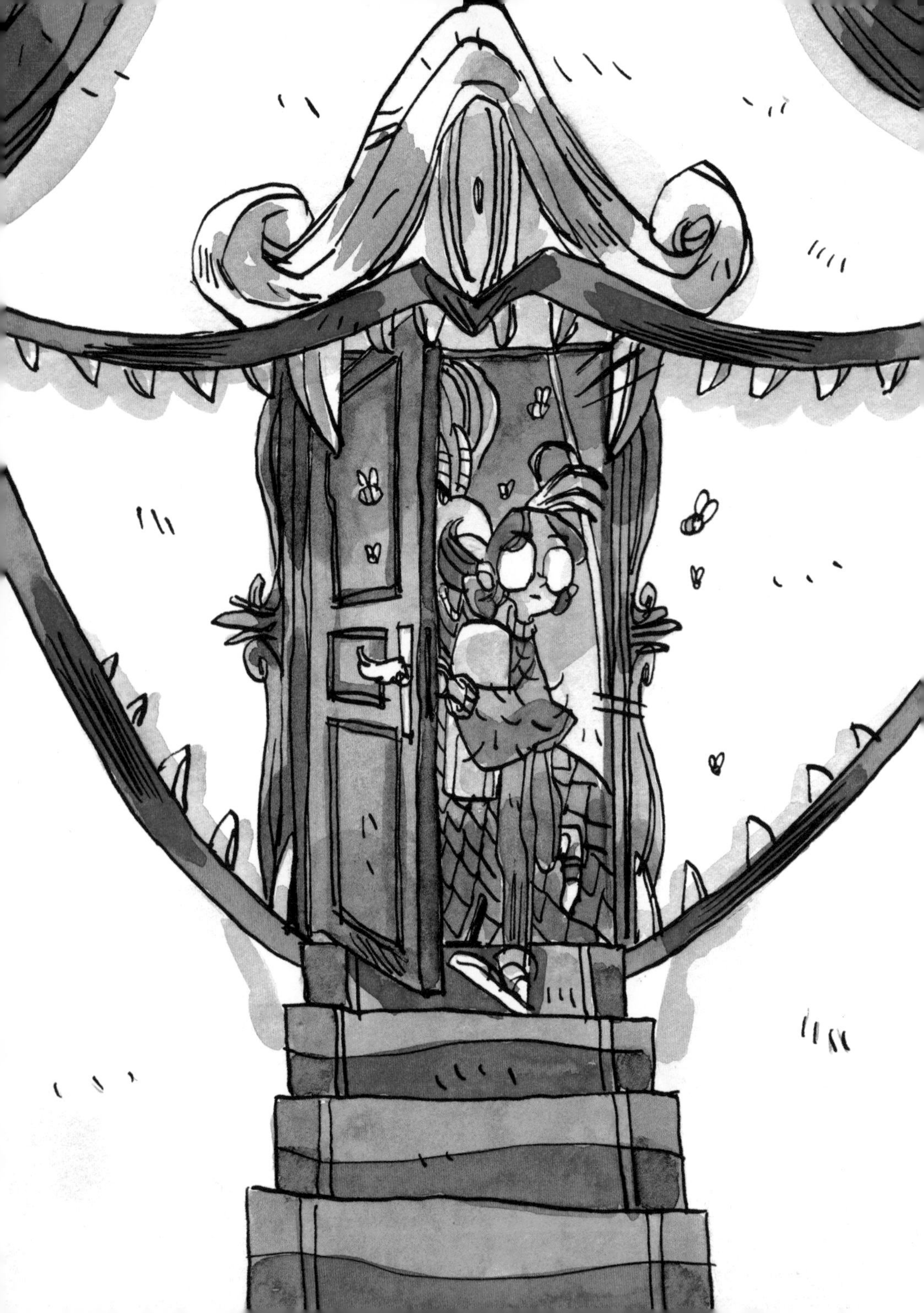

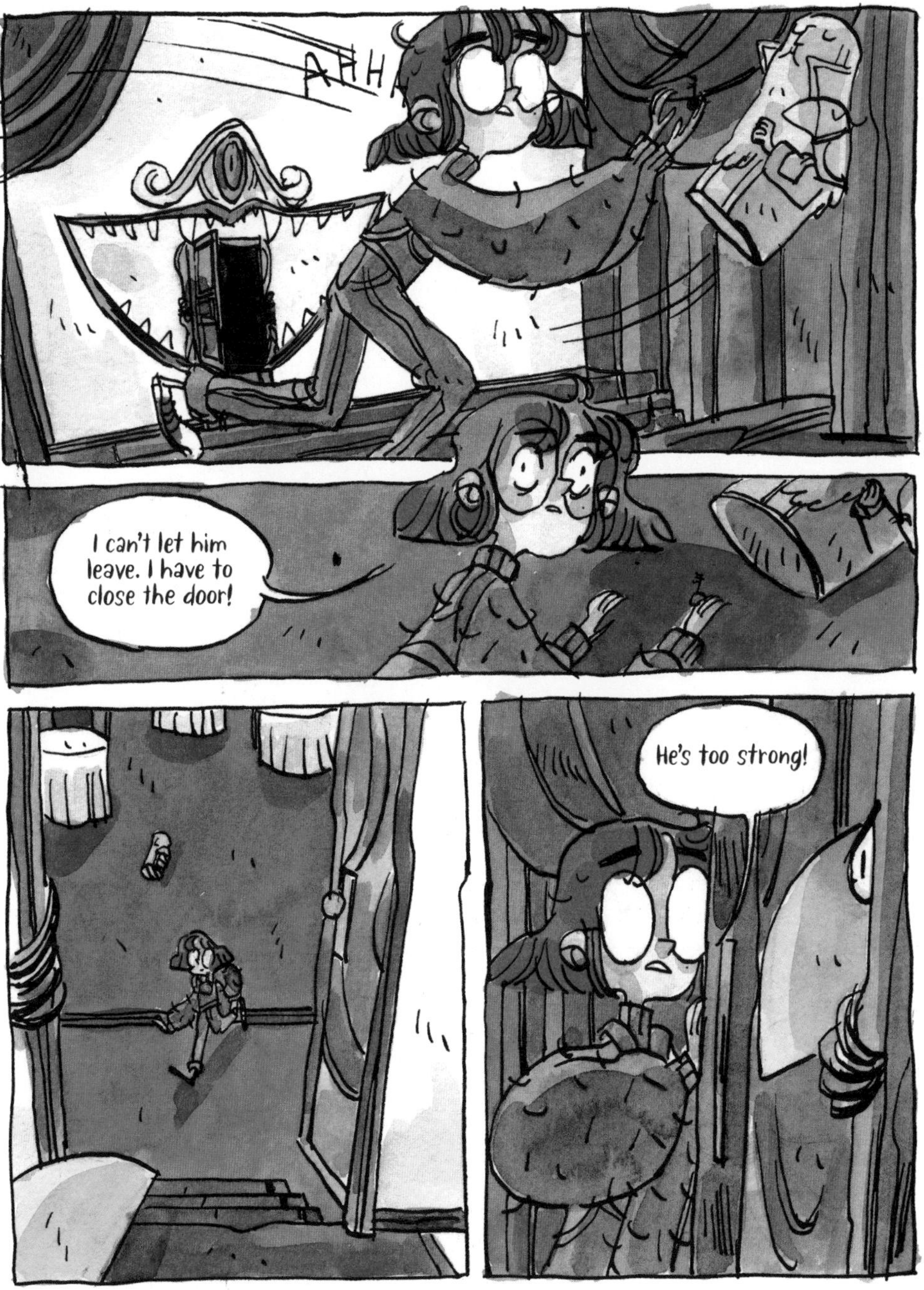
AHH
I can't let him leave. I have to close the door!
He's too strong!

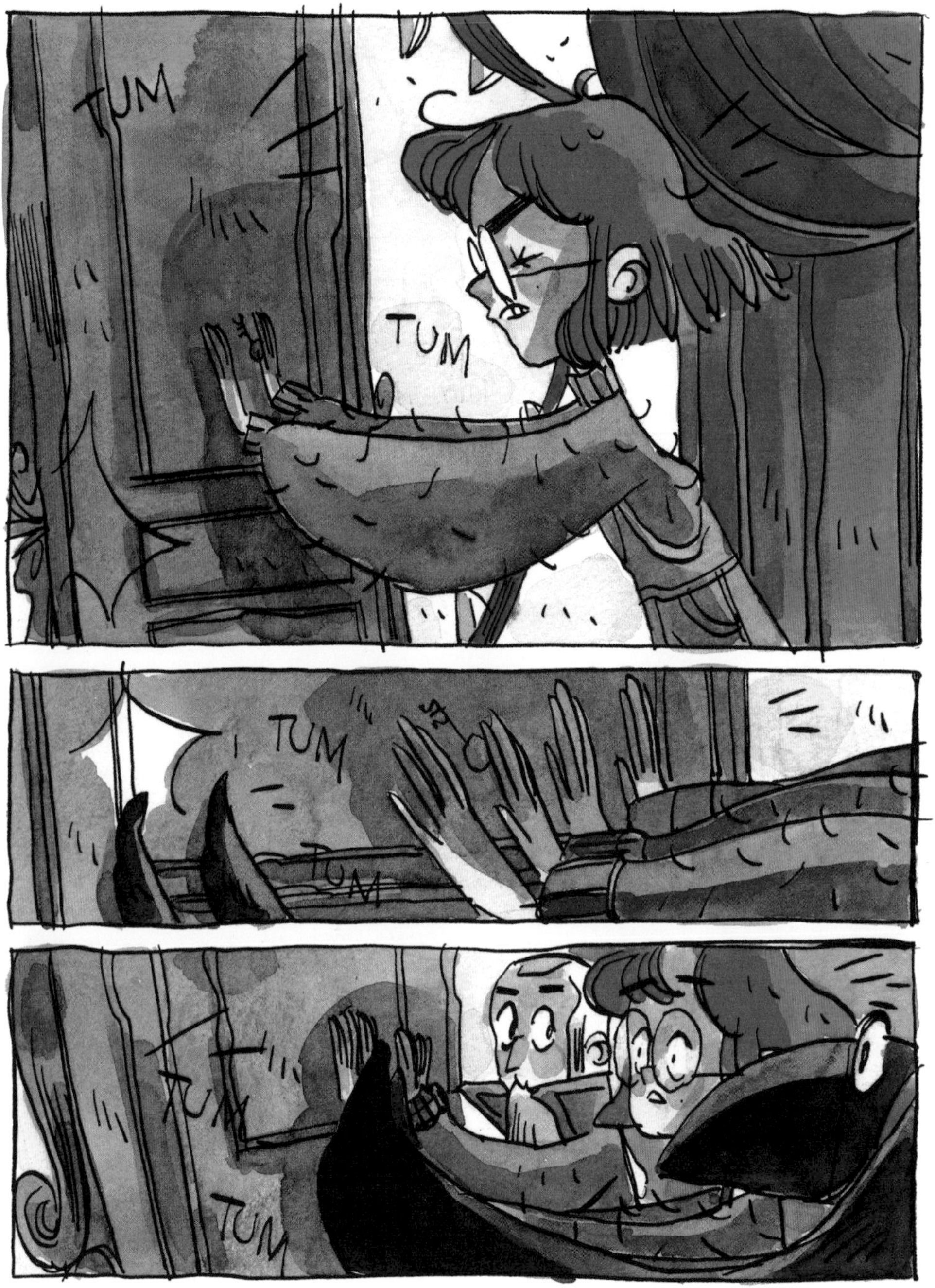
TUM
TUM
TUM
TUM
TUM
TUM

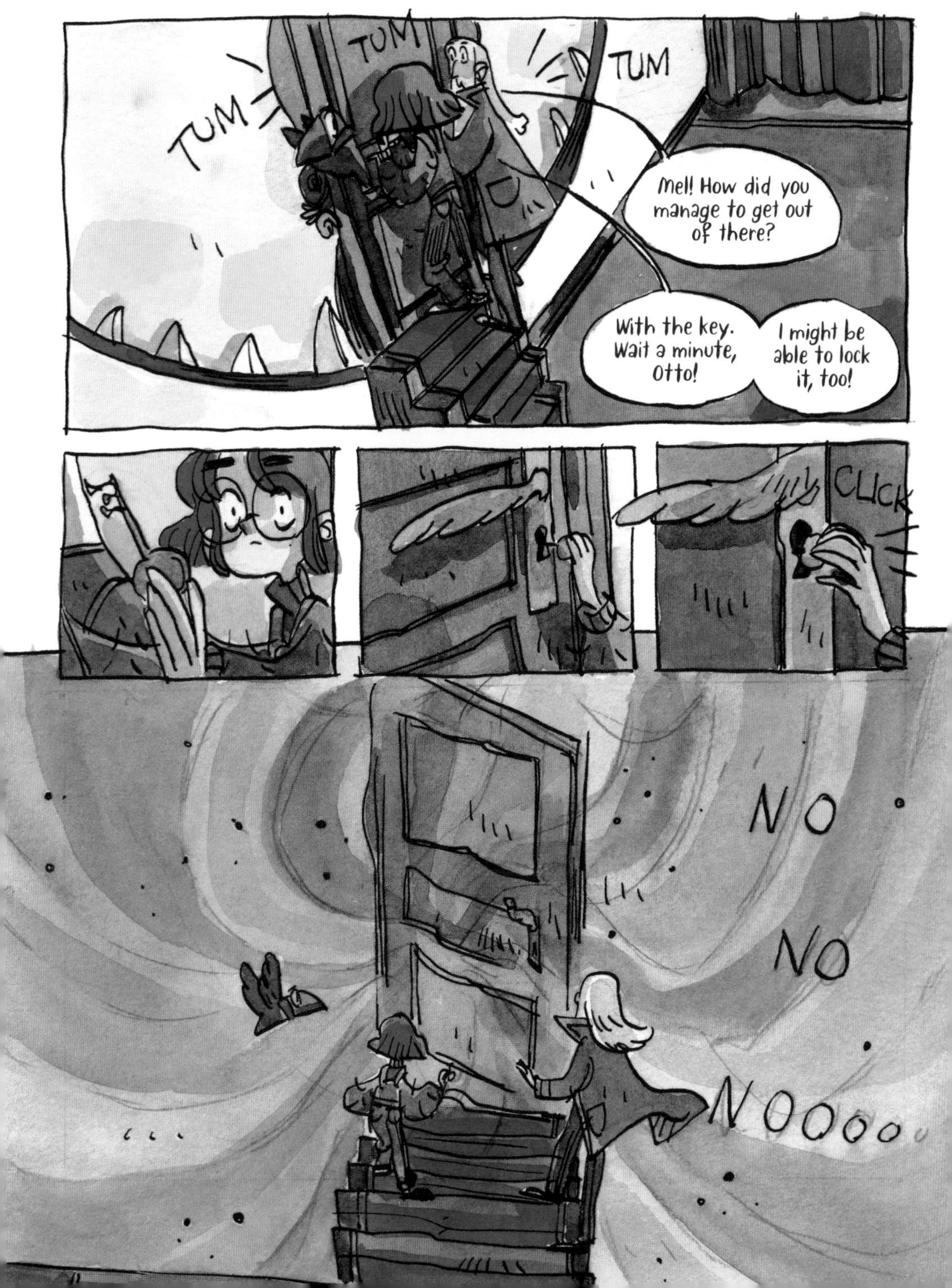
TUM
TUM
TUM
Mel! How did you manage to get out of there?
With the key. Wait a minute, Otto!
I might be able to lock it, too!
CLICK
NO
NO
NOOOO

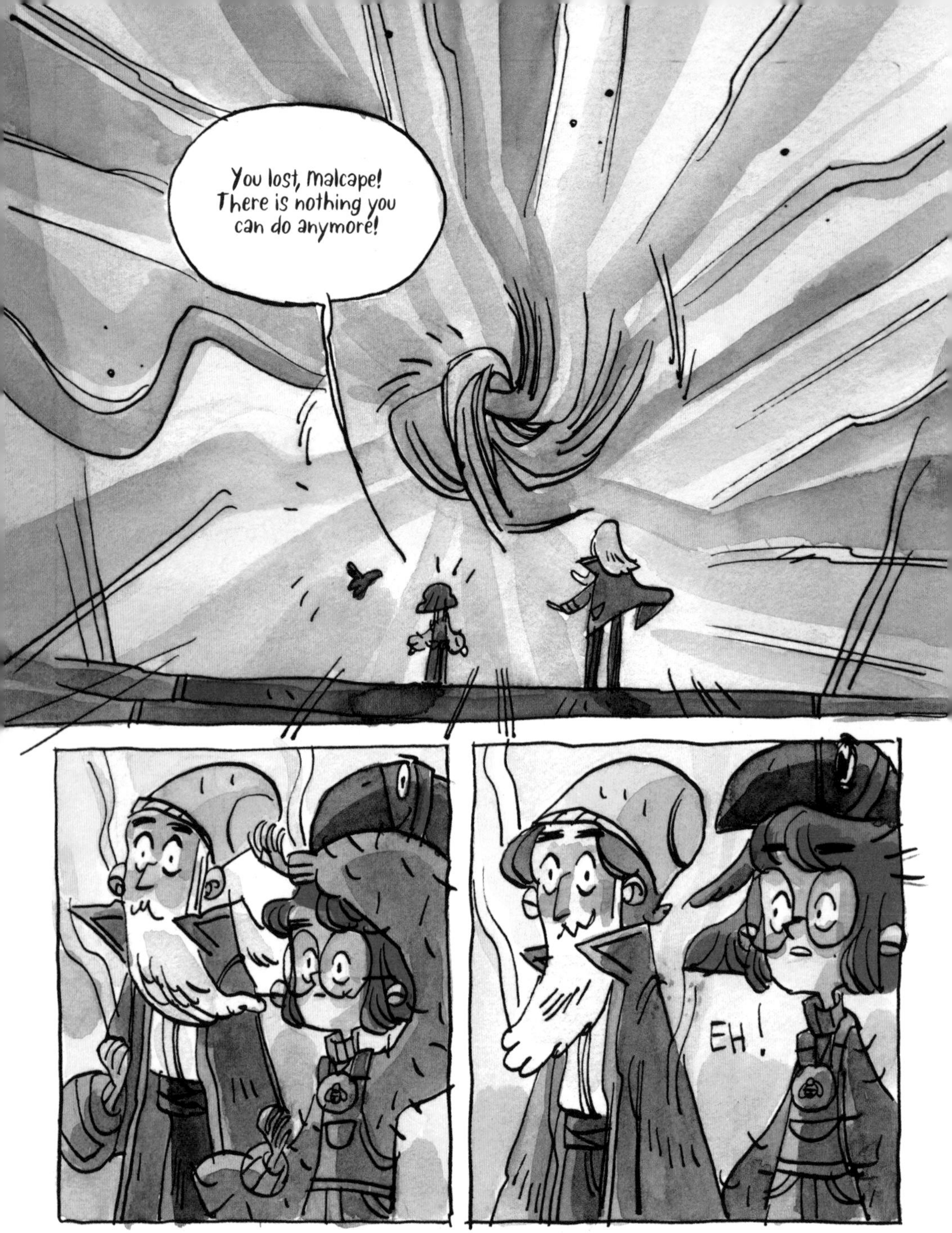
You lost, Malcape! There is nothing you can do anymore!
EH!

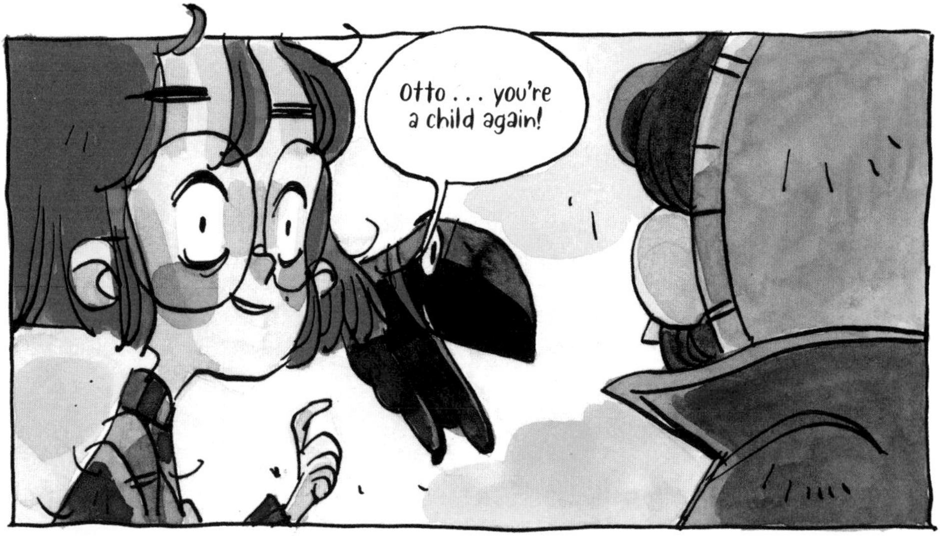

Otto . . . you're
a child again!

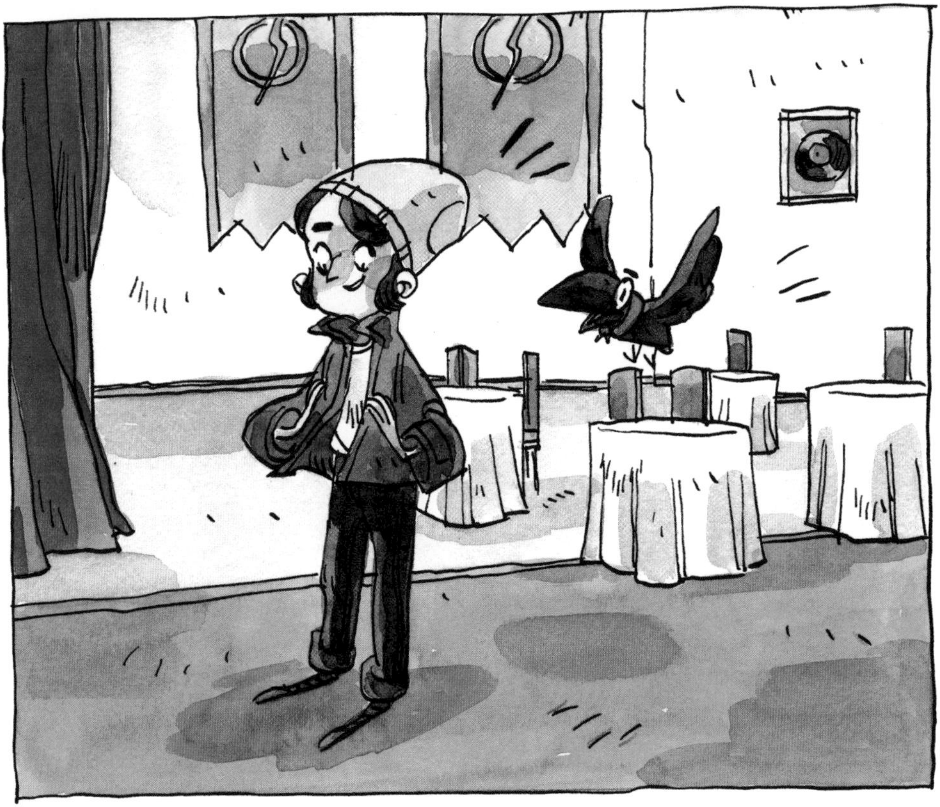

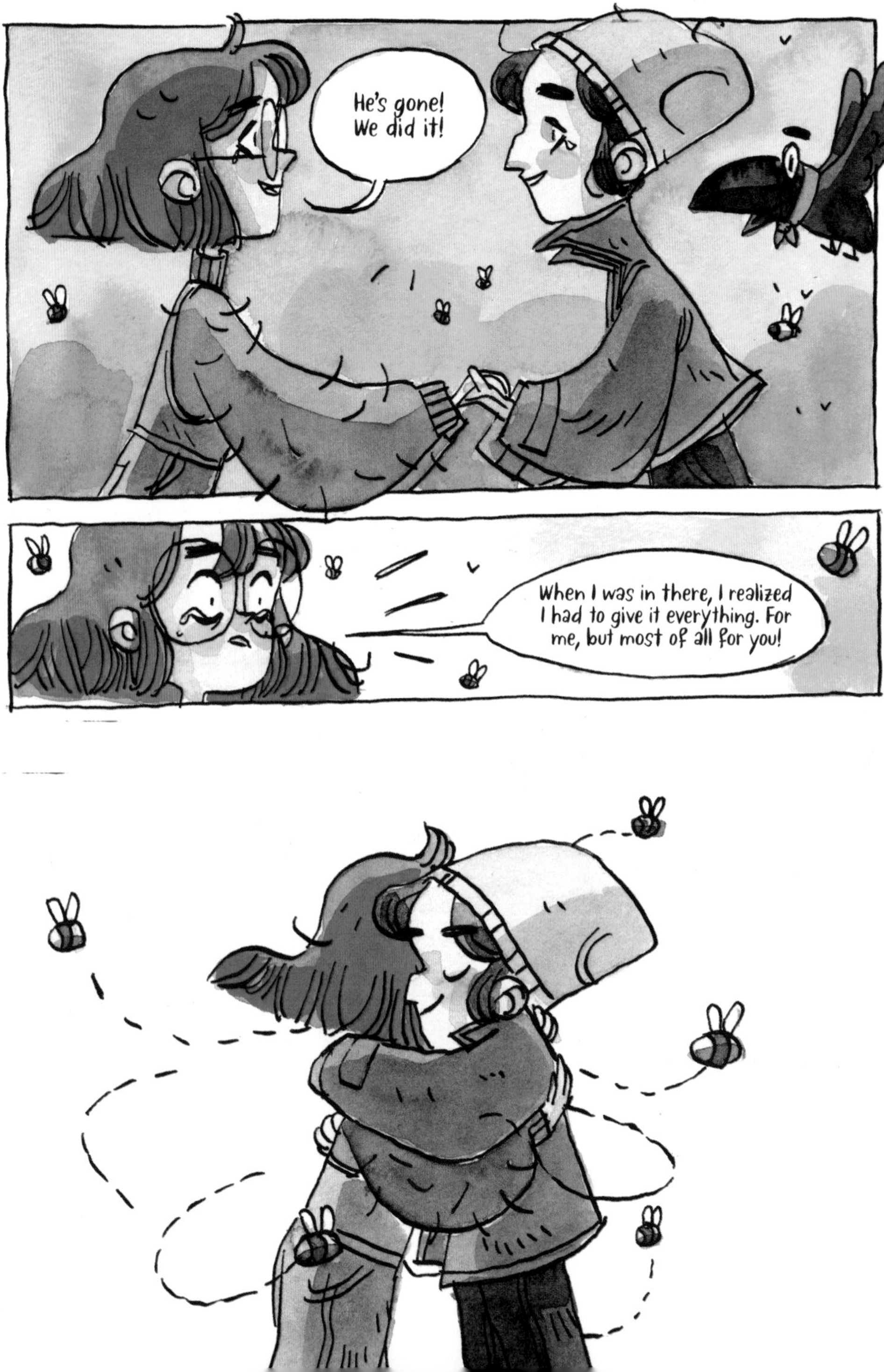
He's gone! We did it!
When I was in there, I realized I had to give it everything. For me, but most of all for you!

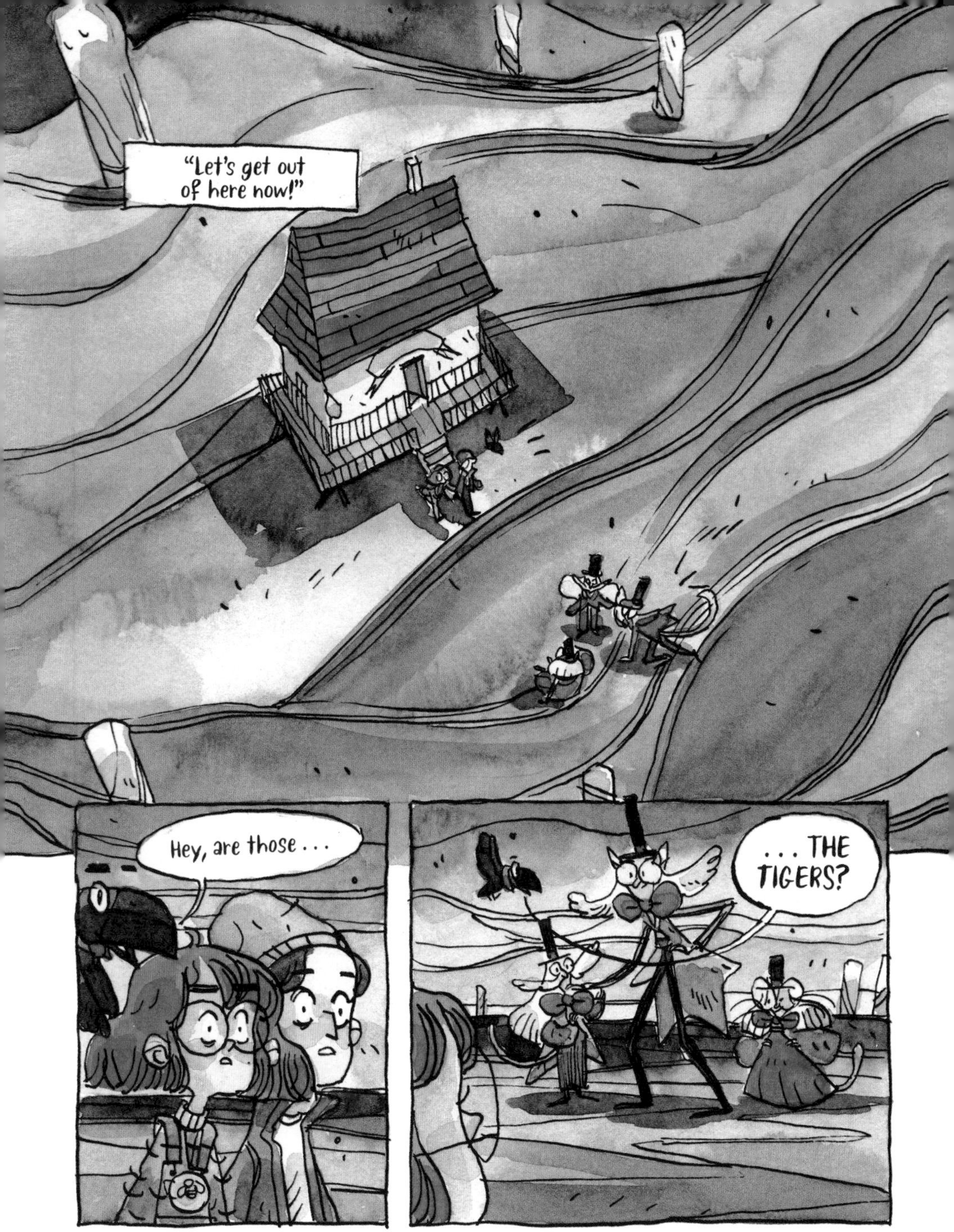
"Let's get out of here now!"
Hey, are those . . .
. . . THE TIGERS?

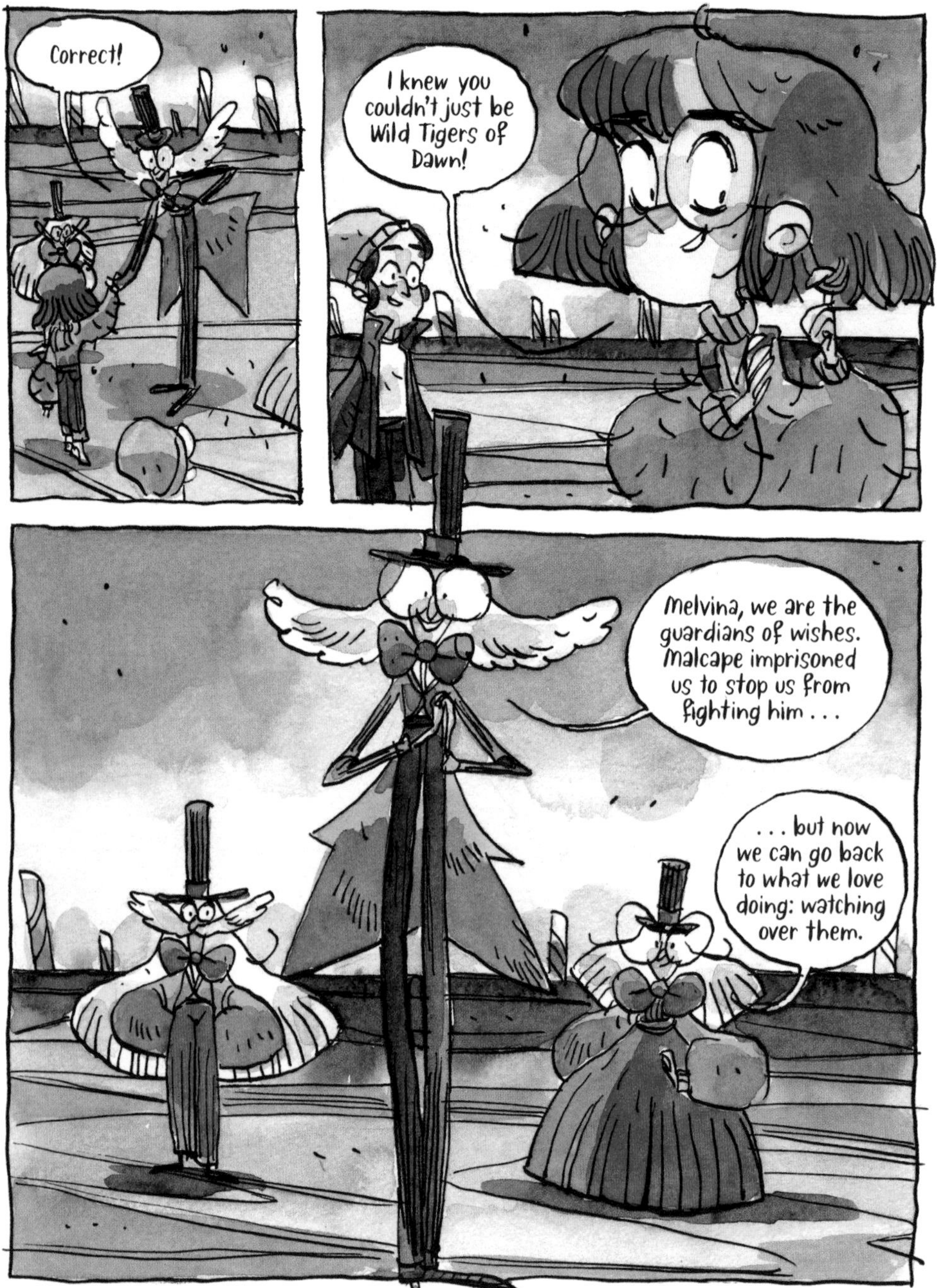
Correct!
I knew you couldn't just be Wild Tigers of Dawn!
Melvina, we are the guardians of wishes. Malcape imprisoned us to stop us from fighting him . . .
. . . but now we can go back to what we love doing: watching over them.

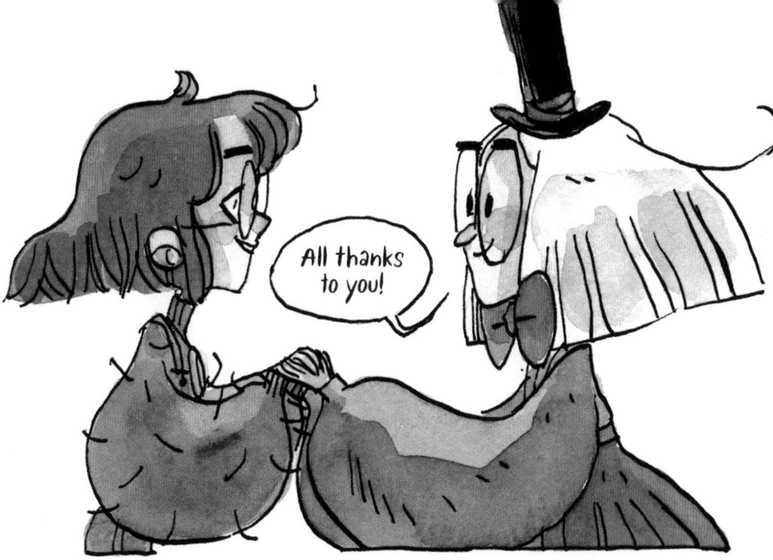
All thanks to you!

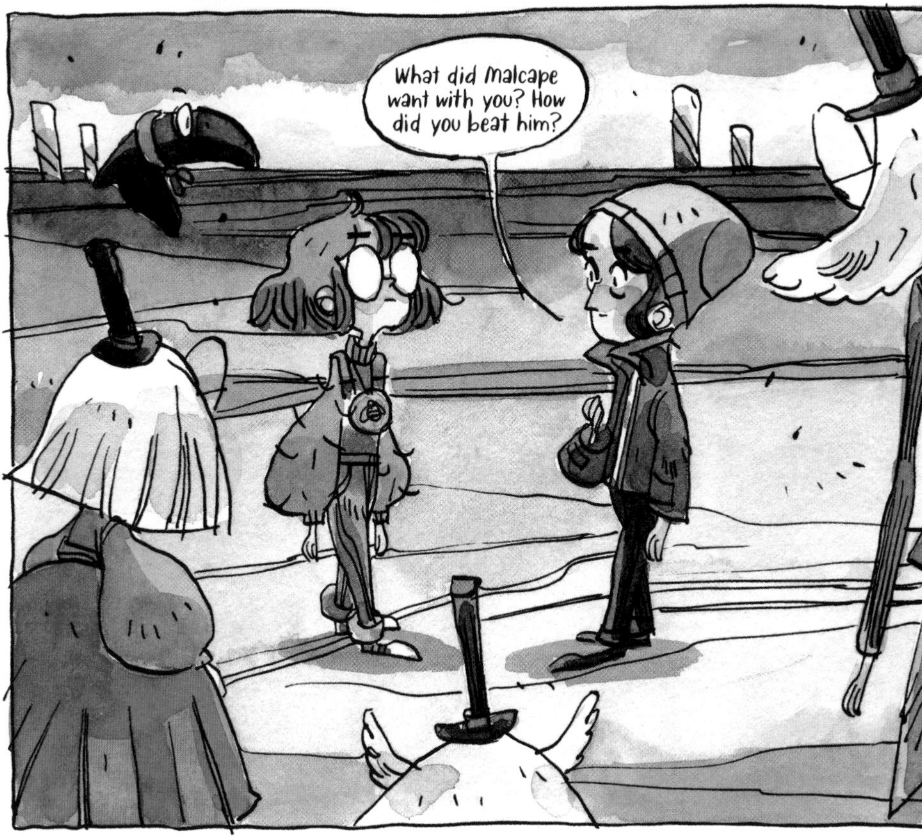
What did Malcape want with you? How did you beat him?

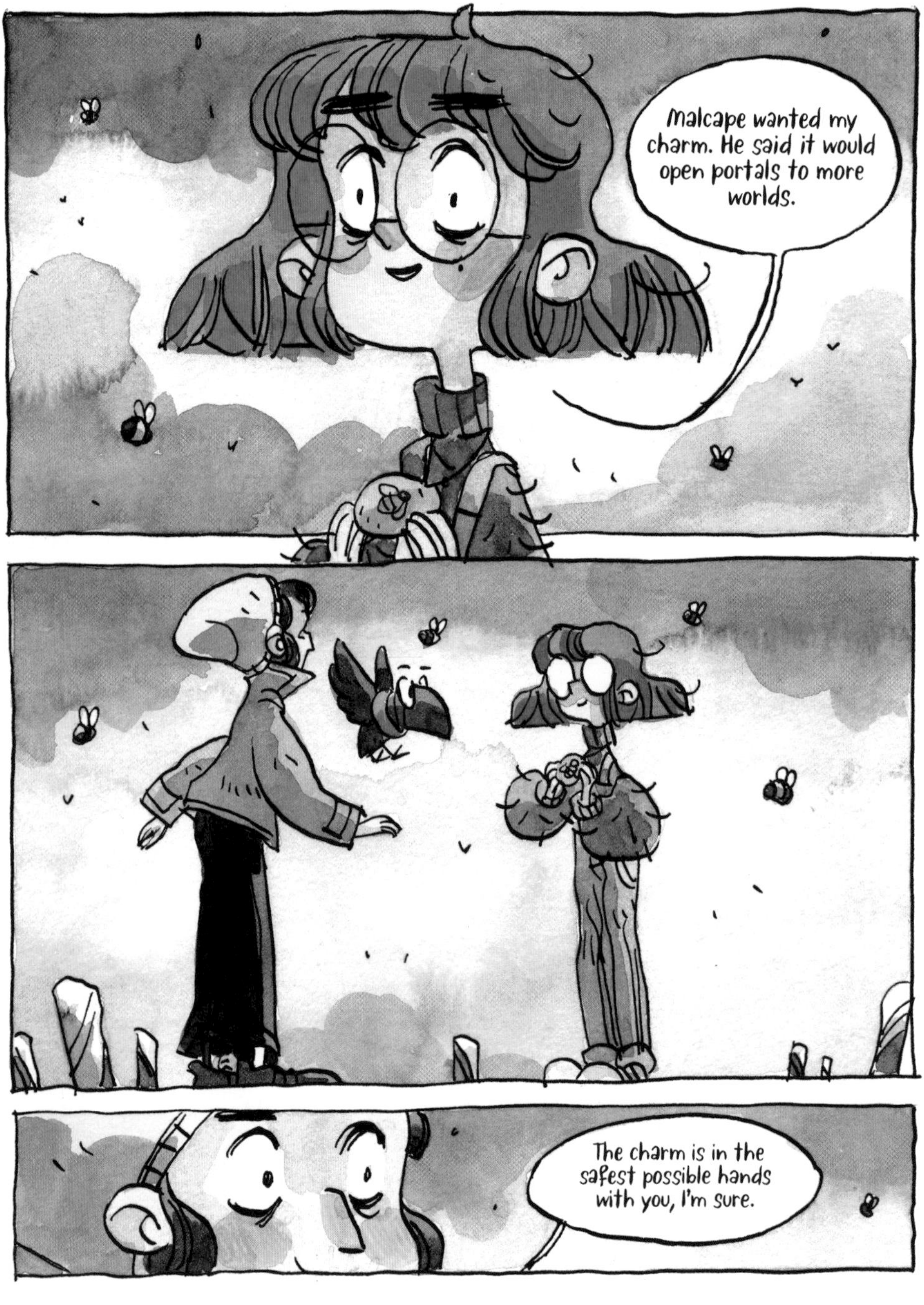
Malcape wanted my charm. He said it would open portals to more worlds.
The charm is in the safest possible hands with you, I'm sure.

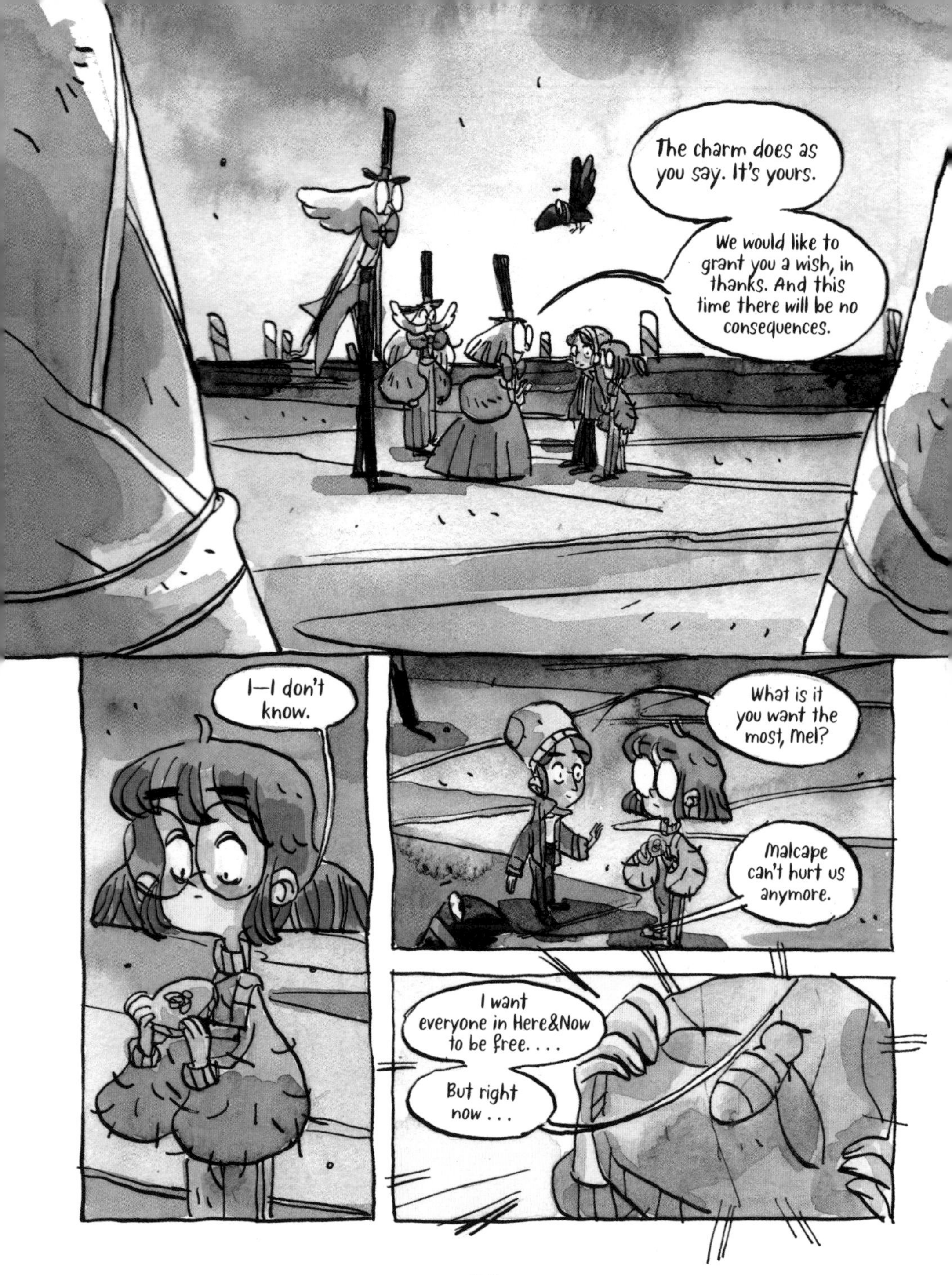
The charm does as you say. It's yours.
We would like to grant you a wish, in thanks. And this time there will be no consequences.
I—I don't know.
What is it you want the most, Mel?
Malcape can't hurt us anymore.
I want everyone in Here&Now to be free. . . .
But right now . . .

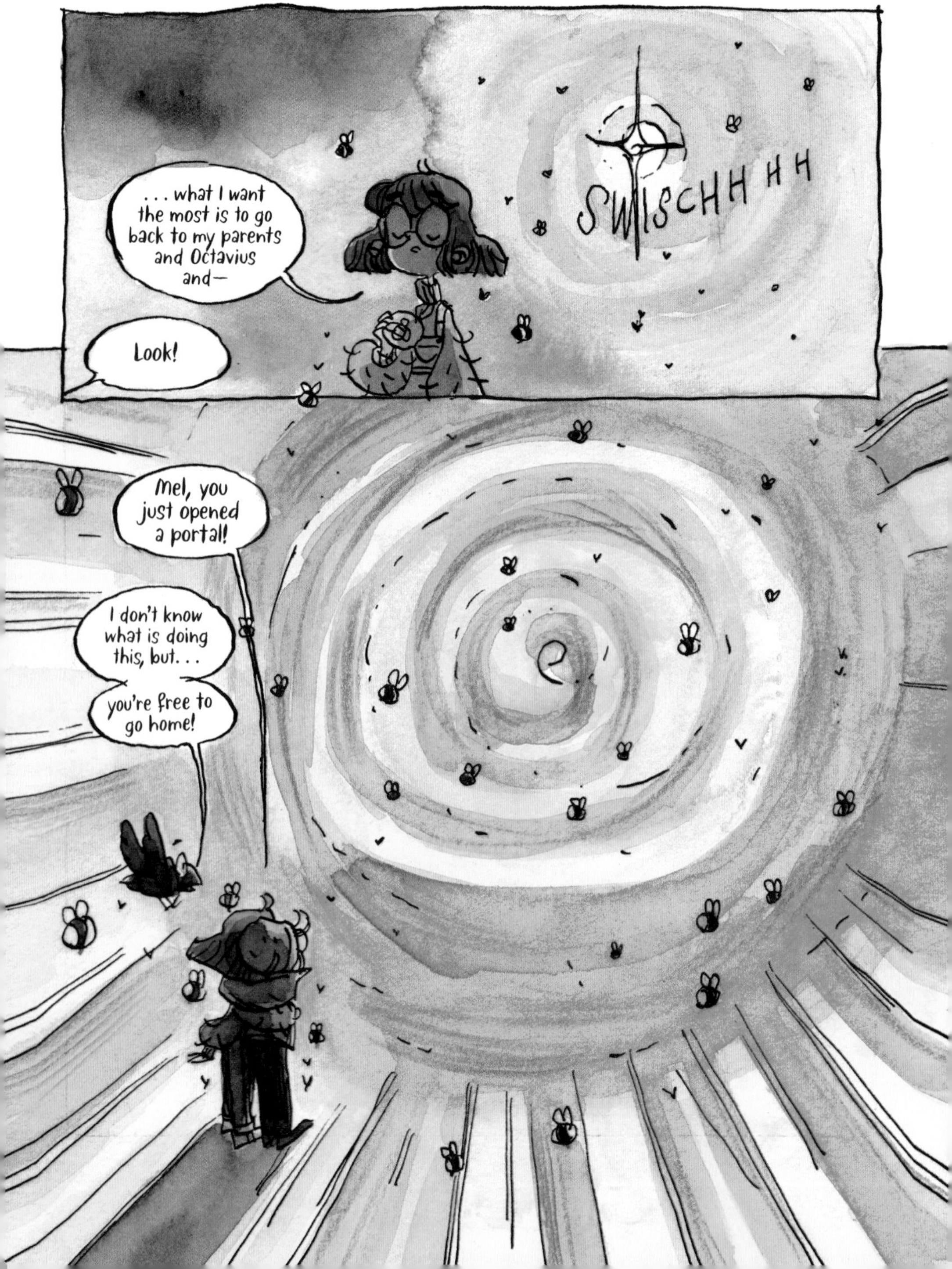
. . . what I want the most is to go back to my parents and Octavius and—
SWISCHHHH
Look!
Mel, you just opened a portal!
I don't know what is doing this, but. . .
you're free to go home!

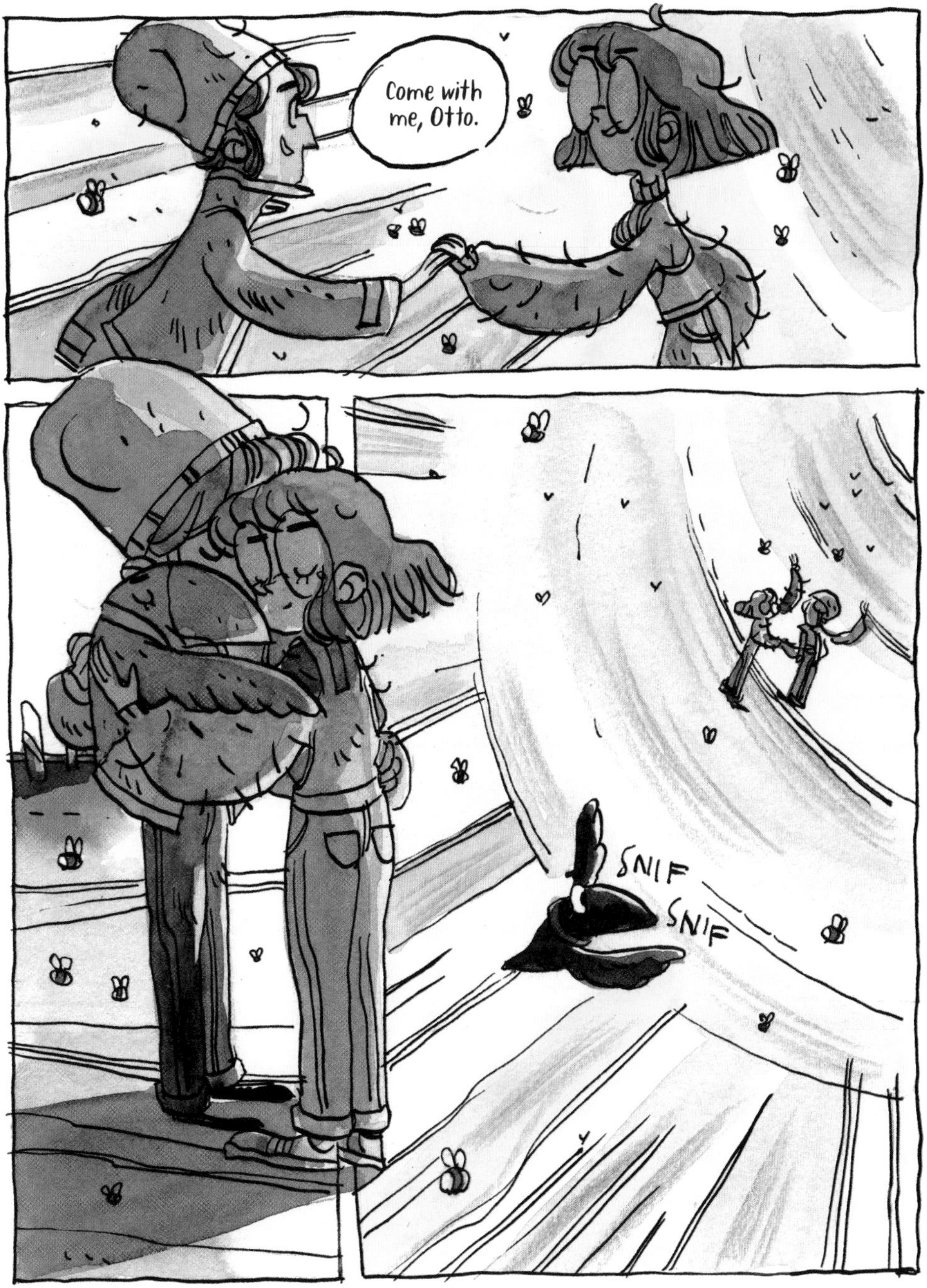
Come with me, Otto.
SNIF
SNIF

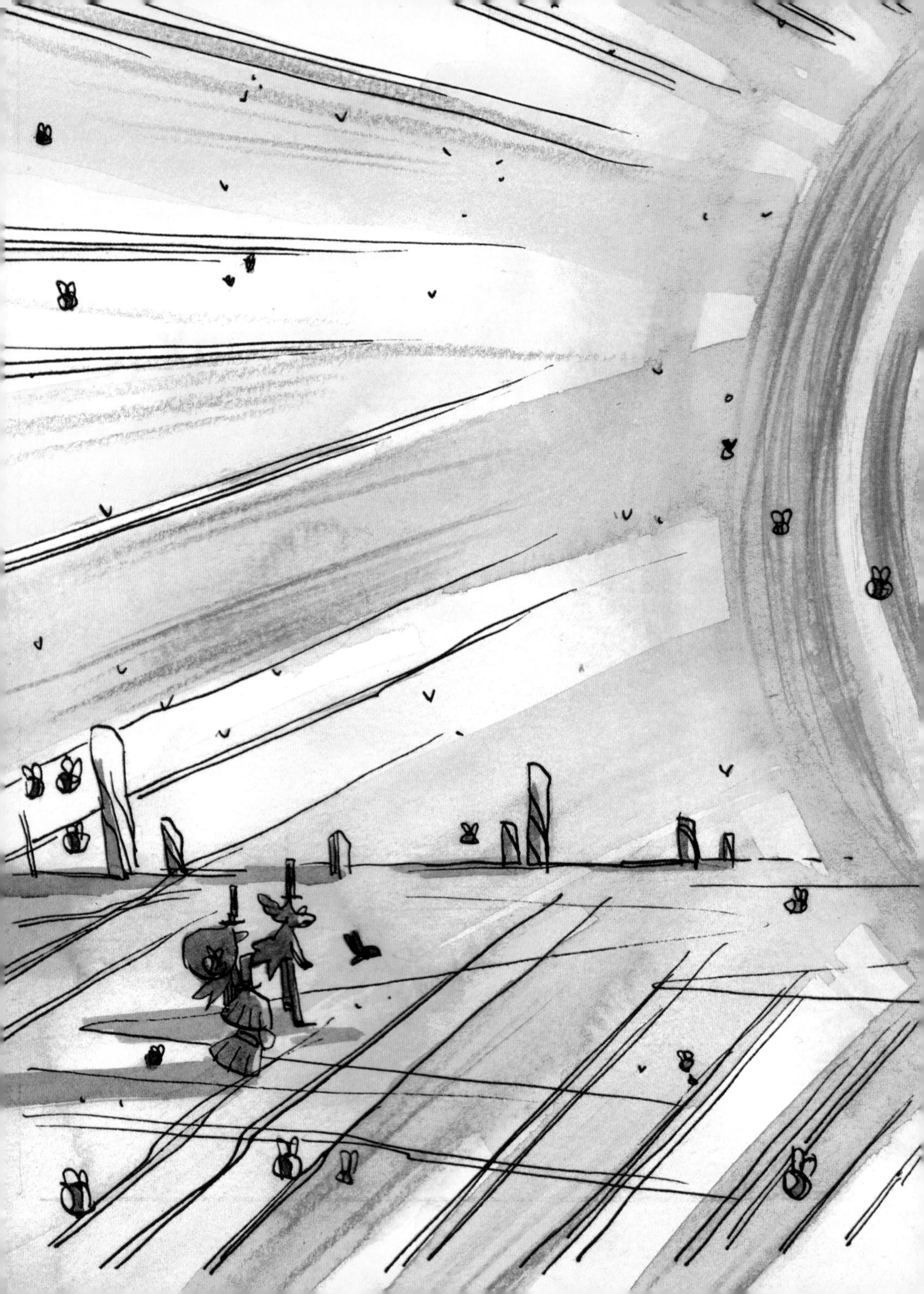

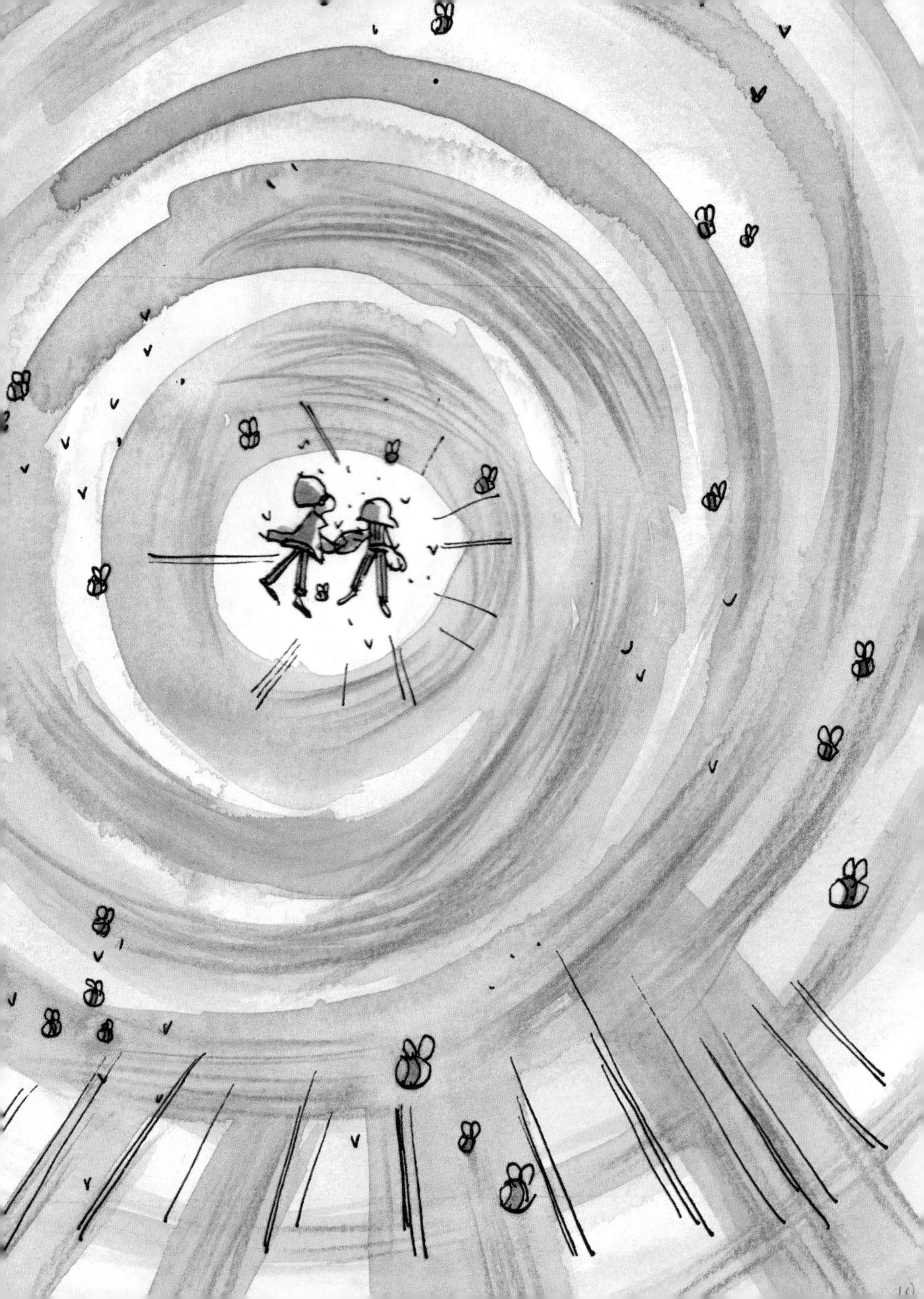

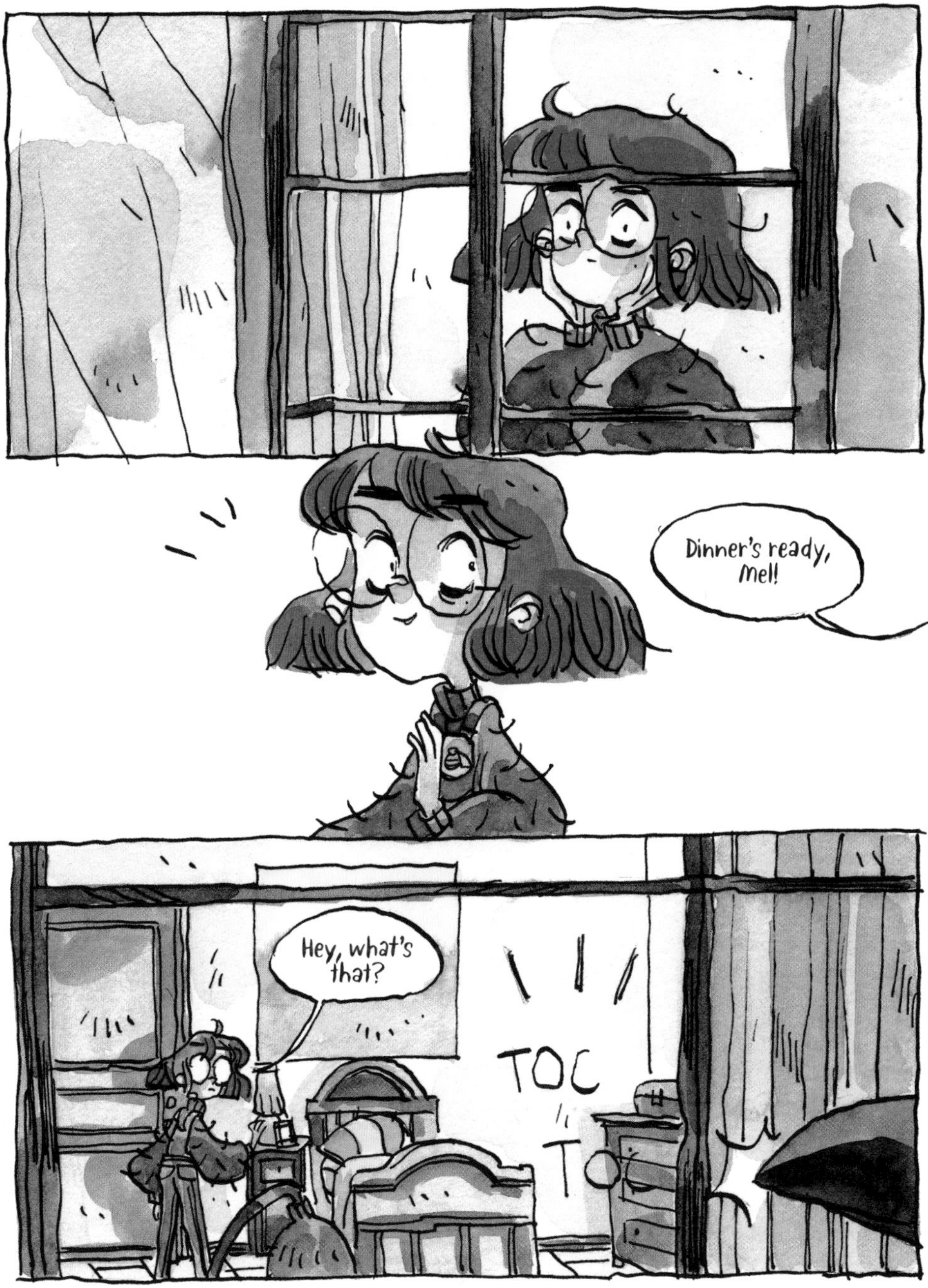
...
Dinner's ready, Mel!
Hey, what's that?
TOC
TOC

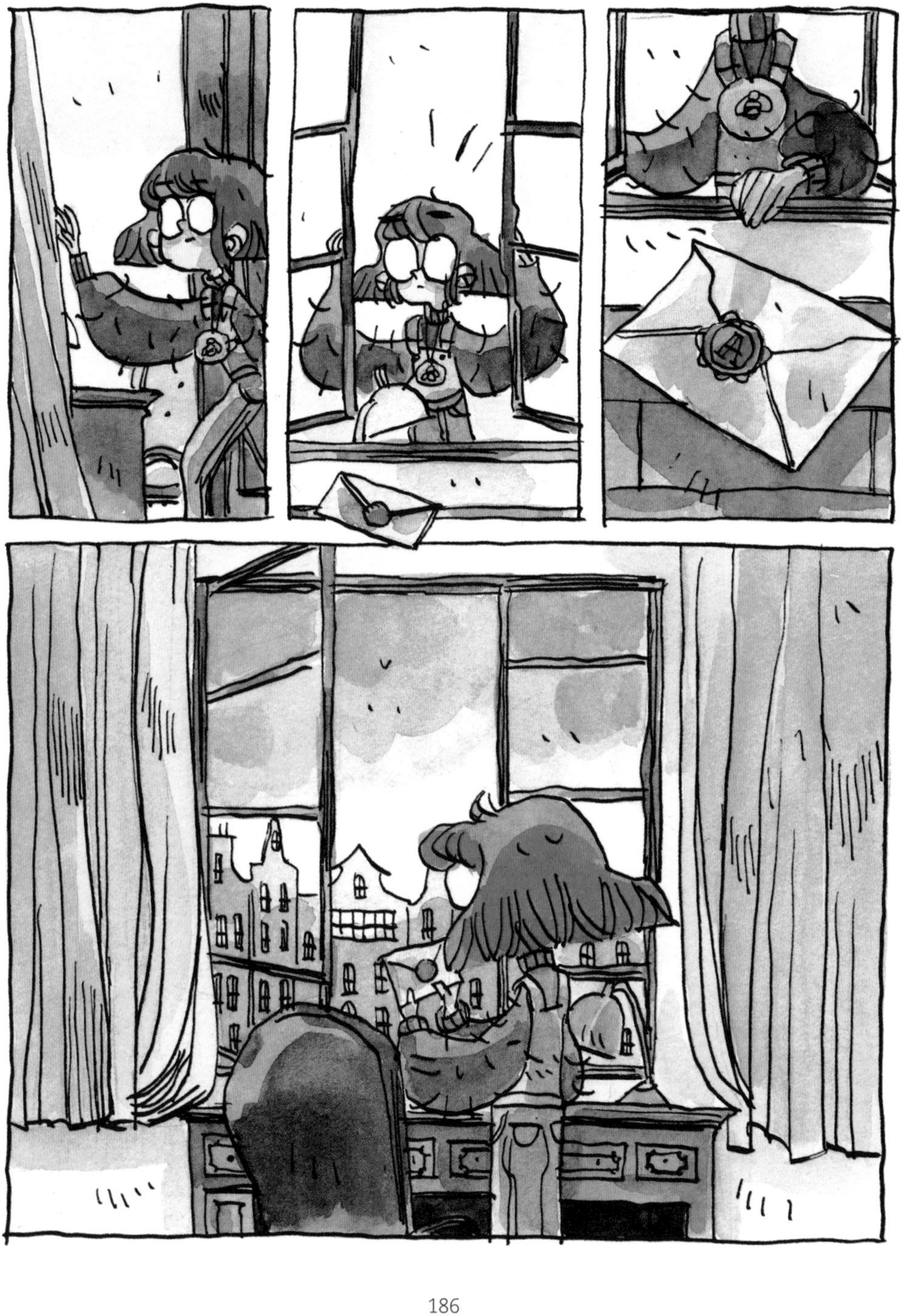

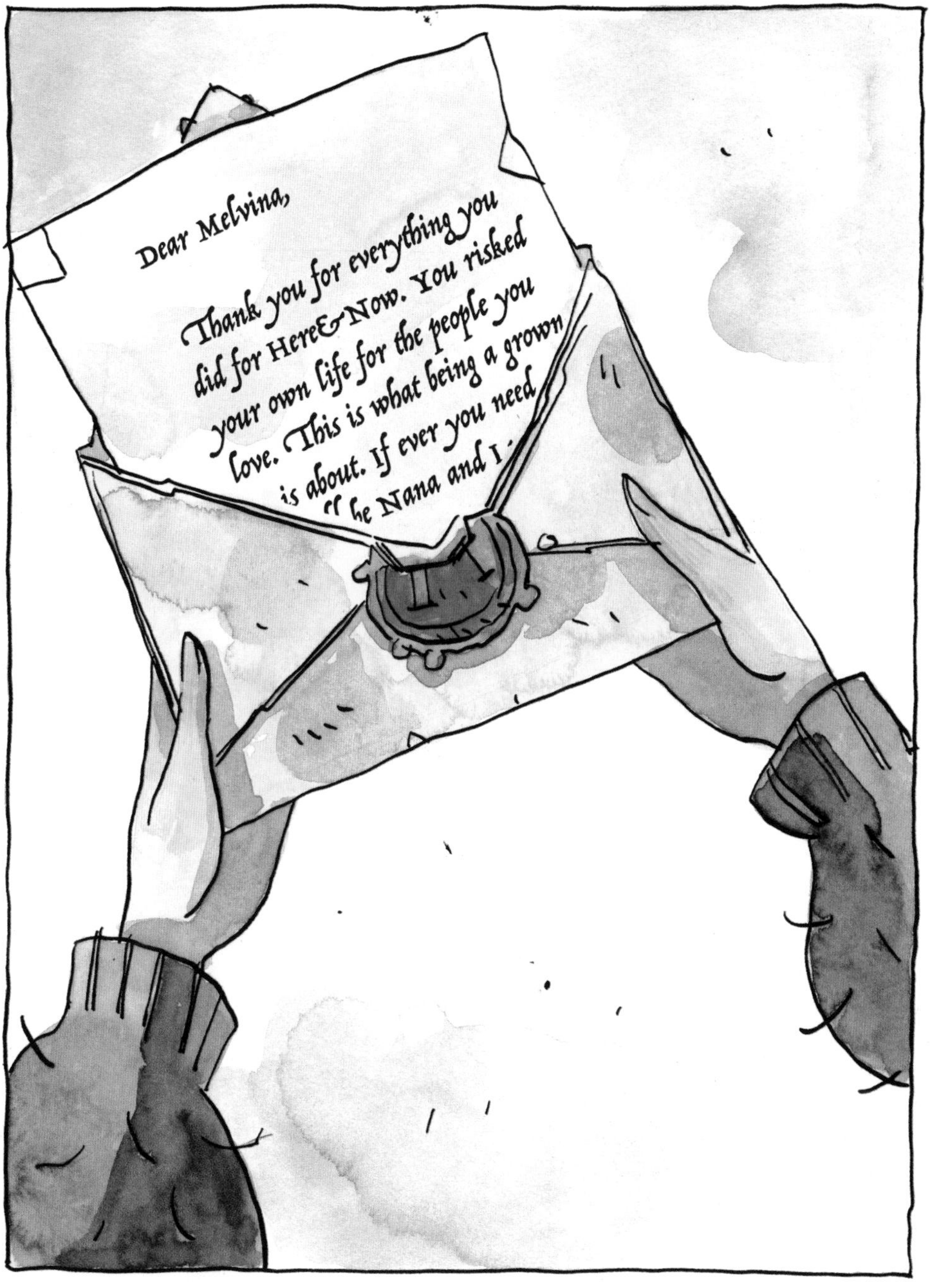
Dear Melvina,
Thank you for everything you did for Here&Now. You risked your own life for the people you love. This is what being a grown is about. If ever you need

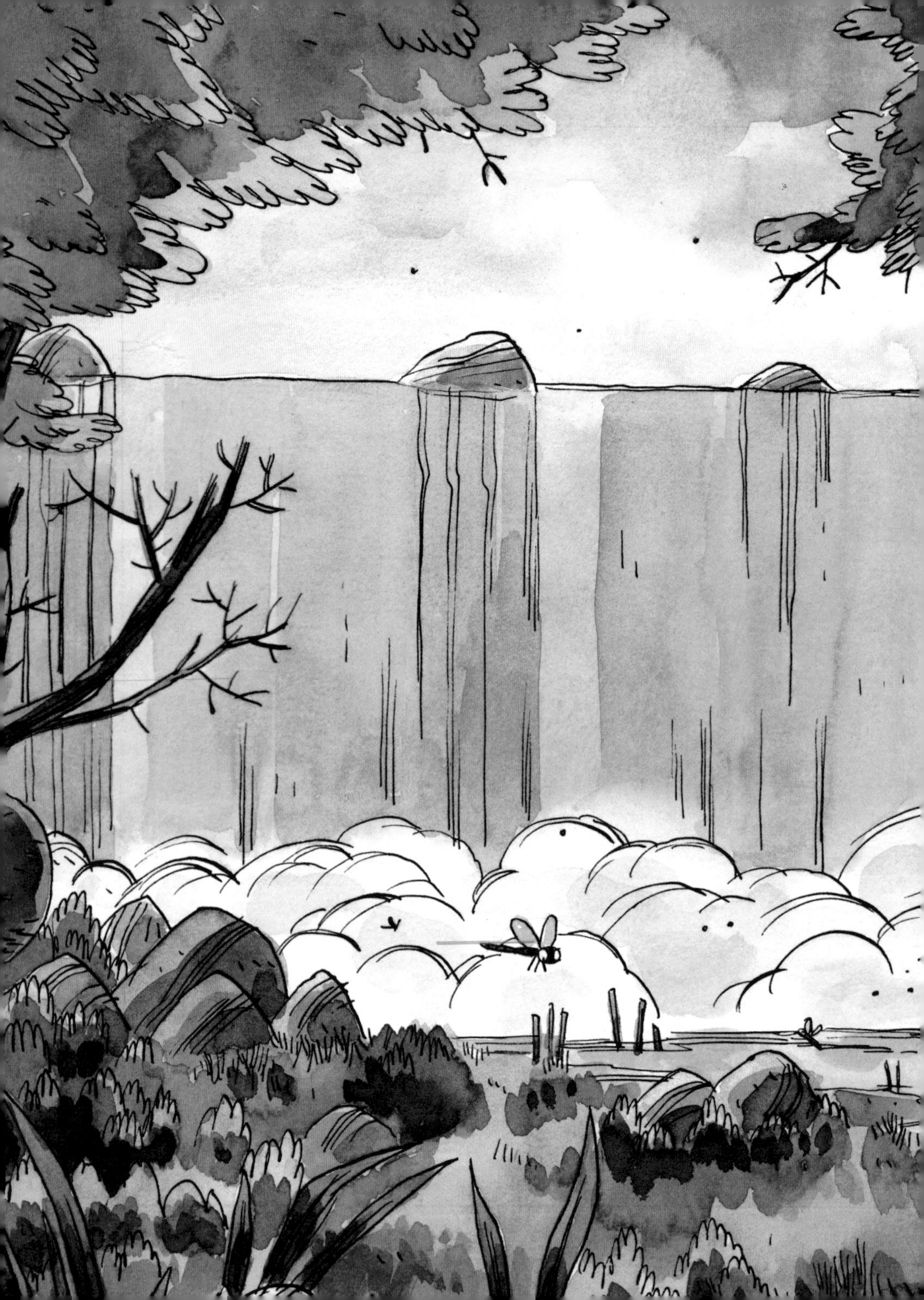

AUTHOR'S NOTE

Mel the Chosen is a very special and deeply emotional project for me. I had been carrying this idea with me for my entire life and am finally able to share it with the world. At the heart of the story are the fears of a little girl, as told by her adult counterpart. Ideally, Melvina will return for more adventures—maybe even as a teenager and then as an adult. Thank you, readers, for cheering on Mel on her journey to grow up—without being in a hurry to do so.

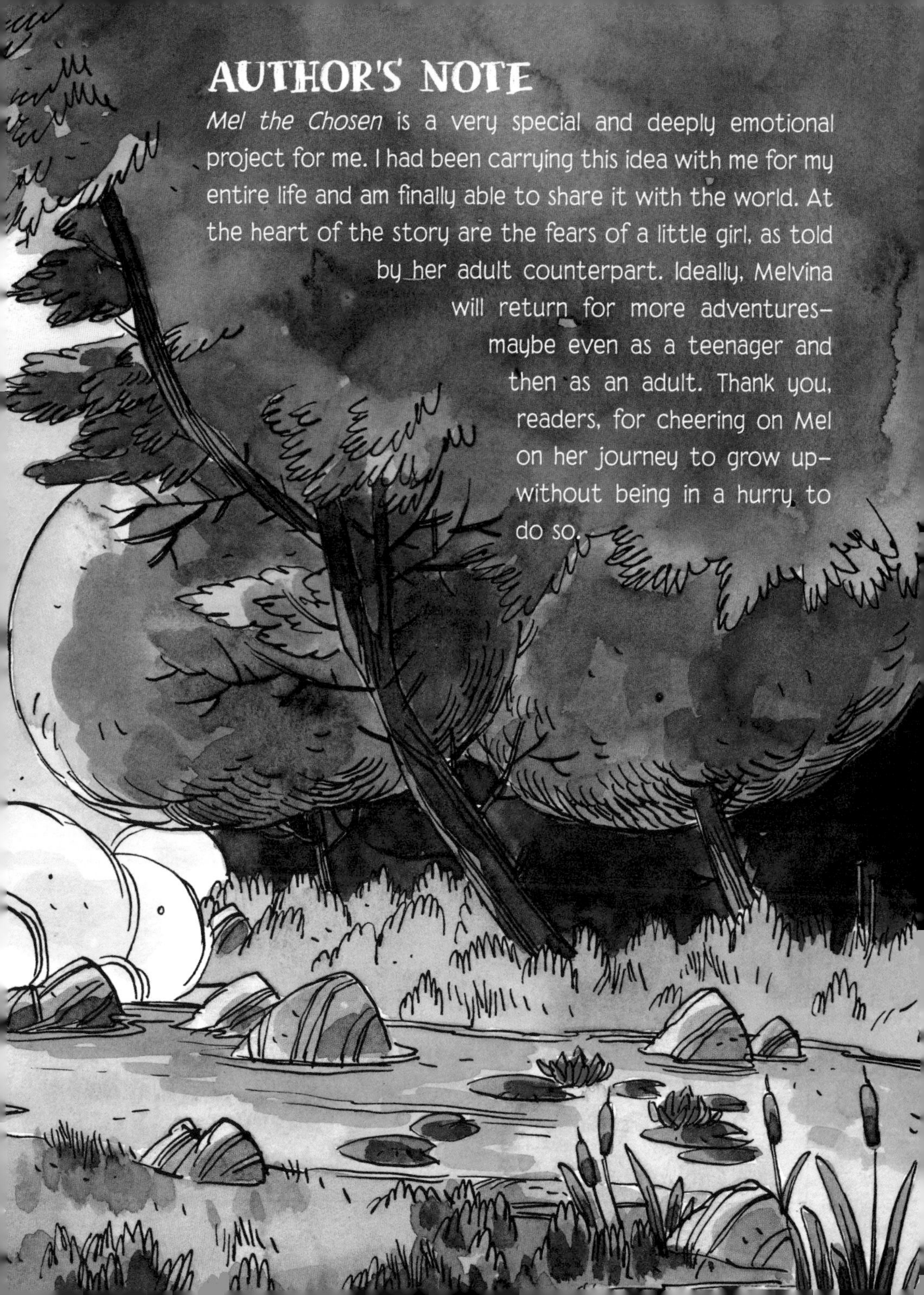

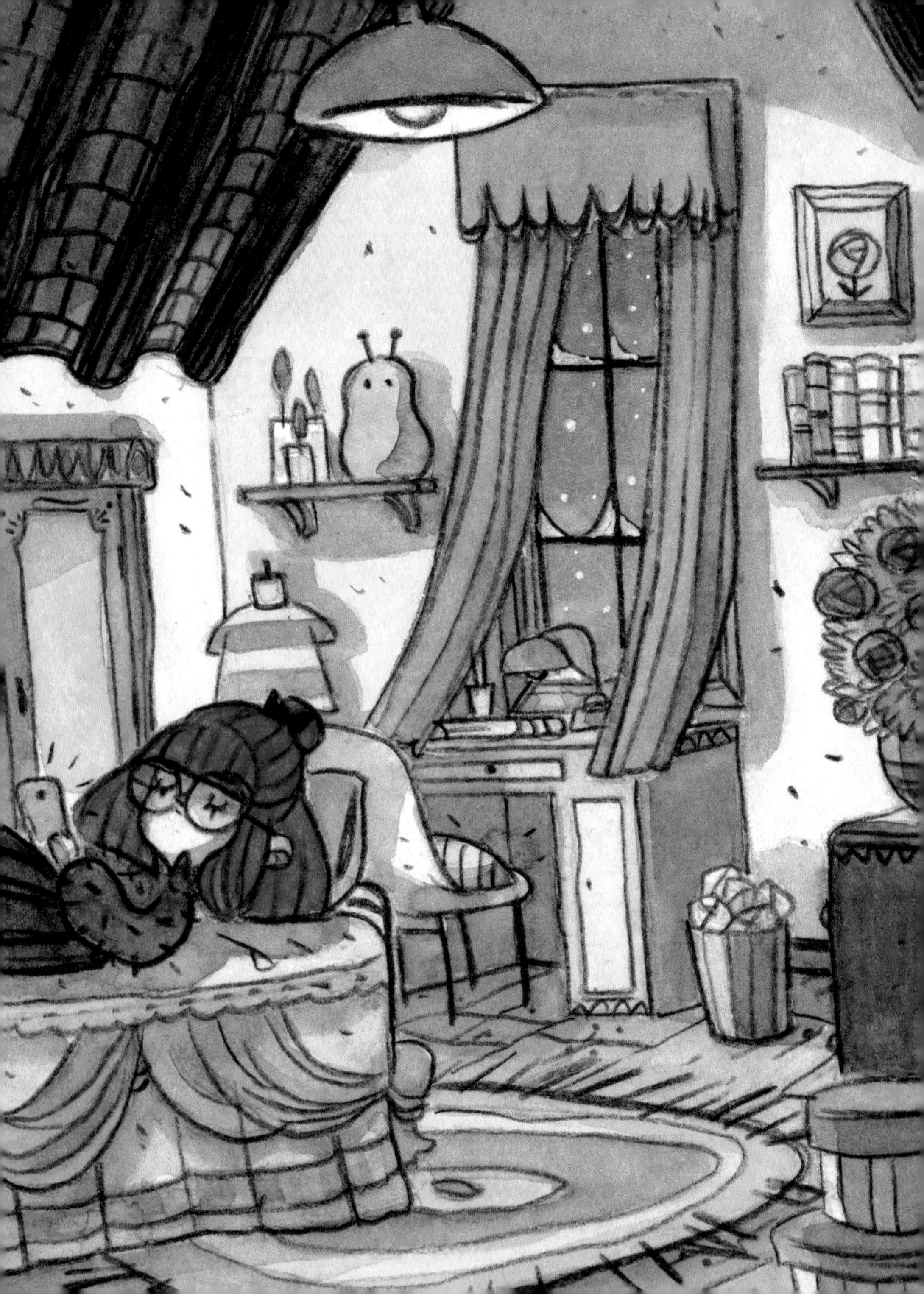

HOW HERE&NOW WAS BORN

or

How Melvina Falls into Otto's Window

I was thirteen when my grandfather passed away; he was like a second father to me. Up until that moment, my childhood had been perfect: a little bubble left untouched by the outside world. For the first time I realized that even in my little nest horrible things could happen—that there were unknown monsters capable of hurting me. It was a delicate moment. Adolescence is a whirlwind of fluctuating emotions that seem unmanageable, and this fracture that I felt inside only made things worse. But one night, Melvina, my alter ego, arrived. She, too, had a lot of problems and did not feel understood, she had lost her grandparents, and she wanted to grow up and escape from the adolescent years that seemed like a burden too heavy for her shoulders. I quickly drew her. Over time I have changed her dress, height, and age, but her rebellious red hair remains unchanged and distinguishes her from the crowd. My teenage self realized that Melvina could do things that were impossible for me, such as traveling to other worlds or managing unlimited ports.

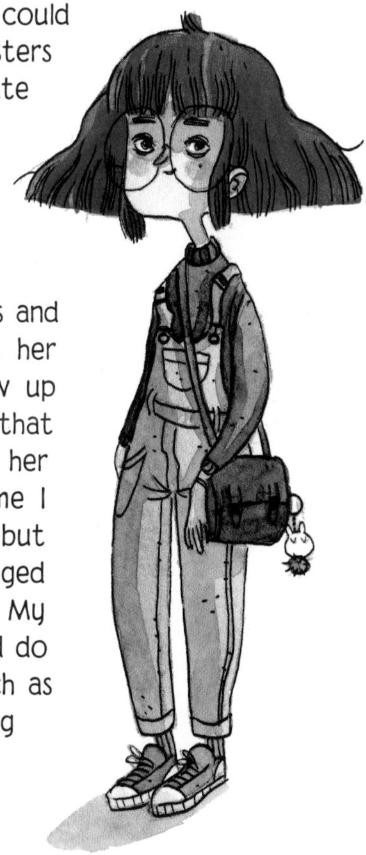

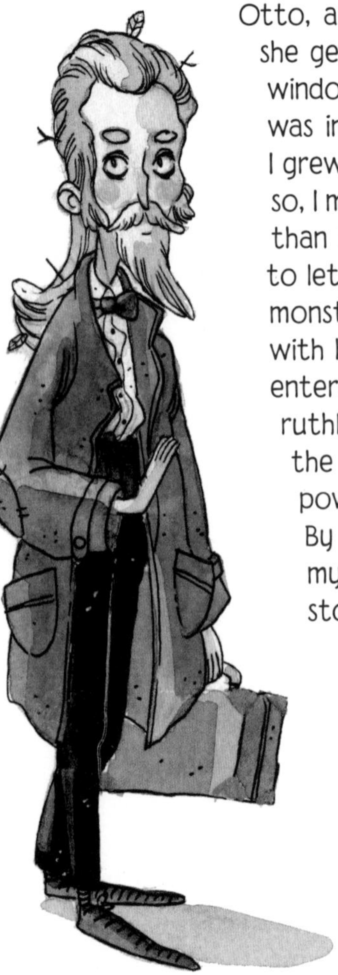

Thus was born Here&Now, a colorful place full of weird characters who do weird things. Here&Now also became the new home of Melvina's grandparents, who are not dead but have just moved there due to circumstances. Here&Now is a new world for Melvina, made up of happy thoughts and incredible adventures that allow her to explore it far and wide. How does she get there? By meeting Otto, an unlikely but very special friend whom she gets to know by falling through a dormer window into his room. (My childhood bedroom was in an attic, and I learned to love roofs!) I grew up while writing this story, and in doing so, I met other monsters, perhaps even scarier than I ever realized they could be. I decided to let Melvina meet a version of one of those monsters so that she could help me defeat it with her power. Malcape, with his long claws, entered the scene about ten years later. This ruthless antagonist allowed me to expand the world of Here&Now, to make Melvina's power grow, and to make her even stronger. By giving Melvina an amulet, I strengthened my own ability to face adversity. Melvina's story began many years ago, and like me, it was immature and angry. In the course of making this book, Melvina grew in awareness and intensity. She and I have been through a lot (and we will go through even more), but now we have our power and our special world.

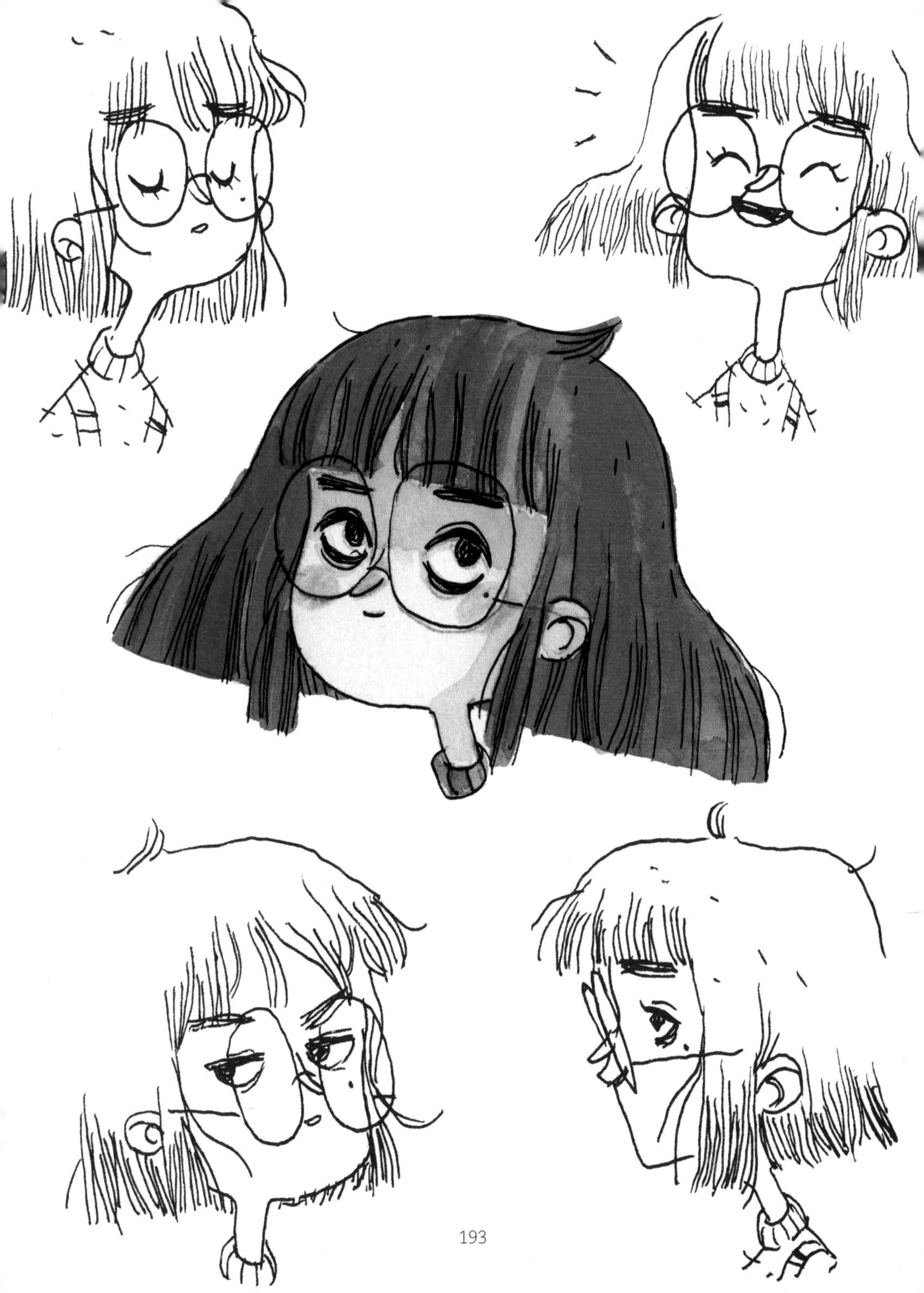

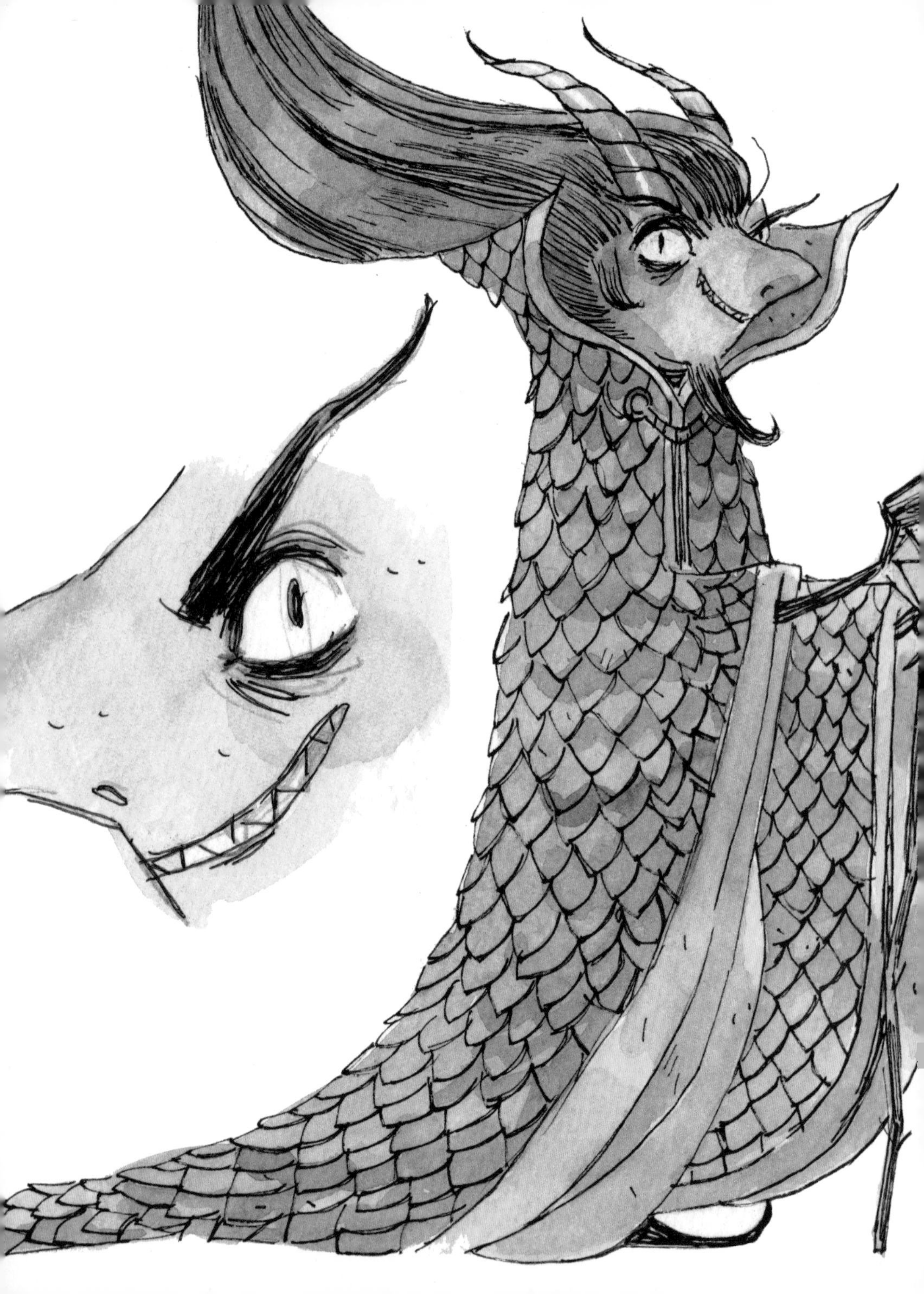

The children of the cemetery
(They are all wearing pajamas.)

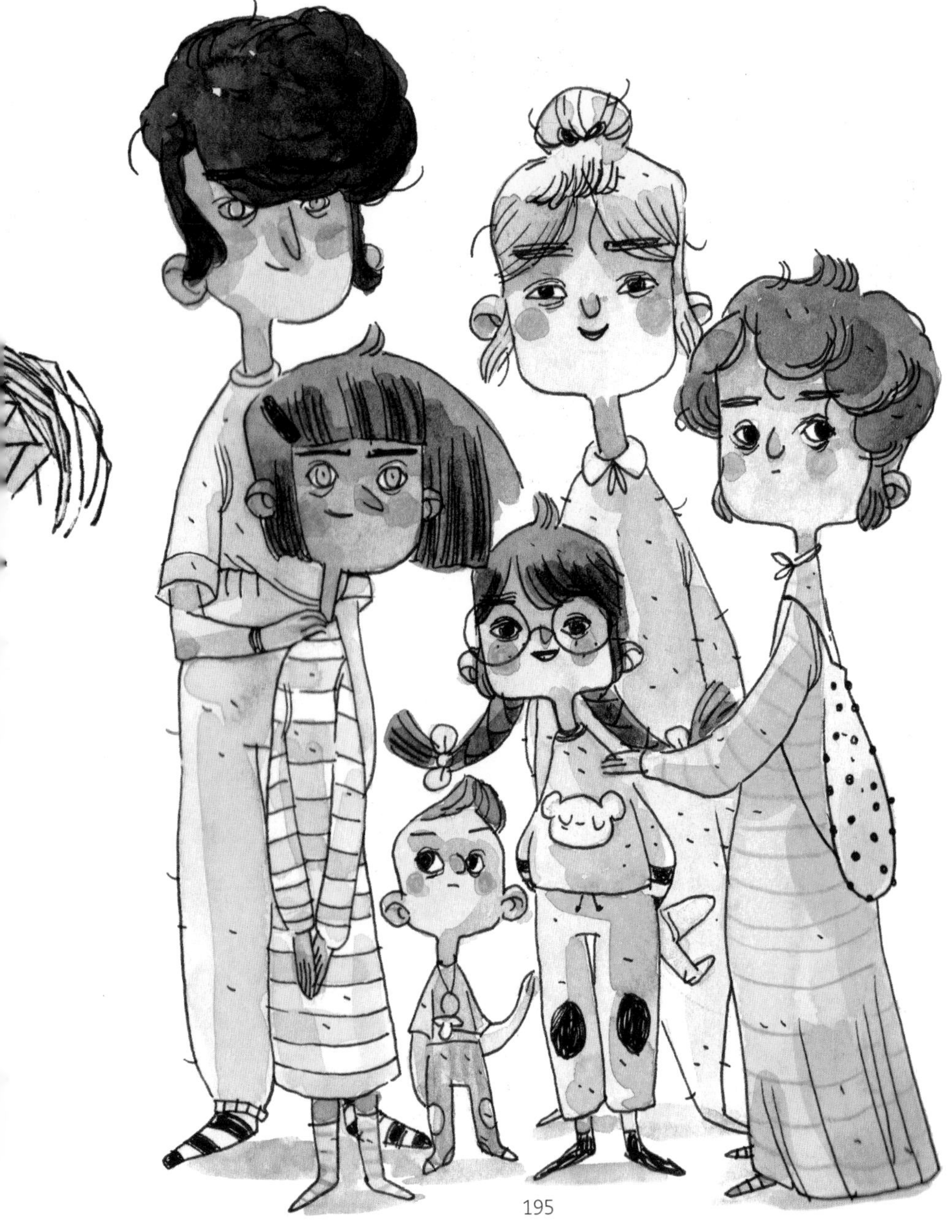

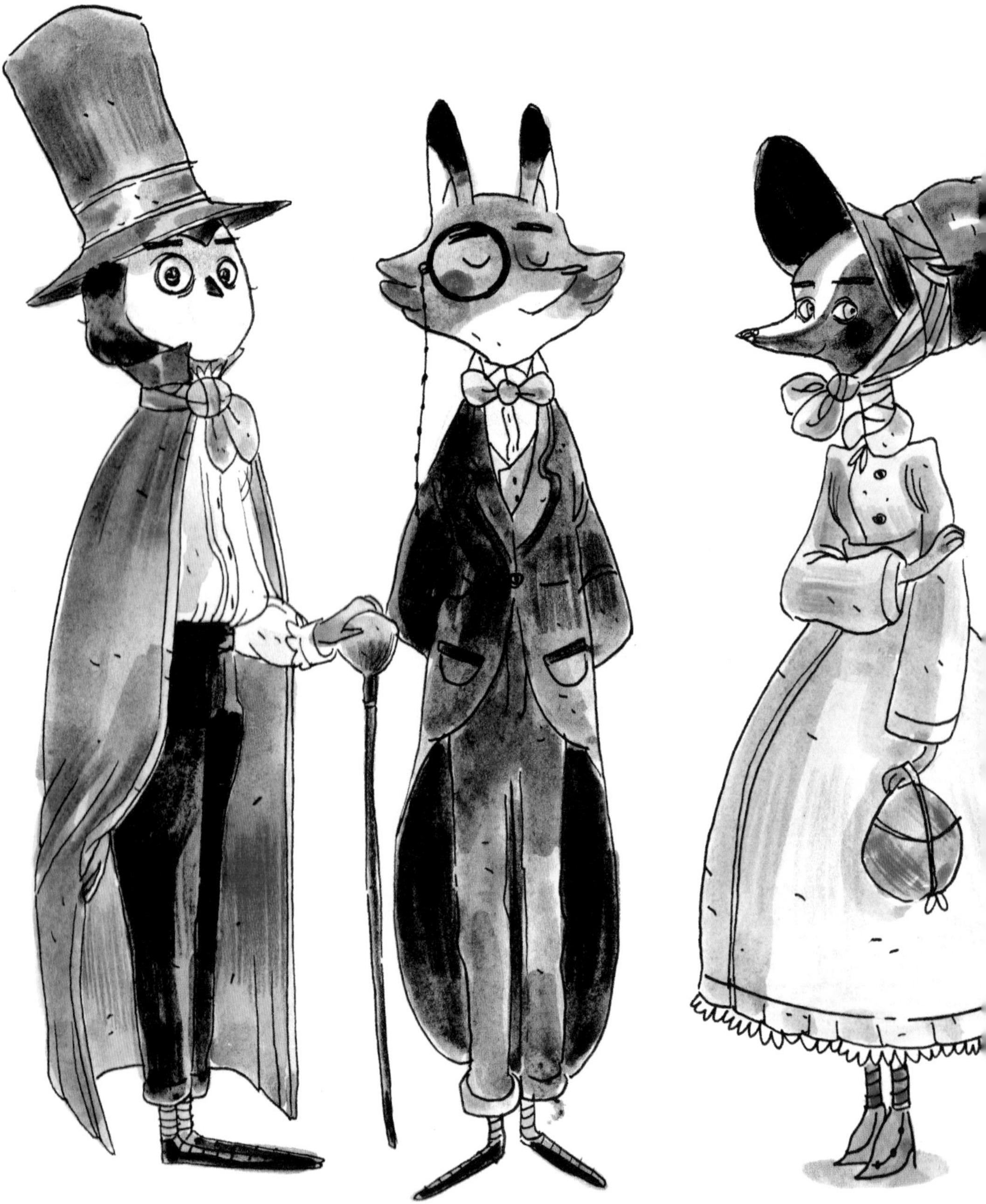

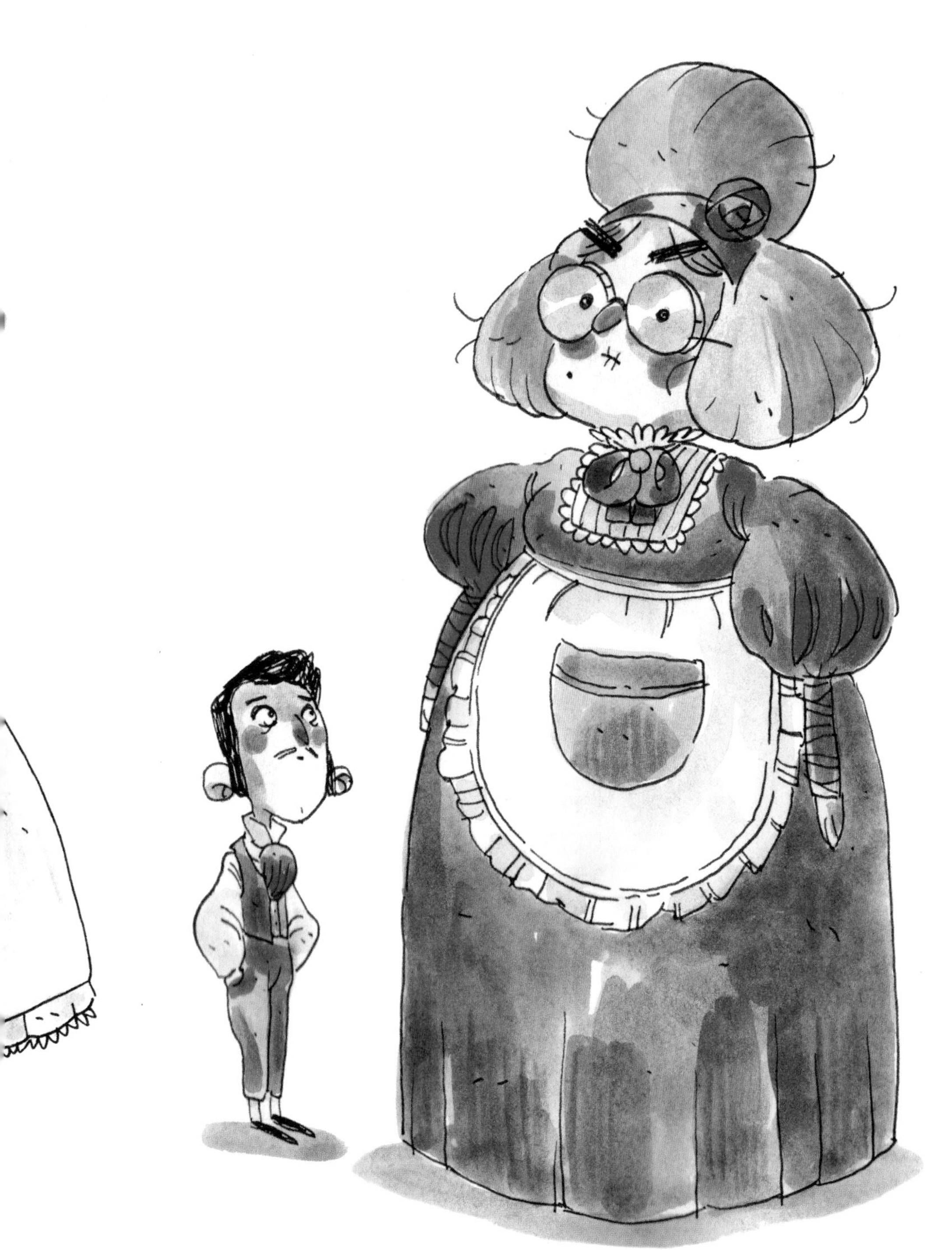

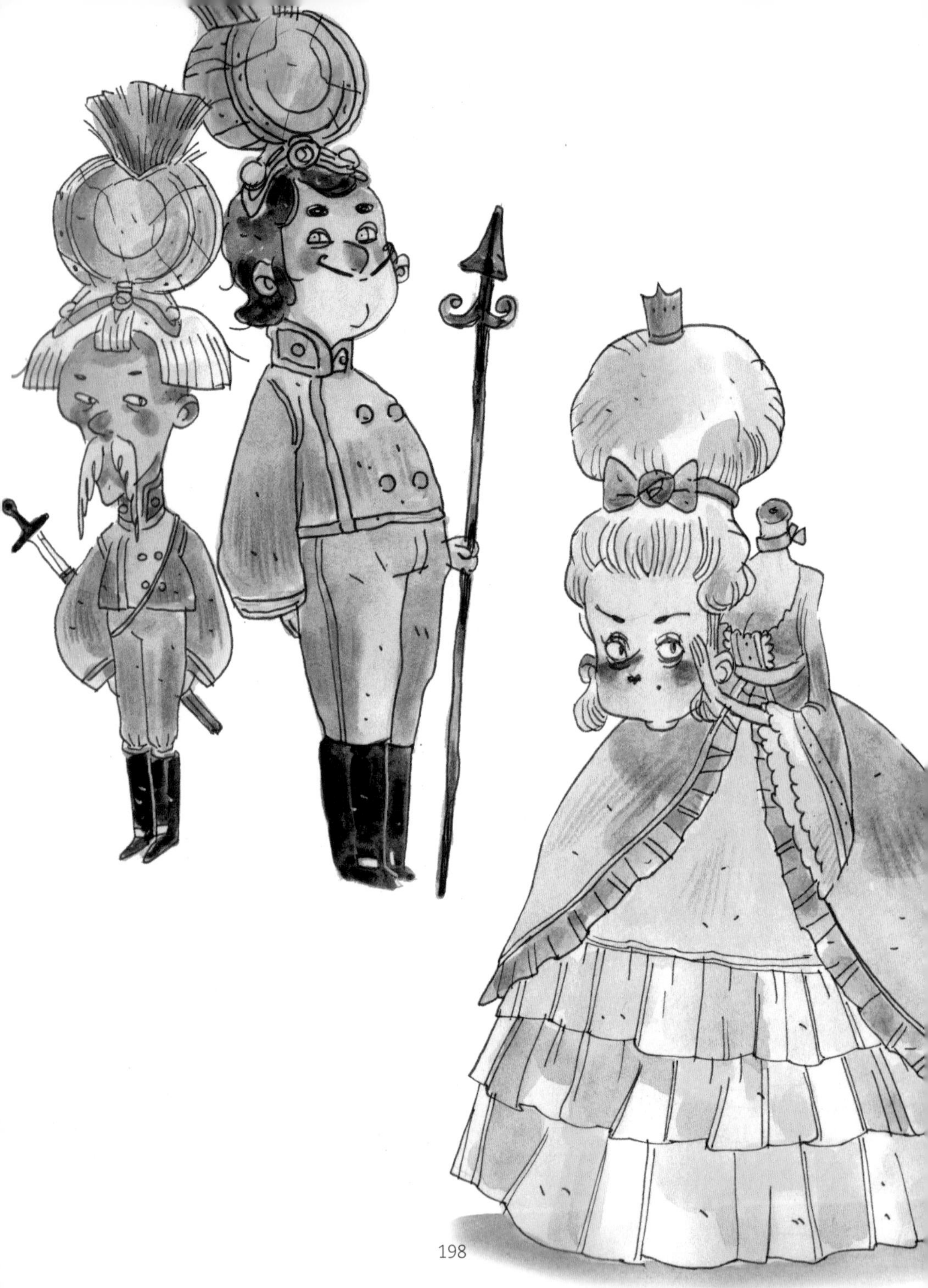

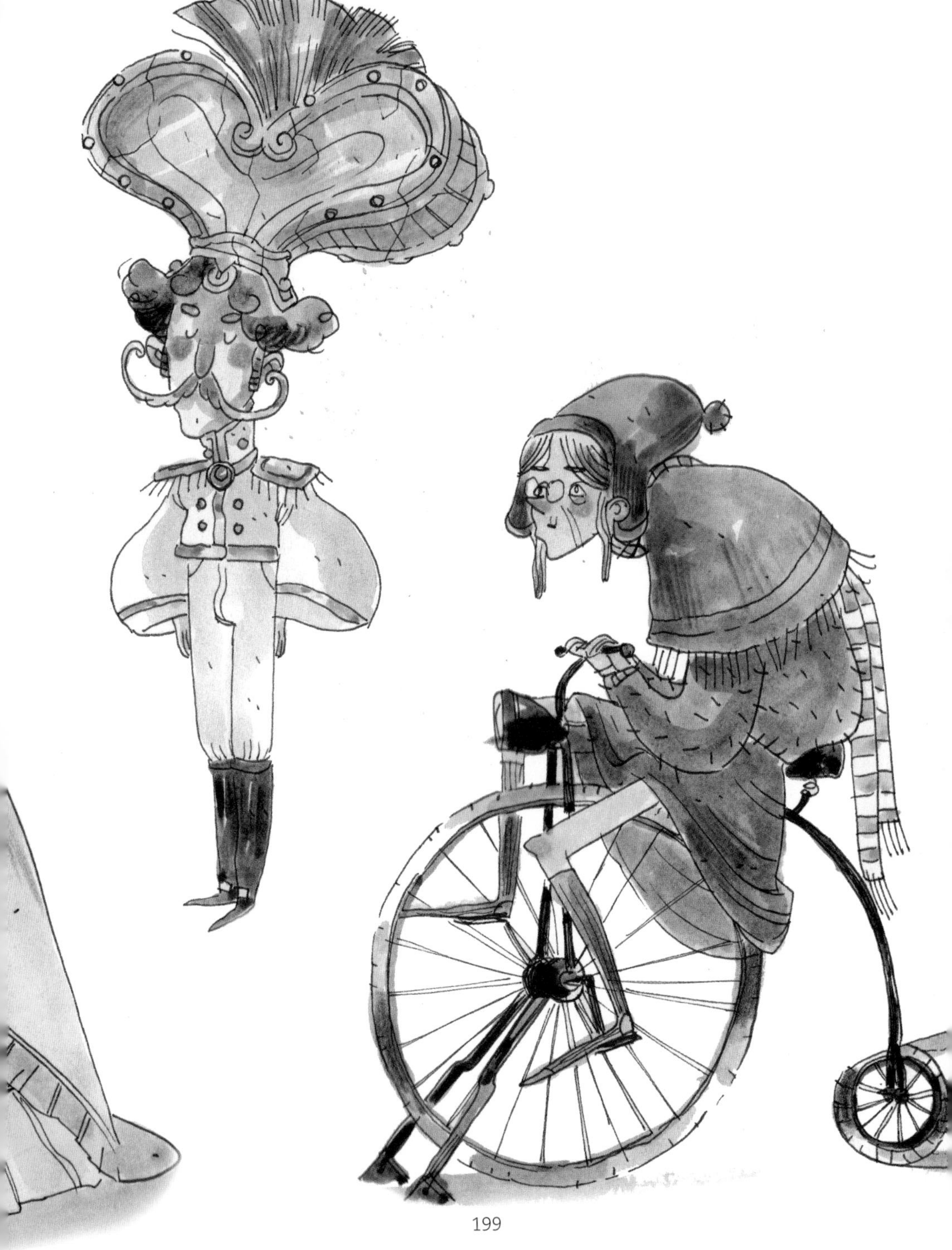

THE MAGIC ITEMS

THE BOOK OF RETURN

This book was created by the Supreme Wizards and brings creatures from any world back to life by transforming them into anthropomorphic beings. It should be used with great caution.

THE TRANSPORT KEY

The key is used to transport someone to places that are dangerous or too abstract for their body. Its origins are lost in the mists of time.

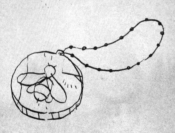

THE AMULET OF THE CHOICE

The amulet was born from the sacrifice of a bee in love with Melvina. It had never happened before, and for this reason nobody really knows its power. The amulet only works in contact with Mel, the Chosen One.

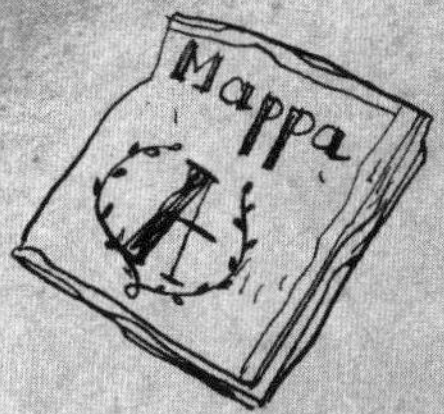
Mappa

THE MAP OF HERE&NOW

The map was created by the cartographer Leompiade de' Sac, an elderly scholar who lives at the court. He created all the maps of the Here&Now universe. It is said that you can reach any place on the map simply by touching it.

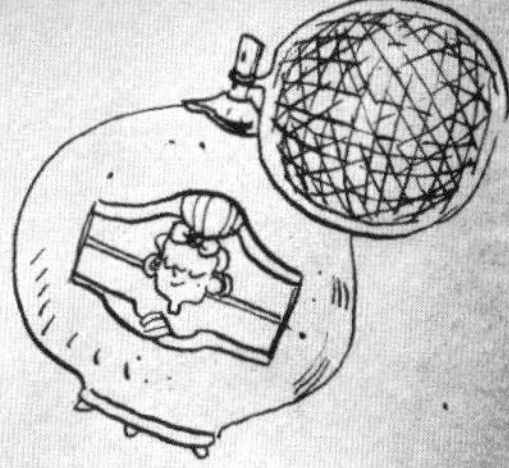

THE PERFUME OF THE QUEEN

It is a magical perfume created by Soffimiellini Mice. It is used to change the height of those who wear it.

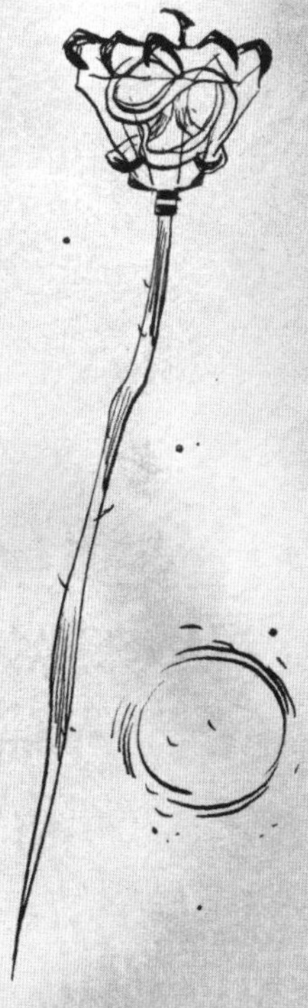

THE SCEPTER OF CREEPING, HISSING LORDS

The scepter belongs to Malcape and the creeping ones. Skilled shape-shifters, they have always stood out for their cruelty and thirst for power. They are known as the Three S.

HAPPY THOUGHTS

Happy Thoughts are made up of emotions and are released from the minds of the inhabitants of Here&Now as they are formed. They can be used as a light source in homes or streets as they flood the room with positive feelings.

THE QUEEN'S CASTLE

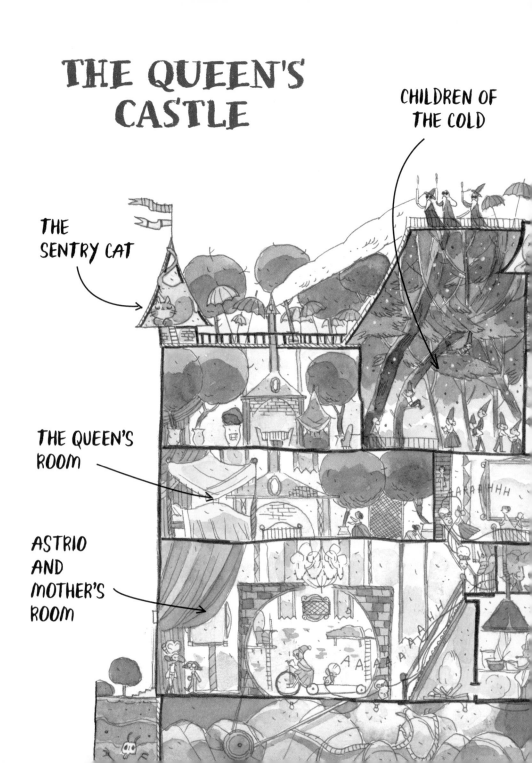

CHILDREN OF
THE COLD

THE
SENTRY CAT

THE QUEEN'S
ROOM

ASTRIO
AND
MOTHER'S
ROOM

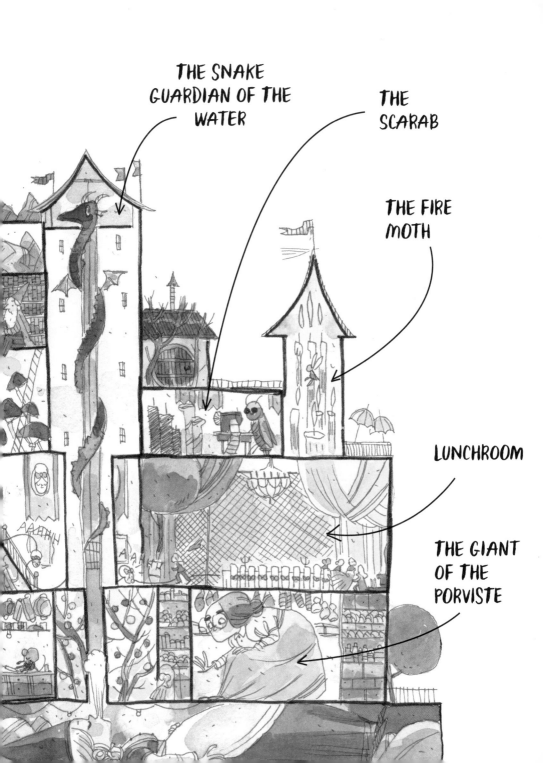

THE SNAKE GUARDIAN OF THE WATER

THE SCARAB

THE FIRE MOTH

LUNCHROOM

THE GIANT OF THE PORVISTE